I0687282

TAKEN BY WITCHES

A HORROR NOVEL BY
NICK IUPPA

Cover art: © swetta, iStock 11261911

Visit the author's website: http://www.nickiuppawrites.com

ISBN: 978-0-9863241-4-7

DEDICATION

To Bill Idelson and Bill Habeeb
who worked with me on those many LA nights
to make something out of this book.

Novels by Nick Iuppa

Bloody Bess and the Doomsday Games

Novels by Nick Iuppa & John P. Mendoza

The Carlos Mann Trilogy
(Alicia's Ghost • Alicia's Sin • Alicia Bewitched)

Avenging Adelita

Acknowledgments

I'd like to thank all the people who advised, sympathized, threatened, condemned, and otherwise helped with the creation of this book, especially Larry Touch, Judy Singer, Seemah Idelson, Kimberly Behl, Bob Gibbons, Alex Singer, Gershon Weltman, Janet Herrington, Roland Lesterland, and Mark Kines. I appreciate the highly supportive, graphic services of Laurie Douglas. Thanks to Janet Grady for her creative suggestions and editorial support, and a special thanks to Clare McGlinchey who brought it all together and polished it up.

WITCHES

"Into the air, over the valleys, under the stars, above a river, a pond, a road, flew Cecy. Invisible as new spring winds, fresh as the breath of clover rising from twilight fields, she flew."

— Ray Bradbury

"I myself have seen this woman draw the stars from the sky; she diverts the course of a fast-flowing river with her incantations; her voice makes the earth gape, it lures the spirits from the tombs, send the bones tumbling from the dying pyre. At her behest, the sad clouds scatter; at her behest, snow falls from a summer's sky."

— Catullus

"I should have no compassion on these witches. I should burn them all."

— Martin Luther

"Witches never existed, except in people's minds. All there was in the olden days was women and some men who believed in herbal cures and in folklore and in the wish to fly. Witches? We're all witches in one way or another. Witches was the invention of mankind, son. We're all witches beneath the skin."

— Ian Rankin

Contents

FOREWORD

Witches exist. Of course they do… in the reemergence of a millennia-old religion that celebrates the mother goddess and ancient practices with a focus on healing and hearth and the strength and powers of women. Of course they do. But what about those other witches… the ones in the fairy tales… those who ride broomsticks and eat little children? Those who cast spells and curses and can turn a man into billy goat or take a plain village girl and make her intoxicatingly, sinfully beautiful? Were these witches merely the concoction of a male dominated society whose purpose was to keep women out of the spheres of power? Were they merely the roles played by frightened old crones who used the image as a way to keep their rough neighbors at bay and buy some small sense of security?

Do witches exist who can call up an army of demons and obliterate an entire city in combat? Are there witches who make love to Satan in the dead of night on All Hollows Eve? Because if they do exist… those witches, then from where does their power come, and to what ends will they use it?

Nick Iuppa

PROLOGUE

I
The Mountains of Poland
1165

A little girl can be very much alone in the woods at night, even if the woods are only a few feet from the cottage where she has lived all her life, even if she has stepped into it for only a moment to snatch one last twig to add to the bundle of kindling she has gathered for her father. For in that moment, when she has stepped so foolishly into the absolute blackness between the tiny shafts of moonlight, she may suddenly catch a glimpse of something that can only be seen in the darkness. Red eyes stare out at her. They terrify her, freeze her, hypnotize her until she is no more than a quivering, speechless little thing who cowers as a hideous monster emerges. Something (someone) hobbles toward her, someone who, in a more distant time, might have been a little girl just like her. The monster is ancient, enormous, even though she can no longer stand upright. She is dressed in black tatters that hang like rags about her. She smells of a strange spicy-sweetness and animal sweat and blood.

The thing reaches out a hairy, twisted claw to caress the little girl's cheek with a palsied clumsiness that accidentally draws blood. The little girl peers from the corner of her eye as those fingers twitch down her cheek and reach for her throat. She lets out a muffled cry that her father hears. He knows it only too well. He jumps to his feet in horror, darts from the cottage and into the woods, cursing himself for letting his daughter go out on such a night.

He finds only the thin blue band from her hair, and her innocent pile of twigs. Her gift of firewood has been twisted into an ancient, evil symbol. The father blusters further into the dark, not caring for himself or the monsters he might face. But he already knows it is hopeless. He already knows that his daughter has been taken into some ungodly family. For evil lives deep in the woods in these dark ages. The ways of monsters and animals run strong in the blood of those who will accept them, who will transform these animal-ways into their own black arts and demon religions, who will stop at nothing to protect their own.

You see, the village where the little girl lived had become a haven for witches. And although that time has long since passed – the village transformed into a city, the woods shrank to the size of a park, and the inhabitants moved to other continents – the witches themselves remain very much unchanged, ... even when they themselves have gone off to distant lands.

II
The Warlock
800 Years Later

Matryoshka's heart pounds as she makes her way through the dense forest. One awkward step on the uneven earth and her ankle twists under her. She stumbles, falls forward, and catches herself on the sharp bark of a massive oak.

"Ouch, damn it," she mutters, grabbing at her ankle. The peasant dress she's wearing seems so inappropriate for this walk in the woods. Puffy short cotton sleeves, gathered waist, bodice that's designed to entice the boys with her full figure. But it isn't offering any protection against the cold as she turns and feels a deeper chill. There's no way out, no path to lead her back to safety.

"Steady," she tells herself, as she feels a pang of desperation, and then suddenly...

She hears music and laughter. There's warmth. She smells a great bonfire. It's crackling song calls her forward. Matryoshka stumbles to the edge of a clearing, then stops, and peers out.

There, no more than a hundred yards in front of her, is a raging pyre that seems to be reaching for the sky. Figures move around it: women: young; naked; exotic; glamorous; spinning deliciously around the wicked blaze. And HE is there too, beyond the fire, sitting in an elaborate, hand-carved, high-backed chair fit for a King: "Wicktor the warlock, YES!"

Matryoshka whispers his name, than calls it aloud, hoping somehow he'll hear her. She calls again... and he does. He stands. Their eyes lock; his gleam with eagerness and desire... for her!

"MATRYOSHKA!!"

She snaps out of her reverie.

"Father, I was just...."

"You were just day dreaming about him again, weren't you?" says the old man as he shuffles toward her. "Back to work, girl!"

Pan Michalowski, her father, moves slowly across the floor of his little gift shop. As he moves he surveys the shelves full of toys, collections of brightly painted cups and saucers, hand carved puppets, and other figures. He reaches the back wall, takes another brief glance around the shop, out through the window to the empty rain-soaked streets, and then he pulls a large book down from the very top shelf of a huge bookcase.

The entire section suddenly swings away, offering a passage into a gallery filled with collectables of the occult: oils; potions; herbal mixes; ritual tools; tarot decks; masks of every kind; crystal balls; runes; spell books filled with ancient secrets from faraway places... forgotten knowledge and wisdom gathered from the four corners of the world... all sold here.

Michalowski and his ancestors have been in the trade for centuries. Their little shop is nestled in the foothills of the Carpathian Mountains, in the small Village of Zakopanski, which now, in 1965, is pressed hard under the thumb of its communist overlords.

"When he comes, let him in at once," says Michalowski. "Then lock the front door, and put the 'Closed' sign up."

Matryoshka has just begun setting out inventory that has recently arrived when the ring of a bell startles her. She turns toward the sound, toward the front door, and her eyes grow wide.

IT'S HIM: a tall, well-dressed man who moves gracefully through the doorway. His hair is coal black, his features: sharp, Polish, and very handsome. A large canvas sack sags heavily from his shoulder.

Matryoshka catches her breath, squeezes her eyes tight for a just moment while she manages to gain control of her breathing and her thoughts. And then she smiles.

"Pan Wicktor," her voice is little more than a gasp. She swallows hard, tries to clear her throat. "Father has been waiting for you."

Wicktor the warlock, who seems to have stepped right out of the girl's dream, winks at the round-faced seventeen-year-old as he glides into the store. There's an aura about him; it's almost electric.

"Did you miss me, Matryoshka?"

The girl feels a tingle in certain forbidden parts of her body, under her traditional Polish peasant garb, under the crisp cotton blouse she was wearing in her dream, under her skirt with its bright yellow and green floral patterns.

"Oh yes, I really missed you," she sighs dreamily. "If only I could join you in one of those...."

"No more of that," calls Michalowski as he makes his way out from the hidden room. He's pointing directly at his daughter, who swallows the rest of her words and turns bright red in embarrassment.

Wicktor's eyes laugh at his companions. He already knows that the girl is his for the taking.

"Get out of here," the shopkeeper growls at his daughter. "Go lock the front door, and then stay out of our way."

"Yes, Papa."

She scuttles to the front of the shop, locks the front door and then continues setting out the display of hand-carved music boxes in the window. Still, she can't help but continue glancing over her shoulder, watching her father and the warlock.

"I've been waiting for these, Pan Wicktor," says Michalowski as he gestures to the sack.

Wicktor smiles, follows the old man into the secret room, and sets the sack down on the broad glass counter to the left of the hidden doorway. He reaches in and pulls out a parcel wrapped in butcher paper, places it beside the bag, produces another package, and then another, until he has twenty-seven of them lined up in front of him.

Michalowski grabs the first package and begins unwrapping it so eagerly that he cuts his fingers on the object inside. His blood turns the paper a deep crimson.

Hurriedly, he wipes his hands and finishes opening the package to make sure that none of his blood has stained its contents. He's pleased to see that it hasn't.

The unwrapped paper reveals an ancient porcelain mask. The face is turned away from him; it's back, a grey-white negative image of what's on the other side. But it does not tell the whole story. The shopkeeper flips the mask over and gasps. The face is hideous: an old woman whose expression is so full of hatred and evil that Michalowski drops it back onto the counter immediately. As he does his own blood spills on to the mouth of the old woman, almost as though she'd bitten him.

Quick, before it stains," Wicktor calls. "She's not as valuable with blood dripping from her lips."

Michalowski doesn't even look up. He's furiously dabbing blood from the ancient face. When he finishes he holds it up, studies it for a moment, and suddenly feels sick with fear. The image of a monster, that's what he's holding, and he puts it down, before moving on to unwrap the next parcel... another mask of the same woman.

"Help here, please!" the shopkeeper calls.

Wicktor shakes his head. "I lugged her all the way from America, Pan Michalowski, past the damn communist border guards. I'm not going to risk my fingers on her hungry mouth."

"I'm calling, my daughter, you idiot," the shopkeeper answers. "Matryoshka! Where are you?"

"Preparing the window display as you asked me to, father." And then, as the girl scurries into the secret room, she stops dead and gasps.

"Oh my God! SHE's here."

The warlock leers at her, and Matryoshka, recovering quickly from the image of the old woman, still can't help but be taken by that leer.

"Excuse me, Pan Wicktor," she says.

The creature gives her a low, formal bow, and then, as the girl tries to slide past him, he pinches her bottom. Matryoshka lets out a flirtatious squeal and bats her eyes.

"No!" the shopkeeper calls. "Stay away from him, girl, or next thing he'll be having you dancing naked in the forests at midnight, asking you to join his band. And after that... THIS!" He holds up yet another witch mask that seems to be smiling defiant curses at them all.

Matryoshka shudders at the sight. "Why would people want such a thing in their homes, Papa?"

"Power my dear," the warlock replies. He has now moved even closer to the girl, allowing her to breathe in his seductive, musky aroma. "It was your uncle that spirited these masks out of our little village. And, I must say, it's been the devil to get them back."

Michalowski eyes the warlock suspiciously. "And does the devil have the missing mask?"

The warlock lowers his eyes. "Unfortunately one of them did slip through my fingers. But only because..." he points to one of the masks, "SHE wanted to keep it."

"Hang these on the wall," Michalowski tells his daughter. The girl obediently grabs as many of the masks as she can hold and goes to the far wall where a sign proclaims "BABCIA MASKS"... and then, in large letters underneath, it translates the word "Babcia" into Russian, German, Hungarian, French and English.

"Babcia – Grandmother," the English sign says, and it shows the phonetic pronunciation of the Polish word as "Bob-cha,"

Michalowski turns back to the warlock. "I sent you to get the masks, and you leave one behind."

"How could I not?" Wicktor replies, "Babcia wanted to hold onto it."

"Babcia's dead," the shopkeeper curses.

"Of course she is, but a dead witch is even more dangerous than a living one. Don't you agree?"

Michalowski is considering the question when, suddenly, there's a shriek.

The men turn to see Matryoshka staring at the wall, unable to look away from what greets her: the accumulated horror of 27 images of the most evil witch who has ever lived.

Wicktor immediately rushes to her, holds her. "There, there," he coos. "You're just not ready to receive her."

"I'll never be ready."

"I think you will. There are many who adore her, who almost worship her."

"It's okay, Kochanie (little girl)." Michalowski steps forward with a huge counter-cloth. "We'll cover the wall. Keep it covered. Only remove it when customers come in with plenty to spend."

"Thank you, Papa," the girl says as her father pulls her away from the lustful warlock.

"And you," Michalowski asks, turning to the creature, "why do I not have every one of these masks?"

"I told you," She wanted to keep one."

"What you say is bullshit!"

"Not really," Wicktor answers with a seductive smile. "But there is quite a story there." He looks at Matryoshka as he speaks. "Let me tell it to you. Then you'll at least understand why I had to leave the mask with the little girl."

"There's a little girl now?"

Michalowski shakes his head while a bewitching smile curls the corners of the warlock's lips once again. Matryoshka smiles too.

"Okay, okay," Michalowski says at last, "Matryoshka, get a bottle of vodka, and two big glasses. Then Wicktor will tell us the story of Witch Babcia in America."

"All over America... Hollywood too!" Wicktor adds, just as Matryoshka leaves to get the drinks. He catches her attention with the name of that fabled city.

"Oh, Papa I just have to stay and listen."

Michalowski recognizes the electricity that flows between his daughter and the warlock, but he has seen many horrors in Poland, and is wise enough to know that the only way to combat the seductive power of evil is with knowledge.

"Yes, get the vodka, and you can stay, Kochanie," he says. "It's time you learned the truth of witches."

He can hear his daughter giggling joyfully as she hurries off to get the vodka.

When she returns she finds the two men seated by the fireplace at the back of the secret room. They are already smoking. Her father puffs on his pipe eagerly. The warlock sucks on a long, menacing, black cigar.

"Now, Wicktor," Michalowski says, as soon as his daughter has poured two large glasses of vodka and taken a seat in the big easy chair beside him, "Tell us the story: Witch Babcia in America."

"I will," the warlock answers. "But, first you must tell me something."

Michalowski shifts nervously in his seat, as if he knows this question and is very much afraid of it.

"Why were the masks sent out of from Poland in the first place?"

Michalowski shakes his head. "Perhaps it is not the time to tell."

The warlock arches a commanding eyebrow and the old man can do nothing but nod.

"Let us just say that their power was growing, that the Nazis showed greater and greater interest. We did intend to sell them one at a time, but not to such evil people."

"Hitler loved the occult," Wicktor adds.

"Yes, there was an incident… that's why my brother, Peter, sent them away."

Michalowski takes a sip of the vodka and feels it tingle all through his body.

Matryoshka, who is so spellbound that she's been holding her breath through the entire exchange, now lets out a heavy sigh.

"Anyway, enough of that for now," the shopkeeper says. "Tell us your story of America, Wicktor."

And so the warlock gathers all his energy and begins.

PART 1

VALENTINE ROAD

CHAPTER ONE

DOMESTIC WITCHERY

"We start our story in 1946, just after the end of World War Two, in Rochester New York, the home of Eastman Kodak Company… manufacturer of everyman's camera, the birthplace of popular photography."

Michalowski suddenly smiles knowingly and nods to an object in the far corner the secret room. The warlock looks and sees a very old Kodak Brownie camera. There's something strange about it though. Wicktor's sharp eyes study it for a moment, before realizing that the lens is not clear but solid... a deep, solid, blood red.

"Made in Rochester many years ago," chuckles the shopkeeper, "by a deranged but brilliant disciple of Mr. Eastman. It can photograph the human soul."

The warlock nods appreciatively, and after a moment, continues his story.

"1946 is an exciting time, filled with hope, promises and peace. Waves of veterans come home and settle down with their young families. Dr. Louis Madonie, a heroic medic during the war, is one of them. He and his wife own an imposing old house on Valentine Road, only a few miles from those legendary Kodak factories. Peace is what the doctor and his young family hope for. But at this time... on Valentine Road... there is very little peace."

"Oh, I like this," sighs Matryoshka, "I really do."

"Then don't interrupt," says her father.

The Warlock brings a finger to his lips as if to shush the girl further. Then he smiles and continues.

Killer was an enormous black Mastiff whose owner kept him chained to a post in the side yard of his home. Valentine Road, where Killer lived, was alive with the excitement of returning soldiers and ecstatic young families. The dog had an explosion of a bark that seemed to ignite deep in his lungs and then blast through the thick saliva that drooled from his muzzle. Killer was not mad, mind you, just insanely angry at being chained in the yard, at that wild excitement he did not understand, at the happy young families parading by, and at every silly cat that wandered close enough to unleash his rage.

One dreary October afternoon, when Killer's master did not return at the scheduled hour and the dog grew very hungry, Killer launched into a series of growls and barks that tore through the neighborhood like an enemy bombardment. More than one former soldier turned to his wife and suggested that someone ought to turn a machine gun on the beast. Certainly more than one nervous housewife agreed.

Killer was well into his second hour of throaty cacophony when little Niko Madonie, the four-year-old boy whose family lived across the street, stopped playing for the day because he couldn't stand the noise any longer.

Niko had been in the side yard of his home, doing one of his favorite things, making mud pies. He had a sprinkling-can full of water that he used to turn the dirt beside the house into mud. He also had an old tuna-fish can that he kept packing with mud and then banging onto the sidewalk until a can-shaped pie emerged.

Niko had been happy and feeling very successful until the barking began. But making mud pies was delicate work, and each time Killer barked Niko flinched and banged the can awkwardly, until the mud pie oozed out of the can and onto the sidewalk in a soggy, unappetizing mess.

It was about the time that his fourth pie went bad, and little Niko was shaking with anger and frustration, that he saw his grandmother hobbling out of the house, across the yard and into the garage. She didn't even look at him.

His grandmother never went into the garage except to gather gardening tools, Niko thought, and she certainly wasn't about to start gardening when it was already getting dark.

"Bob – cha," Niko called. It was what Niko's mother had asked him to call the old woman. If it were up to little Niko, he would have called her 'Witch', because her dark clothes, ugly appearance and strange way of speaking had convinced him long ago that that's what she really was.

Niko got to his feet just as he saw Babcia march across the street directly into the face of Killer's endless barking. She was carrying something. Niko wasn't sure what it was, and so he ran quietly after her, crossing the street between the houses, even though his mother had told him never to. He hunched down as he ran. If Babcia were to see him he would be in trouble.

Niko's grandmother paused for a moment to unfasten the gate to Killer's yard. Niko dove in back of a bush just a few feet behind her. She shouldn't go into the yard, Niko thought. Killer was a dangerous dog that could harm a little boy and probably a scary old woman too, even if she was a witch.

Babcia opened the gate and entered the yard, and as soon as she did little Niko darted up to the fence. He peered through a small knothole even though Killer's wild barking came blasting through it, slamming him in the face and making him shake, just as he had shaken as he pounded the tuna can onto the sidewalk.

Then, the barking stopped.

Niko watched as his grandmother moved quietly in front of the dog. She turned to reveal the tool she had taken from the garage. It was a huge, double-headed axe.

Killer, who would normally have lunged at any intruder, caught sight of the red glint in her eyes, a glint that was far more dangerous than he was. The dog knew it. He whimpered, lowered his head, and backed away.

The old woman was very close to the dog by then. She stepped on the chain that held him to the post. When she did it, she fixed his neck in a tight position near the ground, and then she slowly raised the axe above her head. Niko gasped. Killer whimpered.

"Enough that," Babcia murmured in her thick Polish accent, and then she swung the axe with all the surety of a master butcher. There was a horrible slicing thud as she severed the dog's huge head with one blow, and drove the blade of the axe deep into the ground. Blood spurted up onto Babcia's face and, for one horrible moment, Niko saw the witch turn, smile, and then lick the blood from her lips greedily.

Niko buried his face in his arm to stifle a scream, and then he turned and ran back across the street, through his back door and up into his bedroom, where he threw himself on the bed and buried his face deep in his pillow.

In the yard across the way there was silence except for the spurting of blood as it pumped from the dog's great neck. Killer's head had rolled across the yard, muzzle still drooling, saucer-eyes still bulging.

Babcia did not move any closer to the dog. She did not touch or say anything more. She merely licked her bloody lips again, and smiled with satisfaction, before taking her axe and walking away.

When the dog's owner finally arrived home, he was spooked by the eerie silence that sat on the neighborhood like a shroud. And then he discovered his pet, his watchdog, decapitated. He seemed to go mad himself, almost becoming Killer the dog, barking at the neighbors in wild rage.

He called the police and had them go door-to-door questioning everyone in the neighborhood. No one knew anything about Killer's death, or so they said. And they were surely telling the truth, because, as relieved as they were to be rid of the dog, the neighbors were far more terrified by the specter of an axe-wielding dog-killer among them, someone who might be capable of performing the same swift and sure annihilation on a human being.

For weeks, children were not allowed to go outside and play for fear that they might come in contact with the murderer. This turned out to be quite unfortunate because, as you know, there actually had been a witness to the crime. Little Niko Madonie was traumatized by it to be sure. But he would not say a word about it to anyone. His grandmother had murdered Killer. Unfortunately, she was the very person that his parents decided should baby-sit the following evening. And so they locked him at home with her... for safety's sake.

Chapter Two

Come Play Me

Niko's parents were getting dressed for a night at the movies, and the boy was standing so close to his mother that she could barely move.

Dr. Louis Madonie noticed it, felt that his son always stood so very close to his wife. When she moved Little Niko moved right along with her, as though he couldn't bear to be more than a few inches away from her at any time. That seemed wrong to the Doctor. And then he wondered if the boy was trying to get as far from him as possible? Damn! Where was the affection he had dreamed of all those nights in the foxholes of Europe while the Nazis bombed his position and thoughts of his family were the only things that kept him sane?

"Niko, come here," the doctor said.

Niko glanced at his father, and then took a step backward.

"Helen, send the boy over to me."

Instead, Niko's mother put her arm around her son and drew him closer.

"Give him time, Lou," she said. "He's still adjusting."

The doctor shook his head in frustration. Who thought

coming home to a loving family would be so difficult. Still...
he knew his wife was right. So he walked slowly up to Niko.

"Niko, look at me," he said.

The boy tried to tuck himself in behind his mother's
skirts.

"Niko. Son... You're going to spend the night with Bab
– ka, is that okay?"

The boy didn't move, just stood there with a strange expression on his face.

"For heaven's sake, can't you get my mother's name
right? Helen asked with a smile. "It's Bob – cha."

The pretty, young woman breezed to the closet and back
again, and in the process she was able to find her husband the
perfect tie to go with his new grey suit. Niko didn't follow
her this time. He stood rooted to the spot... in terror.

"Bob-cha, It's Polish for grandmother," said Mrs.
Madonie.

"Should be Polish for witch," the doctor answered. He
didn't like his mother-in-law, and he had the sense that his
son didn't like her either. He was right.

For as long as little Niko could remember he believed
that if Babcia turned and looked directly at him he would die.
Of course she did turn and look at him, and Niko was quite
surprised when he did not die. But he was still very afraid.

#

As soon as his parents were out the front door Niko ran and
grabbed a little toy car and knelt down in the very far corner
of the room, as far away from the old witch as he could get.

"Niko," Babcia called as she dusted the distant bookshelf.

Niko glanced up out of the corner of his eye and saw
that the witch's back was to him. She hadn't seen him, and
he was safe.

"Niko," she called again, and this time she came looking for him.

Niko concentrated on his little car. If he thought about it hard enough maybe he could forget about Killer and the witch. He spun the car's wheels fast, let it go, and watched it fly across the room, directly up to Babcia.

Babcia heard it. She turned and shuffled toward it.

"What this?" she cackled. And then she swooped down in one of her quick witch's moves and grabbed it.

Niko froze as the witch studied the toy. She smiled.

"Niko," she said in her thick Polish accent, "Come play me."

Niko stared at the floor, not daring to look up. And then he heard her hobbling right up to him. "Niko, look me!"

Little Niko looked up into that deadly witch's face, the very face that had licked dog's blood from its lips. Her eyes were glowing red, blood red. Niko scurried into the closet and slammed the door.

Inside the closet Niko could hear his grandmother plodding around the house, humming some ancient tune.

"Niko, come play me," she called after a long while. "Making gingerbread. Drawing pictures."

He let out a muffled groan, pulled an old coat down over his head, and waited.

After a little while the smell of gingerbread drifted in under the door and filled the closet. It was spicy- sweet and inviting.

"Niko, come play me. Drawing pretty pictures. Making gingerbread," Babcia called. She was right outside.

Niko waited. He did not want to be alone with this horror.

He heard his grandmother hobble away at last. There was no sound at all, not even humming. But the tempting smell of gingerbread was growing stronger.

At last Niko crawled out from under the coat. He opened the door slowly. He saw a plate of warm gingerbread cookies sitting on the dining room table far across the hardwood floor. A glass of milk sat beside it. He could also see a big box of crayons and a stack of drawing paper.

Niko slid out of the closet, made his way across the floor, climbed up onto the chair and breathed in the sweet, spicy smell. He grabbed a cookie and jammed the whole thing into his mouth. He was ready to make a quick getaway if the witch appeared again. She did not.

As he drank his milk Niko wondered where Babcia had put the bloody axe. He picked up another cookie and took a smaller bite. He chewed it a little more slowly. He loved the warmth of it and the sweet, spicy taste. Maybe witches who kill noisy dogs don't always kill little boys.

He hoped so.

There was a drawing on the table beside the box of crayons, a drawing that the witch had done. It was a gingerbread house sparkling with pink and white frosting. And yet it frightened Niko. The witch had drawn little black squiggly shapes between the frosting shingles. Only the shapes weren't just squiggles; they were tiny silhouettes of witches: dancing, laughing, flying into the sky.

"Ohhhh, noooooo," Niko called.

Surely any ordinary little boy would have run, but Niko did not. Instead he grabbed a piece of paper, pulled a black crayon from the box, and began a drawing of his own.

He outlined a larger figure: wild, scary with a hooked nose and scraggly teeth, a pointed hat, and claw-like fingers. It was an evil witch. Very good, Niko thought to himself, and then he looked up to see the witch standing right there.

"I frighten you?" Babcia asked. Niko nodded, and then he quickly turned back to his drawing. Maybe if he didn't look at the witch she would go away. Maybe if he didn't draw the headless dog she would not know that he had been a witness. Maybe he was right. Babcia shuffled off into the kitchen and closed the door behind her.

Niko was alone. He tried to imagine what might be going on in that kitchen. What might a witch be doing in there? Niko drew a great dark cauldron. The drawing seemed especially appropriate because there was a new smell in the air: the sickening smell of blood, and heart; gizzards and liver; and garlic; the makings of blood sausage. It was his grandmother's favorite food. Niko would never eat it, no matter how long his mother made him sit at the table staring at it on his plate. He hated it, hated to think about it, hated to smell it even more.

The blood sausage smell collided with the aroma of spicy gingerbread to create a sickening aroma that roiled Niko's stomach and made him want to throw up.

He tried to work through it, tried to concentrate on his drawings. He drew wisps of fumes spiraling up out of the witch's cauldron. But then something else caught his attention, something worse than Babcia's terrifying face or the smell of her sickening brew.

Babcia was singing in her usual off-key way, but now she was using a language that Niko had never heard before. It wasn't the Polish that Babcia sometimes spoke with his mother, and it wasn't the Italian that his father's family spoke. This was a language that was different and terrible, and it was growing more and more terrible by the moment as it shifted from the tuneless rhymes of an old woman to the guttural snarls of an animal.

Get out of here! Niko heard a frightened voice screaming inside of him. You don't want to hear this. Babcia is a witch. She's a monster.

Niko put his hands over his ears and shook his head, but the voice inside of him, calling out for a thousand generations of frightened little children, kept right on screaming.

Run! Babcia's a witch. You saw what she did to Killer. She can do the same thing to you! She can cut off your head, throw you in that pot, boil your liver and make you into blood sausage. Run!

But Niko did not run. He just kept drawing, now almost frantically. And his drawings were growing darker still, inspired by the low guttural sounds coming from the kitchen, the growls that sounded more and more like a vicious, wild animal.

#

When Niko's parents came home they found Babcia's drawing and a stack of eight other drawings all done by Niko. They were all of the witch. Niko had long since sought refuge in his room, and Babcia had completed her tasks and gone to bed too.

"Ancient, Old-Country crap," Niko's father muttered as he looked at the pictures. "She's starting to fill his head with nonsense."

Niko's mother wasn't angry when she saw the pictures. She was terrified.

"He knows," she murmured to herself in horror.

"He knows!"

Chapter Three

Babcia Michalina

Helen Madonie knew her mother was a witch. It was as simple as that. Babcia was not a classic fairytale witch, of course. She didn't ride a broom or consort with black cats. Babcia practiced a darker, more monstrous evil, an evil that had possessed her one horrible night in the ancient forests of Poland.

Babcia was called Michalina then.

She was a girl of only fifteen years. It was nearly eleven years since witches had taken her, and left that little twisted bundle of sticks outside her father's home. The boy who would become her husband, who would give up everything for her, saw Michalina for the first time while hunting in those woods.

He thought at first that she was some kind of woodland sprite who was teasing him, dancing away, just out of reach, almost out of sight, except for those moments when she chose to show herself to him for just an instant, before darting away again even deeper into the forest.

Michalina wore the black and red garments of the Polish witches, but she had pulled them tight around her so that, with every glance, the young hunter saw more and more of her beautiful figure: her shapely hips; thin waist; full breasts and long, inviting legs.

The young man stalked her as he would a doe, and she let him. She led him deeper and deeper into the woods, teasing him every step of the way, and when they reached the deepest part of the forest she suddenly disappeared, only to pop up behind him, spin him around and pin his shoulders against the trunk of a huge, moss-covered tree.

Her look was curious and playful. She was strong (witch strong) and not shy at all. Still, she let the young man pull away, let him turn her around until it was she who was pinned against the yellow-green moss.

The young man kissed her. Michalina did not resist. He pressed his body against hers, harder, more passionately. He let his hands slide up her legs and onto her breasts, and then suddenly he exploded, drenching himself in the sticky warmth of an immense orgasm. He pulled away at once in embarrassment. Michalina giggled.

Incensed, the young man raised his hand to strike her. She merely looked at him, looked at the raised hand, looked into his eyes. There was no sign of fear, none whatsoever. He stopped cold. She smiled and pushed the young man backwards onto the ground. He began to get up, but she was upon him instantly, striding over him, pulling up her skirts eagerly. She had been initiated into the ways of sex very early in her training. It was something she neither feared nor doubted. She yanked the young man's breeches to his knees. She smiled, then knelt upon him, and shivered as she felt him enter her. Tearing her blouse open, she pulled his hands onto her breasts, letting him caress them as she rode.

Michalina moaned joyfully. Her sexual experience was rich enough to know that such a young man could recharge in a matter of moments. And so she brought him to another swift climax and then another and another.

After that, as the shadows grew longer, they talked about who he was, about his dreams, about hers (a husband and children), about her arts and her dark, secret crafts.

Michalina told him how difficult things had been when she first came to the coven, how she had resisted the witches and how they had been so patient, exposing her ever so slowly to their ways, until she embraced them.

The hardest part had been leaving her father. She missed him so, but she could not go back. It would be death for her, and perhaps for him. And so she chose to watch him from a distance, watch him age so much more swiftly than she.

One day Michalina was told that her father had been attacked and beaten by highwaymen, and that he was dying. She was allowed to go to him then. Disguising herself as a hearty young man, she tended to him. She restored his health long enough to become his friend. But it would not be for long. Soon enough the ravages of the attack took their toll, his heart gave out, and he died. But it had been kind and generous of the witches to give her that time with her father, and they had been clever enough to do it in a way that prevented her discovery by the village authorities.

Michalina and her young man would not be as clever and would pay a terrible price for it.

The young man visited Michalina every day from the time they met... to be loved and beguiled by her witchcraft. He abandoned his home and his family to become hers, to accept her ways, to join with her in a witch's Handfasting Ceremony far from the eyes of the village. But foolishly, he spoke openly about it to his family, and to many in his village.

#

It was less than a year later. Little Jarek, Michalina's infant son who had been sucking so sweetly at her breast, was suddenly ripped from her by five men who broke down the door to her cottage and charged in. Waving a notice from the town magistrate, they proclaimed Michalina and her family to be witches. Then, that very night, in that very place, with only the merest shadow of a trial, they began their executions.

The men who had been his friends shackled Michalina's poor husband to the wall. They ripped open the front of his breeches and castrated him on the spot. Then, seizing Michalina, they stuffed the whole bloody mess into her mouth and beat her, chanting, "Eat it, eat it, eat it witch!"

Next, they began to toss Little Jarek like some rag doll from one to the other, the whole gang of them, pitching the baby high into the air, letting him fall almost to the floor before grabbing an arm or a leg and jerking him cruelly upward, breaking bones and tearing muscles in the process.

Young Michalina shrieked as she witnessed it all. She cursed while the men tried to beat her into silence. This was the kind of brutality Michalina had been warned about by her sisters in the coven, brutality that was common in that age of witch-hunts and hatred. Now it was happening to her own little family.

The men grabbed Michalina's snow-white hair and pulled her head back, forcing her to watch as one of them took a spike from near the fire and brought it to her infant son. Their intention was clear: skewer the baby alive, drive the spike through him from head to foot, then throw him onto the spit and roast the cursed child alive.

That was the moment it happened. For Michalina it was not so much the answer to a prayer as it was a surrender.

She did not ask to be transformed. She only gave in to the enormous forces of anger that possessed her.

As her husband bled to death and her infant son was about the be impaled, the sixteen-year-old girl suddenly began to growl, to snap at the air like a mad dog, to change, to grow, to twist and transform. The men suddenly fell back as they saw what was happening.

Thick animal hair sprouted up her neck and down from her head. Claws stretched out from her fingertips. Her legs grew longer and more muscular. Her body became broad and hunched over. She raged at the men. Experienced witch hunters, they were nonetheless far too terrified to escape.

She moved on them one after another. The blood from her husband's organs, still spilling from her mouth, was soon washed away by newer blood from the throats, stomachs and entrails of each and every attacker.

In less than an hour there was nothing left of them. But it was too late, wasn't it? Michalina's husband lay dead on the floor. Her sweet baby, spared the stake and fire, was dead anyway. Michalina gathered up the broken little body and pressed it to her.

"Moj piekny chlopczyk," she murmured, "My beautiful little boy." These atrocities would never happen again, she vowed, not in her village, not anywhere. Never to someone she loved!

It would be almost four hundred years before Michalina would have another child. Four hundred years before Helen and her sisters would be born to Michalina from a new husband in a new land, America. But even in that distant future place and time, she would remember her vow. Atrocities to her loved ones would never happen again.

She would make sure of that.

Chapter Four

The Goal

It was a bright, sunny day on Valentine Road, and an especially important one for the Madonie family. Dr. Louis Madonie, fresh back from World War Two, had hung out his shingle for the first time and was amazed to find that several patients had made their way into his waiting room.

Helen Madonie was in the kitchen trying to deal with the breakfast dishes, but she couldn't really. She had to find a way to tell Niko more about his grandmother, explain that her powers were real, that they were dangerous, but that they would not hurt him, at least not directly.

How could she tell him? The questions so distracted her that somehow she hadn't done much of anything to arrange for Niko's care that day, and so once again the little boy found himself in the company of the witch.

Niko had been so frightened by his last encounter with Babcia that he had finally rushed to his room closing the door against her. And yet she hadn't tried to hurt him, he realized. She hadn't come into his room without asking his permission. And only after a long time, when her voice sounded very human again, did little Niko let Babcia bring him another plate of warm cookies that smelled sweet and spicy, and not at all like the bloody sausage and other evil things that she had been cooking in the kitchen.

Babcia didn't look quite so terrifying this bright sunlit morning, Niko thought, but he didn't dare look directly at her anyway. Instead he busied himself with the little swing that his mother had hung in the doorway of the garage. It was tailored for a four-year-old like Niko. It had a high back and two arms that made sitting in it very comfortable.

Niko sat in the swing and rocked. He could push himself off the garage step and swing just a little bit.

He had to keep busy, if only to keep himself distracted.

The witch was digging in the garden, tending to the cabbage and humming in her own tuneless way. Niko still felt a chill at the sound of her voice. He needed a distraction and decided to try something new, something very daring for a four year old. He got out of the swing and turned to face it. He stepped up onto the seat and then one, two, up onto the arms. It worked very well, so well that he wanted more.

The swing was barely moving as he stepped up from the arms to the back of the seat so that he was standing on top of it as he held onto the ropes.

This was great. Niko turned to look into the kitchen to catch an approving glance from his mother, but she wasn't looking.

Niko peered into the garden for Babcia, but he couldn't see her. And then suddenly she popped up from behind a big rose bush with an arm full of clippings, looking all bristly and wild.

Niko let out a cry and tipped over backwards on the swing. He hit the ground with a great, jarring thud and immediately felt thick, red fluid ooze all around his head and shoulders. It was his own blood.

"Momma!" Niko screamed.

In a second his mother was there. She snatched him up and rushed him into the house, through her husband's waiting room, right into his office where he was listening to a man's chest with a stethoscope.

Dr. Lou could see the terror in his wife's face, and he could see the thick red blood pouring out all over her hands.

"Quick, here," he said tapping his table, as his patient jumped out of the way.

Niko felt his father's strong fingers pushing against the very back of his neck. He felt a soft, wet cloth swabbing the area, and he knew that the bleeding had stopped. But it didn't stop hurting, and he didn't stop wailing.

"It's okay, little Niko," his mother said from across the room. She had pulled back into the corner to watch her husband.

Dr. Louis Madonie had been a medic in the war, and he made quick work of the wound. But Niko kept wailing until his father pulled himself around in front of the little boy and looked directly into his eyes.

"Are you a man or a mouse?" his father asked sternly.

Niko fought hard to sniff back the tears, but it wasn't easy and he continued to blubber.

"A real man doesn't cry like a baby," his father said. "Don't you want to be a real man like your daddy? Don't you want to be a soldier?"

Niko didn't really know what his father was talking about, but he did sniff back the tears and quiet himself. That's when he saw his mother in the corner. The look on her face had gone from uncertainty and concern to wide-eyed love at this latest heroic act of her husband.

Niko's father finished stitching up the wound just as he had stitched up the wounds of hundreds of soldiers during the Battle of The Bulge.

"How'd this happen?" he asked.

"I wasn't there," his mother answered. "He was in the yard."

"Alone?"

"Babcia was there."

"That old witch," Dr. Lou said as though he were cursing.

"She's my mother," Helen Madonie replied. Her smile faded only slightly.

"I'm sorry," answered his father. But Niko could tell by the look on his face that his father really wasn't sorry.

"All done," said the doctor, as he lifted the little boy from the table.

"Say 'Thank you, Daddy,'" Niko's mother told him.

"Thank you, Daddy," Niko whispered.

"You know, Niko," his mother responded with another beautiful, confident smile, "you could grow up to become a doctor like your daddy one day. Wouldn't you like that?"

"I've got bigger plans for this little guy," Dr. Lou said proudly. "He and I are going to write a great novel together, the story of my adventures in World War Two. It will be an American 'War and Peace'. I've been planning it for years. In fact, the idea kept me sane during the worst days of the war."

Helen was surprised to think that her husband had imagined a future for himself and their little boy, and such an ambitious one. She loved the idea so much that she wanted to join in.

"And he could write the movie script, too," she added enthusiastically. Dr. Lou closed his eyes for a moment and thought. "Nah, that's kids' stuff. Nope, no movies. We'll do serious writing: great novels; American Novels; Moby Dick; The Last of The Mohicans."

"But he likes to draw," Helen answered. "I could see him at the Disney Studio working on the next Snow White."

"Helen!" Dr. Lou said sternly, "I've got it all figured out. Niko and I are going to write a serious novel together and that doesn't mean Disney cartoons."

Helen Madonie frowned. Why couldn't Niko figure out what he wanted to do for himself? And it was all so far in the future anyway. The look in her husband's eyes was a little obsessive, wasn't it? The war had done it, she decided. Something happened over there that had changed her husband. And now it would be up to her to help heal the wounds, to make him whole again. What a romantic idea. She smiled lovingly again, and then she spoke to her little boy.

"Do you want to be a serious writer?" she asked Niko without taking her eyes from her husband.

Little Niko didn't even know what a serious writer was, but he knew one thing. What he really wanted to become was the man his mother looked at in adoration.

And the less it had to do with his father, the better.

Chapter Five

The Book

Niko's parents were arguing in the kitchen. Even though all the doors were closed, he could hear them from the living room. He didn't know exactly what they were arguing about, but somehow he was sure that it had to be him.

Suddenly, Dr. Lou burst into the room and looked around frantically. When he saw his little son his expression turned from exasperation to tenderness. It was perhaps one of the most tender moments Niko would ever experience with his father.

"I've got a treat for you, Honey, a real treat," the doctor said.

Little Niko smiled. "Honey?" He felt a slight twinge of affection for his father and knew he had to fight it off.

"Where is it?" Dr. Lou said suddenly, and then he marched up to the bookcase and took down a very large book. He flipped through the pages quickly, smiled and turned to his son.

"Here it is, Honey. How'd you like me to read you a story?"

Little Niko nodded.

"Great!" said the doctor. "And what a book I've got for you. Did I ever tell you about it?"

Little Niko shook his head.

"Well, during that terrible war Daddy fought, the one that kept him away from you and Mommy for so long, Daddy was stationed in London."

Niko looked up at his father. He had no idea what he was talking about, and he still didn't trust him either.

"One day planes flew overhead. It was those damn Germans, the enemy, coming to bomb one of our greatest allies.

"Bombs fell, buildings exploded, people ran around everywhere looking for places to hide. And when it was all over, your Daddy came out of hiding to see what had happened. Do you know what he found?"

"A treasure." Niko answered.

"Be serious."

Niko felt a nasty chill. He looked into the doorway of the room and saw his mother beaming at them. He could feel her pride as she took it all in. It made Niko feel worse. He was starting to hate his father.

"What did you find?" Helen Madonie asked on her son's behalf.

"I found this book, lying in the gutter. It must have been blown out of one of the houses."

"Did you give it back to the people in the house?" Niko asked.

"The house was blown up, Honey," Dr. Lou answered. "There were no people there. So I took the book and sent it back to your mommy. And she got it a brand new binding. So now I can read it to you whenever you want. What story would you like to hear?"

"What stories are there?"

"It's Grimm's Fairy Tales, so there are a lot of your favorite stories: Snow White, Sleeping Beauty, Little Red Riding Hood. Would that be a good one?"

"I like Little Red Riding Hood," said Niko's mother.

"Then I like it, too," Little Niko answered.

Dr. Lou was very happy, and he flipped through several pages, which showed pictures of gnarled old witches and horrible trolls. Niko was relieved to see that his father turned the pages quickly so he did not really have to look at them. At last he came to a very safe-looking page, just words and a silhouette of a little girl in a big cape.

Niko settled into his father's lap as the doctor started to read. Niko's mother smiled and went back into the kitchen.

And so it began, the familiar story of a little girl being pursued by an evil wolf. Niko felt better because it was a little girl and not a little boy. Parts of the story were funny, like the part where the wolf ate the grandmother, put on her clothes and jumped into her bed.

Someone had written the words "Oh No" with a pen at the bottom of the next page, and four-year-old Niko could read well enough to recognize those words. It was a warning of what was to come. Even he knew that.

His father turned the page.

And there it was, the scariest picture in the book, scarier than all the witches and trolls and everything else put together, a picture little Niko would never forget as long as he lived: a huge bed with a grandmother under the covers, only it wasn't a grandmother. It was a WOLF, a scary evil wolf, a scary evil grandmother. A grandmother who was a wolf!

"Babcia!" Niko screamed, jumped to his feet and pointed at the picture. He began to cry.

"I hate that book, I hate that grandma! I hate you, Daddy!"

Dr. Lou was alarmed. "Stop it, Niko. Stop it!"

Little Niko wouldn't stop; he just kept crying. The last thing the soldier wanted was to have his wife hear this.

"Stop it!" he said loudly, and he pulled the boy up right in front of him so that he could look directly into his eyes.

"What kind of a man are you?" Niko's father growled. "A real man doesn't get frightened by pictures in books. A real man doesn't cry. He knows how to keep it inside. You don't want to scare your mommy, do you?"

Niko sniffed back the tears and shook his head. He certainly did not want to do that.

"You don't want your mommy to think you are afraid of pictures in books, do you?"

"No."

"You want your mommy to think that you're a real man like your daddy, don't you?"

"Yes."

"Then hop back up here and let me finish the story."

"NOOOOOO!"

Niko bolted away and ran to his room where he buried himself deep under the covers, clothes and all. He curled up into a ball and stayed there without moving.

He did not respond at all when his mother came to try and comfort him. He did not say a word when his father came to apologize for scaring him. Dr. Lou had been instructed to do so by Niko's mother; even the little boy knew that.

There were two other things that little Niko knew as well:

1 – He wasn't a real man like his mother and father wanted him to be,

2 – He really, really hated his father.

#

Niko had not noticed the pair of witch eyes that watched as he ran from that horrible book with its wicked pictures.

Who knows what his reaction might have been if he had seen Babcia observing it all and knowing that it was her name he called when he saw the wolf-grandmother?

Would he have thought that she, too, wanted him to be a man? Would she be so angry that she would get her axe, chop off his head and then lick HIS blood from her smiling lips?

Niko couldn't figure it out. Except that now he actually did have to be a man. That is, he had to do something important, awful and frightening, something he didn't want to do, but something he absolutely must do.

He had to make his way through that whole, big, pitch-dark house to go to the bathroom, and he had to tiptoe past the wolf-witch's bedroom to do it.

He had twisted himself into knots for half the night, waiting for daylight to arrive. But daylight did not come. He had thought of wetting his bed, but he knew how much that would upset his mother. And so he pulled back the covers and crept out into the frigid, frightening air, past a bed and a shape that was so very much like the scene of the wolf-grandma in that terrible book.

He had to go. And yet, the only thing scarier than the shadowy image of Babcia lying in bed looking just like that wolf was the view down the stairway into the pitch-blackness of the main floor of the house.

Who knew what monsters lurked down there?

Babcia was snoring in frightening wolf-like growls. Moreover, her tiny bedroom was dark and shadowy, with only a bit of moonlight illuminating the table beside her bed. The little end table with its small Tiffany lamp also held a glass full of water, and, in that water, were her yellow witch's teeth. Niko had never seen anything like that before. But at least she wouldn't be able to bite him.

Old clothes hung over the open edge of the closet door. They formed the shape of a hulking monster, like the wolf itself. There were smells too, many of them: blood sausage; sweet, lovely gingerbread, and another smell too — Babcia's own smell, like a great, hairy animal. Niko dared not think about that at all.

"What you doing?" Babcia suddenly growled, as she rose up out of the bed very much as the wolf must have loomed above Red Riding Hood.

"Why Grandma, what big teeth you have," Niko felt like saying, and then he remembered that her teeth were in the glass, so he only whimpered.

"No disturb you parents," Babcia scolded.

"But I have to GO," Niko said in a pleading voice.

"Go?" asked Babcia, and then she smiled a terrible, toothless smile.

"No need go down in dark for that."

And Babcia pulled her huge, animal frame out of the bed, bent down low, and took a white porcelain pot out from underneath the dust ruffle.

"Go here," she cackled. And then Babcia smiled again, a wide, toothless smile, and she turned away to give the little boy some privacy. Niko liked the fact that he didn't have to look into her face. And so he went about his business, and even dared to ask the old witch a question.

"Do I have to do it, Babcia?"

"What?" the old crone responded.

"Be a man like my daddy, write a book for him. I don't think I can."

Babcia cackled. "Such nonsense! Get in bed."

"Can I beat him, Babcia? Can I be better than he is? Can I do stuff that will make my mother love me more than she loves him? Can I make him, you know?"

"Jealous?" The old witch cackled. "That be good, no?"

Niko nodded.

"You can," Babcia answered. "I help you."

Niko got a sick feeling. He feared that he might be entering into some terrible pact. Babcia was an old witch who lopped off the heads of noisy dogs. But even more monstrous was the 'thing' she had become in the kitchen only a few nights before. And now she wanted to help him?

Fortunately, those kinds of thoughts were all too much for little Niko, and so he just nodded his head.

Babcia flipped back the covers, grabbed the little boy and flung him into that wolf-witch's bed beside her.

Niko was frightened and consoled at the same time, and so he spent the night feeling comforted and yet chillingly aware that he could be eaten alive at any moment. And he was certainly very glad when the sun came up the next morning and his mother came to rescue him.

CHAPTER SIX

THE SALE

Babcia woke before the sun rose. She wrapped herself in her musty old grey robe and hobbled quietly down the carpeted stairs and into the doctor's library. The room was ice cold... at least that's what she thought. Why else was she shivering so?

Babcia popped on the overhead light and smiled. There it was: The Book, Grimm's Fairy Tales, back in its usual place on the shelf. She reached up for it, and as she did she felt an electric charge leap from the book and sear into her fingertips.

"Dog's blood!" she cursed, and she swept her gnarled hand in front of the bookshelf, drawing Grimm's Fairy Tales out from its place. Then she spun, sending the book flying without ever touching it, flinging it with all her might hard against the opposite wall.

The book exploded into flames when it hit. Burning pages blasted high into the air. Images of witches and ogres and monsters spun and smoked and sizzled up and down and all around Babcia. The book cover and spine melted into a black knot that seemed to draw itself ever inward until it was little more than a small lump of coal.

Babcia smiled at that moment... actually laughed, mistakenly. For, when the fire had burned itself out, there was the book, cover and pages perfectly intact. There was the reassembled book blasting straight at her head. Only the witchery of nimble footing allowed Babcia to duck out of the way as the book buried itself back into Dr. Madonie's bookshelf.

"Is seeking me out," the witch cackled to herself. "Has found me and wants me. Must be rid of it."

#

Soon thereafter, Helen Madonie learned that she had a job, something she did not want to do, and yet she must. Babcia told her in clear and direct Polish to get rid of that awful book, the book that scared little Niko with its horrible images of wolves and witches, the book that, although she never admitted it to her daughter, held such evil powers.

Helen sat alone in the book buyer's reception area now, clutching the book, almost afraid to look at it, until the receptionist approached her.

"Mr. Mandel will see you now, Mrs...."

"Madonie," Helen answered. "Thank you."

The receptionist ushered Helen into an even smaller room filled from floor to ceiling with books. The desk at the center of the room was piled high with them, and there were more stacks in the corners and on the floor.

"Mrs. Madonie?"

Mr. Mandel peered out from behind the highest stack on his desk. He had a very slight build, almost no hair and a pencil-thin moustache that was not at all in style. Helen could think of only one word to describe him: bookish.

"What can I do for you?"

"I want to sell this book," she said. "It's very rare, valuable, I'm told. My husband found it in a bombed-out section of London during the war."

Helen handed the book to Mandel. The man's eyes lit up as soon as he saw it. He opened the book and turned carefully through the pages, almost caressing them. Then he looked back up at Mrs. Madonie and tried with all his might to hide the glee he was feeling.

"And why do you want to sell it?" he asked.

"It scares my son," she answered. "There are pictures in there that make him think his grandmother is a witch."

Mandel laughed.

"This is one of the very books that helped carry the myth of evil witches into the 20th century," he said. "It was at the heart of the very last witch hunts in England. It inspired fear in thousands, not just your little boy."

"No wonder my mother wanted me to get rid of it," Helen said.

"YOUR mother, Mrs. Madonie? The woman your son thinks is a witch?"

"Yes."

"And do you think she's a witch?"

Helen felt a chill flash through her. She certainly had not anticipated that question.

Bobby McKnight had proven Babcia's powers to Helen when she was only ten years old. And Helen did not want to go back to that terrible moment, not even in her memory, back to the Polish intersection where American kids like Bobby pulled her hair and made fun of her, made fun of her sisters, and made fun of Babcia.

Her mother was truly frightening then, looking like some ancient hag. And she was such a massive woman, bigger in every way than anyone else in her family, even Helen's father. And people had been afraid of Babcia because of that. At least that is what Helen thought at first.

The neighborhood children often taunted Babcia when she visited the general store. The other kids, who were mostly German or English or Scottish or anything other than Polish, called her "Polak!" and threw things at her. But Babcia had a way of silencing them with just a look, a look so frightening that it even scared her daughter.

Bobby McKnight had been the worst of them, Helen remembered; he was the ringleader. He organized the group that decided to commit the ultimate prank one Halloween night so many years ago.

"Steal the Polak's fat old cow, Stella," he insisted.

Helen could just imagine Bobby and his gang planning it all. They were big, strong boys in their late teens. Drag the cow from her pasture and lead her over to the schoolhouse. That would be easy for them. Then get old Stella right into the principal's office, fill her full of castor oil, and let her shit her insides out.

Helen could imagine how the boys must have laughed as they made their plans. Didn't they know they were dealing with a witch?

"Mrs. Madonie, I don't mean to distract you," the bookish man broke in, "But I AM interested in buying the book. Can you give me just another moment to page through it and make sure that it's clean?"

"Of course," Helen answered. She'd much rather talk to Mr. Mandel, as bookish as he was, than to relive her memories of that terrible Halloween night.

The townspeople might have been outraged when the boy's plans were carried out. And the rage would certainly have been compounded by the fact that the cow had actually died there in the principal's office amid all that shit. But the townspeople were distracted by a bigger event, one that completely overshadowed the vicious prank.

Bobby McKnight had been torn to shreds that same evening, ripped apart by a pack of dogs deep in the woods.

"A pack of dogs or a wolf," Helen murmured. "A pack or a single, enormous wolf," Helen said it louder and then suddenly found herself repeating her son's very words: "A wolf who's a grandmother, a grandmother who's a wolf."

"What's that?" the bookish man asked.

Helen couldn't speak; the memories were just too horrible. She had been there. She had seen it all, seen from her bedroom window as Bobby came back to their home to add perhaps one last prank to his Halloween festivities. Maybe he would tip over their outhouse. What a fool! Maybe he didn't know that the cow had died. Maybe he just wanted to add insult to injury. Maybe he just wanted to relive the crime. Still, what a fool!

"What a fool," Helen said aloud.

"Mrs. Madonie, are you all right?"

Helen did not know if she was all right. The horrific scene was deep in her past, and yet she was experiencing every moment of it again: running deep into the woods, feeling the harsh branches scratch across her face as she trailed after her mother. Babcia was chasing Bobby, screaming curses at him in Polish. And then Helen watched Babcia's strides grow longer. She outpaced the girl and yet Helen could still see her, see that Babcia was hobbling, skipping, twisting and then turning, before Helen's eyes, into a full, striding, monster she-wolf.

"DO YOU WANT TO BUY THE BOOK OR NOT?" Helen suddenly shouted at Mandel as she shook herself forcibly from her visions of the past. Her heart was pounding. Her eyes were burning.

"Of course, I want to buy it, of course," Mandel answered backing around behind the stack of books as though seeking refuge.

"Are you sure you're all right, Mrs. Madonie?"

"I'm fine."

"Good then. I just have one question. It's about the very last fairy tale in the book."

#

"Helen, where's my Grimm's Fairy Tales?" Dr. Lou snapped at his wife as she entered the kitchen that evening.

Helen took off her coat and tossed it across the back of one of the chairs. She went to the stove, poured herself a cup of coffee and sat down beside him.

"I put it away," she answered.

"Why?"

"Because it scares him, that's why. It makes him think his grandmother's a witch."

"Well, she is, you know," the doctor said with a grin.

"Stop that!" Helen said loudly, and then she slumped under the weight of the day's events and the memories they brought with them. She just sat there, staring at the coffee cup, doing her best to recover.

"Okay, you're right," Dr. Lou said at last, "She's not a witch, and I've been very cruel in calling her one." He put his hand gently on Helen's.

"But I DO want to read more of those stories to Niko. It'll get him used to facing scary situations. Make a man out of him."

"He's only four."

"Perfect time to get started."

"I've locked the damn thing up," she lied. "No one's

going to see it for a good long time. You can read it to him when he's older, some time when I think he's ready."

"Helen... sweet..."

"I said 'NO' and that's final."

And it was.

Dr. Louis Madonie never mentioned nor saw the book again, because Helen had sold it to the bookish man. And this was in spite of the last heretofore unknown fairy tale in the book, the one called, The Witch and the Soldier.

It told of a witch who loved her grandson so much that she vowed to do everything she could to protect him from the cruel world around him and from his very demanding father. According to the fairy tale, to accomplish the feat she would have to do something witches almost never want to do.

She would have to die.

CHAPTER SEVEN

THE DEATH OF BABCIA

Sunday afternoon, dinnertime, and the Madonie family was seated around the table sharing a meal that Helen was especially proud of, roast pork with mashed potatoes and gravy. Babcia had helped prepare it, and yet she had seemed particularly distant through it all.

Little Niko had said the grace. It was his favorite, one he made up himself. "Thanks for this delicious food, let's eat it, amen." And then he added his usual closing remark, "But not the peas."

It was at the moment, when Dr. Lou was shoveling a mountain of peas onto Niko's plate, that Helen noticed her mother. The old woman seemed to have turned into a statue. Her right hand was frozen in mid-air and her eyes stared into space with a quizzical expression.

"Babcia!" Helen Madonie screamed. Then she turned to her husband in panic.

"It's all right," the doctor answered, and he got up and walked slowly to Babcia. He took her hand, squeezed it, massaged it carefully, and somehow, miraculously, after only a moment, the old woman blinked her eyes, smiled and came back to life.

"It was a mini-stroke," the doctor said. "She'd better lie down."

Helen took her mother, led her to the couch in the living room, helped her lie down and get comfortable. And then she returned to the table.

Helen didn't say another word, nor did anyone else for the rest of the meal. But Helen smiled lovingly at her husband acknowledging this latest miracle.

He had brought her dead mother back to life.

The entire event made Niko angry all over again. How could he be better than a man who performed miracles?

#

Dr. Lou didn't feel like a miracle worker. That evening, as he sat alone after everyone else had gone to bed, he knew exactly what he had done and how he had done it. But he didn't like it. He didn't like saving Babcia's life, even though he knew it was only temporary. Soon Babcia would be gone. (Thank goodness for that.)

In his mind the old woman represented a dark, ancient evil, an evil that he was all too familiar with. He had experienced it first hand on the battlefields of Germany. And it hit him especially hard in Ohrdruf, the German concentration camp.

Dr. Madonie's unit, the 4th Armored Division, had entered the camp, and the sight they found was horrific. The Nazis had learned of the Americans' approach and, before they fled, had executed 40 prisoners.

All those left in the prison were dying, starving or both. The liberating American soldiers where mortified by this evidence of the human capacity for evil. But Dr. Lou had to look at it even more closely. He had to treat the poor wretches who were interned there. And he hated it, hated the old world, and hated the evil that he saw reflected so clearly in the vacant eyes of the victims. He hated the ancient rivalries and the dark human emotions that still blurred so often into the instincts of wild animals.

Sitting there in his home that evening, Dr. Lou knew that Babcia was a part of the undercurrent of that old world. Her death would be a blessing, the elimination of a woman who was tied to those dark forces. She was not a Nazi, of course. She was Polish. If she had been in the Old Country, she might very well have ended up in one of the concentration camps with the two million Polish nationals who were sent there.

How would her supposed witchcraft manifest itself in that situation? He knew that, too. He had seen it. Outside the concentration camp at Ohrdruf, they found the proof: six Nazi soldiers, their heads cut off, their headless bodies torn apart, their entrails strewn across the ground as if they had been slaughtered by some monstrous animal. But all around them were those twisted bundles of sticks, those calling cards of witchcraft.

Wasn't Babcia already gaining a hold on Niko? Dr. Lou asked himself. She loved him too much. It was unnatural. Helen wouldn't believe it. Niko wouldn't understand, but Doctor Louis Madonie did. He had been in Ohrdruf, come face to face with the devil of Europe. This was serious stuff, important, worthy of the great writer he wanted his son to become.

Dr. Lou lit a cigarette, took a deep drag and wondered if he could make it happen. He said a prayer for little Niko, that he would escape the dark forces of his grandmother and her world, and that he would grow up to be a writer capable of creating something really important, An American War and Peace. He took another deep puff, turned out the light, and made his way into the bathroom still puffing away.

He was right about Babcia's health, of course. Sometime over the next two hours, while the doctor lay fitfully awake in bed, Babcia died a peaceful, intentional death... which was only the beginning.

Chapter Eight

Kissing Witches

Niko didn't know what all the commotion was about. He came downstairs surprised to see that his chubby little Aunt Mamie was on the phone making some kind of arrangements. She and her Polish sisters all lived in Chicago, far away from his mother and her Italian-American husband.

When Niko turned the corner he saw that all his aunts were sitting at the breakfast table talking just as excitedly as Aunt Mamie. But when he moved toward the table, all eyes turned to him, all conversation stopped.

Niko's mother stood up from the table and moved toward her son. She knelt down in front of him.

"Niko, I have something to tell you," she began. Suddenly tears came streaming down her cheeks. "I'm afraid we've lost a friend," she said. "It's someone we both loved very much."

Niko wasn't sure whom she meant. His best friend was a little stuffed elephant that Aunt Mamie had knitted for him, and he knew that the little elephant was tucked safely in his bed. Still he had to ask.

"Is it Goggie?" he murmured.

"No," Niko's mother said with a loving smile. "It's someone more important than Goggie; it's Babcia."

"Babcia?"

"Yes, honey," his mother said. "She died last night; she's gone to heaven. We have to go say goodbye to her this morning, then we won't see her again until we go to heaven ourselves."

It was good that Mrs. Madonie put in the part about going to heaven when she explained Babcia's death to her son. Because it allowed her to rationalize the strange reaction she got from the boy when she told him that he would never see his grandmother again.

His face broadened into an enormous grin.

#

Dr. Lou met the boy and his mother at the doorway to the funeral home. He was solemn, as were Mrs. Madonie and her sisters and everyone else who entered the mortuary.

"Let's go see Babcia one last time," Dr. Lou said to his son.

"But I thought she was in heaven," said Niko.

"Well, she is. This is just her body; her soul is in heaven."

Niko's mother shook her head to suggest that Dr. Lou shouldn't delve too deeply into theology with a four-year-old. And so he didn't. The trio just walked slowly and deliberately toward the brightly polished, wooden coffin that was placed at the very end of the long room.

As they moved Niko could hear the crowd talking about him.

"He was very close to her, wasn't he?"

"Oh, yes, he loved her very much."

By then they were standing right before Babcia's coffin. It was rosewood and had a large, silk-lined top that opened. Little Niko could not see into the coffin, even when he stepped up onto the kneeler that was directly in front of it.

"Here, let me lift you," Niko's father offered, and he

raised the little boy slowly up over the edge of the coffin so that, like a passenger in a gradually rising glass elevator, he was brought into full view of the same gnarled, old face that he had been afraid to look at all his life. Babcia's eyes were closed. But those twisted lips were as frightening as ever.

"Kiss her goodbye, Niko," his mother whispered.

This was the last thing that the little boy wanted to do. Kiss her? He dared not even look at her. He squirmed to get away from the firm grip of his father.

"No!" he called out.

"Come on, Niko," his mother continued, "she's gone far away to be in heaven. You won't see her for a very long time."

"If she's gone to heaven, she won't know that I didn't kiss her," Niko said trying desperately to wiggle out of his father's grasp.

"Now that she's dead, she'll be everywhere," his mother answered. "She'll see everything. She'll know everything that happens to us. Now please, kiss her, Niko. She would like that very much."

Niko didn't know what was worse, the fact that he had to kiss the witch or that she would be everywhere and know everything. But then his father obediently moved him forward, pressing him closer and closer to the face of the evil witch.

At last little Niko closed his eyes, stuck out his lips, and felt them come in contact with something harsh and leathery. Most alarming of all, that something seemed to be moving too. Niko recognized a sudden overwhelming smell, a sickening mix of blood and spicy sweetness that hadn't been there before.

Niko opened his eyes. He was only inches from the witch when he saw her smile at him and open her eyes ever so slightly. Then he heard her whisper in a voice that no one else could hear.

"Niko, come play me."

Then everything went black.

CHAPTER NINE

NIKO'S CLOSET

There was no bogeyman in Niko's closet, no goblins or maniacs holding daggers thick with blood. No tigers clawed at the closet door to rip it down so they could pounce on the boy and devour him. There was no soul of a hanged serial killer transforming an innocent pile of sheets into the looming shape of a werewolf.

None of those monsters would have dared hide in Niko's closet, because that's where Babcia decided to stay.

Through the full-length mirror that was hanging on the closet door, Babcia watched and waited, guarding the boy, ready to rise up against any real or imagined danger. She became his own twisted protector.

As the years went by Babcia watched the caravan of toys that danced across the little boy's floor: performers and their circus tent; knights with their castles and dungeons; cars buzzing around little toy gas stations. She could have cast a spell and brought them all to life for him.

But she did not.

Babcia watched as Niko dressed for his first day of Military School. It was not a boarding school, just a day school that provided military training for the little boys who marched in and out of its classrooms every day. She saw him putting on his crisp, new uniform and his shirt with the hard, starched collar. She could have adjusted his hat and cleaned the polish off the back of his trousers where he had rubbed his shoes to brighten up the shine.

But she did not.

Babcia was patient with the comic books Niko read, first Donald Duck and then suddenly Captain Marvel and Plastic Man. She could have helped his efforts to draw as the comics were drawn, whispering charms across the room that would guide his crayons and pencils into more skillful illustrations. But she did not, and yet his drawings got better and better anyway, until they were fine, neat sketches. And all that magic came from Niko himself.

Babcia listened to the speeches that Niko made to the mirror as he prepared for his elocution classes in the third and fourth grades. She was thrilled to see him grow in poise and confidence. Meanwhile, Dr. Lou ranted violently at the boy when his writing was not up to expectations or was not serious enough, or was just a little too original for the old soldier. She could have silenced Niko's father once and for all, put an end to those tirades and destructive demands. But she didn't. And somehow Niko got past the criticism, if only because he had his own goals, the greatest of which was to succeed in ways his father could never imagine.

CHAPTER TEN

KATY HURT

Babcia saw teenage Niko become a striking young man who had his father's curly black hair, intense brown eyes, and his mother's gentle smile. Now Niko turned to more serious sketches of the female form, and the witch realized that this was something new and dangerous. This was not art for the sake of art, but art for the sake of sex. Witches of her era were so close to the animal world and its functions that it was impossible to embarrass them. Sex was as much a part of life as anything else. But in Niko's teenage years Babcia saw that it had become a near obsession with him. She could have distracted Niko or scared him back to more serious matters, but she did nothing about Niko's interest in sex. Until, that is, he brought a girl up to his room.

At 16, Kathy Hurt was the captain of the junior varsity cheerleaders at St. Kathryn's Catholic Girls High School. St. Kat's, as they called it, was the sister school to Saint Ignatius, the all-boys' Catholic high school that Niko attended.

In his senior year Niko was the captain of the Spirit Club. He had wanted to be student body president, as his father had been, but he failed to win the election, and seeing his bitterness after the defeat intensified Babcia's dislike of the doctor and the demands he was placing on his son.

Niko's ascendancy in the Spirit Club however was very much a tonic for him. His success was based first on the clever banners he could draw for the big games; his caricatures of his school's opponents were caustic and very funny. But he then astonished everyone by showing skills at organizing and conducting pep rallies, and turning them into platforms for his own clever speeches. In his senior year Niko managed to make himself more popular than any student body president had ever been. In Niko's mind he had bested his father for the first time in his life. He had to stretch himself to do it. But it was well worth the effort. He was the king of school spirit without being on any team, and he was proud of it.

That's why it was so logical that the captain of the cheerleaders at the nearby girls' school should be in Niko's room dressed in her full cheerleader outfit, showing off her latest (sexiest) routines right there in front of the mirror. It was all very logical, except to a witch who was born in twelfth century Poland.

Niko was listening to Kathy's rather breathless explanation of the new dance moves she had developed for the upcoming pep rally when he heard the front door to the house swing wide open and then slam shut. It was his mother coming back from the grocery store. He hurried down to help her carry in bags of groceries and to explain why it was okay for Kathy Hurt to be in his room in her sexy little outfit.

While he was away Kathy was doing that thing that cheerleaders do instinctively from the time they slip on their first letter sweater. She was watching herself in the mirror, humming the school song and practicing her high kicks and other cheerleader moves. That last move, she decided, seemed especially sexy.

"How'd that go again?" she asked herself out loud. She

counted and flipped her hips to the right. Very sexy, she thought. She stepped through the routine one more time, shaking her pompoms and flipping her hips at all the right places. She'd have to try it on Niko and see how he reacted.

One, two, shake, flip. Maybe if she added a little shimmy she could make it even sexier. Niko would like that... everyone knew he was girl crazy. Kathy stood very close to the mirror, practicing a little shimmy that she'd learned from her friends. "I am so hot," she said out loud. "Niko will be totally bewitched by this sexy bitch."

Kathy smiled, dropped her pompoms, pulled down on her little skirt, straightened her rib-knit sweater, picked up the pompoms again, and began the routine in earnest.

"I will own you, Niko boy," she growled.

Babcia had seen enough.

The room suddenly darkened. The wind kicked up, sending the curtains billowing into the room almost reaching for the girl. Kathy looked back in distraction. She was whispering her song now. She turned and faced the mirror. She looked a little pale. But that was silly. She shook herself and started over again.

One, two, shake, shimmy.

Suddenly, there was a smell in the room. It was odd, sweet, with a hint of spice and maybe of something else, something that reminded her of the smell that had filled the car when her father had insisted that she go out hunting with him for the first time. Kathy's father had forced her to shoot a rabbit and then gut it. The smell was awful. The smell was BLOOD!

Babcia chose to reveal herself at that moment, as slowly and horrifyingly as possible. Babcia's face was now dead and rotting. Maggots and spiders spilled from her eye-sockets, mouth and ears. They crawled towards the girl on a horrid claw-like hand that reached for her as the witch faded up out of the mirror. Still not fully materialized, this deadly Babcia reached a second hand for the girl's throat. The cheerleader froze for a moment. Her eyes grew wide, her lips twisted into a grimace of sheer terror, her arms and hands began to quiver, shaking her pompoms in a new and terrible way. Babcia's fingertips stretched toward Kathy's throat. Then the girl suddenly came to life, shrieked, dropped her pompoms, and rushed from the room.

"Kathy," Niko called as the girl pounded down the stairs almost knocking him over as she ran out the front door and out of his life forever. Niko followed her to the door and called to her as she ran along the sidewalk. She didn't even turn back to look at him.

Babcia heard Niko and his mother coming up the stairs. She cast a quick spell that flipped open Niko's special sketchbook, the one in which he made his secret, sexy drawings. Next, she stirred up the wind and dusted away the heavy smell of blood and gingerbread. And then she vanished completely.

"What the hell? Niko said to his mother. He strode up to the mirror, reached down in front of it and picked up the pompoms that Kathy had dropped in her frantic escape. "What made her do that?"

"Maybe this," his mother answered as she picked up the sketchbook that Babcia's magic had opened to just the right page. It was a detailed drawing that Niko had made of Kathy several weeks earlier. In the drawing Kathy was in her sexiest cheerleader pose, smiling seductively and completely nude.

"Your latest fantasy?" His mother asked accusingly.

"How'd you find that?" Niko responded as he turned bright red.

"Won't you ever learn?" Niko's mother slammed the book and took it with her as she marched from the room. "I think it's time your father had a talk with you!"

"That's mine," Niko called after her, but to no avail.

Babcia said nothing. But she realized that her days in Niko's closet were over. From now on the boy was going to need more active and open protection.

She was, among other things, going to have to save him... from the Kathy Hurts of the world.

Interlude 1

"Oh dear," Matryoshka sighs. She finds that she's shivering all over, staring at the heavy cloth that hangs protectively over the masks. But it doesn't matter. Witch eyes seem to be blazing out from behind it anyway.

She turns to find the warlock studying her.

"Babcia is so horrible," Matryoshka says.

"Not really," Wicktor responds.

"Well, did she ever do anything *nice*? Did the masks ever cause anything good to happen... to anyone?"

Michalowski laughs. "If you only knew, daughter."

"You mean, she did?" Matryoshka giggles hopefully. "The masks did?" Her trembling fingers gesture toward the counter cloth that protects her from the sight of those monstrous faces.

"Who are we to judge the supernatural?" Wicktor asks. He blows a smoke ring that floats off toward the masks. "Who are we to say what's evil?"

"Well, I know the devil is evil," Matryoshka answers.

"Is he now?"

The girl notices that her father gives the warlock a reproachful glance and then relaxes. "We would not be here," says the old man, "you and I, daughter, if not for the power of the masks. They helped Grandpa woo Grandma."

Even the warlock is surprised at this, and he bursts out laughing.

"So many years ago, before the great war, when he was a young man and as handsome as any Michalowski could ever be, Grandpa Aleksander has a mask on display in the store window. And one day he sees a most lovely girl staring at it. The girl tries to walk away, but no, she is drawn back to the window and the mask... bewitched, he thinks.

"Polina is her name, and she stands there all morning long. Meanwhile, Grandpa Alek drinks his coffee and watches her through the window where light reflects outward so she cannot see him.

"Near noon, Alek comes out from the store, approaches Polina, and he sees how, in spite of her great beauty, her eyes look so very far away. He begins talking of witches and masks and other mysterious things. Polina nods as if enchanted. So he brings her inside... into our secret room here, where more masks await. And, while the girl is here, Aleksander begins to...."

Michalowski shakes his head as though he can't quite decide how to phrase what happens next. He's embarrassed, looks down at his hands and then over to the warlock who clearly likes the story's possibilities. But while listening, the creature hasn't been able to turn his eyes away from the shopkeeper's daughter.

The old man glances over at Matryoshka who seems enchanted herself... as much by the warlock as the story.

"Matryoshka!" the old man growls, and the girl jumps at the sound of her name.

"Oh, yes, Papa. Go on, please go on."

"I'd like that," the warlock adds. "Please... do." And he whispers the words as though he is speaking as much to Matryoshka as to the old man. (Please do.)

The shopkeeper clears his throat and begins adjusting his chair so noisily that his daughter is forced to turn her attentions away from the horny warlock and back to him.

"Let's just say that, when the lovely Polina leaves our secret room here, she is more than bewitched. She has the beginnings of a baby."

"That's nice... I think, isn't it?" the girl asks. "And are they happy together, grandma and grandpa?"

"The witching masks keep their empty eyes on both of them. So of course they are true to each other, and yes, they are very happy."

"Wonderful. I like that," Matryoshka says. "And did the masks do other good deeds?"

"Some very important ones... historical ones," Michalowski tells his daughter. Then he reaches over and gives her shoulder a firm squeeze. "But that is another story for another time. For now, Kochanie, let Wicktor tell *his* story."

Matryoshka sighs heavily, and then her eyes brighten. "Maybe Babcia finds a nice, sweet girl for Niko and sees that they both live happily ever after."

"Unfortunately no," the warlock says.

"Matryoshka looks confused and then giggles... "Okay, so then Babcia just boils Kathy Hurt and eats her alive."

"Hardly."

"She goes after Niko's next girl friend then?"

"The truth," says the warlock, "is that it will be three long years before Niko finds a girl to really tempt him, and tempt him she does. She goes to the same high school as Kathy Hurt, but she's a little younger, a little more reserved... not a cheerleader, but far more beautiful."

"And where does he meet this beautiful girl?" Matryoshka asks.

"At a mixer at Saint Kathryn's High School gym. Niko is back from a very successful junior year at the University of Notre Dame. He gets an invitation to the dance, and suddenly there he is, staring at... *her*."

CHAPTER ELEVEN

MEETING AN ANGEL

Niko felt that he was looking at an angel. Somehow, she had ducked out of heaven for just a moment and landed at the mixer he was attending at Saint Kat's gym.

Her lips were sweet and innocent. Her long, blond hair was cut in simple bangs and tucked under so that she looked like a choirgirl. Her green eyes sparkled with a joy that seemed to be right off the face of a holy card, the kind of holy card that priests and nuns were still passing out to Niko, even though he was now a junior at the University of Notre Dame.

As Niko raised his head the angel's expression changed. Her eyes turned mischievous, and she flashed a smile that would have been highly discouraged by the church.

She raised her pretty gloved hand and waved to him. The action drew a rather nasty growl from the thick-necked young man sitting beside her. He grimaced. The angel gave the young man a bothered glance and then slowly stood and floated over to Niko.

"What are you drawing?" she asked as she reached him.

Niko had been sketching in a little book that he took everywhere now that he was studying art (along with serious writing) at the University of Notre Dame. He had closed his eyes for just a moment and squinted so that he could get a better sense of the shadows on the angel's face.

"Just a comic book," Niko answered with a smile.

"You're making a comic book about me?" the angel asked.

"Actually about heaven," Niko answered, and he turned the sketchbook around so that she could see the comic book panels and the deep fluffy clouds that filled them.

"I haven't added you yet."

"Well, then ADD me," the angel said with a fascinated grin.

Niko pulled the book back, glanced up at her and did a quick cartoon complete with choirgirl hair, full lips, heavenly wings and a halo just above her head. Her big, bright eyes were looking heavenward. It was easy.

"Cool," the angel said. "But what exactly am I wearing?"

"The usual heavenly robes, I guess," Niko answered and he added flowing robes and a scoop neckline that showed a heavenly amount of cleavage.

"A little naughty for an angel, isn't it?"

"I think the dress code in heaven is a little more relaxed than here at, uh...."

"Saint Kat's, the Junior Prom, remember?"

"I remember that you're an angel," Niko answered with a smirk. "A teen angel."

"No way," she said. "My name is Holly Blue, and I'm here with Danny Riley."

Riley growled from across the room.

"Are you Riley's girl?"

"Well, actually I am. And I'm not sure what I'm doing here talking to you, except to say that Sue Offenbach's a lucky girl to have a college guy for a date."

"Who's Sue Offenbach?"

"Your date," Holly answered rolling her eyes. "Don't you even know the name of the girl who brought you here?"

"Not since I met you," Niko responded.

Holly blushed. "Well, she's President of the Senior Class, and she's right over there, socializing."

Niko looked in the direction Holly pointed.

"Very pretty. She sprinkled glitter all over herself."

"Looks kinda weird, huh?"

"I like it. And it's definitely not as weird as your boyfriend. He's turning bright red."

Holly looked back at her table just in time to see Riley stand, glower at her and storm from the room.

"Guess we *are* in heaven." Niko drew himself into the picture right beside the angelic cartoon of Holly.

Holly laughed out loud. It was a clear, bell-like laugh as sweet as anything Niko had ever heard in his life.

"I like you. You're a funny guy."

Wow! More praise than Niko had gotten from anyone in a long time, certainly more praise than he had ever gotten from his father who was always complaining about the way he wasted his time drawing comic books.

"Cut that crap," the old man would say. "You've got serious writing to do."

At that moment Niko couldn't think of anything more serious or important than getting to know Holly Blue.

Niko drew a word balloon in his comic strip and added the words, "What's your phone number?" Then he drew another balloon coming from Holly. He turned the book around and handed her the pencil.

Holly studied the scene for a moment, smiled, wrote something and turned the book back around to face him.

"Angels have unlisted numbers," it said.

Niko quickly sketched another panel with the cartoon heads of himself and his angel and the words, "Will you marry me?"

Holly's look turned sour.

"Jeeze! I say four words to a guy and he starts talking about marriage. I hate that."

"I thought you'd be flattered."

"Well, I'm not," Holly answered. "And besides, I have to go. Danny's waiting out in the car. I'm sure he'll be sorry and want to make out... I mean up."

"Which?"

"Both, maybe. With him, not with you."

"What about our marriage?"

"Not a chance," the angel said with a look of annoyance.

"Can I call you?"

"I told you, angels have unlisted numbers," and she turned and headed from the room.

#

It was only a few moments later when old Mrs. Mulroney, Niko's high school art teacher, came and sat down beside him. Niko had continued with his comic book, which now showed him ripping off his angel's heavenly gown so he could get to the new goal of the effort, drawing a totally naked Holly Blue.

"Not nice, Niko," Mrs. Mulroney said as she eyed the sexy drawing.

Niko tucked the book away, blushing as he did.

"It's about your taste in women, Niko," Mrs. Mulroney continued, "That Holly Blue's dangerous. I've watched her operate. Stay as far away from her as you can. She's a flirt, comes on to everybody."

"I'm going to marry her," said Niko. "It's that simple."

"Well, with your father's money it may be that simple, but she'll break your heart. You can bet on it."

Suddenly, Niko didn't want to bet on anything because he felt a cold shiver tingling all through him.

It was the first time in the fifteen years since he had kissed Babcia goodbye that Niko felt her presence, smelled the blood and the gingerbread. And he could sense something else too; she agreed with Mrs. Mulroney.

And she was very angry.

Chapter Twelve

The Date

Holly rolled up her nylon stocking, then lay back on the bed and slipped the end of it over her toes. She unrolled the stocking over her long, perfect leg until she fastened it to the garters on her white lace garter belt. She raised her leg higher, pointed her toes, and turned it this way and that so that she could admire it.

My legs are perfect, she thought. Vogue magazine says so.

The 1962 issue of Vogue had run an article on the perfect proportions for the female body. Holly and her best friend Gina (her partner in crime) had broken out their tape measures and found that Holly was perfect in every way.

Inch for inch, curve for curve she matched Vogue's measurements exactly.

Gina had not fared quite so well, but then dark haired girls were never quite as perfect as their blond counterparts, Holly decided with a self-satisfied giggle.

Tonight she was going to use those curves to get Niko Madonie. What a cute guy, all about comic books and cartoons and having fun. She liked him a lot, and let's face it, she hadn't fared all that well after her breakup with Danny Riley.

He had actually organized his friends at St. Ignatius into a boycott. And they were boycotting HER!

No one called; no one asked her for a date. A girl who had been out every Friday night since she turned fifteen suddenly sat by the phone and waited. And then, magically, there was Niko Madonie, back home from college for the summer. Just when she had forgotten all about him and his comic books and his teen angels, he had called and wanted to take her out.

She'd reward him for that, she thought as she slid into one of the flouncy petticoats that she would be wearing that evening.

Next she stepped into her prettiest dress and wished that she had bigger boobs, like Gina's. That was why her buddy was still having dates while all the boys were boycotting Holly. Gina put out. No wonder she didn't care about Vogue's proportions.

But Niko would want the Vogue girl, the classic model, Holly thought. He went to Notre Dame. He was an artist of sorts, and his father was a doctor (rich probably). She'd show him a good time, a good Catholic School Girl's time, that is: nothing too serious; just flirting; turning him on. Maybe she wouldn't kiss him at all; just tease him a little and drive him crazy.

"Holly Joy," her mother called suddenly, "Niko's here, and he brought the convertible. Better get a sweater."

At seventeen, Holly had never been in a convertible in her life. The boys who took her out came from families that either could not afford them or were too practical to think that convertibles could survive the heavy winters in upstate New York.

Holly walked to the window, pulled back the shades and looked down on Dr. Madonie's enormous, white Imperial convertible. It was almost as wide as it was long, with huge tail fins, gun-sight taillights, and a red leather front seat that seemed as wide as their oversized couch.

"Mmmmm," Holly cooed out loud. "Perfect for making out."

She felt a little gush in her panties and a tingle that went all the way out to the tips of her nipples. Not tonight though, she told herself. Tonight I'm just going to tease and tease until I have him eating out of the palm of my hand.

She flashed her green eyes into the mirror as she left: perfect makeup, perfect legs, and a perfectly sexy, innocent dress.

"No making out though," she cautioned, "No matter how much I want to."

#

Holly and Niko strode around the grounds of the Saint Kathryn's Summer Carnival. She was laughing maybe a little too loudly at everything he said, showing him off to her buddies from class, to the nuns, and especially to the boycott boys from St. Ignatius.

They all knew Niko, of course. He was a big-shot his senior year, not a jock, not class president (as his father had been) but on the student council, editor of the newspaper, president of the Spirit Club that ran all the school dances and rallies. Niko was always the MC. He had a naughty sense of humor that he always pushed as far as it could go. Even the Jesuits had to admire it. And all that Spirit Club stuff helped Niko get to know the jocks. No one dared touch him. Now, he was dating a girl who was perfect for him in every way, a validation of his success and all the successes yet to come.

#

"Right this way folks, play a little game of chance, it's for a good cause, St. Kat's new gym. Whatdayasay? Step right up!"

Niko led Holly to a booth built of wide, rickety planks. White butcher paper covered the entire surface and there were big, colorful numbers drawn on the paper with magic markers.

Beyond the numbers was an enormous wheel of fortune, and beyond that a rack of crazy stuffed animals.

Niko breathed in the rich smell of cotton candy, roasting peanuts and Holly's sweet perfume. He smiled at his date, and then he heard a sudden whimpering coming from beside him. Niko turned to see a chubby little boy of maybe six sniffling back tears.

"No more chances for you," a large woman in a flowery dress insisted.

"Just one more, Mom?" the boy pleaded.

"I said two quarters, Davy," the woman responded, "that's what I gave you and that's what you lost. Now it's time to go home; it's way past your bedtime."

Niko looked at his watch. 7:30. He didn't know if that constituted bedtime for a six-year-old or not. The woman gave a huff in Niko's general direction when she saw him check his watch, and then she turned away. Niko took the opportunity to whisper to the little boy.

"You okay, Davy?" he asked. The lonely look in the kid's eyes reminded Niko of the image he often saw looking back at him from his own mirror when he was six.

"I really like that guy," Davy said, snuffling back a few more tears. He was pointing to a big stuffed figure of Mighty Mouse that sat at the very top of the stack of animals.

"He is great!" Niko answered. "Don't you think so?" he said turning to Holly.

The girl was staring at Niko with a look of great surprise. She really didn't know what to say. Even at the age of 17,

Holly sized up her dates by their ability to relate to children. In the family-oriented days of the early 60s every beau had to pass the fatherhood test for a girl to take him seriously, especially a good Catholic School girl like Holly.

"Miss," Niko asked with an inquisitive smile, "I hate to intrude on this thoughtful moment you're having. But wouldn't you say that that's a really cool looking Mighty Mouse up there?"

"Oh, yes," she finally answered.

"Should I buy it for him?" Niko whispered. Holly shook her head, but the look of admiration didn't fade.

Niko turned back to Davy.

"How about a portrait of him?" he asked.

"A what?"

"Let me show you," Niko answered. And he reached behind the counter of the booth and pulled up some of the markers that had been used to create the numbers on the butcher paper.

"Davy," called the fat lady as she tried to lure the boy away from the booth. But then she saw what Niko was doing, and she stopped.

Right there on the butcher paper, in a space between the large numbers, Niko was sketching a perfect image of Mighty Mouse. Then he added the classic reds and yellows of the hero's costume.

"Like it?" Niko asked.

"Oh, yeah," Davy answered.

"Do you like it, Miss?" Niko asked Holly. That wide-eyed look was still there, and the girl nodded enthusiastically.

"How can I make it better?" Niko whispered to his date.

Holly leaned in toward Niko, "Could you put the little boy in the picture, too?"

"Great idea, Miss," Niko said and he turned back to Davy. The kid looked up at Niko and the young man saw that a big bright smile and sparkling eyes had transformed the boy.

With his black marker Niko sketched in the outline of Davy's features. Then he added a little pink to the cheeks, a little blue to the eyes, a little red to the hair.

"Gee, Mister, you're good!" Davy called as Niko completed the drawing, and his tubby mother nodded in agreement.

"Well then, here you are," Niko responded with a wink at Holly, and he carefully tore the portrait from between the numbers.

Davy snatched the paper and then threw his arms around Niko's lower legs giving him a rather awkward hug.

"Oh, my," Davy's mother blubbered and then, smiling broadly, she moved toward Niko to give her own hug. Niko slipped shyly behind Holly and the mother, after trying to hug them both, backed away.

"Thank you so much," she called as she and Davy headed off into the crowd.

#

"So, what can I do for you, little girl?" Niko asked his date.

Holly gave him her best little girl look. She lowered her eyes and twisted back and forth on her heels coquettishly.

"I'm so lost," Holly sighed in a little girl voice, and then she pulled her hands behind her back in mock innocence. The action pushed her teenage breasts out full in front of her and made Niko swallow hard.

"Maybe I'd better call missing persons," he stammered. "Or the fire department."

"Oh, don't do that," Holly added with a sexy smirk. "I'll be okay. I'm just lonely, you know, need a friend."

Niko stepped toward Holly but she turned away from him. "How about that guy over there," she squealed as she pointed to a little, pink plaid elephant who was looking down forlornly from amid a raft of toy gorillas, stuffed pythons, and Kewpie dolls.

"You want to win the elephant?"

Holly nodded.

"So, let's put a quarter on eleven," Niko sighed. "It's my lucky number."

"Place your bets, folks," the guy who ran the wheel of fortune spoke up. "Place your bets. Okay! We have the good-looking young couple on number eleven. Any more betters? Come on, whatdayasay? Okay, sir, number 99. That's a good one too. And round and round and round she goes, and where she stops nobody knows. And the winner is..."

Niko closed his eyes. Holly cheered as the wheel spun and then magically came to rest on number eleven.

"We did it," she called, and she cheered even louder when the wheel spinner grabbed the little elephant and handed it to her. The pretty girl held the toy, stared into its button eyes for just a moment, and then her happiness seemed to fade.

"He's not smiling," she said. "He looks lost, kind of the way I've been feeling."

Niko looked at her curiously. He didn't know about the boycott boys, and Holly didn't want him to. So she just shrugged and handed Niko the little elephant. Niko took it dutifully, inspected the toy the way his father would have looked at one of his patients: looked behind his ears, checked his feet, and lifted his tail. Then he listened for his heart.

"No heart," he said at last. "No wonder he seems lost."

Holly looked into the eyes of the little stuffed toy. He was so cute, and so was Niko as he bit his lip in sympathy. There was a place for a heart, of course, right on his chest.

"I could make him a heart," she said with renewed enthusiasm. "I could get some pink felt and some thread. It'd be easy."

"He'd be grateful."

Holly cuddled up to Niko as he led her through the crowd with his arm around her. And suddenly she didn't know or care about the boycott boys or Gina's big boobs, or her buddies from St. Kat's, or even the teachers and nuns. But one set of eyes did seem to be glaring their disapproval. She wasn't sure whose they were, someone in the back of the crowd, it seemed. But she didn't like it at all.

"This little guy was really lucky to find us," Holly said (if only to distract herself from the creepy feeling she was getting). "How could he go on without a heart?"

They had now passed from the main fairgrounds to a small wooded area where all the cars were parked.

"I'm not sure it was luck," Niko added. "I think the guy running the wheel really wanted us to have him."

"Well, we are a cute couple," Holly answered.

"Or," Niko added, "It could have been Babcia." And then he wondered immediately why he had said it.

"Who's that?" Holly asked as her creepy feelings intensified at the sound of the witch's name.

"Just my grandmother," Niko answered. "She's dead now, but when I was a little boy I used to think that she was a witch. Maybe she's out there casting spells on our behalf."

"That'd be nice," Holly answered. But things still felt very spooky... not nice at all.

"Never thought of it until now," Niko said. "But it's the kind of thing she might do. Bet she's behind all this."

Niko opened the door to the big convertible and let the blond and her elephant take their seats. Holly did her best to flash just the right amount of leg as she got in. In spite of her spooky feelings, the tease was still on.

"Do you think your grandmother would like me?" she asked.

"I like you," Niko answered, "So she should. But it might

make her jealous. I mean you've bewitched me tonight, so maybe you're a witch too."

"I'm an angel, remember?"

"Right, and that's probably a good thing," Niko added. "There are rules you know. Only one witch per customer."

Holly knew she was supposed to laugh, but Niko's joke just didn't feel very funny; all this talk of witches seemed very unsettling.

#

The white whale of a car pulled into the narrow driveway of Holly's home. It was early; Holly's parents were still awake. Niko could see them watching TV through the front window as he walked Holly to the door. He leaned forward to kiss her, but Holly ducked quickly behind the screen making the kiss impossible.

"Thanks, I had a wonderful time," she whispered, and then she was gone, elephant and all.

"Whoa," Niko said out loud, "a pretty quick getaway." Next time I'll be the one who teases. Next time I won't kiss her. And he walked back to his car thinking of how perfect Holly had looked and how he had never made a plan to tease a girl before.

"It just might work," he said out loud.

#

The next day Holly bought some pink fabric and cut out a series of three hearts, each embroidering with one of the words: "I", "LOVE" and "YOU."

Was that too strong a message? She wondered. Maybe. But somehow, after only one date it seemed appropriate. No kiss, but love: puppy love.

And all the time Holly was making her hearts, she relived the warm, sexy feeling of their date, Niko's perfect interaction with little Davy ("Gee, Mister, you're good!" – Indeed he was.) But she also remembered that creepy conversation about Niko's Grandmother. Worse than that, Holly couldn't get over the feeling that someone quite malevolent was still watching her, someone who didn't like her. And there was another thing, too, a strange smell that suddenly seemed to follow her everywhere. It took Holly a long time to identify the smell, and then she suddenly realized just what it was.

It happened only two days later, when Holly was talking to Niko on the phone. He was trying to coax her into a trip to the Starlight Drive-in Theater (or as his friend Charlie called it, "the ultimate passion pit.")

"Tell me more about your grandmother," Holly suddenly asked. "Was there anything you liked about her?"

Niko thought for a moment.

"I think she loved me," Niko said at last. "She always seemed to be on my side." Except when she wanted to eat you, the voices of a thousand terrified children whispered to him. Niko ignored them.

"Anything else?"

"Well, she made great gingerbread cookies," Niko added. "They smelled terrific."

That was it! Holly knew it. Gingerbread. The smell was gingerbread -- but a very sickening kind of gingerbread, musky and rotting as if it were mixed with... blood.

"Did the cookies always smell nice?" Holly asked.

Niko didn't respond.

"Did they?" Holly asked again, not at all sure that she didn't see eyes staring at her through her second story bedroom window right then.

Don't tell her, don't tell her; don't ruin everything, the inner voices called.

"Niko, I'm scared. Something seems to be looking at me all the time, and, whatever it is seems to smell like gingerbread, only it's more like rotten gingerbread with blood in it. Do you know what I mean?"

Niko held his breath. He knew exactly what she meant. But he also knew that he couldn't let Babcia scare away the most perfect girl he'd ever met.

"No," he said at last. "Babcia never smelled anything like that. Now let's forget her and talk about us, okay? How's the little guy?"

"The elephant?" Holly asked cradling the toy to her.

"Yeah, is he still lost, or is he ready to join our family and go to the drive-in?"

"He'd like to go."

"And how about you? I'd rather not have to sit through Gidget Goes Hawaiian with no one but a lost, little elephant for company."

"I wouldn't miss it," Holly said enthusiastically. Then, feeling a little embarrassed by her enthusiasm, she added a quick "gotta go" and hung up the phone.

And just like that the watching eyes, the smell of bloody gingerbread and the scary feeling vanished.

"He is so cool," Holly said to the little elephant. "We know he likes kids. He'd make a great father, and that's very important." And then she grabbed the little elephant and pressed it into her lap...

in a way that was anything but innocent.

Chapter Thirteen

At the Drive In

The Starlight Drive-In was packed, row upon row of big 1950s and 1960s American cars, some engines still purred as they sat on humps that had been dug into the parking lot to allow the cars to tilt upward toward the enormous movie screen. Other engines had already been silenced. Front seats sat as far back as they could go; many couples were already cuddling before the feature had even started.

Holly leaned over the huge, red leather seat of Dr. Madonie's Imperial convertible and carefully placed the little elephant in the back so that he wouldn't be able to watch what she was about to do. It was time for the big moment: the classic 1962 make out session. At the age of seventeen, Holly was an expert, and it was time for Niko's initiation.

Holly leaned toward Niko parting her lips just slightly, giving just a glimpse of tongue so he could see how generous she wanted to be.

Niko turned away. What was that all about?

Holly sat beside her guy for a moment, talked a little about college, about the movie they were going to see, about her buddies and her teachers, and then she brought her lips close to his again. Same results. Niko turned away.

Holly tried three more times during the course of the next half hour to give Niko a deep soulful kiss, any kind of kiss, but to no avail.

"Damn you, Niko Madonie," she said at last, "You're doing this on purpose, aren't you?"

"What?"

Holly didn't answer. She just looked at her boyfriend with her soft, green eyes. She brushed back her long, blond hair, still tucked under like a choirgirl's, still perfect at the end of a very long day. She turned, and as she did she brushed his arm with her breasts. Surely he must have felt their softness through her loose-fitting angora sweater. Her bra was whisper thin, selected for just this occasion. Holly batted her long eyelashes, looking as inviting and desirable as she knew how. Niko did nothing ... absolutely nothing.

"How can you resist me?" Holly felt like shouting. "I'm the prettiest girl in school, in Rochester, maybe even New York State. Everyone knows it. What's wrong with you?" But she didn't say anything.

Niko hadn't touched her for the entire date, and that was okay; that was in accord with the strict rules of early 1960s courtship. Those rules let beautiful young girls like Holly approach the altar with perhaps a greater knowledge of foreplay than any other group of women before, or since. It was all about making out, Holly understood. Making out was the one way to have a whole lot of sex and still keep your virginity.

Niko was waiting for her to make the first move; Holly was sure of it. But no self-respecting girl ever did that, especially not in the age of Jacqueline Kennedy. Initiating sex was a man's business; the most a girl could do was tease and wait. Except that Holly couldn't stand it any longer. It didn't matter, she realized. Niko might be able to resist, but she couldn't, and if she had to make the first move, that was okay too.

Holly slid her fingers behind Niko's neck, and drew him toward her. She kissed him softly on the lips, then passionately. He pulled back to look at her, but Holly was tired of looking. She pulled Niko to her, letting him watch her lips part, and then her tongue swirled into his mouth just the way Jimmy Ratigan had taught her.

Jimmy was the best French kisser at the University of Rochester, and she was only a high school sophomore when they dated. He had so much to teach her, he had said. And she was willing to learn.

Holly pulled her knees up under her and knelt on the broad, couch-like seat of Dr. Madonie's convertible. She unbuttoned the top of her baby-blue angora sweater, and leaned toward Niko. She took in a deep breath to give him the most inviting view possible.

Niko stared into the depths of her sweater, seeing the lacy edges of her bra. She had purchased it just that morning after a long fight with her mother about the decency (even if your date couldn't see them) of undergarments such as these.

"We're a very hot-blooded people," Holly's mother had said. "Just wearing something like that will make you a little too willing, young lady."

Young lady, indeed! Holly didn't feel like a lady. But she did feel willing. Niko was mesmerized.

What's wrong with this boy? She asked herself. Would she have to lead him every step of the way?

"Don't you want to make out?" Holly asked with that little girl pout.

"Of course I do," Niko answered.

"WELL THEN DO SOMETHING!" Holly shouted, "YOU'RE DRIVING ME CRAZY."

And with that she grabbed Niko and pulled him to her. She opened her mouth and swirled her tongue down his throat. She took one of his hands and pulled it onto her breast sighing, "Oh, yes," as she felt Niko's fingers respond.

"Now, we're getting somewhere," Holly moaned.

Slowly Niko unbuttoned Holly's sweater as though he were uncovering a delicate treasure. And he was, Holly reminded herself.

Niko stared at Holly's lace bra and all that it revealed. He was frozen again.

"Do I have to do everything?" Holly teased as she reached up and opened the tiny clasp on the front of her bra. Then she sighed sweetly as her bra fell away and Niko was granted the incredible vision of Holly's perfect teenage breasts.

"Well?" Holly asked.

Niko looked up into her eyes and then back down at her breasts with that same silly smile. Holly reached up, took Niko's hands and cupped them around her breasts. She guided his fingers to the soft pink cones of her nipples.

"Mummmmmmmm!"

As Niko caressed Holly's pretty breasts her panties were getting absolutely drenched.

The kissing and caressing continued, and Niko decided to take the initiative at the worst possible time. He was sliding his hand up under Holly's skirt and up her thigh to those soggy panties. It was so goddamn embarrassing, so awful. Wasn't there anything to slow him down?

The garter! Yes! He came to the garter, Holly suddenly realized with relief. It stopped his progress.

"What's this?" Niko asked as he fingered the tiny piece of lace that stretched invitingly around Holly's perfect thigh.

"It's the garter from the St. Kat's Junior Prom, remember?" Holly asked. "I wanted you to have it. I saved it for you, wanted to give it to you so you could, you know...."

"Hang it from my rear view mirror?"

"Right," Holly answered with a sigh of relief. "That way everyone will know that I'm your girl."

Niko was panting as he pulled the garter down over Holly's long shapely, perfect leg. And then he flipped it up onto the rear view mirror of his car.

"Now, where were we?" he asked, moving in for more.

Holly felt Niko's fingers sliding up her thigh again, touching the edge of her panties. How had he suddenly become so aggressive? She'd have to stop him. He couldn't go any further. But it felt SO good. What was a sweet, innocent, Catholic School girl to do?

Niko's fingers curled around the edge of her panties as he began to slide them slowly down over her thighs. "What was he thinking?"

"You can't do that," Holly yelled. "I'm not that kind of girl."

Niko had been so wide-eyed and innocent, and now he was all over her. "You were just waiting for me to make the first move weren't you?" Holly asked.

"You made the first ten moves," Niko answered. "And now the next ten are mine."

"I let you feel me up, Niko," Holly pouted as seriously as she could, "That's all you're entitled to."

"That's all?" Niko asked letting his hands slide back up onto Holly's breasts. He began squeezing them softly.

"You've had plenty, Mr.." But then she gave a passionate sigh that did not quite fit her words. "Okay, I'll take care of you... just this once... but never again, I swear."

Holly smiled and turned away from Niko. She wrapped his arms around her as though he were some warm, comfortable overcoat. She leaned back against him, feeling his chin come to rest on her shoulder. He kissed her softly on the neck, kissed her hair, and let his hands slowly glide back onto her breasts.

"Mmmmm, that's nice," Holly responded, and then after a moment she reached back into Niko's lap without even looking, knowing exactly where to go, and she began giving Niko the classic, 1960s teenage hand-job, just the way Jimmy Ratigan had taught her. What else was a good Catholic School girl to do? It allowed her to keep her virginity and still satisfy her man. It was perfect.

Niko was in heaven, smelling Holly's beautiful hair, fondling her breasts, her hand stroking him so surely. He focused on that sexy garter hanging from the rear view mirror; she had saved it just for him. But then something else caught his eye.

Up in the mirror something or someone was out there, outside the car, hobbling down the aisle of the drive-in theater. An old woman, holding some kind of light, looking into car windows and being greeted with cries of shock and outrage. She moved with a sureness that was all too familiar to Niko. And then, yes, there was that bloody, sweet-spicy smell.

It couldn't be, Niko thought. It was impossible. But he could see her.

By then she was nearly at their car, and her expression was one of absolute rage. It was not the look of a human, Niko realized at once, but that of an animal. Her narrow red eyes, her suddenly sure gait seemed exactly that of a she-wolf protecting her endangered cub.

"What is it, Niko?" Holly asked. She turned toward him, her eyes looking both hungry and anxious; her breasts peeked through her angora sweater as invitingly as ever. But somehow Niko's entire body had gone completely limp. His eyes were crazy. Holly was frightened by his expression, and then she too smelled that spicy-bloody aroma.

"Niko!" she screamed.

He pushed open the car door and jumped to his feet, turned, and there was Babcia with the look he had seen just before she had lowered the deadly axe and severed the head of Killer the dog. She was hateful and angry, but not as angry as Niko.

"I wish you'd get out of my life!" the boy screamed ruthlessly. And Babcia held her arms up in front of her face to shield herself from the poison in those words. She stared at him in bitter agony for a moment and then she disappeared.

Niko trembled all over. He clutched the side of the Imperial for support and gasped for breath. Then he turned and looked up and down between the aisles, between the cars. Babcia was gone. Couples in other cars looked away, seemingly ignoring the confrontation. And so he turned back to Holly.

He tried to smile as Holly sat in the enormous car looking up at him. She was as shaken as he.

"Must be hallucinating," Niko managed to stammer.

"Both of us?"

"What'd you see?"

"Nothing; there was just that horrid smell. I thought you said your grandmother didn't smell like that."

Niko tried to collect his wits. He couldn't let Holly know any more about Babcia, or she would never go out with him again. He had to find a reasonable answer for what was going on.

The wind kicked up just a little then, just enough to carry the sweet-sour smell of mustard, caramel corn, hot dogs and pizza to the car.

"The hot dog stand," he said with a sudden smile. "You start worrying about witches and the first whiff of pizza you get makes you start imagining things."

"Bloody gingerbread is not pizza!"

"Okay, pizza and caramel corn and candy and hot dogs all rolled together. Smells like a garbage dump to me."

"But you said you SAW something," Holly responded.

"Thought I did. But it was probably just some old woman getting into a car. Mix in the hot dogs and a fabulous hand job and sometimes you get ... did I tell you that hand job was the sexiest experience I've ever had in my life?"

Holly shrugged. She wasn't buying it, at least not yet. Sweet sex or not, this was all too creepy for her.

"I want to go home." She crossed her arms.

Niko slid in beside her without saying anything, just sat there. They both waited, and then at last Holly's desires got the best of her and she spoke up.

"So, do you want me to?"

"Want you ta what?"

"You know..."

"Not sure I do."

"Finish?"

Niko smiled. "That would be so amazing."

Holly reached up and pulled open her sweater. Her cone-shaped nipples had suddenly turned hard. Niko couldn't believe his eyes. He didn't know they did that... changed shape, how cool.

Holly turned around and leaned back against him. Niko slid his hands up onto those hard nipples and began to squeeze them. Holly let out a sexy little moan and reached down into Niko's lap to find that he was ready... really ready.

That old witch couldn't have been too powerful after all, she thought, as she smiled to herself with sudden satisfaction.

Not as powerful as teenage sex, anyway.

CHAPTER FOURTEEN

FRED BLUE

It was nearly a year since that first haunted make-out session at the drive-in, a year in which Babcia had decided to creep back into the woodwork. Niko was grateful for it, to be sure. Still, none of that seemed to make things any better for Holly. She lay alone in her upstairs bedroom, but her sobs could be heard throughout the house.

Fred Blue was sure he had never seen his daughter this unhappy, and he felt absolutely helpless. He thought of himself as a good father, one who was able to communicate easily with his son and his two daughters. He was especially close to Holly, his youngest. For years the two had had a special friendship; she was his helper when he was in his workshop building things, and even his companion on his occasional hunting trips. He liked to call her Squirt, or Skinny, although he could hardly call her that now because, at the age of eighteen, Holly was a full-grown woman with an alarmingly curvaceous figure.

"What's wrong, Squirt?" Fred asked as he approached Holly's bed. She looked up at her father, sniffled, tried to speak and then began sobbing again.

"Is it Niko?" her father asked.

Holly finally nodded her head.

Fred looked at his daughter who, for maybe the first time in her life, was not beautiful at all. Her eyes were bleary with tears, her lips were puffy and quivering, and her nose was running terribly. Holly snatched a tissue from a little box on her bed and blew into it with a very unladylike honk.

"You look just like a little kid." Fred said.

Holly tried to smile, but all she could do was bury her face in her pillow and start sobbing again.

"Want to tell me about it?" he asked.

Holly sat up to answer. "Niko wants to get engaged," she said.

"Is that so bad?"

"No, it's wonderful. It felt so good when he asked me." Holly smiled slightly for a moment, and then she began sobbing again.

"You just started at Marywood College," her father said.

"I know. That's the thing. So I told him I wasn't ready."

"Probably the right thing to say."

"No, it wasn't," Holly sobbed, as she coughed and choked and buried her face back in her pillow.

"Come on, Squirt," her father said, placing his arm around her and trying to draw her to him. Holly pulled away angrily.

"Go away, Daddy!"

"I will," he answered, "But first I want to know why it was so bad to tell Niko that you weren't ready to get engaged."

"Because Niko was talking to his stupid friends at that summer job of his, and those goddamn guys told him...."

"Don't swear, Honey."

"I will if I want to!" Holly answered with a defiance

that Fred had never seen in his daughter before. He chose to ignore it.

"What did he say?"

"That if I wouldn't get engaged then he was just wasting his time, and he should move on. That's what those assholes told him to say!" Holly sniffed again. "But Daddy, I don't want him to move on, and maybe he's bluffing but... oh shit!"

"Holly, your language."

"Sorry, Daddy."

"Do you love him?"

"Of course I do, at least in the regular way; the way I always say 'I love you' after I've gone with a guy for a while."

"That's not real love."

Holly sat up again. The tears were streaming down her face, and her breath came in quick little gasps between the sobs. "It's not, but...."

Fred Blue heaved a sigh of his own, pulled his daughter to him, and this time she let him. It was something he rarely did. He didn't hug people. But at the moment, holding his little girl seemed right.

"Daddy, when I think of living without Niko, without hearing his silly jokes, or talking about his comic books, or his crazy dreams, or his pushy father, or even his spooky old grandma, I just can't... don't want to...." and she trailed off in sobs again.

"Daddy, isn't that what love is?" she finally got up the energy to ask, "knowing that you can't imagine living without someone?"

Fred Blue hugged his little girl tightly.

"Sounds like it to me, Squirt," he answered. "I'll talk to him."

"When, Daddy?" Holly asked suddenly showing more

than a little bitterness. "He'll probably never call here again. Ever."

"I'm sure he will," Fred answered.

"He said he never would. He was so angry. Why do guys listen to their stupid friends?"

Fred tried to think of a reasonable answer, but he couldn't, so all he did was sit there holding his little girl who was now nearly a full grown woman. Before long she would be leaving him, if not for Niko, for someone else. It didn't matter; she would be gone, and so he cherished the moment for as long as it was his. He was lucky enough to realize just how precious and fleeting it was.

And then the phone rang.

Fred and his daughter looked at each other as Mrs. Blue picked up the receiver in the downstairs living room.

"Niko!" she said angrily. "You've got some nerve calling here!"

Fred looked at Holly and then rushed from the room.

"Do you think Holly will talk to you after all you've put her through?" Mrs. Blue continued. "She's been crying her eyes out all night."

Holly heard her father pounding down the stairs and into the living room. He must have snatched the phone from his wife because the next thing Holly heard was her father's rather stern voice.

"Son, this is Fred Blue. I think it's time that you and I had a talk about my daughter."

There was a very long pause as Niko answered, and it sent Holly's heart plummeting. But then her father responded.

"Okay. Tomorrow's fine. I'll be home from work by 6:30. We can talk then."

Another pause.

"Don't be silly," her father continued. "Of course she

wants to see you. But you and I have a few matters to settle first."

Upstairs in her bedroom Holly was already up, already washing her face, combing her hair, making herself perfect once again.

CHAPTER FIFTEEN

AN AMERICAN
WAR & PEACE

Niko sat in his father's office, waiting eagerly as the old man read his latest creative assignment. Half way through the paper the doctor stopped and looked angrily up at his son.

"This stuff is crap! Who said you could write?"

"Just won the A. A. Milliken Award at Notre Dame," Niko answered with a cautious smile "... for writing excellence!"

"Then A. A. Milliken has his head up his ass! There's not a single serious thought in here."

"It's a comedy, Dad. People liked it, said it was brilliant, original, said it made them laugh."

"Well it didn't make me laugh," his father answered, as he shoved the pages back at his son.

It was April of 1964, and Niko had just rumbled down the three flights of stairs between his bedroom and his father's office complex. He had woven his way through treatment rooms filled with 1960s high tech medical equipment that looked like it belonged on the set of a Buck Rodgers movie. The crazy jumble of sci-fi stuff was one of the few things that Niko actually admired about his father. The old guy always wanted to be in the forefront.

Dr. Madonie's personal office was tiny. Set back from the space age treatment rooms, it was almost completely filled by a huge desk that was piled high with medical books, charts, x-rays, jars of sample prescription drugs and a jumble of bills and paperwork.

Niko sat in the small chair next to the desk, looked at the wild machines in the other room and wondered how he could use them or anything else to make the conversation more positive.

"Always liked that diathermy machine," he said at last. "I used it in a comic book that I submitted as my final creative writing assignment. Drew a giant diathermy that came to life and took over the world. Terrorized everyone with its deadly heat ray... until some superhero unplugged it."

Dr. Madonie smiled, even though he did not approve of comic books, and could not imagine how a university like Notre Dame could recognize such publications as a legitimate form of communication.

"You're incorrigible," he laughed, and shook his head, "Let's hope that graduate school helps straighten you out."

Niko knew that he had to be on his best behavior. On this day, of all days, he needed to get along with the old man. He hadn't come to discuss his writing. It had been almost a year since his long talk with Holly's father: the talk that told him, in no uncertain terms, that he'd better not hurt Holly like that ever again. But there was a more important message too.

Fred Blue told Niko that he liked him, that he would be happy to have him as a son-in-law, as long as Niko went about it in the proper way, of course.

Niko continued to smile now as he talked to his father. He was only a few months away from graduation, visiting on spring break. He had straight As, and had been accepted at the one graduate school that really mattered to him.

"Leland's got a great creative program," he said. "Screen-writing, film production, graphics, fiction, journalism."

"Pretty mixed up, for my tastes," the doctor grumbled. "But what the hell, Leland's reputation is undisputed. So take the screenwriting courses that you and your mother think are so important, and the filmmaking, and the art. But you'd better do plenty of serious writing, too."

"Serious is the word, Dad," Niko affirmed.

"Anything else on your mind?" the doctor asked.

Positive! Be positive, Niko kept telling himself, and then he blurted it out: "Marriage."

"Marriage?" the doctor responded, as though it was the last thing he expected. "Whose marriage?"

"Mine." Niko answered cautiously, "Holly said, 'Yes'."

Dr. Lou's face froze into a quizzical half-smile, and then he gained reassurance.

"After graduate school, of course."

"No, Dad, now. I want to marry Holly this summer so we can go to Leland together."

"Are you nuts? You can't afford that kind of distraction."

"Holly could help me with the work you want me to do."

"She'd help you, all right," the doctor snapped back, "help you to waste your time and ignore what's really important."

So they'd finally come back to the same painful argument they'd been having for years, Niko realized.

"Dad, everyone respects the experiences you had in the war, and we all want you to write something great about them."

"Not me," Dr. Lou answered. "It's something we need to do together, you and I. I've got the story; you've got the skills. An American War and Peace."

God, Niko hated this guy and his nightmare memories. He hated the secondhand dreams and impossible demands. He hated being turned away from everything he wanted to do in favor of some crazy obsession. Of course, Niko said none of it out loud. He thought of Holly and the purpose of his conversation, and he tried to be positive yet again.

"Look, dad," he said with all the sincerity he could muster, "I'll be able to help you some day. But right now I'm just not ready. I've got my own plans and goals, and I have to deal with them before I'm ready to tackle anything as monumental as An American War and Peace."

"Your own plans and goals?" the doctor responded bitterly. "They're all about jokes and comic books, and sex."

"Listen," Niko's father hissed through gritted teeth, pounding his desk, sending an entire five pound glass bottle of Valium into the air and shattering onto the floor, "You've got goals that were set by your family. My father insisted that I become a doctor, and I did. I hate medicine, seeing people's guts, dealing with nothing but pain and suffering. But I did it because he worked so hard to make it possible. Now I'm telling you to be a serious writer. I'm even giving you the goddamn story. I'm handing you greatness on a silver platter. We can work together and do something immortal."

"Dad," Niko tried to break in, but his father wouldn't let him.

"I saw unbelievable horrors in that war," Dr. Lou continued, "Whole nations going out of their minds. I've got to write about it."

"Then write about it!" Niko shouted, breaking down at last. "But do it yourself."

Dr. Lou recoiled for a moment as though he had been punched in the face. Then he gathered himself and spoke slowly and deliberately so that every word rang out as a command.

"We're going to write about it together. That's the plan."

He was standing now, hissing and spitting as he spoke. "I'm not going to stand back and watch you throw everything away for some gold-digger who's just looking for a free trip to California."

Niko caught his breath. He couldn't believe what his father had just said. And he certainly wouldn't allow Holly to be insulted that way. He rushed at his father, but the old soldier remembered his military training all too well. He grabbed his son by the arm and tossed him to the ground. Niko tried to get up, but his father pushed him down.

"You..." the old man shouted, punctuating his word with a good, swift kick to his son's shoulder,

"Are..." another kick

"Going...

"To graduate school...

"You are NOT going to marry that tramp...

"Or you will not..."

"Dad, please!" Niko screamed, but Dr. Madonie continued kicking.

"You will not see another cent of my..."

"STOP IT!!" A sharp, shrill voice rang out above both of them. It was Helen Madonie.

She lunged at her husband and pushed him away from her son. She backed him into a corner and glowered at him with a level of rage that even the doctor couldn't match.

"You've got a waiting room full of patients out there listening to this," she hissed. "You are humiliating your whole family. STOP IT!

"Niko is going to marry Holly and he's going to graduate school and we're going to pay for it, and that's final!"

The two men stared at each other and then at Helen. At that moment her anger had transformed her into the image of her own mother. And they both understood that neither of them was any match for her.

CHAPTER SIXTEEN

THE WITCH
AT THE WEDDING

Niko stood nervously at the altar. He kept looking down at the golden glitter embedded in the sparkling church floor. He didn't dare to take in the crowd that was making its way slowly into pews that were decorated with bright displays of lilacs and lilies. Cousins, uncles, aunts, friends – they were all coming to the wedding: his wedding to the beautiful Holly Joy Blue.

He'd been smiling at the early arrivals for a while, but now that the place was filling up it was just easier to look away, to think about his Holly and the life they'd soon be sharing. And then something startled him: a scuffling... someone moving toward him. He looked up to see his best man rushing across the front of the church in his direction.

"Damn," said Raymond Dallas.

"You're not supposed to swear in church," Niko whispered to the much taller, more muscular man.

"Well, they're not supposed to let witches into churches either," said Ray, "But she's here."

"Who's here?"

"The old witch, right out of Snow White, only worse."

"Where?" Niko asked.

"There, back in the very last pew on the left."

Niko squinted and looked to the very back of the church, just where Ray had suggested.

"Christ! It's her!"

Who?"

"My grandmother, Babcia!"

"Is she a witch?"

"Worse than that," answered Niko. "She's dead!"

Ray spun around and might have fainted right there in front of the altar, but suddenly a series of chords sounded on the organ and the entire congregation stood at once. Niko jumped up on tiptoes to look beyond everyone, hoping against hope that the ugly old woman he had just recognized was really someone's great aunt from Ohio. But it didn't matter; he couldn't see beyond the standing crowd.

Niko turned back to Ray but his best man was now facing in the other direction, totally transformed, goggle-eyed, looking down the main aisle of the church.

"What a babe," Raymond Dallas whispered, and he was right.

Holly was a fantasy, a vision of pure 1960s innocence. Her long, blond hair was still curled under in that sweet, choirgirl look. Her skin was clear and creamy, and her lips still soft and pink. A mischievous twinkle in her eyes added to the allure: naughty sex and sweet innocence wrapped in the same dynamite package. And she seemed to be very much enjoying what might be the greatest moment in her life.

Holly's snow-white wedding dress only enhanced her perfect figure, her smooth shoulders, her round hips, her long shapely legs. Niko knew them better than anyone in the church, and he also knew that for all her sexuality, Holly was still a virgin.

"She's so damn HOT," Ray whispered.

"Goddamn it, you're my best man," Niko responded. "You're not supposed to say those kinds of things to a groom about his bride, especially in church."

"Can't help it, man. She's a Goddess."

At that moment Holly and her father made their way to the very front of the church, and the first thing Holly did when she got there was recognize the leer from Ray Dallas, and so she gave him a playfully naughty wink. Ray nearly melted, but Niko turned sour.

"What is this?" he asked Holly when she slid up to him and batted her eyes invitingly.

"It's our wedding, Niko."

"Not a place to be making eyes at every guy in the crowd."

"Come on," Holly said, "Loosen up!"

"Turn toward me, please," said the priest.

"Stop flirting," Niko insisted.

"If you don't loosen up I'm going to goose you right here in front of the whole congregation."

"Children," pleaded the priest. "Can't we just get on with your wedding?"

The music swelled. The onlookers seemed unaware of the disagreement between the bride and groom, and so they just smiled, cried and envied them.

The couple turned to face the priest, and midway through the turn Holly did grab Niko, to the delight of the only person who could really see it, the wedding photographer.

"Nice move," he whispered to Holly from the side aisle, and in return Holly batted her eyes and gave him a naughty smile.

"Dearly beloved," the priest began.

Niko looked at Holly, and she back at him, and she formed a little kiss from behind her innocent white veil.

"Some consolation," Niko thought to himself. And, as he looked at her, he began to think that maybe his father was right. Maybe this girl was just after his money and a free trip to California. He looked at her eyelids, painted a pale powder blue. Was that appropriate for a bride on her wedding day? She had sequined sparkles sprinkled all over her. They looked cheap, he thought. In that moment, for the first time since he had met the beautiful girl, Niko's feelings were far from those of love. And yet he swore his vows and became husband to this intoxicatingly dangerous beauty.

#

The wedding reception was large, Italian and confusing. Gangs of pre-teen boys roamed the floor looking for mischief and girls to torment. Bevies of sparkly-eyed Italian virgins swayed in their party dresses looking everywhere for boys to tease and captivate. The priest drank as heavily as the groom and stumbled red-faced from table to table blessing everyone. Above it all, Holly sat at the head table, in front of an obscenely large wedding cake offering a vision of heaven to Niko and everyone else in the room.

"She's not here," said Ray Dallas as he ran up to Niko. "That woman we saw in the back corner of the church, no one knows her, no one saw her, and I sure as shit can't find her."

"Maybe we just imagined her," Niko suggested.

"Both of us? The people back there did mention one thing that seemed out of place, though," Ray continued.

"What was that?"

"A funny smell, something like, uh..."

"Bloody gingerbread?"

"Exactly!"

Niko felt shaken. Babcia had made a polite but limited appearance to let him know something. What was it? Niko felt certain of one thing. It had not been to say goodbye.

Just then the tall, handsome wedding photographer made his way up to the head table.

"You'll have great pictures," he began.

"Think so?" Holly asked enthusiastically.

"Always," the photographer responded, kneeling down beside Holly until he was right at her seated height. "But there's something I want to ask you." He almost whispered it. "This may not be the best time, but it's important."

"Anything," Holly answered. Niko didn't like the guy at all.

"I'm a staff photographer for Eastman Kodak Company," the young man said, "And I'm always looking for new models. You look so great that I thought maybe you'd consider posing for me.

"Kodak would offer you a contract. Could be worth a lot of money."

Then he turned to Niko, "Might be just the financial support you need to get started."

"We're not interested," Niko said loudly. "We don't need the money, and we're moving to San Francisco in a few weeks anyway."

"We could have a few sessions," the photo guy suggested. "Bring in a little cash before the trip."

"Not a chance," Niko muttered.

Holly stood and walked over to her husband. She kissed Niko and rubbed her hand up his arm.

"I love you when you're jealous," She whispered in his ear and then gave it a little nibble. She turned to the photo guy. "I suppose there isn't time."

"Now go do your job, or you won't get paid," Niko added loudly.

The photo guy scanned Holly's bridesmaids for an alternate conquest and settled on a sexy, strawberry blond named Pam Kimball.

"How would you like to be a Kodak model?" he asked.

Pam looked at Holly and blushed, then she jumped to her feet, took the photographer by the hand, and tunneled her way deep into the crowd.

"Don't forget you're still working for ME," Niko shouted to the photographer. Then he turned to his bride.

"I can't believe you," Niko said. "On our wedding day."

"Ohhhh," Holly answered, "You know he's perfectly innocent, and so am I. Now let's get out of these clothes and get ready to go to the airport."

#

In no more than fifteen minutes Holly and Niko had made their way to the dressing rooms at the back of the hall. Niko was still complaining.

"You can't tell me that he wasn't after you."

"Of course he was after me," Holly answered with a smile, "So what?"

"So you led him on!"

"Ohhh, I did not," Holly said as she turned and walked back to her husband. She was struggling with a long zipper that extended down the side of her wedding gown.

"So, it's okay to flirt shamelessly on your wedding day?" Niko asked.

"I wasn't flirting," Holly answered. "Well, maybe I was, but not shamelessly." She shrugged. "Please remember two things, okay?"

Niko unbuttoned his shirt and yanked it off in anger.

"First, it's fun, and it's flattering, and it doesn't matter if I don't follow through."

"Follow through," said Niko as he pulled off his expensive tuxedo slacks, nearly ripping them in the process. "You're a married woman, you're not supposed to flirt."

"Second..." answered Holly stepping right in front of Niko and unzipping her gown completely. "You're so damn cute when you're jealous. And third...."

"I thought there were only two."

"And third," insisted Holly as she let her wedding dress drop to the floor, stepped out of it, came up to Niko, and put both her arms around him.

"Please remember this for the rest of your life: I love YOU. You're my guy, and no matter how flattered I am by the attention I get from other guys, you're still the one I'll be going home with."

Then she gave Niko an amazingly soulful kiss.

"Whoa," he said, as he focused for the first time on his new bride and the outfit she was wearing.

"Like my sexy little wedding things?" Holly teased.

"They make you look so..."

"Curvaceous?"

"I was going to say 'stacked'," answered Niko.

"I AM stacked," said Holly sauntering up to her husband and putting her arms around him again. "Stacked in your favor."

"Don't get cute," answered Niko, as his new wife gave him another passionate kiss.

"Now, am I forgiven for flirting?"

"Of course you are," Niko answered. "But you're going to have to wear that outfit every night for the rest of your life."

"Nope," answered Holly. "Not, every night, just on special occasions, when you least expect it. It will be a surprise, like right now."

"Right now?"

"Yes," she cooed.

"Who says our wedding night can't start right now?" And with that Holly turned, walked back into the depths of the changing room and called out perhaps the only phrase that could have sent a frightened chill through Niko at that magical moment:

"Niko," his beautiful young wife called to him, "Come play me."

THE END OF PART ONE

Interlude 2

"She's going to kill Niko's wife, isn't she?" Matryoshka asks.

Outside the little gift shop, only a very few passers-by trudge through the heavy rains that have come this early spring. Most of the people look angry and disappointed. There isn't much to be happy about during these dark days in communist Poland, even in the world-famous ski resort of Zakopanski high in the Carpathian Mountains. There certainly aren't going to be many skiers, or shoppers, least of all gift-buyers, now that the streets are almost flooded.

The warlock can take all afternoon to spin his tale if he wants to. And that's his plan.

"Babcia's going to kill Holly," the girl repeats.

"Listen to you, Kochanie," Wicktor observes with a devilish smile. "Are you really so eager to hear about murder?"

"Oh yes," Matryoshka claps her hands, "it's so exciting and scary."

"You like to be scared then?"

"I didn't think I would, but yes, I do... at least a little."

"Well, don't worry then." The warlock's smile becomes more seductive. "There will be plenty of scary, bloodcurdling murders soon enough."

Wicktor stands and stretches.

He walks up to the huge cloth that covers the display of Babcia masks and lifts the corner. The three masks he reveals send a shock through the warlock as though he'd never seen them before. One is unbearably sad, perhaps the expression Babcia had when she remembered her youth and the death of her first child and husband. The second expression is monstrous, hideous, filled with hatred, the look, no doubt, of the woman who swore vengeance on those who had committed the brutal murders in the name of religion.

But the third mask... the third is worst of all, for there is a look of rage, and defiance. This is the look no doubt that Babcia would give to anyone she thought would harm Niko or anyone else she cared for. This is the she-wolf ready to defend her own.

"Christ!" Wicktor whispers as he drops the corner of the cloth. He shudders, and in that moment even he is awed by the power he's facing.

The warlock walks back and sits down beside the old shopkeeper. "You know, it's still hard to see these masks as matchmakers," he says with a grin. They look so damn evil."

Michalowski sips the last of the vodka in his glass and shakes his head.

"Of course they look evil, Wicktor, but looks are deceiving. I'm sure you know that? Besides, the masks have many powers. Rage is one, vengeance is another, but they can also heal wounds, help foretell the future. With the proper use there is very little that they cannot do."

"Witchcraft," the warlock says as he turns and his eyes begin to burn into the young girl sitting nearby.

Matryoshka's eyes sparkle in return.

"Pan Wicktor, if I learn witchcraft will it keep me young forever? Will I be able to use the masks to cast spells, see the future, become rich?"

Wicktor starts to reach across for the girl... to place his hand on her knee. Then he stops, pulls his fingers back and merely says, "You are so filled with questions, Kochanie? Many would love to have the knowledge and power of the masks? But you...."

The girl smiles back at the warlock seductively. "Tell me?"

"Stop," Michalowski calls to his daughter. "Don't encourage this monster. He is telling us a story. So let him do that... his way."

The old man leans forward in his chair. He has hardly moved at all in a very long time. Of course, the bottle of vodka is now half empty, and his glass doesn't have a drop left in it. Neither does Wicktor's.

Placing his pipe on a small wooden holder that's carved in the shape of a Billy goat, letting the goat's horns support the stem of the pipe nicely, the shopkeeper pours yet another glass of vodka for himself and one for his guest.

Wicktor takes the glass, raises it to the old man, then to the girl, and takes a deep burning sip while Matryoshka studies him. Then she turns abruptly to her father and calls, "Oh, please, Papa, can I just have one sip of your vodka? Please, oh, please. Just one?"

Michalowski looks at the warlock who smiles, shrugs and nods.

"All right then," the old man says, "but just a taste." And yet he pulls out another glass and fills it with the clear liquid, as though once the story starts again he does not want any more interruptions from the girl.

"Sip it slowly, Kochanie," he says as he passes the glass too her.

"Mmmmm, she sighs as she tastes the drink. "It burns, doesn't it?"

"Deliciously," the warlock says. He smiles at the pretty girl. He will coax her into his coven no matter what her father says. And she will make an excellent and delectable young witch.

"So, tell me Pan Wicktor," Matryoshka says as she tries to act as mature as the drink she is holding, "who told you all these thrilling details about Niko and Holly and their lovemaking?"

"An interesting question, isn't it?" Wicktor responds. "After all, some parts give very personal information about Niko, and others speak just as intimately about Holly. Neither of them could have known as much about the other, unless, of course, they talked endlessly about their secrets."

"Did you make up the story?" She takes another larger sip of the drink, feels the warmth of it tickle her throat, and gives out with a dainty little cough.

"I most certainly did not... every word of it is true. If you don't believe me let the masks testify." And with that the warlock strides over to the great sheet and rips it from the wall.

"Whether the masks are good or evil or both at the same time, I can't be certain," the warlock says, "but, as they are my witness, I swear I am telling the truth."

"Now see what you've done, Matryoshka," her father scolds. "You've got him tromping around here, making speeches like some silly actor in a play. And now we're going to have to look at those evil faces as he tells the rest of his story."

"Please cover them back up," the girl asks.

"You said you liked being scared, sweetheart," Wicktor says with a wicked grin. "So let's see how much you enjoy the rest of the tale."

Matryoshka nods without saying another word. And so Wicktor takes another sip of vodka, gives a quick glance over at all twenty-seven masks, which now bring the presence of the hag right into the room with them... and then he continues.

PART 2

UNIVERSITY AVENUE

Chapter Seventeen

San Francisco – 1964

Niko and Holly returned from their Honeymoon to spend two weeks in the home of Niko's parents before leaving for Leland University. It was on the day after their return that Dr. Madonie delivered a surprise wedding gift to the newlyweds. He was so excited about it, in fact, that he drove it over the curb in front of the house, across the sidewalk, and right up to the front steps, almost up the stairway itself. Then he leaned on the horn as hard as he could until Helen, Holly and Niko came running out.

They found him sitting proudly in a big, brand new turquoise blue convertible with its top down and its bright leather bucket seats sparkling in the sun. It was a Plymouth Sport Fury, one of the hottest cars available in 1964, a clean, simple design, whose only accent was a thin, chrome strip with a red, white, and blue inset on each side.

"Whose car is that?" Holly called in amazement.

"I'll bet I know," Niko answered as he bounded past her and right up to the driver's side door. His father looked up at him from behind the wheel. There were tears in his eyes as he pulled the keys from the ignition and handed them to his son.

"No matter what I say, I'm proud of you," Dr. Lou whispered. He could barely get the words out. "You've done a great job; you have a wonderful new wife, and I know you'll succeed."

Niko was speechless. His father opened the door and got out of the car, but before he could even step clear of it, Niko wrapped both arms around the old man and hugged him for an embarrassingly long moment.

"I paid cash for this thing," the doctor added. "Guess following the old man's advice didn't hurt me too much." Niko just smiled and then Holly was beside him, hugging the doctor, hugging Niko, hugging her mother-in-law.

All four of them went for a long ride with the top down then while Holly thought about how nice Dr. Lou had been to them, in spite of all the warnings Niko had given her about his father's nasty temper. Later, when she asked Niko about it, he simply answered, "Yeah, every now and then he really is nice. It's kinda hard to explain."

Two weeks later the couple drove to Leland University. They took their time, and it was a week of joy. As the ocean came into view Holly stood up in the car with her hands stretched out as the wind blew through her long blond hair. The ocean's dampness tightened Holly's curls and turned them into something that resembled a scouring pad. She knew it would. Niko just laughed and kissed her.

"Kinky hair or not," he called above the sound of the crashing surf, "you're still beautiful."

The view of the rolling Pacific was breathtaking for both of them. Niko pulled over, jumped out of the car and ran down the sea cliffs to the beach. Holly was right behind him. He stopped to pick up a large piece of driftwood and then sent it skittering out across the water. When he stood up Holly jumped into his arms.

"How come no one ever said anything about this place," she asked. "It's unbelievably beautiful."

"Guess there are a lot of secrets here that we can discover together." Niko kissed her as the waves crashed around them.

A few hours later and they were in San Francisco. The city and the surrounding area felt magical. Leland University was only thirty miles to the south. The couple rented a little apartment in a brand new complex just off of University Avenue in Los Altos.

The Manhattan Gardens were occupied almost entirely by married Leland students. It was a time when the walls were new and freshly painted, the furniture was right out of its cartons, and the rooms were filled with the intelligent conversations of young people who were optimistic and in love.

Niko and Holly spent weeks building bookshelves, unpacking boxes and getting to know the wonders of the area. Holly thought she might continue college and get her undergraduate degree, but she and Niko soon decided that conflicting schedules made such ambitions unlikely. They talked too about Holly finding some kind of job, but Niko was very much against it and said they didn't need the money. So in the end, Holly said she would give it all up and dedicated her new life to home-making with a husband who would be attending graduate classes for no more than one or two hours a day. What was left for them to do with the rest of their time but explore San Francisco?

The city that Niko and Holly discovered would soon be transformed by flower children and militant anti-war activists, but this was a more innocent time, a time that, in its foolish sense of sophistication and narcissism, was magical enough to drive any thoughts of witches from the minds of Niko and his pretty, young wife.

These were the last fleeting days of Camelot. President John Kennedy had been assassinated, yet the vestiges of his reign still existed, and there were those who argued that the Kennedy assassination was just an aberration. American life would go on as it had before, with perhaps no more than the slightest after-taste of disillusionment.

In the summer of 1964, it was still possible for Niko and his wife to ignore the growing evidence of the coming Vietnam War and the voices of Bob Dylan and other prophets who were singing of the nightmares to come.

Instead, Niko and Holly could drive up to Candlestick Park and follow the San Francisco Giants. The team was in hot contention for the National League Pennant and loaded with superstars. Willie Mays would come up to bat in the bottom of the 1st and swing so hard that he'd fall over from the effort, then do it again before he finally hit a home run, win the game and help the Giants compile a miraculous winning streak that extended through much of September.

On an evening in 1964, Niko and Holly could stroll down Broadway in San Francisco's North Beach and be lured into a nightclub where dozens of mink wrapped socialites sat in awe of the latest, sophisticated evening's phenomenon. Carol Doda, a big, blond, silicon-enhanced mermaid, would come floating down from the ceiling on a huge, white, grand piano, dancing the newest dance (the swim) wearing the latest, most provocative fashion, (the topless bathing suit).

Looking around the club at the stylish young women and their handsome beaus, Niko wondered just how many would return home, bubbling with the joy of too much champagne, and restage Carol's topless swim on their own grand pianos.

Niko didn't have a grand piano, but he did have a fun-loving wife who could do the swim with the best of them and who was more than happy to perform for her husband.

On stay-at-home evenings Niko and Holly could watch Batman and Robin battle the Riddler and the Penguin on television. It was a cool new show and a comfortable escape from whatever fledgling nightmares might make their way into the nightly news.

They loved their visits to San Francisco. The freshly painted, pastel row houses, its unique salt water and eucalyptus flavors, its cartoony hills, its quaint Chinese, French, and Italian restaurants, its winning baseball team, its bright orange bridge, its fog-shrouded forests, and the churning sea all around it gave Niko and Holly an incredible playground for the first few weeks of their marriage. Little did they or anyone else know that the idyllic world behind the pastel facade would be shattered in an instant, like a huge mirror smashed dead center by the thundering hammer of a terrible new age, an age that didn't need witches to make it horrifying.

But, for Niko and Holly, at least, the witches would be there anyway.

Chapter Eighteen

The Reception

A few days later… Niko was pacing back and forth and mumbling about how he did not want to go to the reception for the incoming graduate students at Leland, and how he hated going to parties with people he'd never met. That's when Holly suddenly stepped out into the living room wearing nothing but her sexy wedding lingerie. The sight brought Niko to his senses immediately.

"Relax, Babe," she said. "Everyone will love you. I know… I do," and she put her arms around her husband and gave him a passionate kiss. Niko smiled, and from that moment on he followed her around like a little puppy, all the way to the Sir Francis Drake House on the Leland Campus where the reception was already underway.

#

"The newest members of the Communications Department have arrived," said Billy Bright as he jumped up from the couch and ran up to Niko and Holly. Billy was the antithesis of Niko. He was tall and unkempt, sporting a great shock of red hair and a full red beard. He was wearing a flannel shirt and jeans that somehow did not seem out of place in the splendor of The Drake House.

"Billy Bright, Harvard, '64," Said Billy with a smile and an outstretched hand.

"Niko Madonie, Notre Dame, and this is my wife, Holly."

"Holly Blue," answered Billy, "What a great name."

"How did you know my maiden name was Holly Blue?" she asked.

"He's magical," said a pretty brunette who came up beside Billy. "My name's Nancy Swallow. I'm in Communications, too."

"I AM magical," said Billy with a grin, "But I was also helping Professor Henry organize the student data files. You know, you really need to talk to Professor Henry about your course load tonight, Madonie," Billy continued. "Don't you think so, Nancy?"

Nancy nodded and her eyes sparkled.

"In fact, I could take you over and introduce you to him right now," she said to Niko. "And Billy can tell your wife all about the activities that Leland has for married students."

"Uncovered a lot of great stuff while I was doing that data sort," Billy said. "Spouses' sporting events, medical programs, social clubs, I could tell Holly all about 'em. That's if you wouldn't mind, Niko?"

"Of course he wouldn't mind," Nancy answered before Niko could say anything. "Come on, Niko. Let me introduce you to your new professors," and she tugged Niko one way, while Billy led Holly the other.

Holly turned to Niko, shrugged, smiled, and blew him a kiss.

"Don't worry about her," Nancy said at once. "Billy will make sure that she has a good time."

"I'm a little afraid of that," Niko answered.

"Don't be silly," Nancy said. "Come on. There are a lot of important people you need to meet."

"Like who?" Niko asked.

"Well, like ME," the pretty brunette answered. "We'll be classmates." Nancy was as preppy as a girl could be, with the kind of innocent sexuality that came with cardigan sweaters, knee sox and penny loafers. She had a lithe, athletic shape that could not match Holly's perfect figure, but she was still a knockout.

She wore a starched white blouse and a plaid wraparound skirt that was held closed by a large, gold safety pin. Her deep brunette hair was flipped at the ends and framed a sweet face with bright, sparkly eyes and long eyelashes.

"I drove out here from Boston with Billy," she continued. "Had a great time, just the two of us."

"Are you his..."

"No, I don't think anyone is going to be able to land Billy." Nancy answered. "He's quite a guy; had one of the highest averages of anyone at Harvard last year. Smart, creative, a little wild."

"And he just headed off with my wife."

"Will you stop that," Nancy said. "Come over here," and she led Niko to a spot where they could watch Billy and Holly. By then they were engaged in conversation with a great bear of a man.

"That's professor Mendez of the Fine Arts Department," Nancy said, "He's having his own show at the Palace of the Legion of Honor next week."

At that very moment Holly looked back and saw Nancy and Niko together. She waved happily. Billy turned and gave a thumbs up. Mendez waved as well, even though he didn't know who they were. Billy turned to Holly and said something that made her giggle. Then they turned away as though Niko and Nancy weren't even there.

"If he puts his arm around my wife I'll beat him...."

"To it," Nancy finished his sentence."

"Huh?"

"You'll beat him to it. Put your arm around me and we'll be ahead of them."

Niko didn't move. So Nancy flashed her pretty eyes, put her arm around Niko and turned him toward a group of older men clustered in the corner of the room.

"This is the senior staff of the Communications Department," she said as they approached the trio. "This is Professor Mark Henry, Doctors Anthony Nathan and Walter Stanley."

"A lot of first names," Niko said. The men pretended to laugh at a joke they had certainly heard several dozen times.

"I'm Niko Madonie."

"From upstate New York," Professor Henry confirmed. "Easy trip out?"

"My wife and I had a great time."

"The pretty blond with the green eyes," Professor Henry noted. "Saw you two walking around the campus yesterday. Wasn't sure who you were, but it was hard not to notice her."

"Everybody notices her," Niko answered, with a sad smile.

"The penalty for having a beautiful wife, I'm afraid," Doctor Stanley said. "So, where is she?"

"Billy Bright has her," Nancy responded with a wink.

"Uh, oh," whispered Stanley.

"Uh, oh what?" asked Niko.

"Nothing. Everything's fine," answered Nancy, and she gave Niko's arm a little squeeze. "Believe me, Billy is a true gentleman."

"As I recall, you're the one student who actually wants to work in Hollywood," Dr. Stanley commented. "The big movement these days is toward independent films."

"You've got a minor in art, too," Henry added. "You draw comic books. In fact yours was the first application I ever saw done in the form of a comic. Very clever."

Niko grinned.

"You know when it comes time for your internship, we might want to combine your interests in movies and graphics. How about an internship with Win Mikley Productions? We have some contacts there."

"And also with Chuck Vaughn at Vaughn Visual Arts," Doctor Stanley added. "Chuck told me that he'd like to partner with us on a project. You could be it."

"This all sounds great," Niko answered, "But I may need your help with the old man back home. He wants a serious writer, no comedy, no animation, no movies really. He's planning some epic World War Two novel, and he wants me to help him write it before I do anything else."

"Strikes me as a little stifling," said Stanley. "This is the time when you need to do your own thing. You may never get a chance like this again."

"Exactly," said Niko. "And I've got ideas of my own."

"Besides," added Stanley, "another war memoir? The publishers are flooded with them."

"I wouldn't worry about your father," Professor Henry said. "We know what's best for our students, and we can be very persuasive."

Niko broke into his biggest smile of the evening.

"I see that you're also taking Advanced Design," Professor Henry said, just to make sure that Niko realized how much he knew about each of his handpicked students.

"Billy and I'll be in that class, too," Nancy added.

Niko rolled his eyes.

"Billy loves diversity."

"Billy loves just about everything and everybody doesn't he?"

"Don't worry," Nancy said. "You won't see much of him. He doesn't normally attend classes."

"Is that right?" Stanley asked.

"Oh, he'll be at all of your classes, of course, Doctor," Nancy said, "but he is so good at design he doesn't really need to go to class. He'll just do the readings and work his magic and the next thing you know, he'll get the highest grade in the class, and the instructor won't even know what he looks like."

"Doesn't sound like a real formula for success," said Stanley.

"Billy is always successful." Nancy beamed. And at that moment, almost as an endorsement, Holly's bell-like laughter rang out across the room.

"Another success?" Niko asked Nancy. The pretty brunette shrugged. And so Niko turned to his professors, smiled, nodded and made a quick exit.

Nancy hurried after Niko as he made his way back to Billy and Holly. They were alone together on the couch, and Holly was leaning toward Billy enthusiastically. As Niko approached her laughter rang out yet again.

"I like you," she said to Billy. "You're a funny guy."

"I'm sorry, honey," Niko said as he walked up to his wife, "But it's time to go."

"But I'm really enjoying myself."

"Sorry, but it's getting awfully late." Niko checked his watch and noticed uncomfortably that it was only 9:45.

Nancy walked over to Billy and draped herself on his shoulder.

"They make a lovely couple, don't they," she said. "Let's have them over for dinner some time."

"You two live together?" Holly asked.

"With six other students, in a big old Victorian on Homer Street," Nancy answered, with a smile that grew brighter when she turned to Niko. "I'm sure we'll be seeing a lot of you, Niko. We have so many classes together."

Niko responded with an enthusiastic grin.

It was a little too enthusiastic, Holly thought, and it made her realize that it was indeed time to go home.

#

There was a little bit of a chill in the car as they headed back to their apartment.

"I'd say you have quite a fan there," Holly said at last.

"Nancy?"

"Yes, and who is she anyway?"

"Billy's girlfriend, I guess."

"Billy said he doesn't have a girlfriend."

"Apparently he has lots of them. Please don't join the crowd."

"Well, he is an interesting guy, very interesting," Holly said as she moved closer to her husband. "But I'm much more interested in you than any conceited millionaire like Billy Bright."

"He's a millionaire, too?"

"Said so," Holly answered. "But what does it matter? You're my husband. I love YOU. Now let's go home and I'll show you something Billy will never get to see as long as he lives."

"What's that?" Niko asked with a smile.

"My sexy wedding lingerie," Holly answered.

"Billy will never ever see that."

"Never ever," Holly said with a sexy smile.

Unfortunately, she was wrong.

CHAPTER NINETEEN

BILLY'S BOOK

Later that night, as Nancy and Billy walked home from The Drake House, the girl couldn't stop talking about Niko and Holly, about what a perfect couple they were, and how very attractive.

"You want to add them to your collection, don't you?" Billy asked.

Nancy giggled. It was a warm evening, the kind that only comes to San Francisco in late September or October, a perfect night for a stroll and a fantasy.

"I could see them coming over, along with some other swinging couples," Nancy said with a sparkle in her eyes. "It could be a lot of fun. We could all share them. Wouldn't you like a little taste of Holly?"

"Sweet," answered Billy, "But they're very Catholic, Notre Dame and all. Probably sweat holy water. I don't think our lifestyle has reached Indiana yet, or even upstate New York."

"Doesn't matter," Nancy said.

"Sure it does," Billy answered. "No way we can come right out and ask them if they want to get together for an evening of folk music, pot and communal sex."

"We couldn't do that in Boston, either."

"I've done it," Billy answered, "and it usually worked. But this is going to be a little trickier. We're going to have to seduce these guys."

Nancy's eyes sparkled when she heard the word, "Sounds like fun."

"Yeah, but it'll take time, a plan, a few dangerous liaisons."

"Holly's got the inclination, I think. I helped her get a sexy job this evening. It'll drive her husband out of his mind. But that doesn't mean she's ready for free love."

"Niko's worth the effort," Nancy said.

"And Holly?"

"She's delicious too." Nancy's eyes sparkled even more.

"You want them both, don't you?"

Nancy licked her lips and nodded as though she'd just been offered a double-decker ice cream cone.

"You'll have to lay the groundwork, first though," she said to Billy. "Get to Holly, break down her inhibitions, and make her forget all those marital vows."

Nancy flipped her purse back up onto her shoulder.

"Niko will be so jealous. He's already paranoid because he's got such a beautiful wife. He thinks every guy who looks at her wants to take her away from him. When you actually make it happen I'll be able to wrap him up and stuff him right into my pocket."

"Which pocket is that," Billy asked with a grin, "Breast? Seat?"

Nancy took a swing at him with her purse, and Billy grabbed his shoulder and let out a yelp even though she missed him completely.

They had reached the porch of their old Victorian house. They climbed the stairs, headed through the front door and down the dark hallway to the kitchen.

"Better be nice to me," Billy said rubbing the spot where Nancy's purse was supposed to have struck him. "I've got something important to show you."

"Is it sexy?"

"Not as sexy as you, babe," Billy answered, "But it's incredible. It's a book I picked up from the sale they were having behind the bookstore. Got it from some guy named Mandel."

Billy rounded the corner into the kitchen and pointed to a very thick, volume sitting in the middle of their butcher-block table. It was Grimm's Fairy Tales.

Nancy lifted the book and ran her fingers over the red cover. There was a golden engraving of Arthur Rackham's illustration of The Goose Girl.

"There are stories in there that I've never heard of," Billy said, "and the illustrations are scary as hell."

Nancy flipped through the book, pausing for just a moment at the chilling illustration of Little Red Riding Hood and the wolf-grandma.

"And look at this," added Billy as he snatched the book from her and flipped to the very last chapter. A tale had been added since 'The Witch and the Solider' appeared in 1946.

"The Student and the Sorceress," Nancy read from the top of the page, and then she turned the page and froze. There was a new illustration in the book, a picture of a seductive young woman with long auburn hair and features that were very much like those of Nancy herself.

Standing with his back to her and looking at her over his shoulder was a young man who was the image of Niko. Nancy shuddered as she took in the rest of the scene, the most frightening aspect of all. Behind the two young people, almost hidden in the shadows, was the terrifying figure of an ancient witch. She was looking at the girl with a murderous expression on her face.

"Who is she?" Nancy asked.

"According to the story," Billy answered, "It's the student's grandmother who is also a witch and who doesn't like that pretty young sorceress going after her grandson. The girl uses magic to seduce the student, and when she succeeds the witch decides to punish her."

"What does she do?" Nancy asked.

"Not sure," Billy answered. "The book ends suddenly, as though the story isn't finished."

"It doesn't matter anyway," Nancy said with a shrug, "The picture doesn't look that much like Niko or me; Niko's grandmother is probably long gone, and you and I both know that there's no such thing as witches. Besides, who cares?"

Nancy closed the book and gave it back to Billy with a grin.

"You've got the old itch again, haven't you, Nance?"

Nancy blushed and then she nodded enthusiastically.

"What'll you give me if I help you scratch it?"

Nancy's eyes blazed with passion.

"Guess I'd better help you," Billy said with a chuckle. "But it's going to take a little time, okay? Give me a chance before you go after Niko on your own."

Nancy pouted for a moment and then she nodded as her expression turned back into a sexy smile.

"Good girl. Now, why don't we just go upstairs and see if we can create our own fairy tale!"

This time, when Nancy swung her purse at Billy... she didn't miss.

Chapter Twenty

Design Class

Niko's Advanced Design Class offered no formal instruction. The professor, Dr. Andy Cohen, simply provided a list of projects that the students had to complete in any order that they preferred. Then the students had to bring in the projects, present them to the class and receive what was usually a rather harsh critique by the professor. Cohen mailed out the list of projects before class even began and insisted that the students complete one project and bring it with them on the very first day. Even though Holly did not plan to attend any of her husband's classes, Niko enlisted her help in the first project, and they struggled with the list until they finally settled on one they thought would be perfect: design and bake a unique and original birthday cake.

Three days after the reception at The Drake House, Niko received a call about the design class at 6 AM. It was Nancy Swallow. She and Billy had completed a rather large and unwieldy first project for Professor Cohen, and Nancy was hoping that Niko could pick her up and drive her to class.

"I really do need your help," Nancy said. "Billy never comes to class. I doubt that he'll even give me a hand."

Niko said that he would be happy to pick up the over-sized project and help get it to the campus. Holly was planning to come to the same class so that she could help present their work.

"I'll help serve," she said, as she struggled into her clothes. Even bleary-eyed she looked beautiful, Niko thought.

#

Niko and Holly arrived at Billy and Nancy's Victorian about 20 minutes early, but Niko was still surprised to find that no one was around. Niko turned to Holly only to find that she had fallen asleep in the front seat of their car. So he got out as quietly as he could and walked up the stairs through the porch to the massive mahogany door. It was slightly ajar. Niko rapped on the door and, when there was no answer, called out, "Nancy!"

"Madonie, is that you?" Billy responded from the depths of the house. "Come on in. I'm in the back."

Niko walked slowly through the old Victorian. The bare hardwood floors creaked with each step. As he passed by the rooms off the main entryway he could see the remnants of many nights of partying: half-empty pizza boxes, crushed beer cans, overflowing ashtrays, tangled sweat shirts, a conga drum, a sexy pink bra, and stacks upon stacks of books.

"Over here!" Billy called as Niko approached the back of the house. And so Niko followed the voice and turned the corner into a very large room.

An enormous table took up most of the space. It was piled high with empty boxes of cookies and crackers, moldy cups of coffee, old magazines, pages torn from binders, and in the center of everything, an enormous sculpture: a swirly multicolored hump that looked like a cross between a merry-go-round and a huge grapefruit squeezer. Behind the sculpture stood Billy Bright.

"Welcome to my lair, Madonie," Billy said with a grin.

"Impressive," said Niko looking around and remembering that he had hardly spoken to Billy at all. "Where is everyone?"

"Nancy's upstairs making herself preppy. The others are in their rooms asleep."

"And you?"

"Me, I'm always awake, I can't sleep, maybe an hour or so a night. I hate sleep, waste of time. There's too much to do. I figure if I could just eliminate sleep, I would be able to do twice as much. I've tried it and it kinda works."

"Not me," said Niko.

"Me neither," added Billy with a laugh, "Every week or so I crash completely and go under for a day. But then I'm up again and keep at it."

"What's so damn important that you have to be awake all the time?"

"Everything, man! Everything! Like this design course! Isn't it amazing? Nothing but great projects."

Billy gestured to the wall behind Niko who turned to see that Billy had filled it with finely drawn renderings of the projects on Professor Cohen's list.

Cohen had suggested that the students pick 10 projects from a list of 30 that he had provided. Billy had already sketched 20 of the projects, and some of them had been done over three and four times.

Cohen requested that they design a ring. Billy had done a series of them, gold and silver ones, crested with diamonds and engraved with strange runic letters. Cohen had asked that they design a clock tower for a city square. Billy had three in the same square.

"And how about this?" asked Billy gesturing to the sculpture on the table.

"Yeah, so what is it?"

Billy laughed and then shuffled through a mess of papers near the side of the desk until he found the blue plastic figure of a little boy in a seated position. He picked up the plastic kid and placed him on the top of the sculpture.

"Neeeyyyyowwww," said Billy as he moved the little boy down the curves.

"It's a slide, a great one. Nobody can fall off of the thing, best piece of playground equipment ever conceived."

"Beautiful," said Niko.

Billy got a silly smirk on his face and just stared at Niko. "What?"

"No, man," Billy said with an amused smile. *"Beautiful* is your wife."

Niko just shook his head. Here we go again, he thought. "She is something."

"How the hell did you ever land her?" Billy asked.

The question touched a nerve that Niko didn't even know he had.

"You don't think I deserve her, do you?"

Billy shrugged.

"You don't know what I can do, man. I'm gonna fucking turn the world around, do work that will be immortal: write An American War and Peace."

"Jesus! Cool it, man."

Then Billy laughed. "Niko the Great! Hey, I'm for it. Hope you are great. It'll be fun to have some creative competition for a change. An American War and Peace, huh?"

Niko sunk almost to the floor. He hated the fact that the only dream he could come up with was his father's.

Billy walked up to Niko and put his hand on his shoulder.

"Don't give up on your dreams, man."

"No," Niko added with a sick feeling, "Can't do that."

"And don't worry about Holly either. As far as she's concerned, it's all about you. I watched her at the reception. And so did every other guy in the room. But she was watching you. And don't think she wasn't pissed about the fact that Nancy was hot for you last night."

"Holly was jealous?"

"Yeah, feels good to know that you can make her jealous, doesn't it?"

Niko nodded.

"Only thing is..." Billy began, and then he just stopped short as though there was some secret he was afraid to share.

"All beautiful women are naturally unfaithful, aren't they, Billy? Isn't that what you're trying to say?" It was Nancy Swallow who had entered the room very quietly and had been listening to their conversation.

"Well, aren't they?" Billy asked as he walked up to Nancy and gave her a squeeze. "Too much temptation. Too many guys sniffing around."

"Maybe so," Nancy answered. "Of course, there is a way to have your cake and eat it too, so to speak."

"What's that?" asked Niko, not at all sure he wanted to hear the answer.

"Communal love," Nancy answered. "Sharing. We all get together; you bring your wife or your girlfriend. So does the next guy. Girls like me come alone, just for the fun of it. We have a little wine, maybe smoke a little pot, and whatever happens after that is just nature taking its course."

Billy made a face at Nancy. "How to blow it," he murmured under his breath. And he was right. Niko stood there in total disbelief.

"You know what I mean, don't you?" Nancy asked. Niko didn't move a muscle. The silence was long and ugly.

"Come on, you two," Bill said at last. "I thought you had to get to class." He took Nancy and Niko by the arms and led them from the room. As he did he leaned over to the pretty brunette and whispered.

"This is going to be harder than I thought."

Chapter Twenty-One

Visitation

Dr. Andy Cohen presided over that year's first Advanced Design session like a gallery owner hosting a mid-town Manhattan grand opening. He was short, impeccably dressed and seemed to know everyone there except Niko, Holly, and Nancy. The students all sat at a large table with their assignments in front of them. Several works were under wraps as though waiting for a grand unveiling. Others were displayed rather proudly as they should have been. They were all magnificent: delicate jewelry, small ivory sculptures, and fine architectural renderings.

Cohen gave his introductory remarks and then turned to Niko. "Let's see what kind of contribution we can expect from our would-be filmmaker from the University of Notre Dame. I see you brought us a birthday cake… um humm. Interesting first project."

Niko had placed an enormous cake plate, dome and all, in the center of the table, and at that moment Holly pushed a stack of paper plates and a gaggle of forks onto the table beside it.

"And you brought a wife to help serve it," Cohen grinned. "Very clever, um humm."

Niko smiled and confidently lifted the dome off the plate to reveal a large child's birthday cake built like a great, cream-colored castle. Niko had sketched the cake and Holly had made it for him. She had done something else too. She had created a whole new color pallet using food coloring, egg whites and other ingredients.

"I like the whimsical shades," Cohen added, "They fit perfectly with a child's fantasy castle, um humm. I like those towers too."

"Lady fingers topped with ice cream cones." Holly said immediately.

"Ah, the real designer speaks," Cohen responded. Holly frowned. "I'm only kidding," he said. "This is a very nice creation. Have you taken some pictures of it?"

"Shot up an entire roll," Niko answered.

"Um humm, very good. Then there's no reason not to eat it."

The class cheered, which Holly took as her cue to start serving up the cake to the professor and the class.

"Tastes as good as it looks," Cohen marveled through a mouthful of angel food and frosting.

Holly walked to the head of the table to pass out the last few pieces of cake, and that's when she caught sight of Billy Bright waving at her through the window in the classroom door.

"That's not the end of the projects being offered by the Communication Department," Billy proclaimed as he stepped proudly into the room.

"Billy!" Nancy called. She was delighted that he was there to witness their upcoming success.

"Our project is a cake as well," he said.

With Billy's help, Nancy lifted the project onto the table.

Wrapped in heavy butcher paper, it could have been anything from a mounted sword to a ceremonial canoe paddle, both of which were also items on Cohen's project list. Instead, the unwrapping revealed a huge, scaly, smiling, green and black serpent-of-a-cake with mischievous eyes and a big red candle hanging like a half smoked cigarette from the corner of its mouth.

"A life-size boa constrictor," Billy announced.

"Fabulous!" cheered Professor Cohen. "Can we do a taste comparison?"

"No one said it had to be edible?" Billy answered.

"Of course it is," added Nancy, "But first we want to get a few photos."

"Not a problem," said Cohen, "This is a design class, not a cooking class, and the serpent birthday cake gets an A. The kids' castle was pretty good, too, and tasted delicious. I'll give it a B+."

Billy sat down next to Holly. He smiled and took the last piece of castle cake from her.

"Ummmm," he sighed in exaggerated ecstasy, as he tasted it. Holly blushed. "I worked hard on that," she said.

"As hard as you're going to work this afternoon?" Billy asked.

"Shhhh," Holly whispered, "He doesn't know."

"That's what's going to make it so cool."

"You really think so?" Holly asked, looking down at her hands rather nervously.

"Listen," Billy responded, turning his chair so that he was facing Holly directly, "You're gorgeous; everyone knows it. Here's a chance to remind Niko, right in front of a whole bunch of artists. They'll go nuts. They'll love it."

"His hot little wife up there in front of everyone," Holly said as she closed her eyes and visualized the moment. "It IS gonna be a real turn-on."

"Group-sexiness," Billy added, "You'll love it once you get a little taste."

"Maybe, but I'm not sure Niko will."

"He's gotta," Billy answered. "Sorry I can't be there, but you'll have a dozen guys and gals cheering you on. You don't need my help; you'll be perfect."

"I will," Holly said, and her eyes sparkled with confident anticipation.

None of the moments: the whispered exchange between Holly and Billy; the way they leaned so close together; the gleam in their eyes... none of it was lost on Nancy Swallow, who could feel the sexual tension that was brewing.

She didn't know what Holly and Billy were talking about. But she was sure that somehow Billy was already putting their plan into motion. It all seemed very naughty to Nancy, and very exciting, and that made her tingle all over.

The whispered conversation and all its implications would certainly not have been lost on Niko either. Except that, just as he began to notice it, a rustling in the bushes outside the classroom window distracted him. Someone seemed to be out there. It was an old woman.

She hobbled though the autumn leaves and peered in through the corner of the window. No one else was looking in her direction. No one seemed to notice her. But to Niko her features were harsh and familiar. He felt a cold sweat forming on his temples, felt his chest tighten, his breath grow short. It had been so long, and yet he was absolutely certain.

It was Babcia!

Interlude 3

"She's back?" Matryoshka asks.

"Of course she is," the warlock answers. "What did you expect?"

"Well maybe at least a few more moments of peace for Holly and Niko."

"Can't help it," the warlock responds. "That's not what happened. I have to tell the truth, don't I?" His lips curl then into a seductive grin.

The girl immediately feels it warming her in the secret places all over her body. But this time it feels very uncomfortable. So, she stands and walks to the wall full of masks.

"You bitch!" she yells at the collective images of Babcia, and then, as though she's afraid that the masks will actually come to life and attack her, she scurries quickly back to the safety of her easy chair.

Wicktor smiles and shakes his head. "Oh, Kochanie, how funny you are; you love witches and hate them at the same time."

"Their magic and powers appeal to me," Matryoshka says. "They really do. But I can't decide if they're good or evil or both. Funny isn't it?"

"Witches are not funny," old Michalowski pipes up. "Be very careful... even if you are only thinking about them."

He turns to the Warlock. "Help my daughter understand just how very evil they are."

"But they are not evil," the warlock answers. "They're neutral...they do what they have to do, regardless of what others think."

"For example, Kochanie, can you imagine how – back in that ancient age – Babcia's sisters responded to the slaughter of her husband and child?"

The girl is stunned by the question.

"Well..." she begins at last, as though to offer a highly educated response, but then she just wilts. "Well... no," she whispers.

"And what would you have done if you were they?"

"Oh, I'd get my revenge."

"And would it be bloody and violent?"

"Of course it would."

And would that be evil, my dear?" the warlock asks.

"Absolutely not!"

"Good girl," he says with a victorious grin.

"Now listen."

#

The old women of the village chose five widows and nine maidens to participate in their terrible ceremony. When it was nearly midnight they led them from their homes to the outskirts of the witches' village.

The maidens stripped themselves bare to the waist while the widows covered their heads and faces with white babushkas. Then, taking up clubs, scythes, and the bones of dead animals, they began to march around the village, shaking the bones above their heads, screaming wildly, dragging a huge plow through the dust behind them, digging a furrow to release the spirits of the earth who would surely protect them from the coming onslaught.

It was then that the two Wynofski brothers passed by the village. They had been hunting in the woods for days and had not been able to participate in the capture and trial of Michalina the Witch. They knew nothing of the terrible revenge she had exacted on her persecutors.

Amazed by the spectacle, the young men joked through their fear, drew out a flask of ale and had a draft to bolster their courage. They grew curious, too curious. The brothers then tromped down to the edge of the very path the witches soon would tread. They did nothing to hide their presence. One woman saw them, then another, and then the procession fell on them and dragged them into the middle of the road.

Even though the men were the size of young bulls, women with witch strength outnumbered them.

The women attacked with their scythes, sent great gaping wounds into the young men's arms and thighs. They slit their throats, cut open their stomachs and ripped out their insides. They bashed in their heads until they were nothing but bloody masses of bruised and battered flesh.

Then the procession moved on, still plowing the earth, still shrieking and chanting, but now dragging the young men's mutilated corpses behind them.

The ritual did not save the witches, of course. Other men from the nearby village came soon enough, came to avenge the massacre that Michalina had carried out in defense of her husband and child, and now to avenge the death and mutilation of the Wynofski Brothers as well.

The men burned the village, raped and murdered every witch they could find. Yet Michalina had escaped, or more accurately, she had been saved.

Fearing for her safety, the eldest of the witches (their Babcia) had sent Michalina away days before. She had directed the girl to go far deeper into the woods where she could live in solitude until generations had passed and her acts had been forgotten.

It would be weeks before Michalina had the courage to return to the witches' village to seek advice and friendship. But when she did come back all she saw were the horrors that had been acted upon her sisters: the burnt rubble of the village and what was left of the still unburied corpses. She buried the dead, took the few surviving artifacts that she could find, and then withdrew in horror and despair into the dark forest and centuries of solitude.

\#

Legends sprang up then about Michalina the Witch. It was said that she lured little children to her home deep in the woods; that she seduced them with sweet smelling gingerbread and then captured them to grind them into blood sausage. It was said that she rode her broom through the midnight sky, looking for hunters and other men from the village to capture and murder in acts of revenge.

The truth was that Michalina did none of those terrible things (almost none of them, anyway). But she did become solitary, and, as centuries passed, her age transformed her into a monstrous old crone.

It would be yet another hundred years before she actually encountered a young man who was not afraid of her, who saw something fascinating in her, and who made her the subject of his work.

You see, the young man was an artist, a sculptor... a maker of masks.

\#

Matryoshka suddenly jumps from her seat, grabs the bottle of vodka and pours until the glass is full; then she takes a big swallow, coughs loudly, quivers all over and takes another.

"He made those masks then, didn't he?" she asks. "You're talking about the maker of those hideous things," and she points to the wall of Babcia masks.

The faces look down on the trio, and, for only a moment, they actually seem to smile at this revelation.

"Oh, dear," Matryoshka says, and then she falls back into

her chair shaking her head. "I mean, I do feel for Babcia and Michalina, and all her suffering and, of course, I certainly think that she was entitled to her revenge. But still those… masks!"

The last word is said with a shudder.

"Kochanie," her father says indulgently as he reaches across the table and takes the glass of vodka gently out of her hand, "Are you interested in hearing Pan Wicktor's story or not?"

"Of course I am."

"Then please sit back and listen. Just listen."

Matryoshka nods, straightens herself, and does her best to assume a more dignified air. Then after a moment she adds, "But may I please have my glass of vodka back?"

Chapter Twenty-Two

Masks & Models

Niko went directly from the design class to his freehand drawing course. He was desperate to escape the growing feeling that somehow Babcia was making her way back into his life.

Holly had taken the car and disappeared. Billy and Nancy seemed to have gone somewhere else as well.

Niko was in a dark and nasty mood as he entered the old art room just off the Leland Main Quad. The room was just as gloomy as he was. The walls were a dismal grey and an overhead skylight did little to enliven the place. The San Francisco fog had crept all the way down to Los Altos that morning and was hanging around much longer than it should have.

Niko sat in a small chair at the back of the room and thought. He was early, and only very slowly did the other members of the class straggle in.

A young man in a flowered shirt pulled a chair up next to Niko and gave him a nod. Then, to Niko's amazement, pretty Nancy Swallow moved in on the other side of him.

"What are you doing here?" Niko asked.

"Just developed a sudden interest in freehand drawing," she answered. "Cool room, huh?"

Niko had missed it all. The color of the room and his own feelings had dulled his senses, and so he did not notice the large plaster busts on the shelves along the far wall. There were heads carved in careful replication of the Venus de Milo, Michelangelo's David and other classics. And below the shelf of heads was a shelf full of plaster hands in every conceivable position: fingers pointing, palms open, fists grasping, and on the shelf below that was yet another set of sculptures, ornate vases.

"Great stuff to draw," said Nancy as she stood and moved toward the display. Niko shrugged off his melancholy and moved up beside her. He picked up a bust and studied its fine features. Nancy brushed up against him. The feeling was surprising and nice.

Nancy giggled, reached into a wide wooden box at the end of the shelf and pulled out a plaster mask. It was a Greek goddess, maybe Minerva. She held it up over her face and turned toward Niko. Then she pulled the mask down and smiled.

Niko smiled back, then looked inside the box to see what he could find. There were dozens of other plaster masks of gods and goddesses, drunken old men and scary old women. Yes, scary old women!

Niko shuffled through the box of faces now terrified of what he might find. He turned over some that were facing down or lying sideways in the box. He flipped up a face in the corner, and there she was staring back at him: BABCIA!

Niko flipped the face back down and pulled up another. Babcia again. He pulled up another and then another.

Each face was one more manifestation of his grandmother's presence, and even more horribly, her expression changed with each mask, from wicked accusation to evil glee.

Niko pulled his hand away from the box as though the masks were on fire. Suddenly nothing was in focus. The faces seemed to be swimming and morphing before his eyes. Nancy couldn't understand what was happening to him.

Niko's trembling fingers pointed to the far end of the box. The girl moved toward it and looked.

"Who is she?" Nancy said, wincing at the faces that were staring back at her.

"My grandmother," Niko whispered. "The witch."

"Your grandmother was a witch?" asked Nancy. She felt a harsh terror closing in on her as she suddenly remembered the image in the book Billy had just purchased, Grimm's Fairy Tales. And there was that unfinished story at the very end of it.

Nancy grabbed Niko by the arm and pulled him back to his seat. Suddenly, she was as horrified as he.

"How did you know she was a witch?"

A thousand images flashed through Niko's mind: his grandmother licking the dog's blood from her lips with a smile, whispering to him from inside the coffin, the smell of bloody gingerbread in the drive-in theater, the figure hovering at the back of the church on his wedding day. They overwhelmed him, so much so that he didn't say anything.

"It's okay," Nancy said finally. She took a deep breath and let it out slowly. Then she held out her hands in front of her as though reaching out into the open air to gain control of her fear. Somehow she succeeded.

"The masks only *look* like your grandmother. Look at all the old junk in this room," she said pointing at the busts and other plaster figures sitting on shelves, stacked in corners and piled into boxes. It's been here forever. Believe me, those masks have probably been in that box for years, maybe decades. And I don't believe in witches anyway."

"If you'd known my grandmother, you would," Niko whispered.

Nancy pulled her desk closer to the terrified young man. She wrapped her hands around his and held them.

Gradually the pretty brunette calmed herself completely. Gradually the other students made their way into the classroom. Gradually every seat was filled. Gradually Professor Mendez, the freehand drawing instructor, walked to the front of the room, and just as gradually, Niko's fear subsided and he accepted Nancy's view that the masks in the box only *looked like* his dead grandmother. So too, the apparition outside the design class window must have been nothing more than his imagination.

#

Professor Mendez was ill at ease in front of the class.

"Don't worry, I won't be talking for very long," he said. "In a second you'll have your first chance to do some drawing. But first I want to introduce you to your model. And with that Mendez gestured to the back door, and who should walk in wearing nothing but a thin, flowery cotton robe but Holly.

"This is Holly Blue," Mendez said as Holly walked to the front of the room with her usual sexy saunter. She even bumped Niko with her hip as she made her way to a small riser just behind the professor. Niko stared at his wife in absolute disbelief. Holly gave him a sexy smile as if to say that this public show was all for him. But then she recognized Nancy and saw that her hands were still intertwined with her husband's. She gestured to them and Niko pulled away from the girl as quickly as he had from those horrible masks.

"You will be drawing Miss Blue for the next four weeks," Mendez continued, "And I expect every one of you, men and women alike, to fall in love with her. All artists fall in love with their models. It's the natural thing to do."

Niko didn't know whether to run up to the riser and

snatch his wife out of the room or just leave on his own. As a result, he did nothing.

"Come now, Miss Blue, let's get started," Mendez said. "I've provided some newsprint and charcoal pencils for the first day's work, so everyone get your materials, and let's see what you can do."

Mendez nodded to Holly, and Niko's angelic young wife moved up onto the riser at the front of the room. She stepped matter-of-factly out of her flowery robe to reveal her perfect body, her shapely hips, her up-turned breasts and her sweet mound of blond hair.

Niko rushed toward Holly and the riser, but his wife gave him a harsh, insistent look that stopped him in his tracks.

Holly turned to Mendez. "He's my husband," she said. "He didn't know."

"Ohhhh," Mendez shrugged. The art instructor grabbed Niko by the arm and forced him back to the table of art materials.

"Hang on, young man," Mendez said.

"That's my naked wife up there," Niko answered. "I want her out of here."

"No, you don't," Mendez insisted. "What we're doing here is perfectly honorable and natural. Beautiful women have been modeling for centuries. So have fat old men, for that matter. Don't ruin the class; you and she can work it out later."

"Come on, Niko." It was Nancy Swallow. "Let's just finish the class. I'm sure Holly has her reasons."

"My father said she was a tramp, and..."

"Niko..." Nancy scolded. "She's just modeling. After all, this is 1964."

"She's showing things that only I should know about."

"I understand," Nancy answered, "But she really is HOT."

Niko couldn't believe it. "She turns you on?"

"Sure, why not?" Nancy answered with a provocative smile, and it gave the young man just enough pause for her to lead him back to his desk.

Holly saw the entire scene play out, and now she was as angry and jealous as her husband. She glowered at Niko until Mendez intervened.

"Miss Blue," he insisted, and so Holly struck a pose.

She cocked her hip and clasped one hand on her shoulder. She let her arm drop down across her body in a style that was clearly not romantic or even sexy. But it was athletic: a beautiful, angry, athletic pose.

Niko fumed as he looked at her, and the more he looked, the more he focused on the anger his wife was projecting: her muscular arms, tense and sinuous, her face with a bitter expression on her lips and a rebellious, challenging arch to her eyebrows.

Feeling his own anger rising in him, Niko grabbed a large piece of black chalk and started stabbing at the paper in front of him. And yet, out of what could very well be turning into hatred, out of all that pounding of the charcoal into the paper, the shapes began to emerge.

Niko carved the tense muscles of Holly's arm as though they were preparing to thrust out at him bitterly. It became a huge shape, draping the foreground of his scene and pushing Holly's angry face away, into the upper left quadrant of the page where the same tension tightened the muscles around her eyes, her eyebrows, lips and jaw and contorted them into something that was intense and cruel -- almost witchy.

No one else had that vision. Another classmate built a nearly photographic replica of Holly. Across the room a bearded young man created an equally realistic image of Holly's face with those flirtatious eyes and that choirgirl hair. It had no hint of anger in it whatsoever.

Niko couldn't look at those drawings. It would only

increase his jealousy. Instead he focused on his own work and poured his own emotions into it.

Professor Mendez assessed his pupils and their talents and could not help but feel pleased as he circled around the back of the room to look at Niko's work.

"Ah, hah!" he said out loud when he saw it. The entire class turned.

"You've turned your passion into something powerful," he said. "Very, very interesting, young man."

The more experienced art students smiled at Niko but did not look at his picture. Others moved nearer and peered over the professor's shoulder.

"Now do this," Mendez directed, taking a piece of white chalk and marking out brilliant highlights above the eyebrows and cheekbones.

Niko took a piece of charcoal and pounded out a deep shadow below the professor's lines.

"You're channeling your anger into something great," Mendez said.

Niko said nothing. He just kept hammering the charcoal against the paper, building muscle and shadow that gave the arm the kind of power that you might see in a sketch by Michelangelo. He gave Holly's eyes and mouth his own anger, or perhaps the anger of someone who very long ago had raised an axe above a noisy dog to sever its ugly head.

"That's it!" Mendez said, and he snatched up the drawing, easel and all, and carried it to the front of the room.

"Look at this," he said.

Holly turned toward it and looked, and then she turned back to Niko with an expression that was filled with fear as well as anger.

"May I have this for the gallery?" Professor Mendez asked. "We'll show it at the end of the quarter in an exhibit of the best works of the class. You can have it back after that."

Niko smiled with uncertainty and then finally elation.

"Cool," whispered Nancy and she gave Niko another squeeze that was not lost on his wife.

Niko didn't discourage her at all. Instead he just accepted the praise and admiration of Nancy and Mendez and the class. And in that one brief moment, he suddenly knew exactly what it felt like to be more brilliantly creative than even Billy Bright, more creative than his father could ever have imagined.

#

"I don't trust that Nancy," Holly fumed as soon as they were back in their apartment, "I know what kind of girl she is."

"And now the whole world knows what kind of girl you are," Niko countered. "At least Nancy didn't strip in front of a whole class."

"I didn't strip either," Holly said. "I modeled. It's an ancient and honorable profession."

"Well, why didn't you tell me about it, at least?"

"Because you'd say no. I knew you'd say no. I wanted to surprise you, to have some fun, to turn you on."

"Seeing you naked in front of a room full of guys is a turn on?"

"It could have been spectacular, a really sexy moment just between the two of us with everyone else just sitting on the sidelines," Holly answered. "Billy said it would be so god damn HOT!"

"Billy," Niko shouted back. "Was he behind this?"

"He thought it might turn you on, is all," Holly responded. "But this isn't about him, it's about us, and maybe Nancy. And where did she come from anyway. She wasn't even supposed to be in that class. But there she was with her hands all over you."

"She wasn't the one who...."

"Okay, okay, I'll give it up." Holly interrupted. "I'll tell the professor to find a new model. I'm sure Nancy wouldn't mind stepping in."

"She doesn't have your body. She couldn't pull it off," Niko answered.

"She couldn't?"

"No, she couldn't."

Holly softened. So did Niko.

"She'll never make love to you the way I will either," Holly said.

"I'm sure I'll never know," Niko answered.

"Promise?"

"I already promised, remember? Anyway, why settle for something less then perfection."

"I AM perfect." Holly said with a sudden smile. She was silent for another long moment and then she added: "So why don't I model for you now, and then you can fall in love with your model just the way Mendez said you should."

"I'm already in love with her," Niko answered.

"Then why don't we do what people do when they're in love?"

"I'd like that very much."

Chapter Twenty-Three

The Project

The very next evening Niko was in the kitchen when Holly came up from behind him and put her hands over his eyes. "I have a gift for you," she said. She was still feeling very warm from last night's love making, and she couldn't stop smiling.

"What's the occasion?" Niko asked.

"I don't know," Holly answered. "Make something up. How long have we been married?"

Niko did a quick calculation. "A hundred and eleven days?"

"Okay, then it's our hundred and eleventh day anniversary gift."

Holly reached into a nearby cupboard and pulled out a gift box with a big pink plaid bow on top. "Open it," she cooed.

Niko unwrapped the box quickly only to find their little pink plaid elephant popping out of crisp new tissue paper. There was also a picture of Holly with it, a very sad one with downcast eyes and a somber look. And there was a note. Niko looked up at Holly who was staring back at him hopefully.

"Thank you for finding me and loving me," it said and was signed, "your lost little girl."

"What a pair," Niko sighed. "A lost little girl and a lost little elephant. Well, at least you both have hearts."

He carried the toy over to Holly and gave her a hug. He smiled and kissed her on the forehead. "Now I need your help with my next project," he said.

"Help from both of us," Holly asked.

"Why not?"

Holly turned the little elephant toward Niko so that it was looking at him attentively.

"I have to produce a five-minute documentary film." Niko began. "It can be on any subject. But I want it to be as successful as my work in the art class."

"Maybe you should make the film about the art class," Holly said with a giggle.

"Will you pose for the reenactment?"

"Sure," Holly said, and then she turned the little elephant around so that he couldn't look, put her hands behind her head, and struck a very sexy pose.

"Whoa," Niko responded, "Maybe you'd better not. Anyway, it is a good concept. A model comes in and disrobes. Then I get one of the better artists to draw her picture. I cut back and forth between the artist and his model."

"Could you capture the room itself?"

Niko started to answer and then just stopped cold.

"Something in that room scares the hell out of me," he whispered. "There were faces there …no… masks. You know, plaster masks of real faces."

"Like in the gift shops on Fisherman's Wharf in San Francisco?"

"Right," Niko answered. "But several of the faces looked just like Babcia.

"Nancy was with me when I found them. She saw my reaction; she was trying to calm me down. That's why she was so close to me. "

"Trying to calm you down?"

"Yes." Niko insisted and his expression turned sour. Holly recognized the look and turned the little elephant back around to face Niko. She gestured to the little guy. "Come on... this little guy came out of hiding just to help us be friends again. Do you want to disappoint him?"

Niko smiled with understanding. "Course not."

"Good." Holly thought for a moment. "Was the creepy smell in the room?" she asked, "That rotten gingerbread?"

"I didn't notice it."

"Well, then maybe they were just masks, not The Masks of Babcia." Holly tried to say it dramatically as though she were advertising the latest horror film, and Niko's smile broadened.

"Just throw the masks out the window," she added with a grin. Niko laughed uneasily, and then he fell silent again.

Holly came and sat down beside him.

"Let's concentrate on the project," she said. Niko nodded in agreement. "Is it enough to show the art room and the artist at work?"

"Needs more, doesn't it?"

"You could show how the drawing is coming along in between the scenes of the artist and his model."

"Better than that," Niko responded. "I could show the art DRAWING ITSELF. I could use time-lapse photography. The artist starts to draw and then we see the drawing as it grows right on the page!"

"I like it," Holly said.

"And it's easy to shoot. The only hard part was coming up with the idea. Thank you."

Holly put her arms around her husband. "You have no idea how creative I can be," she said.

She was right.

CHAPTER TWENTY-FOUR

FILMING, EDITING, AND INFIDELITY

The next few weeks were hurriedly filled with pre-production: rent the equipment, buy the film, hire the model, hire the best artist in the class, reserve the classroom, rent the lights, GET THE SCARY MASKS OUT OF THE ROOM!

And so on a Saturday afternoon, a very sweet model named Victoria, and Ron (the best freehand artist in the class) appeared in the studio to allow Niko Madonie to make his film.

He had each of the shots blocked out: the shots of the room, the shots of Victoria entering, the artist bringing in his easel and setting it up, Victoria disrobing and reclining on a low sofa.

Niko took several long shots of Ron sketching; one very nice one was right over Victoria's naked hip.

This preliminary work done, Niko turned to the time-lapse photography. He asked Ron to draw a line of his drawing, then step out of the picture and let Niko take a shot, then draw another line, step out and let Niko take another. The process continued for over 100 shots. By that time Ron had a very nice sketch of the naked Victoria, and Niko had his animated sequence of the picture drawing itself. Unfortunately, a quick calculation showed that Niko had only four seconds of the most important scene in the film.

Niko noticed the twinkle in Victoria's eyes as she watched Ron work. He saw Ron respond and remembered the words of Professor Mendez, "All artists fall in love with their models." Niko wondered about it for a moment, but didn't try to capture the relationship or even the poetic truth that Professor Mendez had described. And so he missed the principal story opportunity of the situation. Days later, when Niko got to the editing room, he came face to face with his problem. He had to build an entire movie around an animated sequence that lasted less than four seconds.

#

Niko drove home from the editing room in a very blue mood. It was raining hard. He found a shivery Nancy Swallow standing outside his door. Holly was not at home, and all the lights in the apartment were out.

"Waiting for me, Nance?" Niko asked.

Nancy beamed as soon as she saw him. "I am. I've come to invite you and Holly to a screening tonight: Truffot's The 400 Blows. Can you make it?"

"Sorry, I'm editing," Niko answered. "Have to get it done tonight."

"I forgot," Nancy answered. "Everyone's got their own little time slot, don't they? Think Holly would like the film though?"

Niko unlocked the apartment door.

"Don't know," he answered, "And where is she anyway?"

Niko flipped on the lights and looked around for a note.

There was nothing.

"She doesn't have a car. How could she have gone anywhere?"

"Someone must have given her a ride," Nancy suggested.

Niko frowned.

"Billy's back at the house, if that's what you're thinking," Nancy said with a laugh. "Boy, you don't have much faith in her, do you?"

Niko lowered his head. "When you've got a wife as pretty as Holly...."

Nancy smiled and stepped a little closer to Niko.

"Can't trust these beautiful women," she teased. "They're all unfaithful, you know."

"I didn't mean it quite that way."

"Would you have more trust if, say, I was your wife?"

Niko smirked. "You're beautiful too."

"Personally, I think fidelity is overrated." Nancy said.

She was very close to Niko now, looking up into his eyes. A smiled turned the corners of Niko's lips.

"You don't think that being faithful to your husband is important?" he asked.

"Or your wife," she answered.

Niko coughed nervously.

"Nancy, are you..."

"Of course I am," she answered. She took Niko's hand and cupped it to her cheek. Then she pulled it to her lips and kissed it.

"Nancy, I'm married."

"I know you are." She turned his hand over and pressed her cheek against it. Niko didn't pull away.

"I love my wife," he said.

"I know you do," Nancy answered. "That's what makes it all so delicious."

Nancy slid her hand up behind Niko's neck. She looked

up at him. Her lips parted and her tongue flicked invitingly between them.

"Nancy, I love my wife," Niko repeated softly... too softly.

SLAM!

The door to the apartment, which had been left wide open, suddenly closed abruptly. Niko and Nancy turned to see Holly standing there.

For a moment she didn't seem to know how to react, and then she just charged past both of them and into the bedroom slamming yet another door behind her.

"Holly," Niko called as he rushed to the bedroom, but all he heard were sobs.

"You didn't hear everything I said," he called, but the sobbing continued.

"Just go away, will you!"

"Let me explain."

"What? That you were going to kiss her and then... Go away! Just leave me alone!"

Niko walked into the bedroom and sat down beside Holly. He tried to touch her, but she pulled away from him. "Honey, I'm sorry."

"Go away, goddamn it."

"Forgive me."

"No! Get out of here and take your girlfriend with you."

"She's not my girlfriend."

"Well, get her out of here, whoever she is."

"Actually, I do have to go," Niko said sadly. "I have to finish my edit."

"Good."

"I'll be back late."

Holly didn't answer.

Niko turned. Nancy was already gone. And so he simply lowered his head and walked from the room leaving his wife in tears.

#

Niko headed back to the editing room, and all the way there he kept repeating the things he should have said to Holly. He hadn't really done anything wrong, had he?

Niko sat down at the editing console and began combing through his film footage looking for something, anything that would help him complete the project and take his mind off of Holly and Nancy. Atmospheric shots maybe, he decided at last. They could help suggest that the spirit of the classroom was helping shape the art. It sounded like an interesting twist.

The sculptures in the classroom were part of the atmosphere. He found plaster models of hands, and he had a close-up of the artist drawing the model's hands. So he cut from the sculpture of a hand to drawing of the model's hand. Feet? The same thing. Faces? Niko poured through the footage. Too bad he didn't get any close-ups of the masks, or did he?

"Any non-witchy masks that I may have shot?" he asked himself out loud. He reeled through the footage even faster.

"Shots of faces should be easy to spot." And there they were. He was talking out loud from then on.

"Now we can make this thing work!"

But it didn't dispel the sadness he was feeling about Holly.

Chapter Twenty-Five

Billy & Holly

Back at the Madonie's little apartment, Holly walked into the bathroom and took a washcloth from the rack. She scrubbed her face, brushed her hair, put on fresh lipstick, and pulled her blouse tight enough to show the outline of her lacy bra. Then she tucked the blouse into her slacks, smiled... and burst into tears.

"What does he see in her anyway?" she asked herself out loud. "I'm beautiful, aren't I?"

But of course, at that moment she didn't look beautiful, and worse than that, she didn't feel beautiful.

How had everything gone so wrong so quickly?

At that moment there was a loud knock on the door. Holly rushed over and opened it. It was Billy Bright dressed in a Hawaiian shirt and sporting a silly grin.

Holly smiled a little when she saw him, and then the tears just began streaming down her cheeks.

"What is it, Holly Blue?" Billy asked. "May I come in?"

Holly nodded and then, as soon as Billy stepped over the threshold, she threw her arms around him. Billy responded, holding her tightly.

"Tell me what happened," Billy said as he led Holly to the couch and helped her sit down.

"They were here, together," Holly sobbed, "Saying romantic things to each other. And they were just about to kiss, right here in our living room."

"You almost kissed me just now," Billy responded. "Is that so wrong?"

"It's the way they were looking at each other," Holly sobbed. "I know where it was going. She wants him. That bitch!"

Holly winced as she said the word. So did Billy.

"Know what I think you should do?" Billy asked.

"Scratch her eyes out!" Holly answered with a little laugh.

"Pretty catty," Bill said without losing his poise or his smile. "But please don't do that. I like her too much. Besides, I have a better idea. Only thing is, you'll have to trust me."

"I don't trust anyone any more," Holly answered. "That modeling thing didn't work out very well."

"I heard. Anyway, this will. And it will be easy for you. Just leave Nancy up to me. I'll get things going between us again; get her mind off of Niko. It's been a while, but I'll bet I can do it."

"I'm sure you can," Holly said with sudden hope. Billy's grin broadened.

"Maybe I'll even talk to that husband of yours. Remind him of what a great little wife he has."

Holly fixed Billy some coffee, and the couple talked for nearly an hour about what makes husbands cheat on their wives, ways to save marriages, Billy's long romance with Nancy. Holly found it all very reassuring. Finally, Billy stood and walked to the door. He was so sweet, so calm, everything she needed at that moment.

"Don't worry at all," Billy said.

"Thanks for coming tonight."

Billy leaned close to her (lips so close). "Trust me."

They didn't kiss. Billy was too much of an artist for that.

CHAPTER TWENTY-SIX

THE ART FILM

Two days later Professor Henry stood before the class and grinned.

"There's been some extraordinary work done over the last few days, he said, "And I want to commend you all. Billy Bright submitted a fine, though largely out-of-focus tourism protest film on the Monterey Peninsula. Nancy Swallow turned in a surprisingly erotic little piece on telephone poles."

"Missed me while I was in Monterey, huh, Nance?" Billy called. The whole class laughed.

"The truth, though," Professor Henry continued, "is that the real masterpiece of this quarter was turned in by our friend, Mr. Madonie."

Niko turned toward the professor in surprise.

"That Art Film," Henry continued, "What brilliant cutting. And the self-control to hold the animation scenes down to a few seconds so you could focus on the way the environment affected the art. Great idea!"

Niko smiled. Everyone was looking at him with admiration.

"The intercutting of the faces was brilliant," Professor

Henry continued, "especially the juxtaposition of that beautiful young model with that hideous old woman's mask."

"What old woman?" Niko asked, as a new sense of fear spun through him.

"What old woman?" Henry responded. "Hell, she practically MADE the film. And the way her expression changed into that evil grin. How'd you do that?"

Niko began to feel weak and a little desperate.

"How did I?" Niko whispered almost to himself, but the whole class heard it and laughed out loud.

"When can we see our films again?" Niko called suddenly. He had to look at it and figure out what had happened.

"Not for a while," Henry answered, "I sent yours off to Chuck Vaughn in Hollywood. He and I have been talking a lot about you. In fact you should stop by after class. I think I have some very good news."

"Sure," Niko answered, not quite certain that any good news could offset the terror that was starting to grow in him. "But I do have to see my film again."

"As soon as I get it back," Professor Henry answered. "We'll look at it together. Then maybe you can explain how you made the plaster mask of an old hag change expressions and smile the way she did."

"I'm not sure I can explain it."

"Just a little bit of the witchcraft that happens in the editing room?" Henry suggested.

"Right on," Niko answered.

CHAPTER TWENTY-SEVEN

CALLING DAD

Niko was almost too stunned by Babcia's latest reemergence to think much about the good news that Professor Henry had passed on to him after class. Leland had arranged a summer internship for him with Chuck Vaughn.

"Chuck has his own company in Hollywood," Henry had said. "You'll have the freedom to do really creative work."

Niko had nodded appreciatively. But he couldn't take his mind off of his movie and Babcia, and how she had somehow managed to make her way into it, if indeed she had. And if not, just what the hell did happen?

And then there was Holly. She had seemed so much better when he returned from his editing session. She had accepted his apology for being with Nancy, both sweetly and lovingly. And she had suggested that they didn't really have to talk about it again if he didn't want to. It was wonderful, except that Niko could see that it was a struggle for her. As much as she wanted to pretend that everything was all right, she wasn't sure. Hell, she had probably never thought about losing a guy to another woman in her entire life.

To get his mind off everything Niko called his father to

share the good news about the internship.

"Doesn't sound like the right situation to me," Dr. Lou grumbled from three thousand miles away.

"It's the chance of a lifetime, Dad." Niko responded. "Professor Henry wants to give you a call, to explain how important it is for my career."

"Important? You're supposed to be doing serious work!" Niko's father grumbled. "Chuck Vaughn makes cartoons about a saxophone-playing cat. How are you going to learn anything from him?"

"Just talk to Professor Henry, Dad."

"I'll talk to him, all right!"

Enough of this, thought Niko. He said a quick goodbye and handed the phone to his wife.

Niko had read Holly almost perfectly. She had done her best to follow the instructions outlined by Billy Bright, but deep inside she was still feeling sad and threatened. Another woman? Was it possible? Now she could speak to someone she admired and who might be able to help her.

Yes, she thought, Dr. Lou was very hard on her husband, and yes, he didn't always seem to trust her or even like her very much. But she knew that he was a wonderful doctor, and she had seen his kind and generous side. The truth was that she needed his advice.

#

Niko walked all through Los Altos that night. He walked past the mansions on University Avenue looking for telltale signs of Babcia in every hedge. He even hiked to the house on Homer Street to Billy and Nancy's never-ending party.

Bongos echoed through the night air, and on the porch Nancy was swaying to the beat. She seemed intoxicated, (intoxicating?). Niko saw Billy come up to her and kiss her.

He didn't want to see or know what happened after that.

CHAPTER TWENTY-EIGHT

SHE'S MINE!

By the next day Holly Madonie was beginning to feel much better. The conversation with Dr. Lou had been a real tonic. Maybe Niko should listen to his father more often, she thought. She had cut through his coldness almost instantly. All she had to do was agree that Niko should help his father write his silly American War and Peace and then offer to encourage Niko to do it. From that point on the doctor was entirely on her side.

It was all in how you approached Dr. Lou, Holly thought. You had to bring out his generosity, not just wait for it to happen through some kind of magic.

There had to be something else going on between the doctor and his son, Holly thought, something that made them natural rivals. Holly didn't know what it was and didn't want to. She had agreed to help the doctor and that was that. The hell with everything else!

Holly bounced down the steps of the Manhattan Garden Apartments in an outfit that was every bit as gay as her mood: a pretty, powder-blue polo shirt with a Playboy bunny on it, neatly pressed white shorts, spiffy tennis shoes. She handed her little suitcase to her husband.

Niko stuffed it, along with several duffel bags, into the trunk of his shiny new convertible.

"Why are we doing this?" Niko grumbled.

"End of the quarter," Holly answered with a smile. "We wanted to see the mountains. Your film is done; everyone loves it. Your art classes are going great. Everything's just fine. So why aren't you smiling?"

Niko mumbled something about witches. Then he tossed the last bag into the trunk and climbed into the car.

Holly reached over and gave Niko's shoulder a little squeeze. He smiled a very distracted smile and pulled the car away from the curb. They headed north to San Francisco, the Golden Gate Bridge and the mountains beyond.

"Mind if I turn on the radio?" Niko asked.

Holly looked over at her husband. He kept glancing at her as he drove, trying to smile. He was sweet, wasn't he, and cute, no Billy Bright though. (Oh, shit! Where did that thought come from?)

Holly wasn't going to complicate this trip with the kind of thoughts she had suddenly begun to have after her evening with Billy, (she could have him if she really wanted to, and she knew it). She wasn't going to talk about them or even think them. As her old parish pastor, Father Newcomb, used to say, they were impure thoughts and desires, mortal sins.

"Sure, turn on the radio," Holly answered.

It was nearly the hour, and that meant the news. Vietnam, though it was not yet officially called a war, was growing more and more alarming and more and more omnipresent every day. Body counts were tabulated weekly and reported daily. The numbers were harder and harder to accept. Ten Americans killed this week, eight the week before. Numbers reported for the enemy were unbelievable: 250 this week alone.

No one knew where it was headed. But for a draft-age student with a college deferment like Niko, the prospects of being required to donate a year of his life to help fight communism were becoming more and more real.

Anti-war protests, which had not yet reached Leland, were already common occurrences on the nearby campus at Berkeley. They were about the evils of war, but also about personal survival and an urgent need to avoid becoming cannon fodder.

In Niko's heart the issue added to his overall sense of foreboding. Coming from a family with a strong military tradition, with a father who had been a war hero and who despised any man who would not serve his country, he couldn't even think of avoiding the draft. He would not do it, would not stay in college forever. If called, he would serve, no matter how he felt about the moral purpose or value of Vietnam. That was his decision. Of course, there was a much more honorable way to avoid what was soon to become a full-fledged war.

"You know I haven't much time," Niko said at last as he turned off the radio.

"What do you mean?"

"I mean Vietnam," Niko answered. "I haven't much time before my student deferment runs out, and I'll be drafted."

"It's a year away," Holly answered. "All this Vietnam stuff will be over by then."

Holly felt wonderful, and it wasn't just Billy's promise to distract Nancy, or Dr. Lou's friendly conversation. She had a great new surprise for her husband. It was something she could do for Niko that would make his worries about Vietnam disappear.

The only military deferment open to someone like Niko besides a student deferment was the classification 3-A.

Holly knew the selective service rules. Every person in America under the age of 35 knew them in 1964. 3-A meant Hardship – fatherhood. All she had to do was get pregnant, not even have the baby, just get pregnant, and Niko would be exempt from the service and the war.

Holly had been going to a fertility specialist in the late afternoons. His office was nearby and she could walk to it. And Dr. Lee had told her what to do. She had a tipped uterus, and that required special exercises. Holly was doing these every night. And now the doctor told her that she was ready (willing and able) to get pregnant, to give her husband a child and a wonderful bonus: it would save him from Vietnam, give him the honorable way to stay home, a way that even a war hero like Dr. Madonie couldn't argue with.

She had brought along her sexy wedding lingerie. It never failed. This was something that she could give Niko that would be all theirs, just theirs. (It would make him forget all about Nancy.)

She didn't want to think about Nancy and Niko. Billy had said that he would take care of it and she knew he would. He'd just turn on that sexy charm of his and Nancy would forget about Niko in a second.

"Oh, Billy," Holly said with a sigh. Niko heard her.

"Billy?" he asked.

"I didn't say anything," Holly answered, and then she blushed. (Shit!) "I heard you," Niko said.

"Must have imagined it."

This was no good, Holly thought, the start of a fight at a wonderful time like this. Holly turned away from Niko completely. He didn't respond, didn't say any more; he just drove on into the mountains feeling another emotion, a growing sense of anger.

If Niko had lived another childhood, one that wasn't scarred by the war in ways he never really understood, it might have been all right. But he had been scarred, hadn't he? By a demanding father, by a witchy grandmother, but neither one of them had done the real damage. (What he really wanted – he remembered – was to become the man his mother looked at in adoration.)

His mother had broken his heart, just as mothers had done to a thousand generations of little boys who were displaced when their fathers came home from the war. The voice of those generations warned Niko that it could all happen to him again. This latest love could be gone in a second when a new man stepped into their lives. Niko had not doubted it for a minute. He was scarred all right, by another kind of witch, his own mother.

#

The little car made its way into the Cascade Mountains of Northern California, up the steep side of Lassen Peak, a sleeping volcano that had blown sky-high in the early 1920s. It had devastated the area all around it, so that now only withered stalks of pine trees and jumbles of granite rocks were left as testament to its anger. Niko identified with it completely.

As the Plymouth Fury topped the crest of the mountainside and began its descent, Niko decided he had to say something.

"Why did you mention Billy?" he asked, as gently as he could.

"I told you I didn't say anything."

"You don't like him?" Niko asked, with more than a hint of sarcasm.

"Well, I like him," Holly answered. "I mean he's a nice person. But he's just another guy really. You and I are married. Billy respects our marriage. And so do I."

"LYING, SHE'S LYING," Niko heard an ugly voice cackle from the back seat of the car.

"Who said that?" Niko called, as he turned to look, and at that very moment… that high up on the mountain… their little car hit a patch of black ice.

Niko jerked around forward as the car went into a skid. They were headed for a broad precipice just across the road.

The car continued to skid. Niko turned the wheel frantically, but the car was moving of its own free will. It was picking up speed, too, and Niko was powerless to change course.

"SHE WANTS HIM," the cackle continued. The car seemed to be filling with a bloody, sweet-spicy smell. Holly turned to Niko. (Did she smell it too?)

Niko opened the car door knowing that soon he might have to jump to save his life. He was just about to take his foot off the brake and jump, sending the car freewheeling across the highway and plunging over the precipice beyond. But in that moment he turned to Holly who looked back at him with both terror and trust. Trust!

"LET HER DIE," the cackle continued.

Niko was sure that he would have yelled, "Jump for it!" as he bounded out the door, but what could Holly have done but freeze in panic as she plunged to her doom in the accelerating car?

Niko slammed the car door shut, and yelled at the top of his voice, "SHE'S MINE! SHE'S MINE!"

Then he grabbed the wheel and jerked it frantically. The car twisted and went into a sideways skid, now moving both across and downhill. Holly screamed. The car fishtailed again, and the couple could see a vast canyon rushing towards them.

At that moment Hank Conroy and his wife Sarah were plowing their enormous Airstream trailer up the mountain on the other side of the road. They rounded a sharp turn just as Niko's Fury came careening across their lane toward the precipice.

Hank's giant vehicle slammed into the very front end of Niko's car. Holly flew almost into Niko's lap. The Fury spun backwards and then slammed into the side of the mountain across the road from the precipice. Hank Conroy's massive trailer was jolted close to the edge of the cliff, but its immense size and weight held it firmly on the highway. After a long moment Hank got out and rushed across the road.

"Jesus Christ! Are you all right?" Hank screamed through the driver's side window.

Niko was shaking all over. He looked at his hands and arms. No blood. He reached up for the rear view mirror and felt a sharp pain in his shoulder as he did. He grabbed the mirror and twisted it to look at his face. No cuts, no blood.

Holly was sobbing hysterically. She had buried her face in her hands.

"There, there, honey," Hank said. Holly looked at him and in doing so revealed a large bruise just below her left eye.

"Let's see, sweetheart. Yeah, I think you're gonna be all right. Just maybe a little banged up is all."

Hank stepped back.

"Your car's a wreck, though." Then he looked back at his trailer and laughed.

"But then, so's mine. And it doesn't matter. We're all alive; that's what counts. Boy, someone's lookin' out for you kids."

"Don't we need to call the police or park rangers or someone?" Niko asked.

"Got a CB in my camper," Hank answered. "I'll call the ranger. We'll get this all taken care of. You just relax. I'll get it done."

Niko looked across at the massive trailer that had come out of nowhere to save their lives. And then he realized that he had to turn around completely. He had to look into the back seat. His shoulder was pretty banged up and it felt painful to turn his body, but he had to do it. He had to see. He twisted. Pain shot up his back and through his arms. But he could see clearly into the back seat, and it was entirely empty.

Babcia was gone.

CHAPTER TWENTY-NINE

NANCY'S RUN

At that very moment Nancy Swallow stood naked in front of her bedroom mirror and looked at her body with a self-satisfied smile.

"Not bad," she said to herself as she slid her hands up and under her small, hard breasts, lifting them as though she were offering them to someone, and she would be soon. She knew it.

"Mmmmm," Nancy thought. She wondered how Niko would like them. Would he compare them to the perfect breasts of that hot little wife of his? Holly's breasts were perfect. Nancy knew it. She had seen them the day Holly had modeled for the art class. "But I'm not bad, either," she realized, as she watched herself slide into her soft, white, cotton panties.

"I've done a lot with me."

Billy was going to make it all possible. Maybe she had come on a little too strong with Niko in his apartment, but Billy had been there a few moments later and made the best of the situation. He had told her all about it. How he had calmed Holly down, helped her trust him. Soon, he would be able to seduce Holly slowly, carefully and completely. Then, once he'd had Mrs. Madonie, Nancy could move right in on Niko.

The important thing now was that she had to give Billy time. She had to be patient and careful and silent about it. Niko had to be the one who was cheated on. Billy worked like an artist. Nancy knew all about it because he'd done it to her. Not the first time, of course. That was the other Billy, the wild one who took her in a small anteroom during the senior ball at Harvard. The artist in Billy had wanted oral sex (ugh), had worked on her so carefully on their drive across the country, had hinted at it, and teased about it until there was nothing to do but give in.

Patience, Nancy reminded herself. But, of course, she could have all the secret fantasies she wanted in the meantime, dream about the fact that Billy would have Holly, then Nancy would have Niko, and then maybe (best of all) the four of them would have each other.

Nancy blushed. She pulled on her jogging shorts, slid into her top, then stepped into her running shoes, and laced them up quickly.

She padded down the stairs and out the front door. No school, a perfect day for a long run past town, past the campus, into the woods beyond, a perfect day to fantasize about Niko. There would be the brief unpleasant moment when she would tell him about Holly and Billy, a crazy angry reaction, and then maybe she'd give him a blowjob right on the spot! Wow!

Nancy ran faster as she pictured the scene, and the more she ran the more she realized just how much she would enjoy doing it with Niko Madonie over and over again.

#

It was thirty minutes later, as Nancy ran up the steep trail past Lake Laguinta, that she began to have an unsettling, creepy feeling, as though someone or something was watching her, tracking her, moving along in the row of eucalyptus trees that flanked the side of the road.

There it was again, something strange and hobbling, but quite capable of moving as quickly as she. Was it some wounded animal not hurt badly enough to be slowed? Nancy stopped and looked into the woods beyond the edge of the trail. There was nothing there, just a slight rustling in the wind, and then there was a shadowy figure, hunched over, hobbling along behind the trees, small, in no way graceful. Nancy felt a cold chill. What could it be, a dog, a coyote, something bigger, something that was not as swift and sure as it should have been; a wounded animal, a mountain lion ... a WOLF?

Nancy broke into a dead run. The thing hobbled along just as quickly as she. For all its thrashing about, it was moving as fast as a marathon runner in an all-out dash for her life.

Up ahead, the trees crossed the trail as it descended into a little wash. The thing seemed to be catching up to her now even though it was still hobbling and cackling, yes, cackling like some crazy old woman – NIKO'S GRANDMOTHER!

Nancy could hear her, and smell her. It was a sickening smell that reeked of blood.

Nancy spun around. She wouldn't run through the trees up ahead, she decided. But somehow the trees were behind her now as well. She didn't remember running through them on her way to the lake, but there they were, encircling her, behind her, in front, on her left, and her right. She was trapped!

Nancy charged on. She would beat the thing in an all-out run; she would get over the wash and through the trees before it could catch her. She felt her heart pounding, her muscles pulling hard, the sweat pouring from her. She could see the humped-over shape trying to move as swiftly as she, the girl who had won three marathons at Vassar felt her muscular legs carrying her forward. The thing hobbled like some kind of crazy crab.

Nancy laughed. She was beating the thing. With all its thrashing, it was falling back, the smell was fading, just a few yards more now to the edge of the wash and then across to the trees, past them, up to the highway and safely home.

Nancy looked back over her shoulder. It was gone. It had disappeared. All that wild hobbling and cackling had ended, left far behind by a strong, beautiful girl who, within a month, maybe two at the most, was going to take that sad, soon-to-be-cuckold Niko Madonie and fuck him like he'd never been fucked in his entire life.

Nancy smiled. She increased her pace as she climbed out of the wash and then charged up the other side into the thin strip of woods that separated her from the highway.

A few feet ahead of her two huge eucalyptus trees flanked the trail. They were dark, shadowy, able to hide things like a ravenous beast that might creep beneath them and wait for its oncoming prey.

Nancy wondered how many sweet young doe had grazed in the pasture at the head of the trail and then been attacked as they made their way between those awful trees. A smell was growing stronger suddenly, not eucalyptus, something else: sweet, spicy, bloody, deadly. Nancy caught her breath in horror.

Red eyes! There, in front of her. She saw them for only a moment... and then razor sharp fangs rose above her wildly as they – it – SHE pounced on the poor, desperate girl snapping her neck and killing her instantly.

Slowly, languidly the beast hobbled around its victim, pushing against her, nudging her, toying with her before it ripped her wide open and began devouring the remains of Nancy Swallow.

Chapter Thirty

Survival

The doctor told Niko and Holly that they were both very lucky to have survived the automobile accident with only minor cuts and bruises. He'd treated them in the emergency room of the Mt. Shasta Hospital, done all the necessary X- rays, and then let them check into a nearby motel for the night.

As Holly sat up on the small double bed sobbing quietly, it seemed like a miracle. One minute they were quarreling, the next their little car was rushing out of control, taking them to their deaths, and then, at the very last second, they were saved.

Holly had never been very religious in spite of her 14 years of Catholic schooling. But this was the kind of event that brought even the most hardened agnostic back to the church.

"We're so lucky," she sobbed. It was as though God reached out and saved them Himself. And with that saving came forgiveness for her impure thoughts and desires about Billy.

Niko was in a far different frame of mind. He was haunted and terrified, and the miraculous accident that saved their lives couldn't make up for the fact that his grandmother was talking to him again, and now telling him to kill his wife. It was madness pure and simple. Could he tell Holly about it, maybe scare her into forgetting about Billy? Not now, he realized. Not ever.

"What did you mean?" Holly asked in a whisper. "When you said, 'She's mine,' what did you mean?"

"I was talking about YOU," Niko said. "I meant that you're mine, that I love you, you're the one I want to be with." In spite of his distraction, the warmth had returned to Niko's voice, and Holly was grateful.

She had such wonderful plans for this trip. And now she looked across the room to her little satchel with her sexy little wedding things packed neatly away, waiting until the moment that she could tell Niko that she was ready to get pregnant with his baby, that she knew she could do it, that she wanted to so badly. And Niko would make such a wonderful father. Not a soldier, a father!

"But who were you talking to," Holly asked as she sat up on the bed and wiped the tears from her eyes. She was wearing nothing but her panties and Niko's oxford shirt. The corner of it made a pretty good Kleenex, she thought.

"To myself," Niko answered in the soft, distracted whisper of someone who was lying. But Holly accepted it.

She turned and looked at Niko. He was sitting in the chair beside the desk. He had turned the chair toward her so that he could look at her. His eyes were troubled, so troubled, but there was no doubt in Holly's mind that they were also filled with love.

That crash was her penance, she decided. It was God's way of reminding her that even though she had committed 'adultery in her heart,' she had a husband who loved her and needed her.

Holly looked back at the suitcase; its contents weren't necessary. The outfit that she was wearing would do just fine, no big production needed. She glided up to her husband and put her arms around him and kissed him.

"You saved my life," she said, "And I'm going to do something wonderful for you right now."

And then she did.

CHAPTER THIRTY-ONE

NEWSCAST

"Niko, get in here!" Holly called. "It's Leland, all of them; the whole Communications Department's being interviewed."

It was 8 AM the next morning, and Holly was watching the early news on channel 2.

Niko gave a muffled call from the shower that made no sense at all.

Holly turned up the sound. She tried to piece together what everyone was saying. There was a reporter standing next to Jennifer, one of the girls from Niko's class. She was answering questions, but her words didn't make any sense, something about tragedy, wild animals, and death.

"Niko! Something awful has happened."

Niko came in, towel around his waist, hair tangled in half-dried Italian curls. He had the glow from a night of endless sex (the best sex of his entire life).

"What's going on?" Niko asked. Holly turned up the sound even louder.

"So the search goes on," the reporter said, "for whatever beast killed the pretty co-ed. But what kind of beast was it? Experts are still not sure. For more on that part of the story we go back to our Studio where Kathy Frank is standing by with Professor Richard Cornell of Leland's Zoology department."

"Jesus," Niko said, and he began pacing nervously behind his wife. "Someone from our class was...."

"Professor," Kathy Frank began, "are there wild animals who could attack joggers on the trails around Leland?"

"Well, that's what happened isn't it," the professor answered.

"Are you saying there are wild animals native to the area?"

"Of course," the Professor answered. "Leland backs up to an enormous piece of wild land. It covers thousands of acres."

"And what kind of animals inhabit the area?"

"Well, coyotes certainly. Rattlesnakes. The problem with this incident is the size of the animal that attacked this girl."

"My God, Niko," Holly said. "Someone was killed?"

"Are there any large animals in the forests around Leland?"

"In the past of course, bears, mountain lions, even wolves. But none of those species has been seen in the area for decades. The tracks in this case indicate some kind of canine: a big dog or a wolf. The direct strides suggest that it was a wolf. But there are no wolves in California now, let alone in the Bay Area."

"Then how could this have happened?"

"My guess is that the victim was killed by some kind of pet, a wolf that someone was keeping. People get these wild animals and keep them in their homes, don't realize how dangerous they are. Most often, when a wild animal attacks, it kills its owner. But when one escapes, everyone's in danger."

Kathy Frank turned to the camera and addressed it directly.

"A Leland graduate student was killed along this trail yesterday while she was jogging. Experts say it might have been by a wolf that someone had kept as a pet. Back to you, Jeff."

Niko paced back and forth even more frantically. "Who was she?" he kept repeating.

"We have another Leland Professor with us," the reporter continued. "Professor Henry, what can you tell us about the victim?"

"Nancy Swallow," Professor Henry began, "she was one of our best...." And then he shook his head, broke down in tears as the camera cut to Nancy's graduation picture from Vassar.

"Nancy?" Niko called in anguish, and he charged up to the television and twisted the volume as high as it would go. But by then Professor Henry was only mumbling.

"Nancy Swallow," he murmured, "sweetest girl in the class." And then he just wandered away from the reporter.

"Let's go to Lake Laguinta on the Leland Campus, where Dennis Raymond is standing by at the scene of the attack."

"Please turn it down," Holly whispered. She had no idea how to feel about the news. (Relief, that Nancy wouldn't be tempting her husband any more.) That was an evil thought wasn't it, unworthy of a girl whose life had just been saved.

"Jeff, I'm standing on the spot where Nancy Swallow was attacked. You can see those trees up ahead. Apparently, as she took her morning run, Nancy passed between those trees where the beast was lying in wait. As Nancy approached the trees it jumped out at her. There are very few signs of a struggle. That suggests that the beast was very large, caught her unaware, and killed her very quickly."

Holly and Niko stared at the television.

"According to the information we have," the reporter continued, "from experts who have been on the scene with us, the tracks that were found at the site are those of a large dog or wolf. We have no proof either way, though dogs seldom, if ever, attack in this manner."

As the reporter spoke, the camera zoomed beyond him and into the trees. Niko moved closer to the TV screen. He saw something there, something deep in the shadows. What was it? Eyes? Glowing blood red?

Niko turned off the television and looked at Holly, HIS Holly ("She's mine!"). He reached for her, and when she put her arms around him, he broke down and sobbed.

"Seems unbelievable," said Niko at last, and then his own haunting words returned to him, words from so early in his childhood, from so long ago:

It wasn't a grandmother; it was a WOLF, a scary evil wolf, a scary evil grandmother, A GRANDMOTHER WHO WAS A WOLF.

"SHE DID IT!" Niko said firmly, and then he pulled back to look at Holly. "And she wants to kill you too!"

CHAPTER THIRTY-TWO

MENDEZ

Niko shook as he lifted the film reel and placed it onto the spindle of the Moviola editor. It was now 7 AM.

Niko and Holly had just returned to Leland from their terrifying mountain adventure only a few hours earlier. He'd tried for a little sleep, but it didn't come. He'd tossed and turned for maybe twenty minutes before he got up, dressed hurriedly, and made his way into the offices of the Communication Department. There, he quickly found the film Professor Henry had left out for him, and took it into the editing room.

His fingers twisted the leader around the sprockets and threaded the film through the gate. Then he stepped on the pedal and sent the Moviola into fast-forward.

He whizzed past the opening scenes of his film. Then, only a few moments in, there she was: BABCIA, her mask looking in on the artist and his model, her horrible face filling the entire screen. She vanished as the artist did his work. Then she was back again, this time with a different expression. The artist drew. His picture completed itself. The model smiled. So did the mask of Babcia, but it was a hideous smile.

Niko jumped back from the editing machine. He hurriedly wound back to the start of the sequence and looked at it again. Babcia smiled. Her expression, frozen on that white plaster mask, changed. Now it was suddenly bloodthirsty.

Niko rewound the film again, looked again, then pulled the reel from the Moviola and pushed it back into the film can.

"Evil bitch!" he said out loud.

He tossed the can on the table and charged down the hall, up the stairs and into the grey morning.

If he hurried he could talk to the one person who might have some answers. Niko ran as fast as he could, across the Main Quad to the art studio where Professor Mendez was preparing for his class.

"You got rid of them, didn't you?" Niko called to the professor as he pushed through the door.

"Got rid of what?" Mendez appeared quite startled at the young man's frantic appearance.

"The masks, Babcia's masks!"

"Whose masks?"

"The masks from the shelf in the corner there! I asked you to take them out of the room before I shot my film."

"I don't remember it," Mendez answered.

"I asked you to get rid of the masks of the old woman because they frightened me."

"Frightened you?" Mendez sounded like he thought the whole idea was silly. "Even if you did ask me I wouldn't have done it. Those masks are too valuable to be shuffled around. They belong in this room."

"But you have to remember?" Niko pleaded. "They scared the hell out of me."

"Well, yes, there have been some scary things going on around here. That poor girl, Nancy, did you know her well?"

"We were..." Niko didn't know how to finish the sentence.

"Well, the campus has been turned inside out with the search for that animal. My God, a killer wolf in the hills around here, someone's monster pet. The police are everywhere. They'll catch it. I'm sure they will."

"I'm sure they won't."

Mendez stared at Niko. "Well, anyway, the masks have always been here. And you should be glad that I didn't take them out of the room. You made good use of them in that art film of yours. Congratulations. Everyone loves it."

"Thanks," answered Niko automatically, as he turned and hurried to the wooden box where the masks of Babcia had been. They were still there, scattered throughout the box. Their expressions ranged from evil contemplation to hideous laughter.

"You could shoot these masks, one after another," Niko said, almost to himself, "and you could bring that face to life with stop-action photography just the way I did with the painting."

"And just as you must have done with the faces in your movie," said Mendez, "It was astounding."

Niko suddenly felt numb all over. He reached out for one of those horrible masks, feeling an electric tingle as he touched the cold, white surface. He turned it over. On the back of the mask the artist had scratched a name into the plaster before it dried. It said, "Michalina Czarownica."

"Michalina Czarownica!"

"Perhaps the name of the artist, or even the model," said Mendez. "Scratching the subject's name into a mask was not entirely unheard of in Eastern Europe hundreds of years ago."

"My grandmother's name was Michalina," Niko whispered. "And Czarownica is the Polish word for witch."

Mendez took a quick step toward Niko. "Are you all right?"

"I'm not sure."

Mendez studied the boy for a long moment. Finally he shrugged and turned away. "You'll have to excuse me. I have to finish my prep. You're welcome to stay, of course."

"Better not," Niko said softly, and he returned to the box full of masks. He shuffled through them again, daring, perhaps for the first time in his life, to gaze fully and thoughtfully at the countenance of his adversary.

Just as he suspected, just as he feared, as he shuffled through the faces he found one that was the most horrifying of them all. It was hungry, bloodthirsty, the last thing poor Nancy may have seen in her life, a face that was both witch-grandmother and wolf.

And now, Niko realized, the monster was after his wife!

PART 3

HOLLYWOOD WAY

Chapter Thirty-Three

VVA

Niko stepped off the elevator into what seemed like a nightmare. It was the 12th floor of the Sunset and Vine Tower Building in Hollywood, California, the perfect place he hoped to get away from Babcia's evil presence. But the floor looked as ominous as anything he had ever seen.

The walls were painted a drab gray, and the dingy metal furniture was hardly what Niko would have expected in an animation studio. There was no one at the reception desk, but a small sign saying Vaughn Visual Arts reassured him that he was in the right place.

Niko looked down the long, dark hallway behind the reception area. It was carpeted in an oriental pattern that made it look like it went on into infinity. Still he decided that there must be someone working down there. He could hear a woman humming to herself in a tuneless, off-key way.

Niko walked slowly down the hallway trying each of the doors on both sides of the hall, hoping that one of them would open and he would see a smiling face looking up to welcome him. (Nancy's pretty face?)

Each door Niko tried was locked, and each responded with an obstinacy that told him he'd never get in.

"Hello," he called. There was no answer, but he could still hear the woman humming to herself.

He tried another door. It was locked. Niko reached the end of the hall and the very last door. He tried it, opened it, reached for the light switch and flipped it on.

BABCIA!

An immense portrait of the witch dominated the room. The walls were a wild mass of drawings, sketches of witches performing their evil rituals. The table in the center of the room was filled with crumpled papers, colored markers, and half-drawn illustrations. A huge black cat screeched and jumped out from behind the table. It landed on the floor beside Niko and scurried from the room brushing his leg with an almost sensual touch. And then...

BLACK!

The room went totally black.

"Scare ya?"

Niko jumped, turned toward the voice that had uttered those words and saw a tall, slender young woman. Her face was a mass of freckles and she wore a heavy wool sweater and a long granny skirt. She smiled nervously at him with a look full of distrust and accusations. She had turned off the light in the room, leaving Babcia in total darkness.

"Who are you? What do you want?" The young woman asked with nervous rapidity. "You're not supposed to be here, you know."

Niko reeled from the attack.

"I'm...."

"Niko Madonie," the young woman answered with a slight shift in expression. Now her look was a little more welcoming, but still distrustful. "You're early, you know; so don't go in there. It's our story room. We call it our WITCH

ROOM. We're developing a new TV show in there. It's secret! Proprietary! Off limits to the public."

"A show about witches?" Niko asked.

"Maybe! Perhaps. Anyway I'm not at liberty to say, you know." She was now tugging at her mousey brown hair and twisting it nervously around her fingers. She was also shaking all over. Way too much coffee, Niko thought.

"My name's Marla," the young woman continued, "Marla Morrison."

Niko held out his hand and Marla shook it far more firmly than he expected.

"Now, come along," she said. "Let's see if Chuck's ready for you."

Niko and Marla spun around and suddenly the office area behind them had come to life as the studio's workers began to arrive. There were production assistants loaded down with piles of artwork scurrying here and there. Two men emerged from the elevator carrying leather attachés and arguing enthusiastically. A striking, redheaded woman in towering heels, studying some kind of a calendar, almost ran headlong into a large, Grinchy-looking man who was busy installing an enormous VVA logo in the entryway.

Niko was dumbstruck by the hullabaloo, and wondered how so great a transformation could have occurred in the few minutes he had taken to find his way to the witch room. Marla's expression brightened as she ushered him into Chuck Vaughn's office.

The room was huge, with a full wall of floor-to-ceiling windows that looked out over Sunset Boulevard and its unending action. The black cat scurried in past Niko and Marla and hopped up onto the broad desk where Chuck Vaughn was poring over papers.

"Behave, CatMan," Chuck rasped, and then he turned his attention to Marla. "Whatyagot?"

He was chewing gum violently.

Charles Martin Vaughn was a short, skinny man with round glasses that matched his leprechaun face and his kaleidoscopic attire. His hair was very thin and combed directly forward; then it was cut off sharply as it reached the edge of his forehead. His shirt was a buzz of multicolored stripes. They clashed violently with the thin, Kelly green tie he was wearing.

"Niko Madonie," Marla answered.

"Great, sit down, kid," Chuck said between chews. "Want a job as a writer?"

"I thought I was coming here for a summer internship," Niko answered as he slid into one of the conference chairs across from the great animator. Marla took the chair beside him.

"Yeah, you were, but we need a writer. And I'd just as soon put you to work full time."

"Hey," Marla tried to interrupt.

"Don't worry, doll, you can keep your job," Vaughn said. "But let's face it, you need some new ideas; WE need some new ideas."

Without missing a chew, Vaughn turned back to Niko.

"This is a tough racket, kid. Creativity is the only thing that counts. We're behind; kinda run dry, need some new blood. We bet the studio on a new animated TV special: Hansel and Gretel. Know the story?"

"Grimm's Fairy Tales?"

"Yep, all about witches!"

"Why me?" Niko asked, feeling he was somehow being sucked into a whirlwind.

"For one thing, you're here," Vaughn answered in that raspy, gum-chewing voice. "And for another, your work is great."

"You liked my comic books?" Niko asked.

"Your comics are pretty good, kid," Vaughn said. "But not as good as your goddamn art film. It's the scariest thing I've ever seen in my life. The old woman is a horror. I tell you, kid, you must know something about witches, 'cos you sure put one on film."

Niko smiled and nodded with the same kind of quirky nervousness that Marla had shown. Must be the energy in the place, he thought.

"Want the job? You get to work with Marla all day long. Calm her down, get a little pot in her or something, and she's a hell of a gal."

Marla shot a vicious glance at Chuck Vaughn, and he burst out laughing.

"Forget that cute freckle-face. She used to be a ballerina, got great legs under that long skirt she's wearing. Show 'em your legs, Marla."

"I will not!" Marla answered as she glared at her boss.

"Okay, okay." Vaughn answered. "Do you want the job or not, kid? Hundred bucks a week. That's a lot of money, plus Marla and witches, what a combo."

Niko looked at Marla, who glowered back at him as much as to say, get the hell out of here. He looked at Vaughn who, in spite of all his bluster, seemed to be pleading with him for help. He looked at the cat, CatMan Due, named for the animated saxophone-playing feline that had made Chuck Vaughn such a success. The cat's eyes narrowed. He had no idea what the hell that meant.

"I'll take it, Mister Vaughn," Niko said with a mixture of joy and horror.

"Wonderful," Vaughn said as he stuffed another stick of chewing gum into his mouth.

"I'll get a contract drawn up for you by tomorrow morning."

"Shit," Marla cursed under her breath.

Vaughn said, "You won't be sorry, kid. Tomorrow morning we'll go to breakfast together, and I'll introduce you to a real, bona fide witch."

"A witch?" Niko asked. Fear suddenly began to twitch its way over his shoulders and down his spine. He shuddered. Vaughn recognized the sign.

"Don't worry, boy," he said, "I think you've already met her. But let's make it a surprise, okay?"

Niko turned to Marla, who was suddenly giving him a frighteningly defiant smile. And then he realized there was more to the horror than just Marla's defiance. It was her eyes. They were stone cold.

#

A few moments after she showed Niko to the elevators and he left VVA, Marla excused herself and made her way back down the hall and into her own office.

Chuck Vaughn had given her a large writer's room with a big mahogany desk and bookcase, a credenza (now piled high with research on witches and their craft), and – best of all – a locking door.

Marla looked out through the wide windows, behind her desk… down onto the corner of Sunset and Vine. For a moment she watched a statuesque blond in an impossibly short micro mini skirt hitchhiking boldly up Vine Street. She shook her head, laughed, then reached up, grabbed the cord to the drapes and yanked them closed.

She locked the door.

Marla stepped out of her skirt, pulled her baggy sweater over her head and and stripped off of her underwear. She felt a tingle that ran down to the tips of her black painted toes. She took a thick sacramental robe from a hook on the back of the door and draped it over her shoulders. Then, she reached into the credenza and pulled out a small silver tabernacle. She placed it in the center of her desk and opened it.

Inside, there was a shrine... to a witch.

Marla took a small vial of sacred oil from the tabernacle. She pulled the stopper, tipped it up, and let the oil spill out onto her fingertips. She rubbed it onto her lips, across the tips of her breasts, down over her belly and lower still.

Her eyes glowed now. She felt transformed. She WAS transformed. And so she closed her eyes, said an evil prayer, and finally announced out loud,

"THEY'RE HERE. IT'S TIME."

Interlude 4

Wicktor tops off his glass, and takes a sip. Michalowski slumps into his chair, eyes half closed, clearly envisioning Marla and her obscene sacrament.

Matryoshka stares at the array of masks that glower back at her from across the room, wondering, no doubt, if it is to one of these images that the young woman prays.

The warlock sneaks quietly behind the girl, does not disturb her, is sure that she doesn't even know he's there. Then he raises up on his toes reaches his hands above his head, and hovers over the old shopkeeper's daughter like some kind of demon.

"THE WOLF-WITCH FLASHED HER YELLOW FANGS," he calls out.

"Noooo," Matryoshka shouts, as she jumps up and runs from the room, only to hear Wicktor laughing heartily behind her.

"You shouldn't scare her like that Pan Wicktor," Michalowski says.

"But it's so much fun to see her scramble."

After a few moments, Matryoshka peers back through the doorway to the secret room, back at the two men and to the 27 masks of Babcia that hang on the wall beyond them.

"It's not funny," she grumbles as she slowly makes her way back.

"I think it is," Wicktor chuckles

"Why not just tell the story?" she asks.

"And miss the expression on your face? You're very cute when you're terrified, you know."

Matryoshka lets out a disheartened sigh and then seems to relax a little as her eyes fall once again on the bottle of vodka. There's still plenty to be had.

"Another sip, please?" she asks her father.

"To make you strong enough to stand up the Pan Wicktor's scary surprises?"

"Um humm."

The old man pours another round of drinks for them all, going a little light on the serving to his daughter this time. Once he's done, he simply adds, "Please continue, Pan Wicktor."

"Yes, but where was I?"

"Back in ancient Poland," Michalowski suggests.

"That's right, with the wolf witch about to attack her latest victim, Julia."

"But what about Holly and Niko and this new woman, Marla?" Matryoshka interrupts.

"Damn it girl, the warlock says, "do I have to lay everything out for you like road signs along a boring four lane highway. This business I want to tell you about now happened centuries before that, I know, but it bears dramatically on what is just about to happen in Niko's world."

"So, let us LISTEN, Kochanie," Michalowski says.

Matryoshka smiles, nods, and soon the warlock's tale takes them back in time hundreds of years.

#

"The wolf-witch flashed her hideous yellow fangs. It moved menacingly towards Julia, but the beautiful girl, like all of Michalina's victims, became frozen in absolute horror.

It was then that the horrible creature raised its bloody claws high above Julia, prepared to lunge at her, to catch her in its monster jaws and destroy her. But the artist would not have it. He threw his body in front of his beloved. Why had he ever allowed Julia to talk him into this, bringing her here to meet this creature that had made him so wealthy, but still had the heart and mind of a monster?

The artist forced himself to face the lunatic snarls of the beast, to stare deeply into her eyes, past the blood-red glow of hatred and destruction, into the soul of the ancient crone who had cared for him enough to allow him to make masks of her.

The artist had once seen the playfulness in those eyes, had found the Michalina inside of Babcia, and she loved him for it, loved him enough to let him visit her again and again, loved him enough to be jealous of any other woman who came into his life, especially the one he intended to marry.

The monstrous she-wolf raged above the artist and his love. Then, slowly, with a tragic wail that echoed through the forest, she melted back into the twisted shape of the crone.

After a moment, Babcia Michalina, Babcia Czarownica, Babcia the great witch, reached up to her neck and drew out her Ladanki...her witch's bag of herbs and spells. She shuffled through it, found a tiny scrap of light-blue paper, unfolded it carefully and began to read from it. She chanted something in an ancient tongue that the artist could never understand.

Her words were hypnotic.

The artist slowly relaxed.

"A spell for cleansing memory," Babcia whispered. "I need a lock of her hair."

She pulled out her witch's knife and moved toward the girl. The hysterical beauty tried desperately to bury herself in the heavy folds of the artist's shirt. But Babcia quickly reached her with the knife and sliced off a snippet of her braid.

"I cast the spell of forgetfulness," she cackled. "It will last forever."

The artist pulled away, clutching Julia to him and praying desperately for salvation.

"Don't be afraid," Babcia whispered. "She'll not remember this." The artist smiled gratefully.

"But never," Babcia demanded, "never bring her here again."

The artist was shaken to his soul. Still he followed the witch's advice, turned, and shepherded his love away from the horrifying scene. By the time they had reached the edge of their village Julia's smile had returned, her step turned gay; she joked with the artist and teased him. She remembered absolutely nothing of what had happened.

Nothing would ever bring that memory back to her. Not even when the artist took one of his many masks of Babcia and transformed it into the image that he had seen that horrible afternoon, an unbelievable image that would bring him his greatest fame and fortune.

It was a mask of the ancient crone, Babcia Michalina, Babcia Czarownica, Babcia the witch on one side of its face, and on the other half the face of a deadly she-wolf.

CHAPTER THIRTY-FOUR

BIRTHDAY GIFTS

Holly was home on Niko's first day of work, unaware of the witchy experiences he was having, unaware, for that matter, of the witch history that so long ago had set the stage for what would soon begin to happen in her world.

The lovely, young Mrs. Madonie was busy arranging furniture in their new apartment. But something was troubling her. Something terrible.

Niko could be losing his mind, she thought.

Holly was becoming more and more certain of it. His reaction to Nancy's death was intense. That was to be expected, but it was also so strange. And then his comments, "SHE did it! And she wants to kill YOU too!"

Holly remembered feeling that she was being stalked by some evil presence when she had first met Niko. And then there was that awful, frightening smell. Niko had talked about Babcia, had claimed to see masks of the evil woman in the Leland art studio where he shot his film. But Holly had begun to convince herself that all of that was a bad dream or a misunderstanding or something. But lately Niko had been talking as though his dead grandmother was back, haunting them again, and that was terrifying!

"I'll snap him out of it tonight," Holly told herself, "Tonight, if only for an evening, we'll have the sweetest loving we've ever had."

Whatever miracle had happened in the accident had made a profound impact on Holly. She said a prayer of thanksgiving every day, cleaned their new little apartment with almost obsessive thoroughness, made suppers that were as fine as she knew how to make, was sparkling and pleasant in her conversation, and made passionate love to her husband every night.

It was just the way the nuns of St. Kathryn's wanted their girls to behave, Holly felt. And yet, through all of it, Niko was spending most of his time in deeply troubled thoughts. The reality was there in his eyes.

Niko could be losing his mind.

Holly was putting the finishing touches on her soft pink lipstick when there was a knock on the door. She checked the large clock on the wall as she made her way through the little apartment: 4:45, kind of early for someone to be coming home from work. Holly's smile faded. Was something wrong? Had Niko gotten into some kind of trouble? She opened the door.

"Registered mail, for Holly Madonie," said a young deliveryman in California shorts.

"I'm Holly."

"Sign here."

Holly signed the form and took the package. It was large and quite heavy. Who could it be from?

She got a scissors and cut away the outer wrapping. Inside she found yet another package in bright "Happy Birthday" paper. There was also a letter addressed to her. She opened and read it.

"Beautiful Mrs. Madonie," it began. Holly glanced down at the signature and smiled. It was from Billy Bright.

"Have you and that handsome husband of yours gotten over the events of the past few weeks? I know I haven't. That's why I'm reaching out to old friends who loved Nancy as much as I did. Hoping we can find some solace together.

I've decided to drive down to Hollywood and pay you a visit. Hope you don't mind. I'll be happy to crash on your couch, or, if that's uncomfortable for you, I'll sleep in my van. I just need some friendship and to see someone really beautiful again.

Your pal, Billy

PS: Enclosed is a gift for Niko, a reward for the great success of his film. Should help him focus on his internship."

Holly took the letter into the bedroom and tucked it into the bottom of her lingerie drawer. No need for Niko to see it; she was sure of that. Might stir up old feelings. Better to be safe.

She returned to the kitchen. The gift was wrapped in silly paper: crazy clowns jumping around, wild streamers, confetti and letters spelling out Happy Birthday. Billy had taken a laundry marker and drawn devilish grins, horns, and beards on several of them. Should she open the gift? Take a peek at least? No. She placed it carefully in front of Niko's spot at the table. And then she went about setting out the plates and silverware and stirring up the spaghetti sauce that would be the heart of their evening meal.

"I need to see someone really beautiful again," She repeated. Holly eyed herself in the little mirror above the stove and was reassured with the vision that was there. She still had it. (And Billy wanted it.)

NO! That thought was a sin. Since the miracle of the accident she wasn't going to let those kinds of impure thoughts enter her mind. This was the new Holly Blue Madonie. And Billy had never once come on to her, suggested that they do anything improper. That was all in her own evil mind.

But the pink dress she was wearing did look sexy, (Billy would like it) and she was far prettier than that Nancy (BITCH).

Stop it! She told herself. It's a sin to think that way about someone who died, especially someone who was torn to pieces. (Only fitting.)

"Jesus, forgive me," Holly whispered in good Catholic School girl fashion. "There, that's better."

Just then Niko walked through the door. His tie was loosened, his sport coat was rumpled under his arm; he looked confused and upset.

"What's wrong?" Holly asked.

"Witches!" Niko murmured.

"What?"

"Witches! VVA is making a TV show about witches. And they want me to write it. They just hired me full time."

"Isn't that good news?" Holly asked, doing her best to smile in the face of her husband's discomfort. "You can write about anything."

"But there's a big picture of my grandmother right up there on the conference room wall."

"Niko," Holly scolded.

"Really. It's right there in the middle of the Witch Room, and Marla says...."

"Marla?"

"She's the other writer. She and I'll be working together, writing a horror story for television."

Holly gathered herself. She wasn't going to jump to any conclusions.

"Would you like a glass of wine?"

"Yeah, sure."

Niko took a series of deep breaths while Holly walked slowly into the kitchenette and poured Niko a small glass of red wine. He watched her doing it.

"Why so dressed up?" he asked.

"Emily Post recommends that every good wife wear a dress to greet her husband when he comes home from work," Holly answered. She sashayed a little as she walked back to her husband (anything to distract him from this crazy new situation).

"Carlo Rossi's best and cheapest," Holly said, handing him the glass.

Niko took a deep draft, held the wine in his mouth, then swallowed and let the warmth of it sweep over him.

"You look really beautiful this evening," he said.

"Bet you say that to all the girls," Holly teased. "Like Marla."

"Marla?" Niko said with a sudden chill. "She's the worst of it. She's probably the witch."

Holly shook her head. Was her husband going mad?

"Did she say she was a witch?" she asked. "Did anyone actually use those words?"

"Chuck Vaughn said that he was going to introduce me to a real witch at our breakfast meeting tomorrow morning," Niko answered. "But I could tell by looking at Marla that she's the one."

Holly ran her long pretty fingers across her forehead. This was more of the same craziness, wasn't it? Try a new tack, she whispered to herself.

"Is she a beautiful witch at least?" Holly asked, trying to humor her husband and do a little probing at the same time.

"Not beautiful at all. She's full of freckles. She hates me, thinks I'm going to take her job. She could be sort of pretty if she wasn't so defensive."

Niko took a deep breath, let it out slowly and realized just how crazy this all must sound to his wife.

"I don't want to talk about her any more, okay. I'd rather look at you. You're beautiful, you know."

Holly smiled. She leaned forward and kissed her husband. "Got some great spaghetti cooking for you. Just like Mom used to make."

"Mom was Polish," Niko said forcing a grin. "So, you must mean Spaghettski. Is it ready?"

"Absolutely," Holly answered. "Oh, and there is a birthday gift too. It came registered mail."

"My birthday's still a long way off. Who's it from?"

"Billy... There was a letter too."

Holly felt stupid as soon as she said the words. She didn't have to mention the letter, did she?

"Billy Bright?" Niko frowned. "What's he want?"

"Says he misses Nancy, says he misses old friends who loved her."

"I'll bet," Niko answered sarcastically. "Let's see it?"

"See what?"

"Billy's letter."

"Oh. It was just scribbled on a little piece of stationary. I don't know where it is, maybe in with the packaging that I already threw away. Want me to look for it?"

"Of course not."

Niko went to the table. The crazy package seemed to smile up at him just as Billy might have. He opened the small card that was attached. It simply read, "A memento of your triumph."

Niko looked curiously at Holly, and then he opened the gift, the gift Billy had purchased from Leland for nearly two thousand dollars, to reward (torment) Niko.

Holly screamed.

It was the mask of Babcia from the art studio and Niko's movie, the worst possible one, a face that was half woman, half she-wolf.

Niko dropped it back onto the table as though it were on fire. He was speechless.

Holly snatched the thing up, folded it back into the happy birthday paper and ran out of their apartment to the dumpster where she threw it deep into the trash. But, as the mask flew through the air, the wrapping came undone; the face pulled away from the paper, and Babcia's witch/wolf countenance was looking back at her with an evil grin.

Holly grasped the edge of the dumpster and hung on for dear life, hung on as she watched the mask sink down slowly into the sheaves of newspaper, puddles of curdled milk, orange rinds, pineapple skin, and other garbage, as though it were lowering itself into a comfortable shroud and settling in for pleasant dreams.

"Pleasant dreams," thought Holly; how long had it been since she'd had them... how long had her life been a nightmare?

"No," she told herself. I'm not going to think like that, and she turned away from the dumpster, stood erect, squared her shoulders, and marched determinedly back to the apartment, hoping that somehow she could salvage something of what she had so hoped would be a wonderful night of lovemaking.

But when Holly entered the little apartment, so rich with the smell of delicious spaghetti and the remnants of that feeling of hope, Niko was nowhere to be seen. Holly looked around the living room anxiously and then saw that the door to the bedroom was closed, and there was a little note sitting on the table.

"Gotta get some sleep," was all it said.

Chapter Thirty-Five

Nightmares

Somehow Niko felt like a high school student again, sitting on the edge of his bed, smiling like a horny teenager.

There, no more than two feet in front of him, Kathy Hurt was strutting through her sexiest cheerleader routine. She had just added a little shimmy, and it was working beautifully.

But still, somehow the vision was here in his Hollywood bedroom... directly in front of him. Niko was watching Kathy shake it, watching her teenage breasts jiggling inside her tight-fitting cheerleader sweater, watching the reflection of her twitchy little ass in the mirror behind her. Niko found himself clapping to the beat, knowing that there was an enormous tent pole pushing up in the front of his pants. He could tell that Kathy noticed it too; she shook her pompoms and everything else she had with newfound enthusiasm as she counted off to the music:

"One – two – three – four – five – Tequila!"

On that word, Kathy did a 60s teenage version of the old Elvis pelvis-thrust with such force that it almost knocked Niko over.

"Whoa!" he cheered, and Kathy dropped her pompoms and ripped her sweater up and off over her head. But when the sweater cleared her face, she wasn't Kathy Hurt any longer; she was Holly Blue.

Holly spun and danced with all of Kathy's skill: the shimmy, the shake and that Elvis Pelvis thrust.

"Tequila!"

Niko cheered again. But, with his call of approval, the mirror behind Holly began to cloud. Holly didn't see it, didn't know it was there. She danced closer to Niko, gave him her sexy pout, stretched out her arms and pompoms and shook everything she had for him. Niko somehow knew that Holly didn't know how to dance like this. She'd never been a cheerleader and yet, here she was:

"One – two – three – four – five – Tequila!"

The room suddenly darkened. The wind kicked up, and the curtains billowed into the room as though they were reaching for the girl. Holly looked back toward the curtains, toward the mirror. And that's when Babcia chose to reveal herself. Her face rose through the cloudy mirror, as it had appeared to little Kathy Hurt so many years ago. It was dead and rotting. Maggots and spiders crawled again from her eye-sockets, mouth and ears. They scurried toward Holly on the claw-like hand that reached for her. Babcia grasped the girl's throat, sinking her talons into Holly's beautiful neck and pulled her back. Crimson blood began to spill down over Holly's naked breasts. Babcia drew the girl to her, opened her ancient mouth with its rotting teeth, reached out her green, slimy tongue and licked the blood from Holly's tender neck and shoulders. And, as the witch swallowed the blood, licking her lips and smiling as Niko had seen her smile when she tasted the blood of Killer the dog, swarms of ants and spiders raced out of her mouth, over the witch's arms, up the girl's neck onto her face and down onto that gorgeous body.

Holly shrieked and turned back to Niko in desperation. "Save me!" she called as the witch tried to draw her into the mirror. Holly's arm touched the surface of the mirror and suddenly, Babcia exploded into a hissing, seething mass of maggots. They spilled out of the mirror onto the girl and began to attack.

Holly's scream was deafening as puss and slime and hungry worms began to engulf her!

Niko suddenly jumped up from his sleep... he was gasping for breath, standing fully upright. And there was Holly across the room from him, scared but alive and whole, pure and beautiful. She was all right.

Niko looked at the terror in Holly's eyes. He grabbed her, and pulled her to him. A dream! It was only a bad dream that came with the horrible package and the witch/wolf mask. It had made Niko so upset that he went to bed almost immediately, without his supper, without the sweet loving that Holly so desperately wanted to give him.

Now, he glanced over at the clock. It was still only 9:30 PM. The dream couldn't have lasted more than a few minutes, and yet, what was that smell... that sweet, bloody smell? And who was that shadowy figure standing across the room staring at him out of the darkness? Was she really there, eyes burning at him from across the room?

Niko knew he was awake now, knew that he had just survived a horrific dream. But still, didn't he hear a voice whispering?

"Niko, come play me."

#

Holly sat with Niko for nearly an hour, soothing him, calming him, letting him hold her tightly, taking love and protection as well as giving it. And when Niko finally pulled away from her, she kissed him with all the sweetness she had hoped to give him in an entire evening of lovemaking. Then finally, sadly, she went back into the kitchen to prepare Niko's lunch for the following day.

It would be brain food she decided: brewer's yeast in orange juice to help fight anger and depression; sliced beef with herbs that her mother had recommended to help Niko think more clearly. Was this the stuff of witchcraft? She wondered for only a moment.

Holly packed the meal neatly into a brown paper bag, and was stuffing it into the refrigerator when she heard a knock on the door. She instinctively glanced at herself in the mirror, fixed her hair and tried to smile. Then she went to the door, and opened it...

AND LET OUT A HYSTERICAL SCREAM.

It was that mask again, there in the doorway... after she had thrown it away, after she had assured Niko that it was gone out of their life forever. Harry Rodgers was standing in the doorway holding it. Harry, the apartment manager, who decided the first time he saw Holly that somehow he had to get to know her better.

Handsome Harry, Niko had called him the first time they had met, because he seemed to spend most of his time posing, posturing and trying to make himself look good.

"Get it away, Harry; I don't want to see it; I don't want to be near it. It frightens me. Niko can't stand it either."

"Jesus! All right," Harry answered, backpedaling as fast as he could. "Thought you'd thrown it away by accident."

"No accident, Harry, no mistake; that thing is evil. I hate it; I don't want it in my house."

"But it must be valuable. It's really very well done."

"Then you keep it. Save it, sell it, whatever you want. It's our gift to you. Just don't let us ever have to look at it again."

"I'm sorry," Harry answered and he lowered his head sadly. "I'll take care of it. You'll never see it again, I promise." And Handsome Harry reached forward and closed the door behind him.

Holly was still shaking. She went to the sink, splashed some water on her face, gathered her wits and headed back into the darkened bedroom.

"Is there anyone in the room with us?" Niko whispered as soon as he saw her. Holly looked around. There was darkness in every corner, but clearly no one was there.

"Oh, Niko," Holly said as she came to him and sat down on the bed beside her husband and stroked his hair. "I need you to be safe and sane for me. Please.

"I know that mask was terrifying, but it's gone; we'll never see it again. Now, try to put all this witchy stuff out of your mind. Tomorrow's going to be a big day for you. It's a great opportunity; you said so yourself."

Niko pulled the beautiful young woman to him. She was right, of course. This was his opportunity to accomplish all the goals he had set for himself, to outdo his father in ways the old man could never even imagine. But there was something more important he had to do too.

Holly felt Niko's body tense, his muscles gripping hard as though they were turning to stone. She pulled away from him for just a moment, and as she did, she caught a look in his eyes that she had never seen before, the steely look he must have inherited from his grandmother: bitter; ruthless; protective.

"I'll NEVER let her have you," Niko told his wife. "I promise."

"Thank you," the girl whispered. "I believe you," and she leaned forward and kissed her husband in gratitude and hope. There was more than a little forgiveness there too, maybe even the beginnings of trust. But as the couple clung more closely, the kiss grew in passion until Holly felt herself almost gasping for breath.

She pushed Niko back onto the bed, climbed on top of him, and – as she did – she flounced her little pink party dress out around her, so that she could press herself against the big steel thing that was fighting to get out of Niko's pajama bottoms. She reached down and twisted her panties aside, letting it snake into her, feeling herself splash the way she always did.

"Happy birthday, lover," she moaned as she jerked open the top of her dress, pulled down the front of her bra, and urged her husband's hands up onto her tightening nipples.

She rode him then, screaming with pleasure, loving every thrust, every moment of love until he exploded inside of her, and Holly fell forward onto her husband, her lover, and they cuddled and cuddled and finally slept.

But as they slept another presence appeared through the mists that Niko's dream had conjured up in the mirror. She was old, twisted, hideous… a witch, but one whose appearance was far from the powerful presence of Babcia Michalina. This witch's face was cut by a huge scar that ran from cheek to chin and then across under her nose. One of her eyes was a cloudy pocket of white, but behind it a sightless dead pupil roamed unnervingly in every direction.

This new witch smiled.

"I have plans for you, Niko. Your Holly too," she cackled.

And then the ancient evil woman gradually transformed into Marla.

Interlude 5

This latest development completely unnerves Matryoshka and she bursts into tears.

"Another evil monster," she moans.

For some reason Michalowski turns away. He's never been able to deal very well with his daughter's sensitive temperament. The warlock, on the other hand, is right there, kneeling by her side, drying her tears, copping a discreet feel while the girl is too distracted to notice.

"Yes, she's a bad one," Wicktor soothes.

"Who is she; where did she come from?"

"Marla's mentor, Babcia's pupil? Remember, didn't I tell you about her?"

I don't think so."

Let's go back then, sweetheart," Wicktor says. "She had something to do with Babcia coming to America... Babcia's Escape."

The girl calms. Michalowski returns to his chair, picks up his pipe, checks his glass and is reassured that there's still enough vodka to keep him satisfied through the next part of the story.

Matryoshka's eyes sparkle. "Make it exciting, though," she says.

Her father rolls his eyes. "You'll just start crying again."

"No Papa. I promise I won't."

The warlock and the shopkeeper exchange a disbelieving glance. Wicktor sighs. "Exciting," he says with a grin, and then resumes that tale.

#

"The hunter drew his dagger and stepped through the witch's doorway.

"Babcia Czarownica had come to live at the edge of the village, brought there by the artist who made masks of her terrifying old face. The townspeople were outraged when they saw her. Yet they revered the artist, knew the value of his judgment and his work. And so they agreed when he asked that Babcia be allowed to live there undisturbed.

Of course, by then the masks of the old witch had become popular across half the world, in Poland and as far away as America.

Many of the villagers secretly purchased and treasured one or another of the masks of the old woman, and they began to treat her with a cautious respect. Until the artist and his wife grew old and died, that is. Then a hateful sentiment began to twist its way into the village.

In the evenings it became common practice to tell horrible stories about Babcia. Children were sent to bed with warnings that Babcia Czarownica would get them if they didn't behave. Womenfolk began to taunt her. Old men kept a judgmental watch on everything she did. But worst of all (most damning of all), some of the local village girls took a serious interest in Babcia skills and began visiting the old witch in secret.

The wife of the Lord Mayor herself, Mistress Maria Goriki, followed her own daughter, Clara, to the witch's hovel late one night, saw that the girl had become a pupil of the witch, and watched the girl spin love potions out of cardamom and clover. That very night, Mistress Maria reported her findings to a meeting of the town elders, and they in turn decided to rid the village of the witch once and for all.

Richard, the ablest huntsmen in the village, a very dutiful young man, an unmarried man, was chosen to seek out the witch and destroy her.

It was Richard then who stepped across the threshold of the nearly seven hundred year old Babcia Czarownica.

Inside, the witch's hovel was thick with the smell of incense. It was sweet, inviting (jasmine and lavender), not at all what the huntsman had expected.

Branches of apple, pear and other fruit-bearing trees adorned the walls. Brightly lit candles formed a circle that almost filled the room. In the center of the circle stood a bed, decorated as though it were an altar with red and white ribbons all around. At the head of the bed, a tall candle, a swirl of red and white itself, waited to be lit. Beside the bed a small table held two silver cups and a silver pitcher. Next to them lay a thick cord (frayed at one end) and a small, double-edged knife.

The huntsman raised his own dagger at the sight of the knife and strode boldly into the room, prepared to meet Babcia in whatever form she chose. He had heard stories of how she could transform herself into a she-wolf, how she was impossible to destroy. And he was afraid.

But there was no old crone, no she-wolf, only a beautiful young woman with Polish white-blond hair and enormous, pale-blue eyes, who giggled as she padded softly into the center of the candle circle. She was dressed in a simple, white cotton gown and slippers.

"Babcia Czarownica!" the huntsman asked hesitantly…. Softly.

The woman only smiled, struck a match and lit the tall red and white striped candle at the head of the bed. Then she gestured to a heap of tattered old clothes in the corner of the room. There was Babcia, the huntsman realized. There were her tattered old clothes and beneath them surely, the broken remains of her body.

"YOU killed her?" The huntsman asked.

"She imprisoned me," the young woman answered, "Trapped me in dark ugliness."

Richard turned to gather up the heap of clothing, but

the young woman stepped forward, stopping him with the boldness of her action.

"Will you enter my circle," she asked, and Richard, who should have been better coached in the wiles of witches, answered, "I will."

And he stepped toward her into the circle.

Michalina, for that is who she was, drew the huntsman to the small table and poured him a cup of May wine. It was prepared, as the circle was, as the incense was, to capture a man's heart and bind it to hers forever.

"To the success of your endeavor," Michalina said, handing him the cup and raising her own toward him. The huntsman raised the cup in a toast, and then brought it to his lips cautiously. He hesitated. Michalina smiled with such innocence that, forgetting all caution, the man took a deep satisfying swallow of wine. Michalina's bewitching smile broadened.

"I have something for you," she said, and she produced a small gift-wrapped package. She handed it to the huntsman.

Richard slit the wrapping with his dagger and saw that it contained a human heart.

"Babcia's heart," she said. "I cut it from her only moments ago. Will you share it with me? Will you taste it?"

The year was 1880. In the distant villages of Poland, life carried on as it had for centuries. Certainly the huntsman had handled the bloody organs of wild game. But this was a human heart offered as food. Richard began to push it away, but the girl stopped him. Her hand clasped around his and around the heart.

"Will you share it with me?" she repeated.

The huntsman looked at Michalina. She drew even closer to him, and he tasted her breath. He saw her large, firm breasts pressing invitingly toward him through her thin cotton robe. His mouth grew dry. He felt the long unanswered call of desire. And he nodded.

"Heart for heart," Michalina whispered as she grabbed the silver cord from the table and spun it neatly around their hands and the heart. She pulled it tight... binding them together. Then she took her athame, her double-edged witch's knife, slit off a piece of the heart, and pressed it between her lips.

Her beauty intoxicated the huntsman.

Michalina's smile was saucy now. She began chewing openly so that Richard could see the blood splatter over her hungry lips and teeth and tongue. He raised their knotted hands to his lips and took a deep bite of the witch's heart, tearing off a chunk and swallowing it whole. More blood squirted across Michalina's face in the process. She laughed like a naughty schoolgirl. Richard laughed too. He took his knife and slit the cord that held their hands together. Pulling his hand away from hers, he thrust the remains of the heart toward the tangled pile of Babcia's body. It landed with a grisly thud.

With both hands free, he tore the gown from Michalina, lifted her and spun her onto the bed.

"I'll have more than your wine and your witch's heart," he said, as he flung himself upon the girl.

Michalina was as eager as he. Her sharp nails tore through the garments that separated them. The huntsman drove himself into Michalina, and she writhed and shuddered in response to his lovemaking. The incense, the wine, the smoke from the candles mixed together, intoxicating the pair as they thrashed wildly on the bed (the witch's altar) until at last, at the climactic moment of their act, Michalina shouted out, "It is done, IT IS DONE!"

They were spent. Richard fell forward on Michalina and they drifted quickly into slumber.

It was nearly an hour later when Richard awoke to see Michalina sleeping beside him. She was as young and beautiful as ever. God, he wanted her yet again. But first there was something he had to do.

He pulled away from her softly and made his way outside the circle to the heap of bones and tattered clothes that was the dead body of Babcia. He pulled back the rags and spun the body around to find that it was not the body of the witch at all, but that of Mistress Goriki the Lord Mayor's wife. She was barely recognizable, torn to shreds as though some vicious animal had found her in the woods and attacked without mercy. Then Richard felt claw-like fingers grasp his shoulder. He swallowed hard and turned.

It was Michalina, Polish white-blond hair, pale-blue eyes, youthful face smiling sweetly. She shrugged with the innocence of a teenager. Richard was terrified. He stood and drew back from the girl.

"Who are you?" Richard asked, as he felt a deep horror spin through him.

"I'm your wife," Michalina answered. "To be the mother of your children. We married just this moment in a witch's handfasting."

"But whose heart...?" Richard struggled to ask.

"Mine," she answered softly.

Richard turned, looked for the bloody heart and saw that it was gone. He drew his blade and slit open the disfigured body of Maria Goriki. Her tortured heart was still whole and in place.

"We ate YOUR heart?"

"Michalina's eyes sparkled in assent. "Magically."

"I'll kill you," Richard cried in terror, and he pressed his blade against Michalina's throat.

The beautiful young girl smiled.

"Kill your wife?" she asked, "Who will love you, who will give you beautiful children, who will care for you and protect you with all her crafts?" She giggled with the knife still at her throat.

The huntsman lowered the blade and stood there solemnly for a very long moment, and then he reached out and took Michalina's hand. She led him back through the circle of lights, back to their marriage bed.

#

That very night Richard and Michalina burned the witch's hovel to the ground and fled from the village forever. With the little money they had, they were able to book passage to America to begin a new life.

True to her word, Richard's wife was always Michalina for him. She gave him five beautiful daughters, and never once, not even when they had been married for decades, did she let him see the hideous creature she had become."

#

"A very nice story," Matryoshka sighs.

"Nice indeed," the old man answers. "But what about this Clara witch?"

"You mean the young girl who had gotten Michalina into so much trouble... whose mother lay dead on Babcia's floor, who peered through the window and watched in astonishment as her witchy teacher seduced the handsomest man in the village... the man she was secretly in love with?"

Michalowski and his daughter say nothing.

"She was outside watching through it all. But she stood too close to the fire that consumed Babcia's home. Smoke from the inferno swirled all around her and blinded her in one eye.

Finally she turned and stumbled away, falling at last against the wagon that Michalina and Richard hoped to use for their escape.

"She was choking from the smoke, eyes burning from it. 'Take me with you mistress,' she moaned, as she caught Michalina coming from her burning home, carrying a great carpetbag.

"We can't. You'll have to stay here."

"But I love him, mistress, and you're taking him from me."

At that moment Richard stepped from the house.

Hurry," he called to his witch wife, "the others are coming. We have to get away, *now*."

"Please take me with you, Richard," Clara cried, as she threw herself at him."

In the distance fiery torches lit the midnight sky. The tromp and rattle of approaching villagers grew ever louder.

"We have to go NOW!" Richard repeated.

Clara wrapped her arms tighter around the man she loved. Trying frantically to kiss him she lunged forward, tripping him and falling with him to the ground. Richard's head struck a bolder; he lost consciousness; Clara was right on top of him.

That's when Babcia reached for her. It was now the witch, the crone lifting her poor misguided pupil up over her head with far more strength than the girl could ever imagine. Babcia pitched Clara out into the front of the house into a patch of brambles that scrabbled up by the side of the road.

Fighting off the thorns, the girl tried to stand but, as if they were under the direct command of the great witch, the brambles grabbed at Clara, holding her down. As she fought to get away, the thorns tore at her face, ripped a great gash across her cheek, and finished the destruction of her eye.

She fell back then and watched as her teacher prepared to take the man she loved away from her... across the ocean.

Clara spat at Babcia, cursed her, vowed that someday she would take revenge. Then she screamed in horror as Babcia the witch, the most hideous of crones, turned once again into the young and beautiful Michalina, who gathered up Richard, lifted him into the wagon, climbed in beside him, set the team moving… to pulling the wagon, and they sped off.

As the wagon left the burning home Babcia waved her arm commandingly above her and, just as the mob reached the blaze, she summoned up great clouds of smoke that spread across the village, filling the lungs of her enemies, dropping them to their knees, watering their eyes, eventually sending them crawling, running, fleeing from the village itself, into the woods… where the wolves were waiting.

Chapter Thirty-Six

Meeting Witch Marla

The elevator doors parted and the eyes of every man in the Tower 12 Restaurant were immediately drawn to the woman who stepped out. A gentleman who had been waiting for the elevator instinctively offered his arm. The woman smiled and accepted. She gestured toward Chuck Vaughn and his table, and her escort was only too happy to lead her there. But what a somber crowd she found waiting for her. They were almost catatonic.

Niko had been staring into space, wondering about visions of witches, masks and red-eyed beasts that tore women to shreds. Chuck Vaughn, equally distracted, was contemplating bankruptcy, divorce and even worse things (suicide).

The only cheerful member of the group was Don Foster, Chuck's supervising animator, who handled the workflow of seven animators and twelve assistants every day. His organization was running like a top, and so Chuck had rewarded him with an invitation to the meeting. Unfortunately, he had a hangover.

The woman who arrived at Chuck's table was, in fact, a brand new version of Marla Morrison. She'd given herself a complete makeover since she'd left Chuck's office the previous day. This was not the mousey young woman in the granny dress that Niko had just encountered. This was a bold, confident Marla with an entirely new look.

She had frosted her hair so that silver streaks highlighted her auburn locks, framed her face and softened the bangs that fell across her forehead. She wore a black, fitted business suit. The jacket had very wide lapels and a diamond pin that sparkled on her chest. To top it off, she wore a broad-brimmed hat with a wide silk band and a high point. It was a mod version of a witch's hat, Niko decided.

Of course the real key to the effectiveness of the outfit was Marla's mini skirt. It was the most popular, late-60s fashion in Hollywood. The mini-skirt matched the jacket in fabric and cut. It barely reached the top of her thighs, but was so well tailored that no matter which way Marla moved, no matter how she bent, she could never be embarrassed.

"It's an engineering marvel," Vaughn joked as Marla approached the table, and it was, a marvel designed to show off perhaps the most spectacular pair of legs that Niko had ever seen in his life, muscular thighs, perfect knees, shapely calves, and they were made even more spectacular because Marla was hoisted up onto five inch high heels.

Marla and her escort made their way to the table. When they arrived, she smiled gratefully to the man. He nodded and backed directly away, almost bumping into a waiter carrying a large tray with several helpings of orange juice, sausages and eggs. In spite of it all, the escort did not take his eyes from Marla who nodded to him and then turned to Chuck.

"Like my new look?" she asked. The men nodded in unison as though they were in some kind of collective trance.

"Sorry the heels are so high," Marla added. "After so many years en point, my feet are so scrunched that these are the only kind of shoes I can wear."

"I wouldn't apologize," Chuck answered. "You're the first woman I've ever seen who can actually walk in those things."

Chuck stood and pulled Marla's chair back from the table. Marla sat and then waved him away when he tried to push it in.

"This is fine," she said. She sat back from the table and, crossing her legs, enjoyed the fascinated look of her partners and every other man in the restaurant.

"Would you like me to cure your hangover, Mister Foster?" Marla said at last.

"Please?" Foster groaned.

Marla rummaged through her little black purse for a moment and pulled out a small vial of liquid.

"Something I whipped up this morning," she said, as she took off the top and poured a few drops into Foster's coffee.

"Stir it, and take a sip," she said. Foster took a cautious taste.

"It's good," he commented. Then he took a full swallow, and a moment later he smiled broadly. "It works. It's wonderful. Can I drink wine out of your navel?"

"Can I turn you into a frog?" Marla replied.

The men laughed.

"So, is this the look of the modern witch?" Chuck asked.

Marla smiled. "Real witches have always been quite different from the images people have of them, you know. Isn't that true, Niko?"

Niko was caught by surprise and he could only manage an ineffectual shrug.

"It's not quite true," replied Chuck as he pulled up his briefcase. He took out a book, Grimm's Fairy Tales.

"Take a look at the volume I just found down at the Pickwick Bookstore.

Pretty standard images of witches, I'd say."

The sight of the book sent a chill through every fiber of Niko's body. It looked like the very book that his father had read to him on that terrible night so many years ago. To everyone's surprise, Marla recoiled as well.

"Let me see that," she demanded. Chuck handed her the book, and she immediately began flipping through it, studying it, shaking her head.

"You have no idea the pain this book has caused my sisters," she said at last. "Oh, and look at this, Niko, the words 'Oh No' written right here in the middle of Little Red Riding Hood."

Niko took the book and studied the page she had pointed out to him. The words were written in ink. (How did she know about Red Riding Hood?)

"This is the book my father found during the war," he said softly. "These exact words were written on this page in the exact same way." And then he turned the page. And there it was, that wolf-grandmother illustration, almost as frightening as it had seemed when he was a little boy.

Niko closed the book at once.

"You don't like that picture, Niko?" Marla asked. "It's the only real picture of a witch in the whole book. The others are only propaganda, you know, used by those in power to turn public opinion against us. I've always hated Grimm's Fairy Tales. However, there is one thing about this particular volume."

Marla turned to the very back of the book.

"It's an additive book," she said. "Some witch somewhere in time – and let me remind you that this book was only printed in 1903 – but somewhere since then a witch got hold of it, cursed it, and enabled it to ADD fairy tales based on what was happening around it.

"Look, here's a story called *The Witch and the Soldier*, where a witch dies so that she can become a spirit and protect the grandson she loves. Here's another called *The Student and the Sorceress*. And here's a brand new tale, just forming: "*The Ballerina and The Cage*. I may have to borrow this and study it, Chuck. The story may have a lesson that can help us, you know."

"Marla," Niko asked, "exactly how did you become a witch?"

Marla smiled. "I learned the craft when I lived in Poland," she said. "I had gone to study ballet with a famous instructor called Raymond Kajenki who lived in a small village outside of Krakow."

"My grandmother was Polish," Niko responded. "Her name was Michalina."

"Yes, I know," Marla grinned, "Michalina Czarownica, one of the most powerful witches in history. Everyone in that village knew of her. She had lived nearby.

"I studied the craft with a woman named Goriki who had been a student of Michalina Czarownica. The woman was ancient when I met her. She taught me how to channel Michalina. It's an amazing experience, like riding lightning as it flashes. Exhilarating, really. And you learn so many new things each time you do it."

Marla shivered with excitement as she thought of her last experience. "Did you like your grandmother?" Marla asked.

Suddenly Niko's face drained of all color. He was not at all sure how to respond.

Marla read his expression perfectly.

"She terrified you, didn't she?" Marla asked. "I knew it. She haunts you every day. And when she met that little wife of yours, I'll bet your grandmother became very angry."

"Holly never met her," Niko answered. "She was dead long before I ever knew Holly."

"But she did meet her. Babcia's everywhere, you know," Marla added. "I'll bet she even tried to kill Holly."

Niko froze. Beads of sweat began forming on his temples. His hands were sweating too. He dried them on his napkin only to find them sopping wet again within seconds.

"Let's change the subject," Chuck Vaughn suddenly insisted. "There has to be a more pleasant topic."

"Of course there is," Marla answered. "Your wife is pregnant, Niko. There's good news. She hasn't told you yet, but she is."

"How could you know?"

"I've ridden the lightning with your grandmother, remember? I know a whole lot about you."

Niko looked at her in stunned silence.

"In the meantime," Marla said, and suddenly dropped her voice into the deep Polish tone of Babcia, "Niko, come play me." And her eyes flashed a blood red.

Niko stared at her for a moment. Then suddenly he jumped from his chair and marched from the table. The door to the elevator had just opened when he reached it, and he was able to charge into the elevator at once. Chuck watched him go with a look of concern.

"What kind of game was that?" Chuck asked as he turned toward Marla.

"Just trying to get things off on the right foot," Marla answered with a smirk. "I want him to respect me and my craft. And if I have to scare him to do it, I will, you know."

"He'll respect you, all right. If he doesn't kill you first."

"He's afraid of me. And he couldn't kill me if he tried."

Chuck drummed his fingers nervously on the table for a moment; he glanced over at Foster and saw that Marla's hangover antidote had worn off. His supervising animator was in no condition to go anywhere or do anything, and so he turned back to Marla.

"I don't want that kid driving home at 120 miles an hour. You'll have to go after him. Give him a lift. Make sure that he gets there safely."

Marla shook her head in protest.

"I said DO IT!" Vaughn insisted.

Marla was startled; her eyes narrowed. But still she got to her feet and headed for the elevator.

"And Marla," Vaughn added as she strode angrily away from him, "put on some fucking clothes."

Marla lips twisted into a saucy smile, and, to the delight of every man within earshot, she replied: "Why, Mr. Vaughn, you know, these are my FUCKING clothes."

Chapter Thirty-Seven

Bewitching Holly

Niko was halfway down Vine Street, almost to Hollywood Boulevard when Marla reached him. A cop had stopped him and was trying to figure out how such a well-dressed young man could be marching along so angrily, slamming his fist into every metal sign he saw, and doing it apparently without the aid of drugs or alcohol.

Marla pulled her orange Mustang convertible over to the curb and rushed to the policeman. She had managed to wrap a long granny dress around herself, and she was glad she did.

"It's okay, officer," she said frantically. "He's my brother."

"What's wrong with him?"

"It's a medical condition, makes him very disoriented. Nothing serious. I can take care of him."

Marla took a deep breath and wrapped herself around Niko's arm. Niko tried to pull away but her witch's strength kept him in his place. The cop eyed the couple. They certainly looked affluent and successful, and Niko hadn't really done anything illegal.

"Okay," he said at last. "Get him to a doctor. If I come

across him in this condition again, *I'll* be the one taking him to the hospital."

Marla flashed a pretty smile and herded Niko back toward the Mustang.

#

As Marla drove Niko to his home, she looked over at him with a strange mixture of fascination and contempt.

The problem was that, in spite of all Niko's strange, desperate anger and confusion, Chuck Vaughn thought the guy was golden.

Niko could pose a real threat, couldn't he? Who knew how ambitious he was. Maybe he even wanted to become the head writer and that was her job, one she'd worked damn hard to earn.

Marla gunned it as she pulled her Mustang onto the freeway. She easily outran a huge tractor-trailer that was bearing down on them. That made her feel better, and she grinned.

It wasn't just Niko's ambition that bothered Marla either. It was his whole grad school style. That kind of look had always meant competition for Marla. She hadn't gone to college, just endless hours of ballet and art school.

In the meantime here was graduate student Niko Madonie waltzing right into her world. Hell, he even had one of those perfect little wives at home. She'd learned of Holly the night she cast her spells and called up the spirit of Babcia.

"Screw you, Miss Perfect," Marla said under her breath. Niko didn't even look up. He was too lost in his own angry thoughts.

Holly's "Miss Perfect Look" didn't really make Marla feel threatened, (the blond hair, the sweet smile, the sparkly eyes). What bothered her was that the Miss Perfects of the world never really had to work for anything! It was all pretty much handed to them. Marla, on the other hand, knew all about work. She'd been a professional ballerina.

Marla was too tall, she felt, with way too many freckles. While guys like Niko were chasing the hottest cheerleaders on the squad, Marla gave up the chase and dedicated her life to ballet, and that's when she fell into the clutches of the one man who had really hurt her.

Raymond Kajenki! What a short, sadistic son of a bitch he was. He had taken her to Krakow where he had trained her in ballet. He wanted to get her away from the distractions of New York, he said. Krakow really was the place for that.

"This is it," Niko whispered. Marla hardly heard him. It was the first thing he had said since she saved him from the LAPD.

"Take that driveway just ahead, then pull into the underground garage." Niko's words were sharp and bitter. Marla ignored the tone.

Raymond Kajenki, she thought, that bastard! He coaxed her, bullied her, seduced her, and when that wasn't enough, he beat her until she became the ballerina he demanded. But when the beatings went on and on and then seemed to happen for no reason at all, Marla began to look for help. She ran away from him, drove through the towns outside of Krakow, drove into the mountains to the little village of Zakopanski, and that's where she found Clara Goriki, an ancient woman, a pupil of Babcia Michalina Czarownica, herself!

Marla tromped on the brakes and the orange Mustang squealed to a stop in the first open space in the underground garage. She shook the painful memories from her head.

"You okay?" she asked Niko.

Niko pulled away from her as though she was a demon.

Marla got out of the car and walked around to Niko's side. She opened the door, reached in, grabbed him, and pulled him to his feet.

"Look," she said at last, "I'm not really a witch, you know."

"You'd better not hurt my wife."

"Why would I want to do that?" Marla sighed. "Listen, I have no intention of hurting you or Holly. I just want you to respect my position. I'm the head writer. I'm in charge. Just trust me and we'll be able to work together just fine."

Niko tried to calm himself. He still didn't like Marla or her games, and he was never going to be able to trust her. Good witch? Bad witch? Non-witch? Unlikely. Still, he nodded and forced a little smile for her.

"Let's go up to your apartment," Marla said. "I want to meet your perfect little wife."

#

Holly Madonie was even more perfect than Marla had imagined: blond hair; green eyes; soft, perfect skin; a pretty face, and a fabulous body; she didn't look pregnant at all.

"Holly, are you pregnant?" Niko asked the moment they entered the apartment. He didn't even bother to introduce Marla, who trailed in behind him.

"Of course she's pregnant," answered Harry Rodgers as he spun around from the kitchen table to face the door. "Hasn't she told you yet?"

Holly turned and gave Harry a look of annoyance.

"I was waiting for the right moment," Holly answered. "Niko's been under a lot of stress."

"Yes, he has, you know," added Marla as she walked around in front of Niko to introduce herself. She smiled a plastic smile and was surprised when Holly responded with a look of genuine interest.

"My name is Marla Morrison," she said. "Niko and I are going to collaborate on Chuck Vaughn's newest show."

Holly nodded sweetly; then she turned to Niko and asked how he'd found out about her pregnancy.

"Marla told me," Niko responded. "She's a witch." And then he fumbled his way to the couch and sat down.

Holly sat beside her husband immediately.

"He's right, you know," Marla added. "I am. I joined a coven when I was in Poland, studied The Craft with a woman who had been a disciple of Niko's grandmother."

Holly stood and moved across the room immediately. The last thing she wanted was more witchcraft and insanity. Maybe it really was time to head back to Leland or all the way to Rochester, New York as she and Doctor Madonie had discussed. You just didn't take a guy who was already hallucinating about his dead grandmother and force him into a situation where he had to think about witches every single day. Especially when his writing partner claimed to be a practicing witch herself. Jesus!

Marla could read every one of these thoughts. Not through any spell or magic, of course, but through the openness of Holly's expression.

The witch realized something else at that moment. Holly would be more reasonable than her husband. Holly might be the key to keeping Niko in line and guaranteeing her success at VVA.

"When did you learn that you were pregnant?" Niko asked Holly suddenly.

"Late this morning," Holly answered. "Around eleven, I guess."

"I quizzed her when I saw her come back from the doctor," Harry chimed in. "She didn't want to tell me anything, but I just bothered her until she did. I was sure she would call you right away, but...."

Holly gave Harry a look that silenced him instantly.

"It's really wonderful, isn't it," she said trying to focus on the very positive news she had for her husband.

"I have a letter that we can send to the selective service. You won't have to worry about Vietnam or the draft any longer."

"Unless," Harry added, "they decide to go to a lottery. Then it all depends on whether or not they make the lottery retroactive for people who have already been deferred, and I think...."

Holly gave Harry another stern look that shut him up once and for all.

"Maybe we should celebrate, Niko," Holly said. "We're free of that old war; we're going to have a baby. I know he'll be smart and handsome and talented, just like his dad. I know you'll make a wonderful father."

Niko smiled lovingly.

"Well, that's it. I'm out of here, you know," Marla said jumping to her feet. "I'm afraid I have something that needs attention right away," And she walked up to Holly and gave her a hug. Holly felt something pull at her hair for a second, wasn't sure what it was, then decided to ignore it as she stepped back to look at Marla.

The witch smiled. "Keep your guy mellow, okay?" she asked. "We've got a lot of writing to do, but don't worry, it will be creative, you know, nothing to get upset about."

"No more witchiness?" Holly asked Marla as though she were pleading.

"Well, I am a witch, you know, but a good witch. Now, I hope you'll excuse me...

"And Harry," she turned to the apartment manager, "Isn't there something you need to be doing, too?"

Harry nodded and then gave in easily as Marla came over and pulled him to his feet.

"Thanks for getting Niko home safely," Holly said as she stood and walked over to Marla. She offered her hand, but Marla pulled Holly close and gave her another hug.

"Everything will be just fine," the witch whispered.

Harry and Marla left together, closing the door behind them, and then moving quickly down the walkway that led to the manager's apartment and beyond to the stairs to the underground garage. As they approached Harry's apartment Marla turned to him. Harry had a very strange expression on his face and his eyes seemed to be scanning her up and down, as though, she thought, he was somehow sizing her up.

"So, Harry," the witch said, undeterred, "I was wondering if you could help me with something?"

"Harry shook his head immediately. "Don't think so."

Marla moved closer, brushed up against him, "Of course you can. Here, let's go into your apartment for a minute so we can talk."

Marla grabbed Harry by the arm and steered him back toward his apartment.

Harry was almost dragging his feet. "You don't want to go in there," he called.

"But I do, you know," Marla answered grabbing the handle of the door, pushing it open…

…and then she stopped cold.

There, inside Harry's living room was a veritable art gallery. Enormous photos hung on every wall: candid shots of beautiful young women in various compromising poses, stripping down by the apartment's pool to their bikinis, sunning themselves topless, strolling around the gardens in short shorts and tight fitting tank tops.

"I see," Marla whispered.

She turned back to Harry who was looking at her in horrified embarrassment.

Instead of commenting, the tall young woman gave Harry a broad grin. She strode around the living room as though she were walking through the Guggenheim. She tapped her chin inquisitively as she studied one photo after another. She smiled, nodded.

"Very nice work, Harry," Marla said. "And none of these women knew that they were being photographed?"

"I don't think so," Harry mumbled.

"How very interesting."

Marla walked to the end of the wall and then noticed a scrapbook lying open on a small table. Newspaper clippings had been pasted into it. The largest clipping on the open scrapbook page featured a headline that read:

VALLEY STRANGLER STILL ELUDES POLICE.

Marla's head jerked back toward Harry.

The big man shifted back and forth on his feet nervously. He hardly seemed threatening.

"You?" she asked. "You... a serial killer... a strangler?"

Harry smiled. His eyes lit up for a moment, and he seemed to puff out his chest, and then he caught himself, slouched, and took a big step backward.

"Of course not. I'm just interested in that particular case, that's all."

Marla took a closer look at the picture in the clipping. Her eyes darted up to the enormous photo on the wall above it, then back to the clipping again.

"It's the same girl," she said.

"No it's not!" Harry's answer was quick and loud and very nervous.

"But..." Marla began and then the witch caught herself and smiled. "Course not." Her smile was so sexy and so... evil, that Harry took another step backwards.

"Are you planning to take any candids of Holly?" Marla asked.

"Don't think so."

Marla turned and walked up to Harry. She stood very close to him. "Why not? She's sweet, pure, innocent, and such a tease... just like all your other..." she paused to think of just the perfect word, found it, and said it... "Victims?"

Harry flinched. Marla giggled. "Do you think the Valley Strangler might be at all interested in Mrs. Madonie?"

Harry's eyes popped open. He took one last step backward but now he found himself against the wall. He shook his head.

"She *is* very attractive, you know," Marla added.

"Yes she is."

"Actually, I collect candid photos myself."

Marla let her body brush very lightly against Harry's. "I might pay a bit for a candid photo of Holly... for my own personal use."

"You like sexy pictures of women?" Harry asked.

"I do, you know." Her smile broadened. "Maybe we can work something out."

#

Moments later Marla made her way down to her car.

"I have her," she cackled. "In more ways than one. First Miss Perfect I've ever been able to OWN."

She reached into her pocket and pulled out a small wisp of hair, Holly's hair. She had snipped it off with the tiny pair of scissors that she always kept in her purse, snipped it as she had hugged Holly.

"And Harry...." Marla added and broke into a loud laugh that echoed through the entire parking garage. It was cold, hard... and evil.

230

All the pieces were coming together nicely, she thought. Niko wasn't going to get in her way at VVA. He wouldn't be able to block her ascent in the company. She would soon have complete control of Holly and through her, Niko. Harry was now probably in her service (one could never tell with a would-be homicidal maniac). And if all that wasn't enough, there was also the book, Grimm's Fairy Tales, and the methods that were spelled out in that newest story.

What was it called? Oh yes, *The Ballerina and The Cage*.

Chapter Thirty-Eight

Caged

The next morning, Niko opened the door to the VVA story conference room (the witch room) expecting a truly horrific vision. But, No, the painting of Babcia, the masks, the witchy paraphernalia were all gone, all tucked behind a partition at the far end of the room by Marla who was sitting at the conference table reading Grimm's Fairy Tales. A month's worth of story sketches were stacked beside her.

Marla was sporting a flowery blouse and another sexy mini-skirt. Her long hair was pulled back in a bun that somehow accentuated her large dark eyes and her red lipstick.

A teapot gurgled on a little table in the corner of the room. CatMan Due sat beside it, eyes narrow and glowing red.

"Tea?" asked Marla with an inviting smile. Niko nodded, and so she put the book aside.

"Celebrate last night?" Marla asked.

Niko smiled nervously, and that told the witch everything she needed to know.

"I'm glad," she added. "You really need to loosen up. Now, let me just get you a cup." Marla searched behind the teapot, finally found a cup and poured Niko a healthy dose of tea.

"All the secret ingredients are mine," Marla whispered as she handed Niko the tea. It looked dark and murky. Niko took a sip: funny taste, but good.

Niko walked up to the table and pulled Marla's stack of sketches over to him. He took another sip of tea. It really was very good.

Niko focused on Marla's sketches for the new animated version of Hansel and Gretel. Each page had two panels; one featured the traditional pair of fairy tale children in classic German folk dress; the other was Marla's interpretation of the story in which the children were much older, in their late teens, lovers, perhaps, rather than little brother and sister.

"Why'd you change the story?" Niko asked.

"More fun, you know," Marla answered, "And a broader audience, grown- ups."

Before Marla finished the sentence, Niko had stopped paying attention. He was staring instead at Marla's long, beautiful legs, which were made even more attractive by the very high heels she was wearing once again. Marla gave him a look that suggested that he really shouldn't stare.

"I'm sorry," he said, and he blushed.

"It's okay," Marla answered. "I was hoping that a more cheerful outfit would help you relax. Do I look like a cheerleader?"

"Not exactly," Niko answered.

"Oh, the high heels," Marla said. "Gotta wear 'em. Remember?"

Niko just nodded and then he took another deep swallow of tea. God, it was fabulous!

"Okay, back to the story," Marla said. "Who's the hero?"

"In your teenage version or the original brother and sister one?"

"Let's start with the original," Marla said with a smile. "It's easier."

"Hansel," Niko responded at once.

"Just what a guy *would* say. Okay, so what'd he do?"

"Left a trail of white stones to lead him and his sister back to their parents' cottage."

"Right," Marla agreed. "In the original Fairy Tale their parents had abandoned them in the woods because the family didn't have enough food to live on."

"I guess."

"And what did Hansel do the next night?"

"Left a trail of bread crumbs."

"That the birds ate so that the kids couldn't find their way out of the woods. Real clever hero, huh? Drink your tea."

Niko took another gulp. Terrific taste. It was giving him a little buzz, too. What was in this stuff?

"So in the original story Hansel leads his little sister deeper into the woods and finds a gingerbread house..."

"The kind that witches live in," Niko added.

"Yes, made from that magical, sweet/spicy stuff."

Niko shuddered.

"He gets them both captured by a witch," Marla continued, "who throws Hansel into a cage to fatten him up so that she can eat him!

"Meanwhile, little Gretel goes to work for the witch, gives her brother a chicken bone that the half-blind old woman can feel when she's checking to see how fat he's getting. The witch thinks Hansel is getting thinner and thinner, so Gretel delays his execution. Then she tricks the witch, pushes her into the oven, rescues her brother and leads him safely home. Gretel is the real hero of the story."

Marla poured another splash of tea into Niko's cup and watched him as he took a big gulp. She added a little more to her own cup and sipped it slowly.

"I almost have the whole thing figured out," Marla added. "But here's where you can help me."

She pulled herself up so that she was sitting on the table, and then she crossed those unbelievable legs.

"How can I make the witch more sympathetic? How can I generate some compassion for her?"

"Are you nuts? She's a witch, she eats little children; why should anyone feel compassion?"

"There's got to be a way," Marla responded. "I mean, I'm a witch and even though I enjoy scaring people, I'll take all the sympathy and compassion I can get."

"On your terms."

"Okay. We'll leave that issue for now. Here's something else that has me stumped: I've changed Hansel and Gretel to teenagers who are in love instead of brother and sister. How can I show what a great hero Gretel is and keep Hansel from becoming a real nothing? I mean, he has to have some value if Gretel's in love with him."

"Girls fall for nothing guys all the time," Niko answered as he watched Marla swim in and out of focus. (What was in that tea?)

"Not in my stories, they don't," Marla said. "A guy's gotta be worth it for me to care."

"Well, he has to have some passions, doesn't he: nature; world peace? He could be a kind of a fairytale anti-war protester."

"That's good."

"Like, he's so into peace and nature and shit that he can't even think straight, so he just follows Gretel around, loves her, does all he can for her, but he has his mind on other things."

"We'll make him a hippie, put him in a flowery shirt and bell bottoms and sandals with long hair," Marla added. "These are the 60s. It'll make perfect sense."

Marla began sketching this new version of Hansel frantically.

"Make sure Gretel is a babe," Niko added, "Like, I think the way you've drawn her is so cool."

Niko took another swallow of tea and felt the world start spinning. It seemed like Marla was aglow.

"I mean, make sure you give her long, beautiful legs, like yours."

"You like my legs?"

"Of course."

"Better than your wife's."

Niko giggled, "Well, actually hers are perfect tooooooo..." the word turned into a long giggle that seemed to last forever.

"Take off your clothes," Marla said suddenly.

"What?"

"Come on, Niko. Take off your clothes. I want to try something."

"Are you crazy?"

"It's okay. It's only an experiment, for the good of the story. The witch kept Hansel naked while he was in the cage. Let's pretend you're Hansel. I'm the witch. Get into the spirit of it, take off your clothes and play the role."

"If you say so," Niko mumbled after a moment of stoned silence. He was a little too high on tea to think about much resistance. So he took another swig, giggled and started the endless process of taking off his clothes.

Marla went to the conference room door and locked it. Then she pulled a cage out from behind the partition. It was not really that big, designed for an animal the size of a large dog. A fully-grown man like Niko would barely fit into it. By then Niko had unbuttoned his cuffs and the first button on the front of his shirt.

"I'd better help you," Marla said.

She undid Niko's shirt and slid it up over his head. Then slacks, shoes, socks, they all came off.

The cage was so small that Niko had to pull his knees up under his chin. Then, as soon as he was in it, Marla closed the cage door, locked it and returned to the conference table. She began to sketch storyboards of Niko (Hansel) in the cage.

"He has to be naked while he's in there, you know."

"Definitely," Niko slurred, and then he realized that he really didn't mind being in the cage at all. For one thing the floor was carpeted, which made it more comfortable than he would have expected. It was actually kind of cozy. And he was so hunched over that the fact he was naked was pretty well hidden. Most importantly of all, being in a cage made him feel safe, as though no witch (not even Babcia), no demanding father, no evil force of any kind could touch him or hurt him while he was in there.

Meanwhile, Marla crossed her luscious legs and began making one sketch after another.

"Marla," Niko giggled, "You really do have the most beautiful legs I've ever seen."

"You DO like them, don't you?" Marla asked, and she began to giggle too. The tea was getting to her as well.

"Mmmmm," Niko said.

"MEOW," said CatMan.

The sound came out of nowhere and caught Niko's dizzy, giggly attention.

"MEOW!" CatMan Due repeated as he leaped up from the far corner of the room and raced toward the door.

Marla turned, followed the cat with her eyes, right over to Chuck Vaughn who was standing in the doorway with his own key in the lock. His mouth was wide open. He had unlocked the door, and now he charged into the room.

"What the hell's wrong with you, Marla? Are you trying to turn this place into some kind of goddamn freak show?"

"And you," he said as he turned to Niko, "Get out of there and put your clothes back on. Christ!"

Marla gave Vaughn a wink that suggested that this was in fact a witchy antidote for all Niko's problems. Vaughn didn't buy it. Niko on the other hand was too far-gone to care, and so his only response was another long, serious bout of giggling.

Chuck eyed the drawings on the table. He went up to the large stack and flipped through it quickly.

"At least the work is good," he said, calming only slightly. "Nice new characterization of Hansel. Seeing him in the cage like that does help. But I can't have any more of this, you two. Hell, if the wrong person walked in here, you could get us all arrested."

Marla shrugged and almost fell over giggling. Niko was gone.

"Kids these days," Vaughn mumbled as he stormed from the room. CatMan was right on his heels, turning and bidding farewell with a loud, nasty "Pfffft".

Vaughn slammed the door in anger but once outside he smiled broadly.

"They make a great writing team," he said to CatMan. "They may be just nuts enough to write something scary as hell... and really great."

#

Back in the conference room, Marla found the keys to the cage and fumbled for the lock. She could hardly get the key into it and that set her off giggling again and, of course, Niko joined in.

"Come on out of there." Marla groaned.

"I kinda like it in here."

"Just get out," she repeated. Niko didn't move.

"We're all outta tea."

"Don't care."

"Well, then let me lock the fucking conference room again anyway," Marla said, and she stumbled over to the door and locked it. Then Marla came back to the table and picked up her sketchpad.

"Okay, since you've decided to stay in there, let's at least get some work done. To start with, tell me, Hansel, how does it feel to be locked in a cage?"

"Safe," he answered. "Even with a witch out there, she can't really touch me unless I want to come out."

"Brilliant," Marla answered. And Niko went on for nearly two hours inventing an entire new story about Hansel's early life and his distrust of his wicked stepmother.

Marla did one sketch after another depicting the story that Niko was spinning. By then it was lunchtime, and Marla insisted once again that Niko get out of the cage. This time he obliged, stumbling frequently as he tried to maintain a sense of modesty while he got dressed.

"You really like it in there, huh?" she asked.

"A lot," Niko answered. The effects of the tea were starting to wear off. "Maybe we can work this way again some time, you know, in the cage, when I really need to get freed up."

"The cage makes you feel free?"

"Oh yeah," Niko nodded.

"Chuck won't approve."

"But it will help us."

"Okay, we can do it," Marla answered. "We'll prop a chair up against the door next time. It will be our secret creative technique."

"Sounds good," Niko said, and then he gave Marla an innocent kiss on the cheek and headed off for lunch feeling like a new man, more self confident, more creative and somehow far less haunted.

After Niko left, Marla pulled out Grimm's Fairy Tales one more time, and she looked once again at the latest story that had been added to the book: *The Ballerina and The Cage*. It told how a young man gained in talent, self-confidence and success when a beautiful young ballerina tricked him into getting into a cage where, for the first time in his life, he was able to feel safe. Of course, the part Marla liked best was the closing scene where the ballerina used her magic to gain control of the young man and make him her slave. She wasn't sure that Niko was slave material.

But it was worth a try.

CHAPTER THIRTY-NINE

BILLY RETURNS

Holly reached for the kitchen telephone and dialed the number of the studio. Through the pass-through of their little apartment she saw Billy Bright staring back at her. Holly felt a sexy tingling all over. Billy looked so forlorn, so needy. It was just as he had said in the sweet letter he had sent along with that terrible mask, "I just need some friendship and to see someone really beautiful again."

He'd driven down from Los Altos overnight, arriving just after Niko left for work. The doorbell had rung within only a few minutes of her husband's departure, and there was Billy, just needing to see someone really beautiful.

Holly felt glad that she'd decided to fix herself up for Niko this morning, put on some makeup, wash her hair, wear her prettiest dress, high heels, and so much more. Her husband hadn't really noticed Holly though, he seemed trapped in his own thoughts... but then almost miraculously, Billy was on the doorstep, and he did notice... indeed.

The phone rang at the studio and Holly heard a female voice on the other end of the line.

"Hello."

"Marla?" she asked, "Marla Morrison?"

"Yes."

"This is Holly Madonie. I'd like to ask you for a favor."

"Okay... sure, maybe... you know."

"I have a friend who's visiting from Leland. His name is Billy Bright."

"Yes?"

"Billy's heartbroken over the death of one of our classmates" Holly said. "Her name was Nancy Swallow, and he was very close to her."

"I'm sorry."

"He needs help, something to take his mind off of Nancy. Actually, more than anything else, he needs a job. So, I was wondering if you might set up an interview for him, with Chuck Vaughn."

"Couldn't Niko do that?"

"I'd rather not ask my husband," Holly said as sweetly as she possibly could. "He and Billy were rivals over almost everything, over art projects, over film productions."

Over YOU? Marla wondered, but she didn't ask.

"Please help us. Billy seems lost. I'm worried about him."

"I'll talk to Chuck before Niko gets in."

Marla could almost hear Holly's happy sigh on the other end of the line. "Thank you," the girl said. "Oh, but please don't tell my husband, okay?"

"Of course not."

Marla hung up the phone and an evil smiled curled her lips. This was the opportunity she had hoped would come. Niko's wife was with another man, a man she felt close to and sorry for. A man she would be willing to lie to her husband about. Marla didn't know the man of course, but all the elements needed for witchy mischief were there.

All Holly needed was a little push, Marla thought, and she was ready to do the pushing.

Marla reached into her purse and pulled out the tissue she had carefully wrapped around the lock of Holly's hair. Then she opened her desk drawer.

Vials of ingredients rattled around inside. Hopefully she had the ones she'd need.

Marla's office was no stranger to witchery, and she didn't have time to go home. The opportunity was staring her right in the face.

Another evil smile curled her lips. "Let's see how Niko likes his perfect little wife now."

#

Holly hung up the receiver. Billy was so worth it. Sweet Billy, sitting there looking so forlorn; he was adorable.

You're a sucker, Holly Blue, in more ways than one, her own voice whispered to her. But how could she think that in the face of the loss Billy had suffered. He was closer to Nancy than any of them, and he must have loved her more than he would ever admit.

The fact that Holly had hated Nancy, that she was sinfully happy when she had heard of the girl's death, made her feel terribly guilty and doubly anxious to help Billy.

Sucker. He's just using you.

"No!" Holly said out loud.

Billy looked up with a troubled smile, and then he just drifted away into his thoughts... his sweet memories of Nancy. Holly was sure that's what was going on.

"Sounds like we can get you an interview at VVA," Holly said as she walked from the kitchen to the couch where Billy was sitting.

His face brightened as she came to him.

"Thanks for setting up the interview," he said. "Nothing has ever stopped me like this before. To have someone you...."

"Loved?" Holly volunteered.

"Cared about," Billy corrected, but then he added, "I guess I did love her, didn't I? She loved me. I know that."

Billy buried his face in his hands.

"Oh, Billy," Holly whispered as she sat down beside him. Billy pulled away, as though he wanted to be left alone.

It's all an act, Holly's inner voice told her. *He's only doing it to seduce you.*

How egotistical is that? Holly asked herself. Here was a heartbroken friend, and all she could think about was how he might want to take advantage of her.

"I want to help you," Holly whispered.

"You're helping just by being here," Billy said. "You're wonderful, you're beautiful," And then he knelt down in front of her.

"What are you doing?" Holly asked in surprise.

"Worshipping," Billy answered. "Worshipping you." And then he placed his hands on Holly's knees.

"No, Billy," Holly called. "We can't. I'm married. I'm pregnant!"

If Billy was surprised he didn't show it. He simply pulled his hands away from Holly and lowered his head. "I understand," he said. "I shouldn't have come. I'm so dumb, just an empty guy with no one left to love me."

"Oh, no," Holly responded.

#

Marla had taken a little saucepan down from the shelf above her desk. It was a souvenir from her days in Poland. She had placed it on a hot plate she had stolen from the coffee room. She put a red candle into it and watched as the candle softened.

Marla smiled. It was time to add the most important ingredient of all, the lock of Holly's hair. Marla's long fingers reached into the tissue, carefully lifted the wisp of hair and then dropped it into the pan. She felt a demon-hiss rise up from the surface.

Marla rubbed lavender oil onto her hands to keep them from burning as she handled the softened wax. Then she took the wax and twisted it, kneaded the hair into it, then shaped it, not only with the skill of a witch, but also of an artist. Soon it had been formed into the shape of a young woman. Even its face bore a resemblance to Holly. A cruel smile once again twisted Marla's lips as she took a sprig of lavender and began to stroke the poppet, caressing it in its most intimate places, ravishing it more and more. Within seconds her witchery had reached its victim.

From that moment on, there were no more warning voices, no more cautions ringing in Holly's head. There was just blind desire for this poor, sweet, beautiful young man.

She reached forward, took Billy's hands and slid them back onto her knees (the knees with the silk stockings that Holly had decided to wear that morning). She was wearing her sexy wedding things, she realized, *for Billy!*

The young man pressed Holly back onto the couch and then, with a hand on each knee, he spread them, opened them so that he could see the vision that Holly had prepared for him.

Billy pulled forward, kissed those beautiful, creamy thighs surrounded by all that silk and lace. And then he just continued kissing. Holly closed her eyes and gave a desperate moan. She felt a wicked passion spreading all through her. She wrapped her legs around Billy's neck and thrust herself forward.

Billy couldn't believe it. He was being raped by whatever sensuous creature had come to possess Holly. Thoughts of her baby, thoughts of fidelity, all were gone in the face of this monstrous passion.

Holly grabbed Billy and pulled his face up to hers. She threw her arms around his neck and kissed him wildly. Her talented tongue did its work, and Billy did not resist.

"Thank you for coming," she panted. "You have no idea how badly I needed you."

Billy didn't answer. He got to his feet, closed his eyes, held his breath, and forced himself to be calm. Then he lifted Holly with his trembling hands, brought her to her feet, and stood there looking at her, sharing her wild, passionate breath, forcing her to become as calm as he.

Then he put a hand on each of Holly's shoulders and pushed down. Holly immediately gave way and lowered herself to her knees in front of him.

Holly stared up at Billy. She was still gasping for air. And then she reached up and gave a hard tug down on Billy's jeans. They fell around his ankles.

"I've never done this before," Holly whispered. "Not even for my husband."

"I'll help you," Billy answered, and then he slid his thumb across Holly's lips parting them ever so slightly. He pressed down on her chin opening her mouth, letting one finger find its way inside. Holly sucked on it for just a moment and chased it with her tongue as Billy withdrew it.

Holly felt Billy's hand reach behind her head, grasp it firmly, and draw it toward him. Holly opened her mouth even wider and closed her eyes.

#

An hour later Holly was lost in remorse. Billy had come and gone so quickly, and now she was left with nothing but the heartbreaking realization of what she had done.

Billy had promised that this was an act of desperate loneliness. It would never happen again. But that didn't matter, did it? She had already betrayed her husband.

As though in a trance, Holly walked to her bedroom closet, reached to the very top shelf and took down a box, a pretty Christmas-gift kind of box with a pink plaid bow on top. She took it to the bed and opened it, pulled back the tissue that was folded so neatly across the top.

She took out the little pink plaid elephant that she and Niko had won on their very first date. She looked at the three hearts she had made for him that she had sewn onto his chest, one on top of the other. She flipped from one to the next.

"I ... love ... you," she read out loud, and then burst into tears.

"What can I do now?" She asked the little creature. "When your daddy finds out, we won't be married anymore. I just know it."

Holly walked into the living room and sat on the couch. There was a big wet ugly stain there, wasn't there? How was she ever going to hide it?

She cradled the toy elephant to her as though she were a little girl. She was so guilty, so incredibly guilty.

SNAP!

Harry Rodgers suddenly poked his head in through her doorway. He had his camera slung around his neck.

"Are you all right?" Harry asked. "I thought I heard screaming." Holly looked up from her reverie. She hadn't even noticed the sound of the camera. But there had been screaming, hadn't there? Oral sex and then wild, dizzy fucking. And now there was a big stain on the couch cushion. It was enormous and it was hers. Harry the landlord was looking at it too.

"I spilled some tea on the couch," Holly said quickly. She felt as though she were about to throw up. "I don't know what I'm going to do about it."

Harry walked over to look at the stain.

"I'll send the cushions to the cleaners for you," he said. "I've got some extras in the store room. I'll get them, have yours back in a jiffy."

"Cute little elephant," Harry added.

"Niko and I won it at a carnival on our first date," Holly said. "When I'm lonely I hug him; reminds me of Niko."

Harry snatched up the cushion and nodded sympathetically. He walked out the door, closed it, then rushed frantically into his own apartment and slammed the door behind him. He buried his face in the cushion and smeared its wetness all over him. He knew exactly how Holly had soiled the cushion. He had watched her from the moment Billy entered her apartment.

He'd taken pictures, too.

Chapter Forty

Handsome Harry

Later that same afternoon: Harry Rodgers had the entire pornographic sequence spread out in front of him: Holly and Billy making love on her living room sofa. It was the most erotic set of pictures he had ever taken. Still, he couldn't take his eyes off of the real, living, breathing Holly Madonie.

From his basement window he could look up at her as she walked back and forth to the laundry in her tight white shorts. He was getting that feeling again, that tingle in his hands, in his fingers, and he knew it was starting.

Harry cleared his head. Thoughts of Holly would not go away. He had shot up four rolls of her wild lovemaking. Thank God he had hung the drapes perfectly to allow that tiny space. Thank God Holly and Niko's side window backed up to the alley the way it did. Perfect privacy for a peeping Tom, but of course Harry was so much more than that... he was a candid photographer with a very long lens. That's why he always reserved that particular apartment for his intended victims.

Carefully, methodically, Harry took his Nikon camera from the top desk drawer. His friend... his accomplice in that forbidden, candid photo shoot of Holly and her lover.

Harry adjusted his longest telephoto. He looked through the viewfinder for something to shoot: The old witch, Babcia's mask. He had hung it in his office after Holly had given it to him. It was perfect. SNAP.

Holly walked by his basement window. The lower parts of her legs were right in front of him. She stopped, reached down and adjusted the buckle on her sandal. What ankles, what legs. She was perfect. A perfect victim.

CLICK – Harry had her on film again: her perfect ankles, her sandals, her long fingers reaching for the straps. Holly walked on. She was definitely wearing those tight white shorts just to entice him, Harry decided. He closed his eyes and pictured her for just a moment, pleading for mercy.

CLICK – Harry grabbed a shot of Holly's curvy bottom as she walked away. He zoomed in and ... CLICK – got one more.

Holly was at the pool now, pretty far away but still within range of his long hard lens. He racked focus... yes, there she was, still within view from his basement window... stepping out of those shorts. Oh, Jesus! Wearing nothing underneath but the skimpiest bikini.

CLICK – CLICK – shorts coming off. CLICK – CLICK untying and removing her halter-top. She *did* mean to tease him, didn't she? Tease and not deliver, tease to drive him mad.

Harry smiled. If she wanted madness, he could give it to her. It would frighten her. It might even kill her.

Harry was sweating profusely and smiling. First, the ritual! First he had to own her.

Harry's telephoto had lost the girl... she was at the pool, but where? He pulled the camera away from his eye and scanned the pool area. Yes, there she was lying out in the sun. He hoisted the camera in front of him, and the viewfinder was suddenly filled with that gorgeous face. She looked sad and desperate though. Not a look that really matched her outfit. Still, it was not as desperate as she was going to look, Harry thought. He tilted down and snapped a quick shot of Holly untying her bikini top, lowering it as far as she dare so she could tan all over.

WHORE! – CLICK.

Harry put his camera down for a second.

"Oh, you're going to enjoy this," he said to the mask of Babcia. He had hung it on the wall to remind him of his own demons, the ones that now demanded the ritual with Mrs. Madonie.

Harry carefully gathered up the shots of Holly and Billy's lovemaking, sexy as hell, but not what he needed for the ritual. The pictures he needed had to be of a woman alone, taken by him, without her knowledge if possible, candid shots of a whore that he could own. He had quite a collection in his safe. There were a half dozen or so beautiful young women he had photographed without their knowledge, before he....

"Well, you know the rest," he said to Babcia as he slammed the pornography into his desk drawer and then hurried out to stalk his latest victim.

Harry crouched just outside the door to the pool area snapping off four more pictures of Holly as she lay in the sun.

CLICK. She must have heard the sound. She looked up.

"Harry, is that you?"

How to fuck up a ritual!

Harry stepped toward the pool and forced a smile. Hopefully she wouldn't notice how much he was sweating.

"Nice camera," Holly called as Harry approached.

CLICK – Harry took a shot of one of the beautiful roses that grew along the fence, Chrysler Imperial (interesting name for a rose). Harry knew the names of his roses better than the names of his victims. He had forgotten most of them.

"I love taking pictures of flowers," he said.

"Can I see the camera," Holly asked, "My buddy Gina and I studied photography together at the Rochester Institute of Technology."

Harry handed it over.

Holly took the camera and panned around with it looking for interesting subjects.

"Pose for me," Holly asked.

Harry gave her a funny look and then struck a pose, some kind of crazy impersonation of a glamorous starlet: lips pursed, eyes flashing, one leg up behind him.

SNAP – Holly grabbed the shot.

"But that's all wrong," she said with a slight giggle. It was the first time she'd laughed since Billy had left her apartment.

"Didn't you ever go to finishing school? Here, do this: stand up straight, keep your knees together, that's it.

"Now put one hand behind your head, the other on your hip. That's better. Hold your breath, stick out your chest, cock your hip."

Harry struggled through the movements.

"Uugghh! You'll never make it as a model, Harry. Here let me show you."

Holly handed the camera back to Harry and struck the pose she was describing. And of course, it was perfect.

SNAP – Harry got the picture. "Very nice."

"Hey, I know," Holly said, "Why don't I pose for you?"

Harry wasn't sure. This was fun, but perhaps not as much fun as grabbing pictures of women without their knowing it. Still, how could he refuse?

"I don't mind," Holly added. "I've been a model. Let me try."

Holly immediately put both hands on top of her head, stood on her tiptoes and smiled.

"How's this one," Holly giggled.

"Perfect," Harry answered doing his best not to stutter. His palms were drenched. He could barely hold the camera. This was getting to be too much. What was she trying to do to him?

"Make me look sexy so that I can give the pictures to Niko and remind him what a...."

"Hot chick you are?" Harry forced the words out far too loudly.

Holly gave him a funny look, then just grinned.

"Right! Maybe he can frame it and put it on his desk at work."

You want to add me to your collection, don't you, Holly? Harry thought. But you'll soon learn who the real collector is.

"How's this?" Holly asked striking a very provocative pose. Harry tried to assume the most professional demeanor he could, tried to hide his excitement. He couldn't wait until he was alone with these pictures.

SNAP – "Very nice!"

"And this?"

SNAP – "Exceptional!"

SNAP – "Delightful!"

SNAP – "That's very good."

Harry wasn't sure he could take it any longer. This wasn't his style. Still the ritual had to be performed and Holly was playing right into it. She continued to strike pose after pose, each more provocative than the next. What did she think, that he wouldn't react? That it didn't register with him? That he didn't matter?

"How about topless?" Holly asked, reaching for the straps to her bikini.

NO!

That was quite enough. Harry couldn't face that, not just now. He had to get back to his lab and study the pictures. And then he had to plan and dream how Holly would be punished for taunting him like this.

"Sorry, out of film," Harry said meekly.

"Are you sure? I was just about to...."

"Tomorrow. Why don't we plan a session for tomorrow? Go get another outfit. Something you husband hasn't seen before, something really sexy," Harry was talking too quickly but if he didn't he had a feeling he would go stark raving mad.

Christ, she was beautiful! Christ, What a temptress! Didn't she realize what she was doing to him?

She doesn't care; she likes doing it.

He had to make a plan, and quickly, but first he had to see the pictures, see what he had. See if he was ready to add her to his collection.

As Harry rushed away Holly's joy went with him. The ominous feelings of dread about her husband, about Billy, about their sin (yes, it was a real sin now wasn't it, a mortal sin, no longer just adultery of the heart); all those horrible feelings came crashing down on her and made her so unhappy... that very beautiful, tragically sad girl in the bikini.

Chapter Forty-One

Darkroom

Harry's hands were shaking as he stood in the dark, loading the precious film of Holly onto the tank reel. He was a good photo processor if nothing else. He would create perfect images of the girl, the tease, the whore!

She doesn't care how she torments you.

Sweat poured from Harry's face, his shoulders, his hair. His hands continued to shake as he placed the reel into the developing tank and then added the chemicals and performed the steps (all in their proper order). Developer (agitate), stop bath (agitate), fixer (the same). Harry opened the tank and let a stream of lukewarm water wash over the film... the precious film.

Harry had the largest, most evil erection of his entire life.

She didn't care what she did to me; I could see that, he thought.

When the washing was complete, Harry's erection was as huge as ever. What a tempting body she had. Harry knew how to deal with temptation, and soon Holly would learn his methods.

Harry finished the process, attached clothespins to each end of the film and hung it up to let it dry. He couldn't help but peek at some of the pictures. There she was. *Whore!* So fucking beautiful and willing!

After the film had dried Harry cut the negative strip into individual shots and put the first one into the enlarger. He turned on the light and focused the image.

It was Babcia!

The full-on face of the hideous mask was staring up at him.

Harry's heart pounded. What was she doing there?

No! Wait!

Harry remembered that the first picture he had taken was of Babcia's mask before he had started taking the shots of Holly. Harry looked back at the other negatives. There was Holly smiling at him, stepping out of her shorts, lounging by the pool in her bikini, flirting with him.

Harry took the most tempting picture of all, Holly reaching for her bikini top, offering to pull it down. He slid the negative into the carrier on the enlarger. He focused the enlarger, adjusted the aperture, slid some photo paper onto the easel and made his exposure. Next he pulled the photo paper from the enlarger and slid it into the developing tray and waited for the image to emerge.

Great! Gorgeous!

He pulled the picture from the developer and slid it into the fixer. But suddenly something was going wrong.

Somehow Holly's image changed when it entered the fixer. Somehow it was turning, right before his eyes, into the image of Babcia. He pulled the shot out of the fixer, tossed it into a large garbage can under the table, and turned back to the enlarger.

Make another picture. Very sweet, very proper, Harry said to himself. He did: just that sweet face with those big eyes and choirgirl hair. She looked so innocent. That was the worst thing about her, innocence hiding all that tempting evil. He found the picture, made the enlargement and pushed it into the developer. Then quickly he made another: Holly's ankle, fingertips reaching to tighten the strap. Fingertips. No face there.

Harry slid the new enlargement into the developer and saw that the latest two pictures were coming along nicely.

Don't know what that witch picture was about, or where it came from, he thought. Don't care. THIS is what's needed for the ritual.

Harry pulled the picture out of the developer and moved it into the fix. The picture began to transform. The photo of Holly's pretty face was becoming the leering image of Babcia, only now her look was even more menacing.

What the hell was going on?

Harry slid the photo of Holly's ankle from the developer into the fix. Babcia emerged again! Even though the picture was of Holly's feet, he got Babcia's face.

Harry was frantic. He tried to calm himself. There had to be a logical explanation. He needed to start over.

He threw the pictures away, dumped the chemicals into the sink and rinsed the trays.

This is some kind of trick, he thought. But who the hell could play a trick like this, and how were they doing it? He stepped back into his office only to see the mask of Babcia now looking directly at him, leering at him with hatred and accusation.

"Witch! I'll deal with you later," Harry screamed. "I can deal with whores like Holly, and I can deal with witches."

Harry snatched up a new set of chemicals and ducked back into the darkroom.

Do it slowly, carefully this time, Harry told himself. He prepared the three solutions in their trays and arranged the trays in the proper order. He selected a new image of Holly, a very tempting one (a proper one for the ritual), a candid shot of Holly stepping out of her tight white shorts when she first came to the pool.

Harry focused the lens, adjusted the exposure. Everything was perfect. He made the enlargement. Beautiful! He moved the paper to the developer. Then he just stared at it for a full ten minutes while the image emerged.

Slowly the beautiful face and body of Holly Madonie became clearer and clearer.

Wonderful.

"Move it to the fixer now," Harry said out loud.

He couldn't stop sweating, and he had been careless with the chemicals. They filled the air, and there was another smell too. What was it? A spicy-sweet smell that became more and more sickening as it grew in intensity, a smell that hinted of blood.

What was he breathing? The chemicals? They caught in his throat. Harry coughed over and over again; he capped the bottles and pushed them up onto the shelf above his w ork area.

He looked down at the image in the fixer, coughing still.

WITCH! Not the beautiful victim, not the girl who would beg him for mercy before he slit her throat. It was the fucking witch.

Harry was growing dizzy from the sickening, bloody smell. He coughed desperately, slammed the tray of fixer against the wall with too much force. A bottle of acid fell from the shelf above him and broke as it hit the edge of the sink. It splattered up onto his face and eyes, burning him terribly.

Harry banged desperately around in the dark room. He screamed in pain, smashing into the trays, dislodging even more chemicals. He grabbed a towel and held it over his eyes as he darted from the room, slamming the door behind him.

He was choking, coughing, and now he could barely see. He staggered out into his office, screaming. He looked up, and there leering down at him was that accusing mask of Babcia. He could hear her laughing at him. The sound followed him into his bedroom where he bolted the door.

"Witch!" He shouted again. "She's after me. And I didn't kill them, really. I didn't kill any of them. I just dreamed of it, imagined it."

"If you're after Holly, you can have her!" he yelled through the door at the mask. "I won't kill her! I won't hurt her! She's all yours. You don't have to hurt me. You don't need to haunt me."

But she did.

Interlude 6

Matryoshka tries to set the vodka glass down, misses the table, and sends it clattering onto the hardwood floor of the secret room.

"Oh dear," she sighs, but she doesn't need to. The thick Polish glass hasn't broken, and, at this point, there's no vodka in it anyway.

"Was it Babcia or the mask who drove Harry insane," the girl asks. "Or maybe Babcia *using* the masks."

"More likely that," Wicktor answers.

"Then Babcia *is* good… and the masks are good too."

Michalowski shakes his head. "Witches and their work are never good, Kochanie."

"I take exception to that statement," the warlock says. "Look at me. I'm a witch, aren't I?"

He turns from the old man, and his eyes blaze seductively at the girl. "Don't you think I'm good, Matryoshka?"

"Oh yes."

The girl smiles for a moment, then she turns bright red and looks away, toward the other room, toward the masks. Wicktor can see her shudder at the sight of them.

"Now, look girl," he says as he goes over to the wall of masks and picks out one of the most terrifying, "Good and evil? Inanimate objects? Even those that are bewitched, what are they?"

He holds the hideous mask right in front of the girl and her father.

"It all depends on the intentions of those who use them. Right, Pan Michalowski?"

The old man studies the mask and the warlock for a long moment. "You want me to tell of the one time I know these masks did good?"

"During the reign of the Nazis, yes."

"And about my brother Peter, and the camp?"

"Not in any detail," the warlock answers with a dismissive gesture. "Just give your daughter a little sense of what happened."

Michalowski sighs, raises his glass to take a sip, and realizes that it's empty, turns it upside down to prove the point, shakes it, sighs again, and then begins.

"After the Nazis came to Poland, many of our people were put in prison camps... Jews, yes, but also our own Catholic religious leaders, and many Polish nationals too.

"We heard of the suffering there and were not surprised. We knew that soldiers would come in the night. They would call all the villagers out of their houses, line everyone up against the wall so that they could watch as a few were singled out for no reason at all: big strong men; young boys; older women; anyone, it didn't matter. They were beaten nearly senseless, and then dragged away. We later learn that they were taken to the camps... to be worked to death.

"My brother and I lived here in Zakopanski. And the Nazis even came to this place. They worked their cruelties, and dragged their prisoners away. Their one mistake, these monsters, was that they failed to notice that we are a healthy people here in the mountains; we are strong, and we are used to taking care of ourselves... and, most importantly, some of us have magic.

"My brother, Peter, was one of those who were taken. He was in his late 20s, and he was as wise as he was strong. When he was captured he happened to be carrying a small vial of an unusual liquid that we had acquired from somewhere in India. He was smart enough to keep it hidden on his person for all the months that the Nazis had him.

261

"He worked hard, did his best to stay healthy, and then one night, when there were rumors that the whole camp was about to be shipped off to another, larger, far more terrible camp in the south, he spilled the liquid out into the prison compound. You wouldn't think that an amount so small, not more than maybe a few ounces, would have much effect. But it did. It was indeed magical.

"Within minutes everyone was asleep, guards and prisoners alike... except for Peter who knew how to combat the magic. That's when he escaped."

Michalowski takes the mask from Wicktor and holds it in his hand. He studies it, smiles at it. "Thank you," he whispers to it. Then he looks up at the others. Wicktor is smiling; even his daughter has a kindly expression as she looks at the old man and the mask.

"Peter did not flee," Michalowski continues. "He came back to our shop, took all 28 of the masks, put them in a great sack, and carted them back to the camp that very night. He re-entered the camp with the masks while everyone was still asleep, and when the prisoners awoke, he quickly gave out 27 of the masks, keeping one for himself.

"Soon sirens blared, Nazis marched, and a review was immediately demanded, even though it was just after midnight. Prisoners were called out of their barracks with harsh German commands. Peter and his comrades entered the compound with the Babcia masks hidden under their winter coats.

"'Sagen Sie uns, die für diesen unnatürlichen Schlaf verantwortlich ist,' the commandant wanted to know. 'Tell us who is responsible for this unnatural sleep... or you'll stand in the center of this compound until you all drop dead!'

"The prisoners stood in one long line. Then the guards began slowly, methodically at one end and interrogated each prisoner they came to. Anyone who gave an answer that was thought to be unsatisfactory was shot dead on the spot. Peter stood very near the start of the line. One of his very best friends was shot before he even knew what was happening.

"So, when the guard came to Peter and asked if he knew what was going on, he merely pulled the mask from under his coat and pressed it up against his face. The guard gasped, he dropped his rifle. His eyes flamed, and then they exploded right out of his face. The guard raised his hands, touched the eye sockets, and his fingers began to melt.

"Even those guards standing a hundred yards away had the same experience.

"The commandant roared, machine guns were turned toward the crowd, when suddenly twenty-seven more masks were pulled up over the faces of the prisoners. The guards on the gun turrets wailed. Their eyes exploded; their heads split; their hands and fingers melted. Very soon they, like the guards in the compound, were little more than masses of melting flesh.

"Peter gestured to the prisoners with the masks, to all the prisoners in fact, so that they would follow. And they did, out through the doors of the prison camp and into the nearby woods... into the night.

"When Peter returned to Zakopanski he was crazed with the idea that the Nazis would find the masks and somehow gain control of them. We had a cousin who had immigrated to America then, who worked as an art instructor at Leland University. We sent all the masks to her, and then we ourselves boarded up the shop and went into hiding, higher in the mountains, for the rest of that long terrible war."

Chapter Forty-Two

Encounter

Niko was still in shock.

It had been one of the most heated arguments he had ever known; one he could not believe had actually taken place. He was screaming, cursing, saying things he never thought himself capable of saying, getting responses that were equally harsh and cruel. From Chuck Vaughn!

It was all about gingerbread. Chuck had had a new idea for a gingerbread house, one that was huge and Gothic and scary, a gingerbread house that would warn Hansel and Gretel about the witch and make them think twice about approaching. Of course, their hunger would draw them to it anyway.

Marla loved the idea, liked the thought that stupid Hansel would be getting his prudent girlfriend into trouble once again.

Niko somehow knew that it just wasn't right. He had a much different idea, one that came from God only knows where, maybe from that evening so long ago when his grandmother lured him out of the kitchen with the sweet-spicy smell of gingerbread.

He had spent that evening drawing witches, he remembered, and the smell of spicy-sweetness and blood sausage had inspired him.

Niko couldn't see the duality in a Gothic gingerbread house as much as he could see the horror of a cute little cottage that was hiding a witch who ate children.

It was 1 AM when he arrived home. He walked to the kitchen table to see that it was still set for dinner.

Shit! He hadn't called Holly to tell her that he would be arriving late, that he was locked in a creative struggle with the boss.

There was a greeting card on his plate. He opened it. "Happy Anniversary" it said. He flipped it over and there was a note from Holly.

"Wake me when you get in."

Niko sank into his chair. It was so late, and he had not only forgotten to call his wife but also forgotten that it was their first anniversary. (God, think what had happened to them in that year.)

Still, the argument was worth it, and in the end he had won, more or less. Chuck had said, "Okay, show me! Show me the kind of house you're talking about, and if it works we'll use it."

Niko was proud that he'd had the conviction to win an argument with the greatest animator who had ever lived. Did all this come from creating while locked in a cage?

Hell, Niko didn't even need the cage anymore. Three or four hot story sessions with Marla and he learned that he could be just as creative outside of it with his clothes on.

Niko took a piece of paper from a huge stack he kept on the kitchen counter. He began sketching cottages made of gingerbread, and as he did, he relived the childhood moment when Babcia lured him from the closet to eat cookies and draw witches.

"Making cookies, drawing pictures."

He could almost hear her tuneless humming, almost taste the gingerbread, and almost smell the blood of the sausage that mingled with the spicy sweetness. He could almost feel Babcia's haunting presence. And he could almost see her drawing of a gingerbread house, a gingerbread house conceived and drawn by a witch far more real than Marla could ever be. No wonder he was so certain.

The house he was drawing wasn't Gothic at all, only a cute, little cottage that somehow warned of the wickedness within.

"This'll show them," Niko said out loud. "Hell, I can run the creative side of that house better than Marla or anyone."

Where were these ideas coming from? He didn't know. But he was starting to believe them.

Niko drew the gingerbread house very much as his grandmother had, with dark little flecks of black in the gingerbread that were in fact silhouettes of witches. As he drew the cottage he made it more and more his own, adding harsh shards of dark chocolate that cut into the cute curly shapes of the white frosting shingles.

He added smoke coming from the chimney and then drew sparks and cinders flying up in the smoke, sparks and cinders that were really dancing witches.

"I'll show them something," Niko said as he drew sketch after sketch. "I'll teach Marla not to challenge me in front of Chuck."

Then slowly, frighteningly, Niko began to realize that Babcia was with him. He heard her tuneless humming, smelled her bloody sweetness, saw her eyes glowing blood red in the darkest corner of the room. And this time he dared to stand and approach her. He dared to walk right up to her.

Babcia was there, hunched over, crone that she was, watching him. Niko looked directly into her eyes. He dared to do it. And what he saw was a look he would never forget. She was proud of him. She agreed with his boasting. He could someday be as great as Chuck Vaughn if he wanted to, and she would help him.

"Niko, come play me," she said.

Niko nodded. But suddenly her gaze shifted past him. She tilted her head curiously. It was more the move of an animal than a human. And then a snarl curled the corner of her lips. They started to quiver; her teeth began to chatter as though she were a hungry beast trying desperately to hold back a vicious attack. Low, guttural growls burned from her throat. Rage began to glow in her eyes. Her quivering lips pulled back to reveal monstrous, yellow fangs. She snapped at the air, shook all over, tensing herself before she lunged forward to strike.

Niko turned quickly.

Holly had entered the far end of the room. He spun back, stepping to his left to try to block the charge of the ravenous monster...

But she had vanished. Niko was stunned. He grabbed the arm of a chair to calm himself. He had been ready to fight back against his grandmother, and she knew it.

"I didn't hear you come in," Holly said softly. She hadn't seen or heard the horror Niko had faced. The young man took a deep breath and closed his eyes.

"I tried to be as quiet as I could," he whispered at last.

"You saw my card," Holly said, flipping it over on Niko's plate.

He sighed, smiled and walked slowly toward her. His breathing was becoming more normal now.

"I didn't get one for you, I'm sorry."

"It's okay," Holly answered. "I saved the dinner, a pretty great pot-roast, but it'll be even better tomorrow."

"I'll come home early, I promise," Niko whispered, hoping that Holly could not see that he was still shaking. "I have something special picked out for you. You'll love it," he said.

Holly could tell that he was lying. But it didn't matter.

"I have a new outfit to wear," she answered. "Got it just for you. I call it my sexy, *anniversary* things."

She smiled weakly. "You'll love 'em too. I know you will."

"I'll love them, and then I'll love you... all night long," Niko answered.

Holly was suddenly overcome with guilt. She ran to her husband and put her arms around him quickly so that he couldn't see the tears in her eyes. Niko responded, squeezing her as though he knew he had almost lost her forever.

"Oh, Niko," Holly whispered, "Thank you."

"For what?"

"Just thank you."

Niko held her tightly, kissed her desperately, and felt her hug him just as desperately in response. And in that moment he swore in his heart that no witch was ever going to take her from him, no matter how powerful her magic...

No matter what kind of rewards she promised him in return.

Still it wasn't that much later when the young husband pulled away from his sleeping wife, walked slowly out of the bedroom, and made his way to the window. He opened the living room shades and stared out onto the courtyard.

"Please," he whispered, "Babcia, can't you accept the girl I love. Can't you help keep her safe instead of always seeing her as an enemy who should be..." he paused for a moment not willing to even say the words (killed, destroyed, murdered, mutilated).

"Babcia, I can see that you're trying to protect *me*, but how about my wife, huh? If only because I love her...

"If only because I love her."

Chapter Forty-Three

Billy's Job Interview

It was the day of Billy's big interview at VVA, and, as he sat across from Marla Morrison in Chuck Vaughn's office he found that he was entranced by the look in her eyes, her expression, even in the way she sat in that chair... so upright and self-possessed. He knew instinctively that the witchy young woman was bold, ambitious, and sexy as hell. His eyes flashed at hers. Marla turned even more fully toward him.

"I AM Babcia, you know," she said, and then she crossed those dangerously long legs of hers in his direction.

Chuck Vaughn wasn't used to being ignored, and he didn't like it. The rate of his gum chewing increased dramatically, and then, just to interject himself into the unspoken conversation, he asked a question.

"So just who the hell is this Babcia, anyway?"

"Babcia?" Marla whispered without taking her eyes off of Billy, "Why, she's the witch who's been haunting Niko, you know. She's the mask that took over his art film that you liked so much; she's the picture that you hung on the wall of your Witch Room; she's the monster that slaughtered Billy's girl."

Billy's head snapped back to the witch. She had broken the spell. "My girl?"

"Nancy Swallow," Marla continued.

"Nancy was killed by a wild animal," Billy said.

"Is that what they called her?"

"Her?" Chuck Vaughn interrupted.

"Babcia, the beast that killed Nancy." Marla's eyes narrowed. Her pupils flashed a deep blood red. Her features froze, stone cold. Billy was suddenly shaken to the core. He looked down at the sketch he was making. He had asked Chuck for some drawing paper when he had entered the room.

"Sketching is a nervous habit of mine," he had said.

"I think that's great," Vaughn had answered and handed Billy a whole stack of punched animation paper. Marla suggested that Billy make a drawing of her.

Billy was not the quick-sketch artist that Niko was. He couldn't sum up a person with a few brief lines. But, given time, he was a far better technician. His drawing of Marla captured the complex young woman completely; plain, yet somehow beautiful; nervous but somehow very self-assured.

"I'm channeling Babcia, you know," Marla added suddenly. "Have been for days. It's exciting!" Her eyes lit up. "We'll have to do it together some time, Billy."

"I'd like that, Billy responded, and, just like that, their eyes locked once more, and they were in perfect union again.

"Well, this is all wonderful," Chuck said, mashing through another mouthful of gum, and he used the moment to change the subject. He began talking about his favorite topic: the history of VVA. He told how he had come up with the character of CatMan Due on a train ride from Kansas City to Los Angeles.

Marla's eyes were still locked on Billy's, but then they began moving quickly from Billy's eyes to the stack of papers on his lap, then up to his eyes and then back again.

Without a word, Billy realized what she wanted, and so he turned back to his drawing, finished it, and then he took a second piece of animation paper and placed it over the initial work.

Billy had time to sketch and listen. He kept looking up at Chuck and then Marla and then nodding, but something horrible was happening in the new image he was sketching. The outline of Marla, which he had traced from the original drawing, was now taking on the horrific features of Babcia herself. Billy shuddered. He was doing it intentionally. (He hoped.)

"And that's the story of VVA," Vaughn concluded, "What do you think?"

Billy was so wrapped up in his work he didn't realize that the question was directed at him.

"Billy," Marla called. "Answer him."

"Oh, yes," Billy answered. "What do I think about..."

"Working here," Marla injected.

"Sounds like fun." Billy said.

"Delicious fun!" Marla added. "Chuck, you know, I need another assistant, someone different from Niko, someone who can delve into The Craft of the witches with me and make sure that it's well represented in our show. I mean, Niko's good at scaring people but what's really needed is an apprentice witch."

"Wouldn't you like to be my apprentice?" she asked Billy.

The young man grinned at Marla. Their unspoken communication was perfect.

Chuck stared at the witch for a moment, and then he turned to Billy. "Marla and I need to talk about the details of the job before we can make you any kind of formal offer," he said. "Let's see your sketches, kid."

Billy handed the sketches to Vaughn. The famous animator looked at the top drawing of Marla, the one that captured her complex personality so perfectly.

"Very nice," he responded.

"I'll be worth the investment," Billy said.

"I'm sure you will, son. But I have to tell you that we're already way over budget on this project, I've mortgaged the whole damn company to get it done, and things are pretty tight around here. The last thing we can afford is another head."

"I see," answered Billy. (Shit!)

There would be no job. He felt sure of it. He wanted to punch the old man right in the face, and then just take Marla and go on that wild ride, that channeling thing she was tempting him with.

"Let me study your drawings," Chuck added. "Let me talk things over with Marla. Maybe she can convince me that we need you enough to incur the added expense."

Billy looked at Marla who was starting to revert to her more nervous persona.

"I'll get back to you tomorrow," Chuck said.

Billy nodded, said a polite, "Thank you," and walked out the door.

"Damn you Chuck!" Marla hissed as she looked angrily at the old master, but Chuck didn't even return her gaze.

He had lined up Billy's drawings so that they were right on top of each other. He was flipping the pages the way animators do when they are working on the action in a scene, back and forth, back and forth. The effect was amazing. With only two drawings he could see Marla transform into Babcia right before his very eyes. It was terrifying.

Vaughn jumped from his chair and ran out of the door and after Billy shouting, "Hey, wait a minute, kid."

"Wait just a goddamn minute!"

Chapter Forty-Four

Surprise

"Niko Madonie," Billy said, as he walked into the office of his old rival the very next morning. Niko was stunned and not especially happy to see him.

"Billy?" he sighed.

"That's me. Just been hired. Marla needed a little more help, so I'm joining the team."

"You're going to be part of the writing team?"

"Not exactly," Billy answered. "She said she needed someone to help her add more witchcraft to the story."

"Do you know anything about witches?" Niko asked.

"Only what I saw in your movie, pal. But I can learn."

"How did you manage to get in to talk to Chuck and Marla about a job?" Niko asked, as he motioned for Billy to take a seat in the chair in front of his desk. Billy sat down and immediately put his feet up.

"A few influential friends," Billy answered.

"Great to have you here," Niko lied. "Oh, and thanks for the mask," he lied again.

"Bet it really creeped you out, huh?"

"As a matter of fact it did, and Holly, too."

"Too bad, I'd hate to scare her... but you? Hell, a good horror writer needs to be scared all the time." And then Billy turned to his tour guide, Sally Fukes, Chuck Vaughn's rather chunky receptionist. She was standing politely near the door studying the two men.

"Don't you think horror writers need to be scared all the time, Sally?"

"Oh yes, of course," she answered.

Niko wondered if Billy had already made a pass at Sally. Probably not.

She was cute but a little too heavy for Billy's taste. And besides, he knew his old friend was way too smooth to do anything like that on the first day of a new job. Sally would have liked it though. That much was clear.

Strawberry blond, Sally Fukes wasn't really chunky; she was *downright fat* (her mother's words). But Sally didn't much care. She had her own personal style as well as a huge appetite for ice cream, donuts, and for a certain kind of cowboy that frequented the country-dance clubs around Pomona.

Chuck Vaughn had given Sally the job with the understanding that she dress her very best every day, and that she never, under any circumstances, "play that goddamn cowboy music while at work."

Sally obliged, and was generally considered excellent at her job. She was masterful at operating the switchboard, but what was far more important was that Sally understood men on a very basic level. Even at nearly 200 pounds she could charm the most irascible sponsor, New York executive, or underpaid animator. There was a kind of magic about her.

There was one other very special thing about Sally that almost no one knew, and she intended to keep it that way. Coming from the backcountry of Tennessee as she did, she had made the acquaintance of a certain little circle of mountain women. One old black woman in particular, Mother Black everyone called her, befriended Sally and had taught her The Craft. At least that's what Sally finally admitted to the outraged ranchers and growers who had forced her to leave their community for consorting with the old woman. Sally was heartbroken. She liked Mother Black and the skills she taught. They made her feel special, and she felt they were beneficial, even necessary, far less toxic than the remedies being handed out by certified doctors, for heaven's sake.

Sally set her sights on Hollywood for the kind of excitement she always saw in the movies. She was afraid that she would have to give up the things Mother Black had taught, of course, but then she read about the job as a receptionist at VVA. It was a place where they were doing a TV special on witches. It said so right in the job ad. It fitted right in with her knowledge of The Craft. She came in, met Chuck and Marla, and the deal was done.

When Marla asked Sally to give Billy the tour that morning, the chunky receptionist thought he was the most handsome thing she'd ever seen in her life, better looking than any of the boys at the country-dances. She could also tell that Billy was the kind of sophisticate who might not be too interested in a full figured, Tennessee country girl. But boy he sure was cute. She'd just have to see what developed.

As far as Niko was concerned: Wow! He was a living doll too. And he seemed to understand things about The Craft that no ordinary man should know.

"He's putting the scare back into Hansel and Gretel," she said whenever she introduced him to visitors. Sally, of course, noticed the tension between the two men as soon as she led Billy into the room. Somehow she could sense that the last thing Niko wanted was to be around Billy Bright. Billy would be challenging him every day.

Just then Niko mentioned someone else, and Sally knew at once that it was someone Billy cared about very much.

"Nancy?" Niko asked. "Any more news?"

Billy's face darkened. "Lab reports are all in. Identified the creature that killed her. Definitely a wolf, a very strange kind though, nothing like it in the US. More the kind of wolf they have in Europe, the Black Forest, in...."

"Germany or Poland?" Niko asked.

"Must have been somebody's pet. They did a canvas of the area but were never able to find it."

"Well, a real animal, anyway," Niko answered.

"Right on," Billy said. "Not the kind of witch-wolf that was on the mask I sent you."

"Of course not," Niko replied. "How could it have been?"

"Holly said you thought it might be," Billy answered, and as soon as he mentioned Niko's wife he realized that he shouldn't have done it.

"When did she tell you that?" Niko asked.

"Couple days ago. Just stopped by for a minute on my way here. Wanted to say 'Hi,' that's all."

Niko turned away from his desk.

Keep away from my wife you son of a bitch!

He wanted to scream it at the top of his lungs. But this was hardly the time or the place. He held it in.

"The question I keep asking myself," Niko said at last, is, 'Why Nancy?'"

Billy seemed suddenly distracted by the question, heartbroken, lost.

Sally (Billy's chunky Tennessee tour guide) came up to him, took him by the arm and led him from the room.

She did understand men, didn't she... in all kinds of ways.

#

Marla was wearing a completely different version of her usual bulky sweater and granny dress. On this day she had unbuttoned the dress up the front so that her high-heeled boots were on display.

"Like your footwear," Billy told Marla as Sally led him into the room. He flashed just a hint of his million-dollar grin, but he still had that distracted look in his eyes. (He really had loved Nancy, hadn't he?)

"They're not too comfortable," the witch responded as she stepped forward to show them off, "but they do look good, you know."

"They do," Billy agreed.

"Thanks for the help, Sally," Marla said to the receptionist. "I'll take it from here."

Sally smiled, "What a doll he is," she whispered as she shuffled from the room.

"Ready for a serious assignment?" Marla asked as she turned back to Billy.

Billy nodded.

"I have to go out for the day, but I've got piles of stuff for you to read and I'd like to quiz you on it tonight. Can you come over to my place at eleven o'clock this evening?"

Billy smiled. It was an interesting invitation wasn't it? "Sounds good."

"We're having a meeting of my coven. Hollywood witches," she said. "They'll want to know just how much you've been able to learn from your readings."

Billy tried to respond in a businesslike fashion, but the prospects seemed so sexy that he was getting an enormous erection. He couldn't help it.

Marla glanced down at it. "That's very nice, you know," she said, "but this is serious. Here's a list of things that you'll need to pick up for me on the way over."

Marla took a neatly bound notebook from her pocket. She pulled a page from it and handed it to Billy. Then she recited the list from memory: a viper, two newts, three tarantulas, four rats and twenty five bats.

"The rats can be store-bought, the cute and cuddly kind," Marla said. "Pick them up at the local pet shop. Get the ones with the sweet, friendly personalities."

"You'll have to get the bats and other stuff at Hollywood Wranglers. They've been helping me a lot lately. Just charge it to my account. Sally can give you all the information."

"Right," Billy answered. He felt like saluting. He was still rock hard, but Marla didn't seem to be paying any attention.

"And the exact number of each species is important," she continued. "You know: one, two, three, four, twenty-five."

"Thirty-five," Billy answered, after a quick calculation. "Bats, snakes, spiders, rats? What are they for?"

Marla laughed out loud. "They're ingredients, you know."

"For what?"

"Didn't I say I wanted to make you my apprentice?"

Billy nodded.

"I guess you'll find out tonight then, won't you?"

Chapter Forty-Five

The Initiation

Billy opened the trunk of his car and hauled out two large, black wire cages. They were full of "Marla's ingredients", as Billy now called them. The creatures scurried around hissing and chattering and making Billy feel very angry. What was he doing buying cages full of vermin? It had taken him all afternoon. But he was okay now. It was 10:57 PM, and he had just arrived at the sprawling bungalow that Marla had rented on Beachwood Drive... right under the old Hollywood sign.

Billy lugged the heavy cages up the long, winding sidewalk that led to the porch. The house was in mint condition. Must have been renovated very recently, Billy decided. The body of the house was a dusty ocher with dull red trim and dark grey shutters. It was amazing how a home in such perfect condition could seem so ominous.

Marla's ingredients scurried, slithered and flew from one side of their cages to the other. They were making the cages unbalanced and hard to carry. The ingredients were not getting along either. In spite of the fact that they were partitioned off from one another, they still continued to fight, chatter and squeal loudly. Billy carried the cages as far away from his body as he could so that the rats, especially, couldn't lean out and bite him. They tried, as did the viper, but her partition was of a much finer mesh and so it offered better protection.

Billy hoisted the heavy cages from one step to the next until he'd climbed all thirteen of them and arrived at the front door. It was painted black. On the door a silver knocker was fashioned in the face of a man who was half human and half vines and branches.

"Earth guy," Billy grunted. "Hope this is a friendly place." The knocker didn't respond.

Billy wiped the sweat from his forehead. Hell of a way to arrive at a party. He banged the knocker and the door creaked open very slightly. Billy knocked again and waited. In the distance he could hear the strains of medieval folk music, almost a kind of Virginia reel, music for dancing anyway, but with a very eerie quality.

Billy decided not to wait any longer for an answer to his knock. He stepped through the door and into the dimly lit entry. Then he reached back, grabbed the cages, and lugged them in as well. When he dropped them onto the floor he set off a nasty flurry of rats, bats and spiders. It fitted in perfectly with his surroundings.

Only a few candles provided any light at all. Still Billy could see that the ceiling was immense, vaulted. A great winding stairway snaked its way up into total darkness. Hallways trailed off into shadowy rooms where oriental carpets, huge tables, and cluttered bookshelves offered refuge to dark, shadowy figures.

Suddenly the door slammed shut behind Billy, trapping him, he realized, inside the house. But worse than the realization was the being that had closed the door.

She stood there, small, hunched over, a woman so old

that her body seemed no more than a hollow shell. Loose fitting skin hung over ancient, twisted bones. Her fingernails were long and curled; her face was slashed from her left ear to the corner of her narrow mouth with a seemingly open wound that looked to have been there for centuries. A thin, crooked, line ludicrously highlighted with bright red lipstick formed her smile, and yet her eyes still seemed to sparkle with the nervous excitement of Marla Morrison.

This could have been Marla's great-great grandmother, Billy thought. And then the creature shuffled toward him, and Billy kicked the cages out of his way as he ran away from her and off into the depths of the house.

Half way into the nearly pitch-black living room Billy recognized another figure. It was towering, cloaked only in dark robes, and standing by a huge table filled with bottles and jars of odd shapes and sizes.

The grim reaper, Death itself, Billy thought as he tried desperately to feint away from it. Death did not take the feint. Instead it grabbed Billy by the arm and dragged him closer.

Death was a woman, Billy suddenly realized, as the overpowering strength of his adversary drew him toward her. The enormous hollow-cheeked creature shook off her hood to show her magnificent ebony skin, her silken black hair, and her smile of absolute surety.

Death dragged Billy to the table. She spun him around so that he was facing away from her, and then she slid one hand down over his belly so that she could press herself tightly against him from behind... in some kind of unearthly embrace. Now her free hand was at his throat.

Billy grabbed for her hand and tried to release her grasp, but Death was too strong. She had him at the table now. Billy's right hand was tearing at the long fingers that squeezed his neck so tightly. His other hand flailed wildly, trying to find some way to strike his adversary. There was none.

The struggle became more intense. Death reached onto the table. Billy's strength was making her task more difficult; still she was able to reach between the bottles and plunge her free hand into an enormous jar of creamy ointment that smelled very sweet, almost intoxicating. She brought the handful of glop to Billy's face. He screamed as he saw it coming and then suddenly it was all over him, smearing across his forehead, into his eyes and nose and his open mouth. He looked like some kind of giant insect larva as he struggled even harder to get free.

The hand pulled away from Billy's face. He was choking now, and nearly faint from shortness of breath. A second handful of the stuff suddenly splurged down onto his groin, covering the front of his jeans, his belt, and his belly. Death suddenly let go of Billy's throat, and she pushed him away from her and across the room.

Billy raised both hands to his eyes, and tried to clear his vision. Death was laughing at him. Her smile was broad and joyous; her raven hair swirled around her face; her hollow eyes sang of victory. Her robes had not completely escaped the splash of the ointment, and now they hung open, revealing the naked muscular body that had so completely dominated him.

Death took in a deep breath, rested against the table, and broke out once again in wild, high-pitched laughter. Billy bolted from the room in terror. There was moonlight streaming through the patio doors at the back, and so he darted through them and out into Marla's garden.

The garden was filled with women, about a dozen of them, Billy guessed, as he gazed out through the thick filter of ooze that still covered his face.

He was feeling a little better now. He could see much more, and there was a sweet cooling property to the glop as it seeped into his cheeks and forehead and in through his jeans.

Many of the women in the garden wore robes similar to the one worn by the woman who was Death. The robes were black with large hoods and golden braids for belts. Some of the women had their robes open and Billy could see their breasts, their hips, and the dark mounds of hair between their legs.

Was this Marla's coven? Were these her Hollywood Witches? They were just what anyone would expect in Hollywood, Billy thought: teachers; waitresses; secretaries; all wannabe starlets, he guessed; all of them studying The Craft; each of them just a little more beautiful than women in those professions might normally be anywhere else in the world. This was Hollywood, after all.

How could nervous, insecure Marla (ballerina legs notwithstanding) run a coven filled with these kinds of women? Billy wondered. But then the answer came to him immediately: she was a real witch, and had learned witchcraft from an even greater witch, who had learned it first hand from the greatest witch in all of Poland.

Billy stopped to catch his breath for a moment and to marvel at the gathering. The women ranged in age from their early-twenties to mid-fifties. Each was in magnificent physical condition and each seemed to be lost in the music. They had coated their face, breasts and other parts of their bodies with the same sweet, creamy ointment that Billy felt chilling his face -- not nearly as much, of course -- but enough to give them a warm radiance. The ointment was making them glow.

To the left of the dancers fiddle, flute, and guitar players provided the odd medieval music to which the dancers swayed. They stood inside a circle of candles, which encompassed the entire yard. Behind the whole group there was a marble platform with an altar on top. The marble was very old, and the top of it was stained red with blood. Billy looked closer and saw that the hideous old crone who had met him at the door now had a huge butcher knife, and she was slitting open the rats, snake and other vermin, spilling their blood on the altar and then tossing their remains into a huge cauldron that hung from wrought-iron railings just in front of the altar.

The cauldron was bubbling, and the aroma from its brew gave off the same sweet smell as the ointment, although now it was mixed with the stench of the crone's bloody ingredients.

Billy took a step toward the dancers, feeling very much more comfortable than before. (Was it the ointment?)

"Here I am, ladies," he called, with a boyish grin. Big mistake. They saw him and rushed toward him, squealing with excitement as though he was a rock star. They grabbed him and threw him to the ground.

"Wait a minute," Billy tried to scream, but it didn't help. He was swarmed under. The women cared little for the deep gashes and other wounds that they inflicted as they tore his clothes from him. Billy fought to get away, but there were just too many of them. They ripped off his shirt and, yanked off his boots and jeans. The chubbiest of the women grabbed his shorts and jerked them away too. She seemed especially delighted with the prize. And then she turned her sweet, round face toward him.

"Howdy," she sang out. "Welcome ta the party!" It was Sally Fukes. "Why ya fightin like that? It's gonna be lotsa fun."

Billy suddenly agreed. Fighting off the dancers was not only useless but also unnecessary and maybe dangerous. Why not go with the flow. And so he just relaxed and let these big, strong, beautiful women strip him naked. Suddenly he was doing just fine, looking forward to the proceedings as they lifted him and carried him to the great marble platform and the altar on top. And then Billy noticed the crone standing there with her bloody butcher knife and her hideous facial scar. The altar was already drenched with the blood of her victims. Was he next?

Billy began to struggle again, kicking, screaming, and flailing back and forth. It didn't help. He was overpowered. The old crone swept away the last remains of rodent flesh and entrails, and made way for Billy to be lifted onto the altar and pinned down on a bed thick with blood.

Billy was held tightly in place, and now the old woman walked to the foot of the altar. She dropped the knife. She also dropped her robes to reveal an ancient body that, as Billy had sensed at first, was nothing more than pock marked folds of wrinkled skin hanging from twisted and misshapen bones.

The old woman, the crone, the witch, (Clara) smiled a toothless grin at Billy and hobbled to the lower edge of the altar. She climbed up onto it somehow and began crawling up over him. Billy screamed and renewed his struggle. He couldn't move an inch. There was something unnatural about the strength of the women who were holding him.

Billy looked into the old witch's eyes. They were familiar, weren't they? There was something about them that was more than aged and terrifying. They were wild, neurotic, excited. Was it Marla, the witch, who had become the crone? Suddenly, Billy was aroused, very ready to fuck this monstrous creature.

The crone kneeled above Billy. He could not move. Dozens of hands with claw-like nails held him in place. Then, with a hideous cry, the hag lowered herself onto Billy.

She squealed with pleasure. Billy felt a rush of sexual energy as she rode upon him, slowly at first and then more and more wildly, but as she did, a transformation began to take place. She began to turn into Marla. Her matted, ancient hair became wild auburn locks. The breasts, which were no more than empty sacks bouncing upon her chest, became firm and beautiful. Her skin tightened until it was sweet and young. Her face was radiant. But that was only the beginning.

The auburn hair that graced her head and her pubic arch grew and it continued to grow. Suddenly it was extending down onto her face and over her back. And it grew up from her loins as well, across her belly and up to the very edges of her breasts. Billy was now under Marla's control.

The women loosened their grasp. Many moved away and began dancing with each other or by themselves. If Billy had looked up toward the bright silver moon, he would have been able to see them dancing skyward. Others spun in the air and grabbed the bats that had escaped the witch's butcher knife and were now transforming themselves into sprites and imps.

Billy could not enjoy the full effect of the experience, however. Fear began to grow in him because suddenly he was being raped, ravaged, literally, by Marla (who in some way perhaps) had become Babcia and harnessed her vast power, and who was now transforming herself into something even more horrible, something more monstrous, half woman, half she-wolf: the very image on the mask Billy had given to Niko.

CHAPTER FORTY-SIX

THE MEETING

Niko was sketching as fast as he could, pulling various magic markers from the vast array in front of him, slapping a little color onto his drawings to brighten them up. This was a new sequence that he really liked, and now Marla, in her own high-strung, twitchy way, was fucking with it.

Teenage Hansel alone, naked in the cage, the witch drooling and hungry, ready to turn him into a tasty dinner. Is he plump enough? She wonders. She reaches her scraggly hand into the cage to determine if he's ready to eat. She's nearly blind, can barely see shapes and, in this dim light, not even that.

Suddenly Gretel reaches out over the top of the old woman and gives Hansel a chicken bone. He sticks it out for the witch to feel.

"Scrawny!" she cries, "No good ta eat." She tries to look closer, sees nothing, rubs her eyes and reaches to the other side of the cage.

Hansel turns the bone over, gives her the other end, but in her blindness she pushes past it and grabs a good healthy chunk of his shoulder.

"More like it," she cackles. "We eat tonight, Gretel," and she turns to find the girl.

Gretel dances around the room calling to the witch. She's deep in the shadows where the old witch can't see her.

Suddenly Gretel moves into the doorway. She pulls a flute from her pocket, raises it and begins to play sweetly, hypnotically. The witch hears the music, smiles, follows the sound. She has to dance, even if she doesn't want to, because Gretel's tune is magic.

Gretel leads the witch away from the Gingerbread House where Hansel is caged, up onto the meadow, and into the silver moonlight.

The witch can now make out Gretel's form against the enormous moon. The girl is tall, young, beautiful, growing close to womanhood, and yet she is skipping along like a child, dancing, playing her magical tune. The witch dances along, too, in crazy, tangled steps. She does silly pirouettes.

The full moon gleams as Gretel leads the dancing witch through the meadow, across bridges, over little brooks that sing in harmony with her melody. She leads the witch on through the woods and then right into a thorny briar.

The witch can't stop dancing. She twists into the briar and is caught up in it as she spins deeper into the thorns. Gretel picks up the tempo. The witch is dancing furiously now, tearing her clothes, her flesh. She's caught, falls over, still dancing frantically though she's down. Instead of helping her escape, the dance only catches her on more thorns, and draws her deeper into the brambles until finally she is raked with wounds, bleeding, nearly dead. Even then she is still twitching to the music.

At last she becomes silent. Gretel finishes the tune. The witch does not stir. Gretel approaches the briar, and looks into it for proof that the witch is dead.

BUT SHE'S NOT.

Her deadly hand reaches out, grabs the flute from Gretel and casts it deep into the briar. Then she grabs the girl and begins dragging her into the thorns and certain death. Gretel fights wildly for her life. At last she manages to wrestle free from the witch. She takes off running, back to the house.

The witch, torn and bloody but with no music to hold her back, escapes the briar and hobbles after her. But as the two approach the house, they can hear music again. Hansel, during all his hours in the cage, has fashioned a flute of his own, and now he begins playing the same magical tune that Gretel played, and with the same results. Gretel turns to see the witch spinning and dancing again without any way to stop herself.

Gretel races into the gingerbread house and closes the door. The witch bounds in through the window. She dances around Gretel, doing her best to close in on the girl.

"Don't stop playing, Hansel. Please don't stop," Gretel pleads, and then she sees the witch's oven. It's enormous, the size of a full-grown man. She races to it, opens the door. Inside, the oven is deadly hot. The witch recognizes the danger but is unable to stop her frantic dance.

The next time she spins past Gretel the girl pushes her into the fiery oven and locks the door tight. The witch perishes and they are saved.

#

Niko smiled and handed Marla the thirty-five drawings he had sketched for the sequence. Marla responded with a dissatisfied smirk.

"I don't know," she said. "I mean, what is it? Just exploitation of another one of our supposed weaknesses."

Niko slumped back in absolute disgust.

"What about this?" she asked, tossing Niko's drawings onto the conference room table and then striding across the room as though she were taking center stage in one of her grand ballets.

The witch is at the cage. She feels the chicken bone; she thinks it's Hansel's arm. He's not ready, she decides, and so she just leaves the room bringing Gretel along with her.

"No food here," she says, "But there'll be plenty tonight at the Witches' Sabbath. Let's go. We'll get something to eat, and then you, my dear, can learn a thing or two about witchcraft."

The witch takes Gretel to the Sabbath, she meets some wonderful witches, is charmed by them, and.... We can figure out the rest later."

"I like it a lot," called Billy from the head of the table where he had been doing a master sketch for Marla's story. It showed the Witches' Sabbath as Marla described it, but it was filled with details from Billy's own initiation: witches nude or in unbound robes dancing with each other, flying up into the sky, riding on brooms over an altar where a muscular young man whose face could not be recognized was being driven into wild sexual madness by a shapely young woman who, nonetheless, was part wolf.

He handed the drawing to Marla who passed it on to Niko immediately.

"This is way off track," Niko said as soon as he looked at it.

"Nonsense," Marla replied. "It's perfect, more in keeping

with today's audience and the real spirit of a modern Gretel. Maybe she should become a witch. And if it's sex you want, there's nothing sexier than a Witches' Sabbath, believe me. We're having one on the next full moon. You should come by. It'll be a chance to get some fresh ideas. Bring that perfect little wife of yours along, too. How pregnant is she, anyway?"

"Seven months," Niko answered instinctively. And then he shook his head. "No, absolutely not."

"Billy, see if you can get Chuck to come in here and settle this little creative argument we're having," Marla called.

"Right!" answered Billy jumping to his feet and heading out the door. He shot Niko one last look of defiance as he left.

"Well, it's just you and me now you know," Marla said. She grabbed a pointer that had been leaning up against the corner of the room and, walking up to Niko, she touched the pointer to the side of his face and drew it slowly down, past his neck and over his chest.

"You spent your whole life being afraid of witches, Niko. Why don't you try tasting one? And I mean that in the most outrageous way possible."

"I'm a married man." Niko said firmly.

"Oh, please." Marla snickered.

Niko thought of Holly at that moment. "I love my wife," he said.

"Of course you do," Marla answered, and she let the pointer drop below Niko's belt. "But then, what's this?"

She pressed the pointer against him.

"Stop it," Niko said as he grabbed the end of the pointer. Marla let him jerk it out of her hand. Then she smiled.

"There's just one thing," she added.

Marla reached back into her hair and unpinned it from the tight bun that had become so much a part of her daily business attire. She shook it free, and it cascaded around her face in large auburn locks with broad silver highlights.

She slipped out of her bulky sweater to reveal the top of a flattering black lace corset.

"My favorite color," Marla said. "Thought I'd dress like a bride today, a witch-bride, you know, in black. I was sure we'd have this opportunity."

"There is no opportunity," Niko said coldly.

"Isn't there?" Marla asked. "I'm afraid there's something you don't understand, Niko."

"NO!"

"Oh, yes. Do I really have to spell it out for you? Can't we just play a little?"

Marla walked to the door of the conference room and locked it. Then she turned toward Niko, advancing on him, strutting as she came. She unsnapped her heavy granny skirt, let it fall to the floor and then kicked it with the tip of one of her very high heels.

"Niko," she whispered. "Come play me."

Marla looked spectacular, Niko had to admit. Her skin was smooth; the sexy corset squeezed her waist into a classic hourglass form and lifted her breasts high. The witch aroused Niko far more than he ever thought she could.

"I love my wife," Niko repeated, with all the nervous certainty he could muster. "I'm married."

Marla arched her eyebrows and grimaced. This was an affront to her witchcraft and her beauty... and then she laughed.

"Is that right, Niko? Are you sure Holly's worth it? Think of US, you and me, working together as a team; we could run this place. We could jerk it away from that silly old man and his ridiculous cat. It could be ours."

"And Billy?" Niko asked.

"You know what?" Marla sneered, "Fuck Billy!" And then she giggled. "Speaking of that... Guess who's been doing just that?"

"You!"

"Well, of course, me, you know. But besides me?"

Marla waited for her message to sink in. And as she did, she continued to pose and preen for Niko, now pursing her lips, now putting her hands on her hips and twisting them invitingly. Niko felt the sexual excitement growing. He closed his eyes and forced himself to turn away and stare into the distance. Marla's vanity was wounded again.

"Better face the truth," she shouted. "Your wife's a whore!"

"Don't say that!"

"You don't want my opinion, I know," Marla said as she walked around in front of Niko again. She let her hand glide sensuously across his shoulders and onto his chest.

Niko grabbed her wrist and held her firmly.

"No!" he insisted.

"All right, then," Marla answered, her eyes now ablaze with anger. "Go ask someone else about your little wife if you don't think she's whoring around. Go ask Billy Bright."

Marla turned and stormed to the far end of the room, to the partition that was still concealing the portrait of Babcia and all the other witchy paraphernalia. She pounded those high heels as she went, gathering her clothes in the process. She ducked behind the partition. She hadn't even bothered to unlock the conference room door, but it suddenly sprung open as Chuck Vaughn used his own key to enter once again.

"What the hell are you two up to this time?" Vaughn grumbled. Billy followed him into the room. He was wearing that boyish grin as though it were a badge of triumph.

Niko charged right around Chuck Vaughn and grabbed Billy by his lapels. "My wife," Niko demanded.

"Oh, Jesus, here we go again," said Vaughn.

Billy stood as tall as he could so that his imposing size might intimidate Niko. "What about her?" Billy asked.

"Have you, has anyone done... tried..?" Niko's anger garbled his words and even his thoughts.

"What he's trying to ask is whether or not anyone has DONE Mrs. Madonie?" Marla said as she stepped into the room. She had dressed in her granny clothes again, pulled her hair back and looked much more like her usual mousey self.

"Other than Niko himself, that is," Marla added with a giggle. "Because if they have, then there's certainly no reason for him to be so fucking chaste."

Billy laughed.

Vaughn began drumming his fingers loudly on the conference table. "Wish I HAD done her," Billy said, "but...."

Niko was red with rage. He grabbed Billy by his shirt and pulled the big man down to him. Billy had never seen Niko like this. He seemed much stronger than he should have been. And those eyes, a deep blood red was burning within them. Billy recoiled. He was the one initiated at the Witches' Sabbath. So what the hell had happened to Niko?

"Please," Marla called. "There's no need for violence. And if there is, I'd like to be the one to provide it."

Chuck Vaughn was now pounding his hand on the table. Everyone was ignoring him, which brought him closer and closer to the boiling point.

"Never touched your wife, man," Billy lied.

"If you ever do...." Again that blood red glare in Niko's eyes told Billy how real and dangerous the threat had become.

"THAT'S ENOUGH!" Vaughn bellowed as he jumped to his feet and stared daggers all around the room. "What is this, a fucking soap opera?"

Marla gave a nervous laugh and then twisted her smile into a disarming pout.

"I was merely trying to bring a little authenticity to our story by inviting Niko and his wife to my next Witches' Sabbath," she said with all the innocence of a black widow spider.

"Christ, Marla," Niko hissed.

"All right," she responded. "And I was trying to get you to buy into my ideas. But that was all, you know. I merely wanted you to consider my story line. Does that seem so unreasonable?"

"And you don't like Marla's ideas?" Vaughn asked turning to the two other men in the room.

"Yes/No" said Billy and Niko respectively, at the same time.

"Which is it, goddamn it?" Vaughn growled.

"There's a little disagreement," Marla said with a witchy smile. "But we'll be able to work it out, you know."

"You'd better," Vaughn answered. "We have a presentation to make to the sponsors and the network in New York City, next month. I want agreement. I want a single storyline, and if you can't get there, then at least give me two very well defined options that I can choose from. Got it?"

"Of course," Marla answered with vapid sincerity. "Niko, Billy and I have always been able to find creative agreement in the end, you know. We'll work it out for you. Won't we, Niko?"

Niko was stunned. This was pure unadulterated Hollywood bullshit. He had seen traces of it in every meeting he'd been in since he joined VVA. Now Marla was suddenly showing pure mastery. She nodded to Niko, as much as to say, go along with me on this, and so he finally took the cue.

"Yes, we'll work together and get it settled," he said.

"Good," said Vaughn.

Niko turned to Billy. His rival seemed as exasperated as he was. It didn't matter what Billy said, of course. Niko knew that he was a snake. (And what do you do when a snake gets into your home? You kill it!)

Holly was another matter. Niko felt the old pangs of

jealousy and mistrust. But he forced them away. No more hysterics. No more accusations. No Inquisition. He loved her. He'd put her through hell already. Maybe it was time for him to show a little trust. No one had admitted anything, and so the best he could do was not make too much of it, not try and put pieces together that didn't fit… that maybe weren't even there. He'd never been able to exercise that much self-control before Niko admitted, but maybe this was the time.

"One more thing," Vaughn added as he turned to go out the door, "I don't want to hear another word about who's fucking whose wife or any of that kind of shit! Got it? Or *you* are the ones who'll be fucked… not your wives!"

"Wish I had a wife not to fuck," Marla murmured with a sarcastic grin. But Vaughn was already out of earshot.

CHAPTER FORTY-SEVEN

HAPPY BIRTHDAY, DAD

AN AMERICAN WAR AND PEACE
Manuscript Outline By Doctor Louis Madonie

1 – Bombing of Pearl Harbor
2 – Decision to enlist
3 – Angry response from family
4 – Patient petitions to keep me home

Niko shuffled through the 100-page outline his father had sent him, knowing that parts of it were very good, knowing why his father had chosen to send it just before his 60th birthday.

Dr. Lou had to make some kind of statement, Niko realized. He had to offer some tangible evidence of the value of his idea if only to keep his dream alive.

Niko's father knew that he was losing his son, maybe this time for good. Those other old threats to their combined success: comic books, cartoons, even marriage were minor compared to the allure of Hollywood.

Holly was now on the doctor's side since that conversation that seemed so long ago, (Before the car accident, before

Hollywood, before adultery). She had agreed to help him win his son back to "the book project," as she called it. She did it subtly, telling Niko how nice it would be to go home after they had finished at Leland, talking about a cozy life in upstate New York where writers could write during those long, cold winters. But even Holly's gentle seduction did not seem to be doing the trick. Niko just smiled sweetly whenever she talked about leaving California, as though his mind was already made up.

The doctor knew that Niko was becoming more confident in his abilities, too, and less dependent on his family. *An American War and Peace* was in great danger. And so the doctor had sent this 100-page outline, detailing his adventures, how he had won his medals, risked his life and saved so many others. It was all there in that unusually neat, doctor's handwriting of his, and a lot of it was damn exciting. The camaraderie was often funny. The concentration camps were drawn in a way that would induce horror and outrage, teach lessons about humanity and its capacity for evil. And then there was that overpowering message about breaking with the old hatreds, destroying that terrible heritage before a bright new world could ever be fully realized.

It was, Niko understood, a noble endeavor, one worthy of his highest ambitions and greatest talent, one far surpassing anything he could achieve in an animation house making horror kiddy cartoons. So why didn't he want to do it? Why couldn't he at least give up a year or two to help the old man reach for immortality? The doctor would even support them financially, he knew. He and Holly could live at home with his parents or right around the corner. (Ugh!)

An American War and Peace had always been a point of contention between father and son, a source of anger and resentment. It was as though the project only existed so that they could fight about it. And when they weren't fighting about how to do the project they were fighting about its content.

The evils that Dr. Lou was so fond of describing in the cities and towns of Europe, didn't they exist in Vietnam, in the Middle East, in America itself?

"Isn't evil alive in our own government?" Niko asked.

The doctor had turned red with rage. How dare his son question the authority of The United States of America?

"My country, right or wrong," Dr. Lou intoned.

"Just what the Germans said as they joined the Nazi party," Niko responded.

Niko missed those fights now. He couldn't believe it, but he did; he missed his father for the first time in his life. He knew that the old man would call soon (hopefully not tonight), check on Niko's reception of the outline, and hint around trying to gauge his reaction to it. Dr. Lou would start suggesting ways they could get started. Niko would resist; his father would press, more resistance, more pressure, and then open hostility.

Niko had to prove himself on his own before he could take time to help his father. But there was an important new element in his thinking now, something he learned just by watching the way things happened at the studio. You didn't just walk away from Hollywood, not even for the best and most noble intentions. You don't leave a golden opportunity in a place where opportunities are nearly impossible to come by. You don't lose your momentum.

Maybe once he was established, then he could work on his father's book, but he was sure that his father didn't want to wait any longer. That's what came of hitting a milestone birthday like 60, Niko realized.

Yes. There would be an argument, and in the end they would continue to hate each other, feel more hatred then love anyway even though, somehow, love was finally starting to work its way into their relationship.

Four hours later that relationship between father and son was as dismal as it had ever been.

#

"Happy Birthday," Dr. Madonie whispered to himself at 11:30 that same evening. "Happy goddamn birthday." His 60th birthday had in fact been one of the worst days of his life. It hadn't been Helen's fault. She had done her best, except for that stupid suggestion. Wouldn't she ever learn?

Helen had tried to make it so romantic, had prepared a candlelit dinner: filet mignon, baked potatoes, strawberry shortcake, his favorites. She had mixed his martini, one of three martinis he would drink that entire year. And she had purchased some special lingerie just for the occasion. She kept hinting about it through that long, wonderful dinner.

"Wait till you see it," she had said. "But first let's call the kids?"

Call the goddamn kids.

Dr. Lou was as eager as anyone to speak to Niko about his outline. But not tonight, not on the day he had probably just gotten it, too risky to do it tonight. It had been nearly six months since Niko and Holly had moved to Hollywood for that internship with Chuck Vaughn, the doctor realized. That internship was the problem. It was ludicrous. No! More than that, it was dangerous, distracting, the kind of thing that turns a bright young mind like Niko's (with all that fine, expensive schooling) away from its intended work.

The kids had sounded distracted during the phone call. Holly's health was good and she wanted to talk about the baby. But there was a sadness about her that made both the doctor and his wife very uncomfortable. She had the definite attitude of a woman who had been, what? Unfaithful?

Then Niko got on the line, said that he had received the manuscript, joked about how good it was and how he'd get back to his father soon, with "comments."

Comments? Shit! Sounded like pure Hollywood bullshit to the doctor.

After that Niko talked on and on about the TV show he was working on: Hansel and Gretel and he raved about the great success he was having at VVA.

"Chuck Vaughn seems to be very impressed with me, Dad, and I've got a really interesting writing partner, Marla Morrison. She's a former ballerina. I'm sure you can imagine the fabulous legs she has."

Dr. Lou wondered if Holly was still in the room and if she could hear her husband raving about his colleague's *fabulous legs*. Maybe that was the reason for her melancholy.

"Our story sessions are a little unorthodox," Niko continued.

"Here, talk to your mother," the doctor responded. He didn't want to hear about unorthodox story sessions or leggy ballerinas. He'd had more than enough of Hollywood.

"But one thing, Dad, one thing I have to tell you before you go," Niko added. "I'm dropping out of Leland."

"What?"

"I am," Niko answered. "Chuck Vaughn has offered to extend my contract at the studio; he's offered me a big raise. I'm taking it, Dad. I may never get a chance like this again."

"But what about your real job, your destiny, all the things we planned for you? *An American War and Peace*?"

"Sure, Dad, we can do that too, okay? Your outline is great. I'd love to work on it with you. I'll get back to you with details as soon as I can."

Dr. Lou felt sick to his stomach. His son really was in Hollywood, wasn't he? And he'd learned a few things there, too, nasty bullshit things.

Dr. Lou lowered his head and handed the phone to his wife. Tears were in his eyes. She could see them.

"What's wrong?" she had asked.

"He wants to drop out of Leland," he said softly. And then he just turned and left the room. Now his dream really had slipped away, in spite of all of his long, hard work on that goddamn outline. What a waste.

Helen spent the rest of the night trying to salvage something of her husband's hopes and dreams, at least for this one special night, getting Niko to agree to delay his return to Leland rather than dropping out completely, getting Dr. Lou to acknowledge that Niko was now willing to work on the book (what a turn-around that was, if you could believe it), getting Niko to say *Happy Birthday* before she hung up the phone. The doctor went through the motions without much heart. And if his attitude hurt the feelings of their spoiled, selfish kid on the other end of the line, well then fuck him... FUCK HIM.

That was it for the lingerie and the birthday celebration, and all the rest of it. Helen was in bed crying while Dr. Lou was in the bathroom brushing his teeth and cursing everything he could think of, including himself for not being firmer with the boy, for not insisting that he stop sketching comic books, for letting him marry that Holly Blue. Some help she'd been.

When the chips were down she couldn't deliver either. She had saved Niko from the draft, at least, gotten pregnant, and now she was going to have his grandchild.

"That was really what your reconciliation was about. Right, Helen?" he asked the thin air. "It was all about grandchildren, all about babies. Add babies to the equation and suddenly everything is about them."

Dr. Lou dried his face and looked at it more closely. It was drawn and wrinkled, and he, doctor that he was, knew that it was the face of a man much older than his years. The war had taken its toll. His son and his wife had made their emotional demands, too. And his dream, his novel, keeping that alive might have been the most demanding thing of all.

He trudged to bed.

"I'll write it myself if I have to," he swore under his breath. "Happy fucking birthday."

He looked at Helen; she was wearing her new lingerie, but she was now fast asleep. She was beautiful, even at 60, beautiful, loyal, faithful, intelligent. More intelligent than he. What more could a man want? (Greatness, immortality.)

He was pulling the covers up around him when he turned to give one last smile to his beautiful wife.

But suddenly it was BABCIA who was lying beside him in the bed, as hideous and evil looking as when she had been alive.

She rose up and stretched a twisted hand across his chest letting her long talons spread and fall. She pressed her claws into his flesh. Pain radiated into his chest, into his blood vessels, and into his heart. She lowered her face to his until their lips nearly touched and he could feel her spit as she spoke to him through gritted teeth.

"I be back. And not be as gentle next time."

And suddenly she was gone, leaving him sweating and gasping for breath, the victim of the first in a series of heart attacks that would grow in deadly intensity... with each subsequent visit from the witch.

CHAPTER FORTY-EIGHT

HANSEL & GRETEL

Marla watched Niko pitch his version of Hansel and Gretel to Chuck Vaughn. The handsome young man was a showman, no doubt about it. His eyes sparkled, his curly black hair had become delightfully tangled, she thought, giving Niko just that much more charm. His smile was infectious.

"And they all lived happily ever after," he said with a concluding grin.

"Happily ever after?" Marla groaned to Vaughn. "It's so friggin sweet, you know, it makes me want to puke." She turned back to Niko and stared at him, and in return he cocked his head and gave her more of that silly charming smile.

"Prick!" she whispered.

Niko turned back to the boss. "Anyway, there are your two approaches, Marla's and mine, Chuck. Which one do you prefer?"

Chuck Vaughn eyed Marla in exasperation. As far as he was concerned, Niko's work had been nothing short of miraculous. He had wound the original story of Hansel and Gretel carefully with Marla's vision of a sexy teenage horror film featuring a young hunk of a Hansel and the feminist Gretel who was in love with him.

Niko had presented the storyboards that were now pinned in careful, sequential order across the conference room wall. He had shown perfect timing, excellent choice of words and great use of voices as he told the story and portrayed each character. He had been a godsend, a genius.

Hell, someday he could run this place, Chuck thought to himself. He should be grooming Niko for the role of Creative Director right now.

Billy Bright sat at the far end of the table, hollow eyed and gaunt. He had been awake for four straight days and nights creating the storyboards for the version that Marla had presented first, the version that was clearly overshadowed by Niko's.

"Our ending was great, you have to admit," Billy said.

"Are you kidding?" Niko responded. "It was too damn gory: Witches' Sabbaths, unborn babies torn from their mothers' wombs. Do you really think that any broadcast network would put a show like that on television?"

Chuck Vaughn eyed his dysfunctional little family. He was scared. He had to admit it, at least to himself. He had just put up his property in Malibu as collateral to get the last piece of funding he needed for the production. He cleared his throat and everyone turned toward him.

"I like what I see," he began. "I like it a lot. Now we just have to get it across to the execs in New York. The cocksuckers! Not an ounce of creativity in any of them, and yet they'll end up deciding the fate of the project." (And my studio and ME, Vaughn realized.)

"Niko," he bellowed. "I think you should present your storyboards in New York. You've never faced a crowd like that, but I think you can do it. Don't you?"

"Absolutely!"

"Mr. Vaughn," Billy added, "You really should give the job to Marla. She's got great presentation skills."

"Don't think so," Vaughn said gruffly. "It's Niko's story we're going with. He should tell it."

"Now, I think most of the storyboard drawings are fine." He gestured to the hundred and fifty sketches on the wall. "I like what you've done with the characters, cute but sexy. That's always the best formula."

"Niko, your drawings are a little cartoony, but they work great in the action sequences. Marla, help him out, see if you can clean up some of them, build more character into Hansel and Gretel. We have a lot of work to do. I'll get the studio plane to take us to New York before the end of the week.

"Niko and I will present this thing to the brass in New York. Billy and Marla stay here to provide any last minute support we need."

"NO!" someone said, and it was a surprisingly commanding 'NO' that came from Marla.

"What do you mean 'NO'?" grumbled Vaughn.

Marla walked up next to him. She put her hand on her hips and let her sharp talon fingernails twitch threateningly, as though she could easily sink them deep into her boss and rip his face off.

"Niko has the ending all wrong," she said through gritted teeth. "Gretel shouldn't push the witch into the oven. She should convert and become a witch. Can't you see how much better that is?"

Vaughn just shook his head.

"Look," Billy said, "it's simple. Gretel reads the witch's books, talks to the witch, decides she wants to become a witch herself, and then we celebrate with a spectacular Witches' Sabbath, and, in the end, Gretel and the witch roast Hansel and share him for dinner."

"Ludicrous," bellowed Vaughn. "Nobody's going to buy that!"

"I know it sounds crazy," Billy added, "but I'm sure we can make something out of it. Give us a chance to rework it. I'll do the sketches myself. We'll get it to you before your plane leaves for New York. If you like it you can include it, or present it as an alternative, or whatever."

Marla walked up to Billy, and now her hand was on Billy's shoulder, and her nails were digging into him.

"Begging isn't becoming, you know, Billy," she said. "Not even for a writer."

"I know what he means though," said Vaughn. "And we could use a big climax. Billy, you and Marla work up that Sabbath thing; see if you can figure out a way to get it into Niko's story. Don't make it too goddamn grisly though. And set it up as a separate option. If it's great, we'll include it; if not, it's shitcanned. I'll let you know about our departure time as soon as I can get a meeting set in New York. Good work, everyone."

Chuck Vaughn stood, walked over to Niko's story sketches, studied them for just another moment and smiled. Busty, long-legged Gretel; muscular Hansel, naked in the cage; that crazy witch dancing her way into the briars. He could make something great out of that. Good shit. Very good shit!

Suddenly he was feeling more confident about it all, much more confident. And so he left the room all smiles. Marla followed him, turning to say something to Niko just as she reached the door.

"Nice job, Niko," she said with sarcastic venom. "I'll be in my office whenever you want to bring your sketches by so that I can help you clean them up, you know?"

"Thanks," Niko answered, deciding to ignore her attitude. "Sorry the old man didn't like your idea better."

"That's all right," Marla answered. "There are other, more powerful people, who might be interested in it."

"Like who?" Niko asked.

Marla let out a long, deep, nasty laugh. But she didn't say another word.

Chapter Forty-Nine

Billy's Drawing

They dragged Holly Madonie into the Witches' Sabbath. Her clothes were stripped away until she was naked. Monstrous witch talons dug into her flesh. Her unborn baby was torn from her body, then held high above the throng of hideous ghouls.

Chuck Vaughn studied the maddening images as he sat in the back of the room during Niko's presentation to the New York executives. Marla and Billy had slipped the pages to him as he boarded the plane for the trip back east.

The pictures were troubling, very troubling, he thought. No! More than that, they were terrifying. Vaughn flipped through them one more time. What the hell were Marla and Billy thinking?

He had never met Holly Madonie, of course, but he recognized her face from all the snapshots pinned to Niko's wall. And here she was, drawn in the fine, careful hand of Billy Bright.

Never! Never in a million years would anything like this make its way into one of his television specials, no matter how adult the world had become. Thank God he had been smart enough NOT to include Marla and Billy's hideous new ideas in today's presentation.

He glanced up at Niko as the kid talked his way through the final images in his pitch, then Vaughn folded the drawings and tucked them into the very back of the book, Grimm's Fairy Tales. He had only brought the volume with him as a prop, for effect, because it looked so good and would make his presentation seem more authentic.

On an early cue from Niko, Vaughn had held the book up for the executives to admire. Then Niko took over and told his story. He hadn't missed a beat during his pitch. It was just as he had written it, which was plenty sexy enough, not this horrific abomination that Marla and Billy had concocted.

Chuck Vaughn would deal with those two as soon as he returned to Hollywood! He'd end their involvement with his studio forever. There would be no more of their kind of sick shit, and that was certain.

Suddenly, Vaughn was shaken by loud applause that turned into a standing ovation. Niko bowed. He'd sold their story to the New York execs, the sponsors, the network, all in one brilliant presentation. Acting, singing, showing off, he had won over some of the highest paid TV executives in the country.

Chuck was standing and applauding too, although Niko deserved most of the credit. His athletic, action-packed drawings were terrific. Vaughn had to admit it out loud, had to tell Niko to his face. Time to be a little nicer to the kid. There would be a handsome bonus coming his way. And Niko had shown some real leadership ability through the whole process, even stood up to him and proven his point.

What had happened to that frightened young man who walked into his office eight months ago, a kid whose insides seemed to be like fine china? Vaughn knew the answer. He'd gotten it together in a hell of a hurry.

"Great work!" John Quincy Fuller said to Vaughn as he came up and patted him on the back. The second highest man in the television network was more cheerful than Chuck had ever seen him.

"Talented kid," Fuller added. "Hear he's a Leland man."

"Was," Vaughn responded. "Right now he's working for me full time."

"Not one of these crazy San Francisco hippies we keep hearing about?" J.Q. asked.

"Hell no," Vaughn answered. "Niko's solid, married, got a kid on the way, and from the pictures I've seen of his wife, I have to say that she's really...."

"Hot stuff?"

"Spectacular."

"I'd like to come out and meet her," Fuller added. "In fact, I was thinking I should spend more time with your whole studio. Maybe include you in my monthly visits to the coast.

"Why don't we get together late this afternoon and do some planning, look at ways that we can get more out of your operation? Maybe a little added investment could help bring things along."

"I'd like that," Vaughn answered, trying to show as much restraint as a man could when his empire (not to mention his soul) had just been saved.

"Should I bring Niko along to this afternoon's meeting?"

"Whatever you want." J, Q. answered. "Don't need a story/sketch man there, but if it would be awkward not to, then sure."

"Niko's more than a story/sketch man," Vaughn responded. "Got a lot of management skills, really good instincts. He wrote most of the presentation himself. I'm starting to think that he might be my next Creative Director."

By this point Vaughn and J. Q. Fuller had made their way into the lobby outside the big network conference room.

Vaughn looked back. There was no one left in the room except Niko.

"SHIT!" Vaughn shouted so loudly that half a dozen executives turned and looked at him. Niko was looking at the book (the additive book), and he had unfolded Billy's set of drawings. Niko hadn't seen them before. Vaughn had decided not to show them to him. Didn't want to queer the presentation. So why didn't he hide the damn things better, or just throw them away? Why was he looking at them while Niko was in the middle of the biggest presentation of his life?

Niko was studying the pictures now, with a look of sheer, absolute horror. And it wasn't just because of the drawings, Vaughn realized. It was the book, too, the additive book with its new fairy tale that Vaughn had barely noticed. He had somehow accidentally stuffed the pictures into the very start of this newest grim tale with its own original illustration that somehow mimicked Billy's most horrific work.

Niko's flesh crawled as he read the title of this newest, most gruesome fairy tale: The Unborn Sacrifice!

He looked up and saw Vaughn. His lips were moving but no words were coming from them. Chuck walked back into the room with an expression as horrified as Niko's.

Then Niko found his voice. "They're going to do it," he whispered.

Chuck Vaughn closed the conference room door quickly and turned to face Niko.

"No," he said firmly. "Those are just storyboards. They don't mean anything."

"But the book...." Niko answered. "My wife's in the book."

Chuck Vaughn looked more closely at the pictures in the additive book. There was a very pregnant Holly being stripped naked by leering witches.

"I know exactly what it means," Niko said, "I have to get back there."

"Isn't there someone you can call?" Vaughn asked desperately. "Call Holly."

"I can't," Niko murmured. "If I tell her about this, she'll go nuts."

"Then call the police."

Niko stared at the floor. "And say what? That a picture in a 70-year-old book tells me that my wife is about to be murdered?"

Vaughn wrung his hands in desperation. "Don't you have any friends in the apartment building?"

"Harry!" Niko said with a sudden look of relief. "The apartment manager. Haven't seen him for quite a while, but if he's there.... Please God, let him be there."

Niko raced to the phone at the rear of the conference room. He dialed Harry's number quickly. There was a long painful wait: seven, eight, nine rings. Niko's expression came closer and closer to despair. And that's when Harry's weak voice came on the line.

"Harry? Harry Rodgers?" Niko asked.

"Yes," came a soft, almost haunted answer.

"Harry, this is Niko, you have to help me. It's about Holly."

"But I can't...."

"Listen Harry, I think Holly's in grave danger."

"From whom?"

"I can't explain. But listen, can you go over there?"

"I can't. I just can't go out," Harry whispered desperately. "I've been very sick, and I've been instructed to stay inside."

"By whom?" Niko asked.

"Sorry, I just can't tell."

Niko ran his hand back through his hair in exasperation.

"At least keep an eye on her then, will you? Make sure she's all right, make sure she stays home."

"I can watch her," Harry answered with as much determination as he could find. "I promise I'll do that."

"I'll be there as soon as I can," Niko responded. "In no more than five or six hours. But in the meantime, just keep an eye on things, and if anything weird starts to happen, if anyone you don't recognize goes into that apartment, call the cops right away."

Harry mumbled something that Niko hoped was agreement, and then he hung up the phone. Somehow he didn't feel as relieved as he thought he should.

"Okay, look," Vaughn said nervously, "there's a commercial jet leaving JFK in two hours. I know. I used to take it all the time. We helicopter you from midtown Manhattan to the airport. The flight's direct, gets into LAX around 10 PM."

Niko gave Vaughn a desperate look.

"I need to be here for a meeting this evening. It means the survival of the studio." Vaughn's voice was now as desperate as Niko's. "I'll take the private jet home as soon as I can. A commercial jet will be much faster for you, believe me."

Niko nodded.

"Gets me home before midnight at least, gotta be there by then," Niko said as he gathered up his things and rushed to the door.

"Midnight?" Vaughn asked.

"Right," Niko answered. "The witching hour."

CHAPTER FIFTY

HOLLY'S HORROR

Holly moved cautiously toward the window. She pulled back the drapes and watched in horrified fascination as bony fingers of lightning crackled across the nighttime sky. Reaching desperately for the ground, she thought, groping, feeling their way toward her!

She turned and looked back into the living room of their little apartment, and suddenly she began screaming hysterically.

She was there! She was there! That wicked mask of Babcia was there, hanging on the wall, leering down at her, having come from God-only-knows-where to torment her.

How could Niko have left her at such an important and dangerous time? She was so damn pregnant.

Holly ran to the closet and grabbed a broom, a broom to chase a witch. She poked at the mask. It didn't budge. She jabbed at it, rammed it wildly. It leered back at her in defiance.

Hysterically, Holly tossed the broom aside and grabbed at the mask. Sticking her fingers into the holes in its mouth and eyes, she tore at it, tried frantically to pull it from the wall. It seemed welded in placed, fused into the wall. Holly dropped to her knees, hung from the mask, used all her weight and her unborn baby's weight to drag upon the hideous thing. It cut her; it bit her! Holly screamed and let go.

That's when the power went out.

"It's okay," Holly sobbed to herself. "It's okay." Thunder, lightning and wind were sure to knock down some power line somewhere.

But still it wasn't okay. In the next instant lightning shattered the darkness, and the horrific face of Babcia was smiling at her again.

Holly stumbled into the bedroom, to the nightstand. There was a flashlight. She grabbed it, turned it on, peered into the darkness. Nothing! She saw the little crib that she and Niko had purchased for their baby.

The baby, Holly thought to herself. I can't hurt my baby. Can't get too scared. Don't want to traumatize the kid.

FLASH! Lightning! Right on top of her! And then thunder shook the entire building. Sheets of rain slammed wildly against the window, waved like treacherous grey-green ribbons across the sky.

Holly looked back into the living room to see that the mask had come free from the wall, had fallen onto the soft carpet and somehow had shattered.

She was okay now; Holly tried to tell herself. She was safe. The thunder had destroyed the mask and she was all right. Her baby was all right. All she had to do was make it through the night. Survive the next few hours. Be calm.

She was calm. Except for those eyes, those blood red eyes staring out of the darkness from across the way. Red demon eyes. Witch's eyes.

Holly dropped the flashlight and ran into the living room and then across it to the front door. She opened it. Across the way Harry's apartment was dead black. No light in any window. No sign of any life. It had been that way for months. Not a living soul. But what was that thing beside Harry's doorway?

Witch eyes were staring back at her from across the rain-drenched court. Lightning flashed. A dark terrible figure stood there, hunched over, cackling some evil curse.

"Gotta get outta here!" Holly screamed. She slammed the door and ran to the phone. It still worked.

Billy. Call Billy, he could save her. He would be there for her. The phone rang.

"Billy?"

"Holly?"

"God, Billy, I'm so glad you're there."

"Are you all right?"

"I'm terrified."

"It's only a little thunder and lightning."

"No. It's the witch... that damn witch mask you gave us. It's here."

"Maybe she's looking out for you, trying to protect you," Billy tried to joke.

"It's not just the mask, there's some*thing*... someone out there, looking in at me, stalking me. You've got to come here and help me."

"I'm trapped here," Billy answered. "My van's a wreck...."

"Billy, someone's after me!"

"Okay," Billy's voice suddenly sounded as terrified as Holly's. "Okay listen, I can take a cab, be there in twenty minutes."

"That's not soon enough. I have to leave now. Maybe I can get out of here myself, get into the car, drive over there."

"Be careful."

Holly looked out of the window. The red eyes seemed to be gone for the moment.

"Just a minute," Holly whispered. She ran to the front

door and opened it. Nothing. No one. Just sheets of rain. Lightning lit the night for a moment. No one was there. Holly ran back to the phone.

"Billy, I'm coming," she said. "I'll be there in a few minutes."

"I'll look for you."

Holly hung up the phone and closed her eyes. "Mother of God, please help me."

Lightning illuminated the mask of Babcia, as it lay shattered on the carpet. The eyes still seemed wide and evil, still glowed blood red. Holly walked far around the shattered mask as she moved through the darkness to the kitchen. She gathered the keys, her wallet. Time to think clearly. She clutched the little flashlight desperately. The closet. She had to open the closet to get her coat. Who knew what was hiding in there. Shattered masks, red eyes in the night, hunched-over figures in the darkness, anything horrible was possible.

"Mother of God, please help me."

Holly snatched the closet door open only to be confronted with...

... clothes, coats, nothing else.

She grabbed her raincoat and put it on. She had to move quickly. She had to get out of there while she still had the nerve.

"Mother of God!"

She flung open the front door and dashed out into the darkness. Rain and wind blasted into her face and tore the hood of her raincoat from her head. It drenched her hair and streamed into her eyes. Holly raced into the parking garage. It was dry. It was warm.

Blood red eyes peered out at her from the distant shadows. A dark figure hobbled toward her. Holly pulled on the car door. It was locked.

"MOTHER OF GOD!"

She juggled the keys as the creature crept closer.

Jam the key into the lock, God damn it!

LIGHTNING FLASH and there was BABCIA, only a few yards from her, waving her hideous, gnarled old hands with their bloodthirsty claws.

Turn the key! Get into the car!

Slam the door.

Put the key in the ignition.

Start the car.

Start the car!

MOTHER OF GOD! START THE FUCKING CAR!

Holly felt the engine catch. She crunched into reverse, wheeled out of the parking space and slammed the car into drive.

Babcia raced toward her, waving her bony arms!

OH MOTHER OF GOD, JESUS, SAVE ME!

The car roared across the parking garage away from Babcia, toward the ramp leading up and onto the street.

An enormous black wolf moved slowly across Holly's path and stopped in front of her. Its red eyes glowed, and yet it lowered its head and looked almost... what... concerned?

In a moment of sudden clarity a new thought crossed Holly's mind. It was ignited by the memory of Billy's sarcastic words: "Maybe she's looking out for you, trying to protect you."

She wants me to stay here... to stay in the apartment... she doesn't want me to go to Billy's... there's danger there!

The wolf raised its head and looked at her; it whimpered.

Thunder exploded right above Holly. The wolf didn't move. It lowered its body and planted its feet.

"It's blocking me!" Holly sobbed. "God damn it! The bitch is blocking me."

Holly's hands were trembling as she clutched the steering wheel. Her eyes strayed to the rear view mirror. Another flash of lightning, a crash of thunder! Holly jumped and suddenly saw a new shadowy figure lumbering up from the depths of the garage… another hideous old crone.

Not Babcia though, Holly realized… another witch limped along toward her.

Lightning flashed again, and for a split second Holly could see a twisted ancient face. A deep cut healed as though it were an open wound, a white blind glassy eye, tattered old witch robes. Her mouth was drawn in a hard determined line and she was coming for Holly.

The girl heard the witch's long, twisted, broken fingernails drag across the back of the trunk lid… then they began moving slowly up the driver's side of the car.

Holly jerked her head forward and looked ahead. The wolf was still there, growling now, yellow fangs bared, hair standing upright on its back. It blocked her way.

The claw-fingers of the witch scrabbled up to the door handle; they reached for it.

"MOTHER OF GOD, SAVE ME," Holly prayed, and she floored it.

The car pounded ahead and into the snarling wolf. She heard its body ricochet out onto the street. The front of the car was smashed in. Wolf's blood poured toward her across its hood. But the car kept running.

And it ran and it ran… and it ran all the way to Billy's house.

Holly pulled up in front, turned off the ignition and, without stopping to catch her breath, she raced from the car and into the apparent safety… of Billy and Marla's sprawling home in old Hollywood.

CHAPTER FIFTY-ONE

THE PLANE RIDE

As twisted fingers of lightning clawed at the Hollywood Hills, Captain Jack Moran taxied VVA's little twin engine Beechcraft onto the New York City runway under glorious, star-bright skies.

As Harry Rodgers watched a hobbling, cackling shape menace Holly in the darkness, Chuck Vaughn waited for the arrival of the beautiful companion J. Q. Fuller had asked him to "give a lift" back to Hollywood.

Moments after Holly charged her car safely out of the garage and over to the residence of Billy Bright, Chuck Vaughn's companion arrived and breathlessly buckled herself into the seat beside him. Chuck asked her name.

"Michalina," she answered, "Michalina Czarownica."

As Holly rushed up the steps and into the arms of Billy Bright, Michalina and Chuck were getting along famously.

"Wouldn't you like to get out of that coat before we take off?" Chuck asked.

"No, it's fine really," she answered with only the slightest trace of a Polish accent.

At that very moment Billy led Holly to a softly lit little

room in the back corner of the old Hollywood bungalow that he now shared with Marla.

"It's very interesting fur," Chuck said. "Not sure I've ever seen anything like it before."

"It's wolf," Michalina responded, as she ran her fingers over her coat. "It's very rare. In fact, the only place you can get a coat like this is in Poland."

Holly looked up at Billy. He had been so understanding. But there was something frightening about him now. He looked different somehow. Maybe it was just the scary thunderstorm. He seemed excited but very much afraid.

The VVA plane reached cruising altitude as Chuck Vaughn cracked open a bottle of vintage champagne and toasted the person who had made this all possible.

"To Niko Madonie," Chuck cheered.

Billy tucked the beautiful Holly under the soft coverlet of the bed he had provided for her, and she went quickly, deeply, desperately to sleep.

"To Niko Madonie," Chuck repeated.

"Tell me about the young man?" Michalina asked. "I want to know just how you feel about him."

CHAPTER FIFTY-TWO

MARLA & BILLY

"Can't we just slit her throat and be done with it?" Billy asked angrily.

"Of course we can't," Marla responded. "We have to follow the ritual, you know. The bitch has to suffer. She has to see us tear the baby from her. She has to see us boil it alive. After that you can kill her any way you want to."

Marla's eyes were wild, her hair completely disheveled. She turned to face Billy, and as she did her black witch's robe swept open, revealing the thigh-high boots she had chosen to wear for the occasion. Like her sisters at the Sabbath, she wore nothing else. Her flesh blushed red with excitement. Beads of sweat glistened over her forehead and across her chest. Her breath was heavy.

Billy would normally have been excited by Marla's appearance, but not tonight, not with things spinning wildly out of control. He turned away in anger. A deep fire was burning within him, one he was powerless to express.

"The ritual requires that she be alive when we kill the baby," Marla said. "Then the wolf/witch will come. She'll share her powers with us. She'll guarantee our success. But only if we do it the way she wants us to."

"How could you know what she wants?"

"I've channeled her enough," Marla answered. "I've breathed her breath, I've become her. She wants to be with her beloved grandson, and Holly is in the way. The witch is looking for a vessel that will allow her to be near him always. "I CAN BE THAT VESSEL."

Marla's eyes glowed with the sheer exhilaration of the prospects.

"This is no ordinary witch," she continued. "Her powers go back for Centuries'. To have her power is to have EVERY-THING!"

#

Holly cowered in the far corner of the bed, curled up in as small a knot as possible. Her hand rested on her large pregnant belly, on her unborn baby. She had been listening in growing terror to the conversation in the next room for at least an hour. She was trying to formulate a plan of escape, but her head was so muddled with fear.

Still, as long as there was a conversation, there was hope she thought. But there really wasn't any hope left, and she knew it.

Thunder rumbled its threats and accusations at her. Witch-finger lightning tore the sky. Its brightness illuminated the room every now and again so that Holly could see the horror she had fled to.

Bloody writing filled the walls.

"Die! Unfaithful Bitch!"

She had started to notice something else in the dark, too. A small mangled creature torn open near the foot of the bed. What was it? She didn't know. She didn't care. Holly whimpered, softly, hopelessly. That poor mangled thing was the source of the blood that decorated her walls.

"It's getting late; we have to call the witch!" Marla commanded.

"All right, all right" Bill grumbled.

"Oh, Billy," Holly thought as she listened, "You betray me so easily." The end had surely come. Holly reached to her head to tangle her fingers in her golden hair. It wasn't there! Her head had been shaved. Her beautiful hair was gone.

#

Niko checked his watch. 10:15, not much time till midnight. Why were his greatest fears targeted on the witching hour? He knew the answer very well.

Niko's plane had just arrived in Los Angeles. He had rushed through the airport, found a taxi and ordered the driver to take him home: 45 minutes. But was that the best place to go?

If Holly were frightened would she have stayed at home or would she have reached out for help from someone else? No! That didn't make any sense. Holly would stay where she felt safest, if only to protect her baby. Maybe she would run to Harry. They hadn't seen him; he had been sick he said. Still, of all the possibilities on this most horrific night, Harry was the safest bet. Niko was sure of it.

The taxi sped along the freeway that arched across the Hollywood Hills; then it dropped into the wind-raked San Fernando Valley and sped to the apartment where Holly would surely be waiting. Niko prayed that he wouldn't be too late.

#

"I can't do this," Billy suddenly shouted at Marla.

"You'll do what I tell you!" the witch shouted back without looking. She did not see Billy pick up the huge silver candlestick that they had brought along for the ceremony. It was the size of a baseball bat.

"I just can't."

Marla turned toward him. She saw the candlestick.

"Murder too much for you, Billy?" she jeered. "You're a sorry excuse for a witch's apprentice. Oh well, I would have only had to kill you later anyway, you know. You'd only be in the way."

And then she laughed, a nervous high strung-laugh that now crackled with the growing brittleness of megalomania.

Holly listened from her chamber, daring not to give in to the illusion of hope. And it was an illusion, wasn't it? Still this was Billy, Billy Bright, Billy the deceiver, Billy the seducer, HER Billy.

Swinging the candlestick like a broadsword, Billy charged at Marla, but she slipped easily out of his way. She was a ballerina, after all.

Billy's momentum carried him into the wall. He crashed half way through it, splattered lath and plaster everywhere. He had to yank hard on the candlestick to pull it from the wall. He did. Then he spun again and charged the witch, this time adding a slight feint, an old high school football move. Marla was not fooled. Instead she danced across the floor again as though she were floating over it with absolute grace. Billy went sprawling into a bookcase, and his impact brought a torrent of ancient books cascading down on him.

Holly listened in sheer terror, knowing that Billy's struggle, the struggle to save her life, was not going well. She must save herself, she realized. She must save herself and her baby.

Marla turned toward Billy just as he was about to charge her again. She whispered a spell at the candlestick. The spell took hold of it and made it her weapon.

Billy charged one last time, but this time the candlestick spun up, out of his hands, and away from him. Then it swung around and came crashing into him, clubbing him, bludgeoning him, pounding him.... into a bloody, lifeless pulp.

CHAPTER FIFTY-THREE

HARRY RODGERS

Niko told the cabby to wait in front of the apartment building as he rushed up the stairs and across the courtyard to his home.

His worst fears were realized. The door stood wide open. Inside, things were a shambles, as though Holly had barely escaped. There was no sign of a struggle, but drawers and cabinet doors were wide open. Coats lay scattered across the floor as if she had struggled to get to hers, then taken it and rushed out.

Beside the phone he saw a note pad. Scrawled into it was the imprint of an address. Niko grabbed it and stuffed it into his pocket. Then he turned and made his way across the courtyard to Harry's apartment.

There were no lights on inside. Niko was reaching forward to pound on the door when he saw that it was open. He pushed against it, and the door swung wide. Niko entered.

The place reeked of sweat and urine and vomit. White sheets were draped over couches and chairs. The floor was a tangle of old clothes, wine bottles and dust. Blinds were drawn and taped shut. Harry's home had become a dismal cavern, a hideout for someone afraid to go anywhere. Only one small window let in any light at all, and that window provided a direct view into Niko and Holly's apartment.

None of that made any impression on Niko at all, however. What overpowered him and everything else in the room were the photographs hanging on every wall. They were enormous, many of them six feet in height, and they were all of Holly: Holly tightening the strap of her sandal; Holly in her bikini by the pool; Holly about to lower her bikini top. Some were candid, but most were not. Holly had posed for them!

Just then a shriek startled Niko and turned him around.

There, draped in a white sheet, was the huge figure of Babcia walking slowly toward him. She staggered, not with the movements of Babcia, but with the shaken steps of someone who was about to faint.

It wasn't Babcia, Niko realized. It was Harry wearing the mask of Babcia that had somehow been shattered and pieced back together again. Harry was grotesque. The shroud did not entirely cover his white T-shirt or his naked legs.

Niko placed his hand dead center in Harry's chest and stopped his advance. Harry's body was little more than skin and bones. The six foot three inch man couldn't have weighed more than 80 pounds.

Niko reached up and pulled off the mask. Harry's real face was even more horrid. He looked like the undead. His hair was matted, his beard long and scraggly as though he hadn't shaved in months. His eyes were set back in great hollow sockets. His cheeks were gaunt, his mouth an ugly gash barely hiding nasty, rotting teeth.

"God, what happened to you?" Niko asked.

"Haunted," Harry answered breathlessly. "By the witch. Haunted for months. Look at her pictures all around you."

Niko looked up at the pictures. There were none of the witch.

"All I see are pictures of Holly," Niko answered.

"My God," Harry whispered in disbelief. "Really?

"Well then," he added in some kind of misguided desperation, "If you want pictures of Holly, if you want shots of your whore, have these!" And he reached to the end table and grabbed an array of wallet-sized photos that had been sitting there... face down. He flung them into the air and sent them cascading across the room. The pictures were hard-core pornography: Holly fucking Billy Bright; riding him in some wild, animal ecstasy. Niko's worst fears, Marla's cruelest warnings were realized, there... alive in those photos.

"Jesus!" called Niko, as he fell to his knees and then collapsed against the foot of Harry's leather couch. He groped around, grabbing one picture and then another and another. He wailed as though he were at the funeral of his loving wife. (Perhaps he was.) Still, he kept grabbing pictures, looking at them as he sat there in the darkness, now sobbing bitterly.

"She's not worth it, old man," Harry sighed as he slouched down beside Niko. "She's a whore, she's just a whore. She deserves to be punished for the way she teases and...."

A hand grabbed Harry by his throat with incredible strength (witch strength). It pulled him to his feet. Then it thrust him back against the wall smashing his head deep into the wallboard.

"Didn't I ask you to keep an eye on Holly?" Niko demanded.

"Yes, and I did," Harry gasped in desperation. "But she asked too."

"She? Babcia?"

"No, of course not... that girlfriend of yours."

Niko clenched his teeth so quickly that he almost bit his tongue.

"I HAVE NO GIRLFRIEND."

"No, of course not. I meant Marla. I think she wanted me

to kill Holly for her, but the mask took over my mind, started to drive me mad... I had to hide, but then Marla told me she just wanted me to watch Holly, see what she was doing, look for opportunities and, above all else... just stay out of her way."

"Her way?"

"Yes hers, Marla's, and today the witch was here for Holly, trying to scare her."

"Marla?"

"No."

"Babcia."

"Yes, but there was another witch here too, smaller, darker with a great scar across her face and a dead white eye."

The last words made Harry shudder almost uncontrollably.

"Were they together?"

"Oh no... Babcia, I think was trying to scare Holly back into the house. But that blind, scarred old witch, whatever her name is, wanted Holly to go, to get out of here, to drive away."

"And what did Holly do?"

Harry moaned in pain and desperation. "She's fucking gone isn't she? Can't you see that? She's gone!"

Harry lifted himself up as though he had one more important thing to say, and then he slumped forward, unconscious. Niko caught the withered man and lowered him slowly toward the floor. Then he stood, turned with great purpose, and rushed back to his cab. In his hand he had a single picture, one he had found among the filth that Harry had sent cascading across the room. It was a shot of Holly but a different Holly, a loving Holly, looking so guilty, clutching that crazy little toy elephant and sobbing.

"My lost little girl," Niko murmured.

CHAPTER FIFTY-FOUR

MARLA'S SACRIFICE

Marla had taken the racks of sulfur, brimstone and other chemicals, as well as cages full of scurrying, hissing, rattling creatures, to the huge cauldron that bubbled on the fireplace at the far end of the room. Now, she was carefully preparing the potion she would use to summon Babcia.

In the next room Holly had gone to the window and pulled up on it desperately, hoping that somehow she could open it, crawl out onto the roof, find a way to jump down even from two stories. The window had not budged. It was painted shut, she realized. She had found a small nail file in the drawer of the end table, taken it, brought a chair, stood up at the window and was now digging at the paint with all her might.

She tried to do it as quietly as possible because she did not want the witch to hear. But the window wasn't budging, and the paint was chipping off so very slowly. Still she dug at the window with the nail file, missing sometimes and tearing the flesh of her own hands, spattering the window frame with blood.

Was there no way to break the window? Holly had asked herself. But embedded within the glass she could see a tight wire mesh that would surely make it unbreakable. And so the poor, desperate girl dug at the paint around the window edges, hoping she could chip away enough to set herself free, while in the adjoining room a witch prepared to tear her open and sacrifice her child to a greater, even more monstrous evil.

#

Inside the cab Niko was able to make out one of the words that was scratched into the note pad, the most important one of all, the only one that really mattered: "Billy!"

She was running to Billy, who now lived with Marla. No need to decipher the rest of the note. Niko knew the address of the witch, the witch whose storyboards showed his wife as the victim of a human sacrifice.

Holly would be running right into her trap. It was the kind of thing Babcia might have wished, he thought, but then Harry had said...

"My God," Niko called out loud. How could a man in Harry's condition offer an accurate perspective on anything? What the hell was going on? But then Niko realized that it didn't matter, nothing mattered, because Holly had betrayed him. He had absolute proof of that, and now she was running to Billy and Marla who intended to kill her.

Niko lowered his eyes and just sat there for a moment. "Where to, Bud?" the cabby asked.

Niko looked at the picture again, the only one he had taken with him: Holly and the elephant, his lost little girl. Niko raised his eyes, cleared his throat and ordered the cabby to drive to old Hollywood, to Beachwood Drive, to Marla's home.

#

Holly had nearly scratched through the paint around the outside edges of the window. She tugged again. One side of the window gave. The other was still very stuck. She jammed the nail file into the paint on that side of the window, tearing into her thumb in the process and adding more of her blood to the mess of chipped paint and tears and sweat that were congealing on the windowsill.

Don't panic, Holly told herself. She had to succeed because, within minutes, the door to the bedroom would fly open and that beast of a woman, a woman she thought was her friend, would make her way into the darkness, grab her, drag her into whatever demonic chamber she had created in the other room, slice her open, pull her baby from her, and slaughter it.

"Oh, Niko," she whimpered.

Now there was a banging in the other room, an inhuman screech, a howl and then a low, snakelike hiss. The kettle was bubbling over. Marla was chanting horrible, inhuman incantations.

Holly sobbed; she turned toward the door, lost her balance, teetered for a moment on the chair and, in the process, dropped the nail file. It bounced under the bed.

Rain roared out of the nighttime sky. Thunder pounded heartlessly at Holly.

"Niko," she called. "Oh, Niko. Oh, Blessed Mother of God, save me."

#

"I'll give you a thousand dollars if you get me there before midnight," Niko said to his driver at 11:40.

"I'd love that, mister, but look at the traffic. If I can pull up onto the shoulder we might have a chance, but I'm not sure. Who would have expected a backup on the Hollywood Freeway at this time of night?"

\#

Holly was down on her knees reaching under the bed, her huge pregnant belly blocking the way, limiting her reach. Her fingers touched the tip of something metallic, the file. She pressed down hard on her stomach, harder than she ever should have for the sake of her baby. She reached with all her might and, as she did, she repeated her prayer over and over again.

"Mother of God, save me."

A hissing sound now filled the other room. And then the familiar smell was everywhere. It was sweet at first, but then it became more and more sour, more bitter, until it was sickening, horrible, the smell of spicy sweetness mixed with blood. Rotting gingerbread.

Holly grabbed the nail file and stood. She hoisted herself onto the chair and began chiseling away at the narrow little strip of paint that held the window shut. And that's when she heard the deep, cruel, guttural growl of a huge, angry wolf.

Babcia had joined them.

\#

"It's 11:50. Where the hell are we?"

"Just another few blocks, mister. I'll have you there at midnight."

"Not AT midnight. Before midnight."

"I'll do my best, don't know how we're going to make it, but I'll try."

\#

Now there was a deep growl that was growing into an angry, bloodthirsty roar, then the sound of running, of claws scraping on the hardwood floor, of something somehow launching itself into the air and then landing with a monstrous, heavy, bone-shattering crash.

"OH, MY GOD! OH MY GOD! SAVE ME FROM THE WITCH!"

#

"God, Babcia," Niko pleaded as the cab slogged its way along the base of the Hollywood Hills, "if Harry was only right, if you were really trying to scare Holly back into our home, if you really were trying to save her, then stay with her now. Save her now!"

The cab once again ran into a wall of traffic and stopped dead.

"That's enough! I'll run from here," Niko shouted as he jumped from the taxi. "It's midnight already. It's too late. I know it."

"Hey, what about my fare?"

"Call me!" Niko said. He was running now, running down the street to Marla's home where horrible things must be happening.

"Call my office," he yelled to the cabby, "Vaughn Visual Arts. VVA!"

"VVA? CatMan Due? I love that guy."

#

The room became almost silent now except for a soft hideous gnawing, tearing, swallowing that seemed to go on forever as the smell of that raw, spicy sweetness mixed more and more with the coppery stench of blood.

Holly continued to scrape at the paint and pull up harder and harder on the window. It was part way open now but nowhere near enough for her to squeeze through safely.

Then the doorknob to her room began to turn very slowly. The door was locked. There was no sound of unlocking, and yet the knob turned. Holly stopped working on the window. She froze in fear and turned toward the door.

#

Just one block to go, Niko told himself. It was past midnight. It was already too late, but he had to keep trying. He had to get there.

Vomit lurched from his stomach and up into his mouth. He turned his head to the side and blew it out across an expensive Hollywood lawn as he ran along, barely stopping at all.

#

The doorknob turned. Holly, as terrified as she was, had to defend her baby. The hell with herself; she'd get what she deserved, but she had to defend her baby. She stepped down from the chair, grabbed the little lamp off the nightstand and yanked its cord from the wall. It was the only weapon she could think of. She raised it above her head just as the door began to open, slowly at first and then fully!

Holly screamed.

Babcia stood there! No longer a wolf, now a hideous crone, eyes bulging and bloodshot, long hairy fingers, nails that were claws dripping with blood, a monstrous mouth with crooked, slimy teeth, and a face caked with blood and chunks of flesh. Marla's flesh!

Holly dropped the lamp in terror. The monstrous apparition hobbled toward her. Slowly, inexorably Babcia raised her hand and pointed a twisted finger at Holly, at her belly, at her baby.

"SHE'S MINE," the old witch cackled. "SHE'S MINE." And then she let out a long shrill, hideous laugh and vanished into thin air.

#

Niko heard Babcia. He rushed up the steps and burst into Marla's room, and what a horrible sight he saw: Billy's smashed-in head, Marla torn to pieces, ripped open, entrails strewn everywhere. Floor, walls smeared with blood.

Holly was standing in a doorway at the opposite end of the room. Her eyes were wild. She couldn't speak; she could only tremble.

Niko ran to her and lifted her into his arms. He rushed from the room, slipping only slightly as he did, just enough to lose his balance; then he caught himself on the edge of the great table of ingredients that Marla had set up before the cauldron. He jarred the sulfur, brimstone and other chemicals that were sitting there, and they toppled over, splattering into the great fire that still burned under the witch's cauldron.

Niko rumbled down the stairs, carrying his pregnant bride. He raced out the door just as the chemicals ignited and spread. They blasted sparks through the bloody room, and then exploded into crazy pinwheels. Fire erupted. It destroyed Marla's chamber within seconds, and then it consumed the rest of the great old bungalow before the firefighters and police ever had a chance to arrive.

Interlude 7

Michalowski is thrilled with the outcome of the story but still sleepy from an afternoon of conversation and vodka.

"Not quite so fast," says the warlock. "You think that's all there is to it?"

The shopkeeper looks back at Wicktor nervously. "Perhaps not."

"Definitely not," Matryoshka answers.

"*Why* not, beautiful?"

The girl blushes, flutters her eyelashes, and smiles sweetly. No one has ever called her beautiful before. "Because of that other witch," she says… or was that some other part of Marla… maybe a disguise."

"No disguise, Kochanie," the warlock says. "Clara Goriki was a pupil of Babcia's but then she turned against her."

"But why did she hate Babcia so much," the girl asks.

The warlock smirks at the pretty teen. "Perhaps I just provided too many information too quickly," he says. "Don't you remember?"

"*I* remember," Michalowski says smugly as he makes his way back into the secret room. He had been on his way up to bed. You said she was in Poland, watching her teacher take the man she loved away from her… across the ocean."

"But then where was she when Marla was being destroyed," Matryoshka asks, "When Babcia was saving Holly?"

"Babcia was eight hundred years old, one of the most powerful witches who ever lived," the warlock answers. "Clara was a little more than a hundred. Do you think she would really challenge the great witch in a direct confrontation?"

"Of course not," Michalowski answers, as he reaches forward, takes the vodka bottle, spots a few more drops in it, removes the stopper and drinks them directly from the bottle."

"So, where was Clara then at the end, Matryoshka asks. "Where did she go?"

"Interesting question, sweetheart," the warlock said. "Interesting indeed... a story for another time, perhaps... meanwhile..."

"Meanwhile?" Matryoshka says, as though troubled by the idea that there could be more.

Chapter Fifty-Five

Six Years Later

It had been almost too easy. Frighteningly easy, Niko thought, as he straightened his tie and pulled on his suit coat.

The fire, the birth of little baby Joy had been over six years ago, and though he was still haunted by the events that occurred, Holly seemed to overcome them with ease, frightening ease.

She had confined herself to bed for about three days, or was it a week? He wasn't sure. She wouldn't eat, hardly spoke to him, seemed almost catatonic. And then on the fourth day (or was it the seventh?) she woke up with a big smile and never looked back.

She seemed to grow stronger and healthier the closer she came to giving birth. Her hair returned quickly, more lustrous and beautiful than ever. The birth, the delivery was a dream as though the baby herself was fighting to make her way into the world and to strengthen her mother as she did so. It was so easy, almost frighteningly easy.

Niko was quick to call the authorities about Harry. Oh, he had gathered up the pictures, put them in a safe place to be destroyed at a later date. He never mentioned them to Holly. In his mind it had all ended with the death of her lover on that terrible night. Still, he fought nearly every day to maintain that conviction and his trust in Holly.

She had broken his heart.

In the meantime his career flourished. With Chuck and J. Q. Fuller fully aware of the role he had played in the successful development of Hansel and Gretel, Niko gained the title of Vice President and Creative Director. Boy Genius was what Sally Fukes called him, and she wasn't the only one.

Hansel and Gretel became an international television hit, a classic. And Niko's follow-up, Snow White and Rose Red, was even more successful. Niko wrote the script himself. Ideas had just poured from him with frightening ease.

#

"How's the proud Papa?" Holly called from the doorway to their bedroom.

She was still in her lingerie, the 1970's version of her sexy wedding things.

"Give you any ideas?" Holly cooed as she brushed her shapely hips against him when they passed. "Time for a new baby, I think."

"It's the baby-making that appeals to me," Niko added with a grin.

Niko heard a loud coughing from downstairs. It was his father. He was not doing well at all, Niko thought. He glanced uneasily at Holly and did his best to finish getting ready.

Dr. Madonie had suffered a series of debilitating heart attacks that culminated in a massive myocardial infarction. It occurred on the very night that Marla and Billy had met their untimely deaths.

"What a horrible night," Niko said out loud.

"What did you say?"

"What a horrible, terrifying night," Niko repeated.

Holly froze. A cold shiver passed through her. She shook her head, shook it off.

No, she thought. This was all a figment of her husband's imagination. She wasn't going to buy into it.

That night was blocked out of her memory completely. Sometimes, on those very rare occasions when she tried to think about it, it was like watching a play from the worst seat in the house, from behind a pillar. Her memory was blind to those moments. (But it wasn't deaf, was it?)

Like that view from behind the pillar, she couldn't see the action, but she could HEAR it. And whenever Holly listened to the sounds coming from that deep, dark, terrible place, what she heard was screaming: (Oh, God no, save me from the witch!)

There was one other thing she knew about that night, though, that night so horrible that she had to hold onto the belief that it was all a terrible dream. It had changed her life completely. From that moment on, things had gotten so much easier, FRIGHTENINGLY EASIER.

Niko hurried down to the bottom of the stairs where his father was awaiting a ride to church. The doctor and his wife were visiting California to attend their granddaughter's First Holy Communion Ceremony.

"Ready, Niko-boy," Dr. Madonie said. The doctor had been calling his son "Niko-boy" ever since the young man's first great success with Hansel and Gretel. On that day it became clear that Niko-boy would surpass his father in wealth, notoriety and achievement. But he had done it all through cartoons and comic books and witches. Trash!

The old man sank into a chair. He could barely walk. There were times when he hardly knew where he was or who he was. But during those moments, when he was able to think clearly, the first thought that always struck him was that his life was over. His ability to achieve was at an end. His son didn't need him any more. But Niko would never become the great writer that Dr. Madonie had envisioned. They would never write An American War and Peace. And that, in the end, was the tragedy of Dr. Madonie's life.

#

Niko went to the nursery, to Joy's room. She was six years old. According to Catholic Church teachings she had reached the age of reason when she knew right from wrong. And so she was ready to receive her First Holy Communion.

Joy looked up as her father entered the room. Her grandmother, Niko's mother, was brushing the little girl's long, blond hair, tucking it under at the ends so that she looked like a choirgirl. Joy grimaced and growled with each brush stroke.

Niko's mother smiled, in spite of Joy's protestations. Helen Madonie was still a very attractive woman, though she was showing more and more traces of the look that she would have in her very old age, the look of her mother, Babcia. Niko shuddered.

"Do we have to do this, Daddy?" the little girl asked.

"Of course we do. Don't you want to meet Jesus personally?"

"Don't give me any of that, Daddy," she said with a voice that seemed to come from very far away.

"Uh, excuse me," Niko's mother said, as she sensed an oncoming struggle. "I'll just wait downstairs." And she hurried out of the room and down to the first floor, leaving Niko and his daughter alone.

"What did you say, young lady?" Niko asked.

"Never mind, Daddy. But I don't want any part of this. I'd much rather practice The Craft."

"The Craft?" Niko asked. "What are you talking about, Joy?"

"Never mind," she answered, "but can't I just stay here and play with you? Daddy, come play me."

Niko was dumbfounded. (Those words!)

Joy had always been a precocious little girl with an immense vocabulary and a unique point of view, a little girl whose favorite character in Sleeping Beauty was Maleficent, who would rather pretend to make eyeball soup than hold imaginary tea parties for her dolls.

"And look what I found," Joy continued. She raced back to her toy box and pulled out a large, white object wrapped in tissue paper.

"Look at this."

Niko did look at it, and then he pulled back in horror.

THE MASK OF BABCIA.

Where the hell did it come from? "Joy, you can't have that! It's evil," Niko stammered. "We have to get rid of it."

Little Joy turned, looked at her father and her eyes darkened. It was not at all the look of a little girl.

"I need it, Daddy."

"And look what else I have." Joy raced to her toy box and pulled out another large object. Niko couldn't believe his eyes. It was the book: Grimm's Fairy Tales. Niko had tried to get rid of it after he took over VVA, had sold it to a guy named Mandel, a rather bookish man, Niko remembered.

"Joy, we don't need a book like that either," Niko said. "It's too scary."

"No, it's not, Daddy; it has a lot of wonderful stories. I have three favorites. Want to know what they are?"

Niko shook his head, but Joy answered anyway.

"Well, I like Little Red Riding Hood, of course."

"Of course," Niko repeated feeling himself growing numb.

"And then there's The Witch and the Soldier. I like that one a lot." "Of course," Niko repeated.

"But my most favorite in all the world is the one at the very end of the book. It's called Witch Girl. Want to read it to me, Daddy?"

Niko was dumbfounded. NO! He did not want to read it. It had not even been in the book the last time he had seen it. And yet he sat down beside his daughter and read her the story about a witch who loved her grandson so much that, after she had fulfilled every one of his heart's desires, she took over the soul of his little girl so that she could be with him for the rest of his life.

Joy smiled as her father read the story. She looked up at Niko, and he was smiling, too. As he read the story he began to experience a feeling that he had only known fleetingly before that moment. It was a feeling of peace, confidence and safety.

In a very objective sense Babcia was cruel, ugly evil. But she loved him. She listened to him and tried to help him in her own unique (murderous) way.

Niko's smile broadened, as he read more and more of the story. Joy rested her head onto his shoulder and cuddled close to him. He was invincible, Niko realized. Babcia had made him a success and would go on helping him.

Niko wasn't sure how many of these thoughts or feelings were radiating from the little girl who sat so attentively on his lap, but he didn't care. As far as he knew, this was only the beginning of his greatness. Fame and fortune were his, far beyond his own desires, even beyond his father's noblest ambitions.

In that moment he embraced his lineage, all of it, including the ancestry that was born in the dark, ancient forests of Eastern Europe so long ago, where his grandmother, as a little girl, had once been taken by witches.

As had they all.

THE END

Epilogue

"So, there's how you get the other mask," Michalowski says as he taps his pipe on the bowl beside the wooden pipe holder. "You go to the little girl, offer her a lollipop or something in exchange for the witch mask. And while you are there, get the book too: Grimm's Fairy Tales."

His words hang in the air for a long moment before the entire heavens seem to answer him with a resounding, "NO!"

Lightning flares and crackles through the shop. The glass case beside the front window shatters, and a small fire breaks out near the witch masks. Wicktor jumps to his feet and stamps it out at once. A bombardment of thunder then begins shaking the building, and it seems to go on for ten minutes or more.

Once he has stomped out the flames, the warlock turns to Michalowski.

"The little girl is the witch, you old fool." He gestures toward the masks. They seem to have taken on even more menacing expressions in the strange darkness of the storm.

Then the warlock slouched back into his chair. "I'm sorry. I don't mean to insult you in front of your daughter," he whispers.

"It's alright," Michalowski answers. "Sometimes I am an old fool."

The three sit near the fire in silence, motionless, thinking of the story and the fierceness of the storm. They listen to the rain as it ravages the little shop.

"She was the one, wasn't she?" Matryoshka whispers finally, as she gestures toward the masks. "Babcia told you the story, not Niko or Holly. Babcia told it to you through the little girl."

"When I went to her and tried to buy the mask," Wicktor answers, "the little girl gave me that red-eyed witch look. I realized that she could do anything, become anything she wanted to be, and she would just as soon boil me up and eat me as sell me the mask. There's no way anyone this side of hell can get it away from her."

Again there's silence except for the pounding of the rain and thunder, which finally seems to be moving away from them.

"Shop is officially closed," Michalowski announces as he struggles to his feet. He takes the empty bottle of vodka to the counter and drops it into the trash. He then shuffles over to the shattered display case and sighs.

"Tomorrow," he says. "Now, come, Matryoshka. I will not leave you alone with this creature. You will not become one of his witches. I will see to it."

He turns his back on the two and hobbles to the door. But Wicktor comes up behind the girl as she starts to follow her father.

"Come see me the first Halloween after your eighteenth birthday, Kochanie," he whispers in her ear. "I'll give you a proper initiation into the Craft, and I'll help you gain all the powers of the great witch."

Then he glides around in front of the girl never losing touch with her body, always trailing his fingers sensuously across her back, her shoulders, her chest. "All the glorious beauty of witchcraft can be yours."

He says it softly so that the girl's father can't hear him.

"And Babcia's ugliness and cruelty as well, Pan Wicktor?" Matryoshka asks.

"If you wish."

"Come now," Michalowski calls to his daughter as he turns back to the couple.

But Wicktor is already busy throwing the counter cloth back over the display of masks. And, amazingly enough, once the masks are covered the rain stops abruptly.

Twilight pushes through the dampened gray streets, turning little puddles and run-off into rivulets of purple and gold. Birds are quick to announce that the storm has finally ended.

"Thank you for your service, Pan Wicktor," Michalowski says, "and your story. Tonight my girl and I will sleep well. Tomorrow we fix the shop and find out what it's like living with a store full of witch masks."

The warlock nods to the old man and then bows to the girl. She curtsies.

Wicktor smiles. He is certain that she's his.

The Witch Within Her

Prologue I
Zakopane Poland – 1509

Walter Sapalski began riding in the nighttime. The year was 1509, certainly not a safe era to be night riding, and yet he did. And, if ever his friends would ask him why he had undertaken such a dangerous practice, with all the brigands that were on the roads and all the wild beasts in the forest and the witches too, he would answer with one of three reasons.

The first was his horse, Arra. Won in a lottery at the village fair, she was surely one of the finest horses in the countryside, finer in fact then her owners knew when they had offered her up as a prize. Surely, Arra would let him outrun any evil creature who set out to do him harm.

The second reason was his daughter, little Michalina, taken by witches in only her sixth year of life. Much of it was his own fault, and he knew it. He had not watched closely enough, had not seen as she had slipped out the door of their cottage to gather firewood so that her father could be warm on that blustery night, a night when witches were surely about.

The third reason for the night rides, which Walter might admit to no one but himself, was the absolute despair of it all. For, in those dark moments, he was certain that he had forever lost his little girl, the one person he had lived for after her mother had died in childbirth.

Everyone he loved had been taken from him, it seemed. So, why not be caught by brigands, destroyed at their hands, suffer the punishment that he knew he deserved for his carelessness in losing his daughter. Better to pay the price in this world than face eternal punishment in the next.

"A rough night," Walter grumbled to his horse as he pushed the bit into her mouth and pulled the reigns around her head. Arra didn't seem to care. She was eager for the run.

"Will you find her for me tonight?" he asked his horse, "Or will it be evil and destruction in her place?"

Arra whinnied, shook her mane, and pawed the ground.

"It'll be somethin', I wager," he added. "Now let's be off." And he flung himself up onto his steed, and together they charged from the stable.

"Michalina!" he cried as they burst into the open air. "Find me, sweetheart!"

But Michalina had already found him. She stood only yards from the entrance to the stable. She watched her father astride Arra bolt from the door and charge off into the night. And almost as quickly as he, she ran through the forest alongside him. A girl who was somehow more than that, a girl with the power of the animals she lived with; strong, young, twelve years old now, drawing nearer to womanhood, and as beautiful as the moonlight that spun through the swirling mists.

Michalina was with her father, but he could not know it. For she was a witch, converted to the ways of the coven and hated for it by everyone, especially by the Polish church. The institution sought to exterminate her kind and anyone who cared for them. Walter was in mortal danger, should he ever be known to come in contact with his beautiful daughter. And so she chose not to allow it.

But oh, how she yearned for that reunion.

Prologue II
The Forests outside of Zakopane
Poland – 1970

Twenty young witches made their way around a huge marble circle that had been set into the base of a quarry many centuries before. Above the circle, narrow rows of stone seats looked down, turning the place into what must have been an ancient amphitheater. To the right of the circle, a freshly pressed velvet cloth covered a low, flat surface, perhaps some hidden altar. To the left, a great, unlit bonfire stood dark awaiting only a torch to set it aflame.

Starlight, the only illumination at that midnight hour, offered a magical glow to the setting. The stars seemed huge, brilliant... so close that it felt as though they were pressing down upon the circle and its attendants. And all around, giant trees hunched like ogres standing guard on all those present and the evils they had come to commit.

In the background, the sharp, snow-covered ridge of the Carpathian Mountains sliced up into the night rising higher it seemed than the stars. Much closer, an enormous tower jutted equally tall into the blackness.

The witches wore coarse, black robes that reached their ankles but were unbound at the waist so that every step exposed a glimpse of thigh, a peeking breast, a hip or a delicate ankle.

Most of the girls were Polish, and their white-blond hair and pale blue eyes glistened in the starlight. Only one of them was over the age of nineteen, an ebony girl from the inner city of Los Angeles who was long-fingered, bright-eyed, skinny, and almost invisible in the dark except, that is, for the bright whites of her enormous eyes and ivory teeth that bit her lower lip while she tried to navigate the trail up from the circle and into the seats.

Twin highborn sisters had come from England to join the preparations. Their chatter made them sound like royalty, and their turned-up noses and haughty gaze seemed to offer a harsh judgment on all that was happening around them. Still, they were as stunning as the other young witches, as though beauty itself was one of the principle requirements for becoming a member of this coven.

Some of the witches rushed in excitedly, seemingly anxious to have a hand in whatever great evil was about to begin. Others giggled and chatted, appearing unaware of why they had been asked to attend. But there were also those who seated themselves slowly, fearing this night and all it would bring.

Eventually, all found places on the cold stone and fell silent as a keen sense of anticipation filled every young woman at the gathering.

"He's here," one of the girls whispered, and it was true. Wicktor the Warlock had arrived.

He made a dramatic entrance, leaping high into the air, spinning around three times, and coming down in the middle of the circle.

The warlock stood then and surveyed his helpers. They were all so youthful, so childlike. All he could really see were wisps of the blondest hair, eager eyes, and smiles of anticipation.

He flashed his left hand, and an enormous fire exploded in the great pyre that had been built at the very back of the clearing. The flames illuminated his muscular body and the thick black hair that covered it. He strutted out into the crowd, up the stairs, and into the first row. The young women instinctively pulled back from his animal presence.

"There is no time to waste, my young witches," he said. "SHE is coming very soon, and we must be ready."

"Babcia is coming?" gasped one of the highborn, young witches who expressed the hope of every member of the youthful coven... that they would soon meet Michalina Czarownica: Babcia, the greatest of all witches.

"And what is your name?" the warlock asked.

"Megan Cummings," she answered.

"And I'm Morgan," said the twin who sat beside her.

"Come all the way from England, then?"

The girls nodded.

"Well, if you've come to meet the great witch, then too bad for you, because Babcia has other business. She has left a very delicate task to us, and we must complete it successfully. Still, don't worry, ladies, there will be plenty of evil doings to satisfy you, believe me."

The twins looked at each other and giggled at the news. And then the warlock turned and looked across the crowd to a sweet, round-faced, Polish girl who had just made her way to the very edge of the gathering.

"Can you guess who is coming, Matryoshka?"

The shopkeeper's daughter stood and smiled flirtatiously at the warlock. She had been dreaming of joining his coven for years and had just now managed to escape a possessive father who had warned her incessantly about the dangers of Wicktor and his brood.

"Is it Holly Madonie?" she asked.

"Ah," answered the warlock. "Mistress Matryoshka knows much of this story. Holly Madonie is the wife of Niko, beloved grandson of the great witch."

Matryoshka smiled proudly and began to inch her way past the other girls until she was right beside the warlock.

"But if you know so much, how could you be so stupid?" he jeered and, with a wave of his hand, sent Matryoshka sprawling right on her backside with her heavy apron, skirt, and half a dozen petticoats thrown embarrassingly up around her waist.

The other girls might have laughed except for the fear that such humiliation might also happen to them. And so they remained silent.

"Anyone else care to venture a guess?" asked the warlock.

The young, black woman raised her hand.

"And what is your name?"

"Chantel, sir. Chantel Brown."

"Stand up, Chantel Brown, and tell us who you think it is that we must prepare for?"

Chantel stood. The front of her robe fell open and revealed large, youthful breasts that were completely bare. The warlock watched them rise and fall more quickly as the girl drew in one nervous breath after another. Finally, she turned to him and whispered, "Marla... Marla Morrison."

The assemblage fell silent. Most of the women thought they knew the story of Babcia and her battles with Marla. It was a war for Niko's very soul.

"She's dead," Matryoshka called. "Babcia killed her. She can't possibly return."

There was yet another long pause as most of the young witches nodded in agreement. This made the warlock look unhappily from one to the other to the other.

"Well, you're almost right, Chantel Brown," he said at last. "But almost is never quite enough is it?" And he let out a wicked laugh startling a flock of ravens that had gathered at the darkest edges of the circle. The birds launched themselves skyward in a single, ominous cloud. They flew in a great arch around the high tower and roosted on its topmost parapet. Their motion set off the braying of goats and horses penned in a nearby coral.

"I don't understand," murmured Chantel. "Tell us what's going to happen?"

"You're such a great storyteller," sighed Matryoshka. "You have to tell us."

Flattered, the warlock smiled and may have even blushed beneath the darkness of his coat.

"There's work to be done, young witches," he said. "But perhaps you will work harder if you have some understanding of what we're about... and there will be time enough to get things done... though you may end up working far into this night and the next and the next."

"Oh, we'll work gladly, Sir, for a bit of the story," said Megan. And the others echoed the sentiment.

"All right then," he answered. "I have your commitment, and believe me I'll make sure you honor it. But now, let me spin a tail as wicked as any you've ever heard... a cautionary tale to be sure: one that is not quite yet finished, and one in which you all may soon play a part."

The women in his coven murmured in astonishment. Illuminated as they were by starlight and firelight, they gazed in rapt attention at the warlock as he returned to the center of the circle, sat cross-legged in front of them, and began to tell his story.

ABOUT THE AUTHOR

Nick Iuppa *is the former Creative Director of Paramount Pictures' Digital Entertainment, Head of Apple Computer's Learning Technologies Group, and Writer for the Wonderful World of Disney. He's the author of 5 novels, 4 technical books on new media, and a humorous compendium of management tactics called MANAGEMENT BY GUILT. Nick's an avid international traveler, hiker and adventurer. He and his wife, Ginny, live in the San Francisco Bay Area.*

I love hearing from my readers and learning
what they like or don't like about my stories.
I'd be very grateful if you would send me a quick e-mail
and tell me your opinion of *Taken By Witches*.
I promise to answer personally and directly.

Tell me who you are and let me
thank you for reading my novel.

Contact: nickiuppawrites@gmail.com

www.ingramcontent.com/pod-product-compliance
Lightning Source LLC
Chambersburg PA
CBHW061305170626
46817CB00001B/53